DONN FLEMING

MANGROVE MURDERS

A BIG BEN MYSTERY

Mangrove Murders
FROM THE BIG BEN MYSTERY SERIES

Copyright c 2015 by Donn Fleming

FIRST EDITION

The scanning, uploading, and distribution of this book via the Internet or via any other means without the permission of the publisher is illegal. Your support of the author's rights is appreciated.

All rights reserved. No part of this book may be reproduced, stored in or introduced into a retrieval system, or transmitted, in any form, or by any means (electronic, mechanical, photocopying, recording, or otherwise), without the prior written permission of both the copyright owner and the publisher, except by a reviewer who
may quote brief passages in a review.
This book is a work of fiction. Names, characters, places, and incidents either are the products of the author's imagination or are used fictitiously. Any resemblance to actual events or locales or persons, living or dead, is entirely coincidental.

CreateSpace
ISBN: 978-1507553824

Published by:

PALMWIND PRESS
1674 University Pkwy
Sarasota, Florida 34243
P.O. 222 West Brookfield, MA 01585

Printed in the United States of America

Cover Photography: dos Ene
Author photo: Maddison
Cover Design and Book Layout: Eli Blyden

www.DONNFLEMING.com
Author correspondence: FLEMWRIGHT@AOL.com

for BettyAnn

(for all we've been through)

and the kindiegarten club

(my band of brothers)

Mangrove Murders

PART I

Retribution

*... I stood behind an isle of trees
Listened for the whetstone on the breeze ...*

Robert Frost

PROLOGUE

The body had washed in with the rising night tide and gotten tangled in the spider roots of the mangroves. Naked, Caucasian, female, not a blemish on her. With the late morning tide low, she was out of the water, stretched on a thin, tan blanket of sand beneath the shade of the mangroves. She looked like she was snuggled in for a nap. Her hair was long, butterscotch blonde, and fell across her dry, crusted back, with the ends thin and spread out and dipping into the murky green water.

Neither man said anything. Big Ben slid over the gunwale and sank into the water to his knees. MacLaren grabbed an oar and pushed the boat into the sandy strip of shoreline and jumped out. Ben was kneeling next to the woman with his fingers on the side of her neck. "She's gone, probably not too long, maybe only a couple of hours. Early morning or pre-dawn."

"Geesus," MacLaren said, looking around the small lagoon for a boat or a canoe or something. "What the hell was she doing in here?"

Ben gently turned her by the shoulders and carefully untangled her hair to get a better look at her face. He squatted there for a full minute and then slowly rose to his feet.

MacLaren stood with his mouth open. Big Ben looked over to him. His look said, *You've got to be shitting me*.

MANGROVE MURDERS

1

Hannah

Hannah Hunt Everett left her husband in the driveway washing his car. It was a hot Saturday afternoon. The sky was crystal blue. The kids were at Grandma's. The dog panted in the shade beneath the pygmy palms.

"I'll be home by six," she said.

Clayton Everett III was rinsing his bronze Mercedes with the white convertible top. "Don't cut it too close," he said, "I'd like to leave no later than seven." They were going to the Opera House.

Hannah went to him, rose on her tiptoes and gave him a peck on the cheek. "See you later."

She got into her Lexus two-seater and pulled away from their luxurious home in Meadow Ridge, one of the newer gated enclaves in sunny Sarasota, Florida. She wasn't going to return home.

This is insane, she thought. *How did I ever get involved in this?* Hannah exited through the south gateway of Meadow Ridge and headed west on University Parkway. She didn't have a clear answer, but Hannah knew one thing for certain. It had to end.

If her husband ever found out, the outcome would be unbearable. She could no longer continue this secret life of lies and deception. Her family was too important. Hannah wanted her life back. Simple day-to-day life, without jeopardizing everyone and everything she loved. The ruse had been going on far too long and there were too many perils, someone was destined to get hurt and if it all came to light, there'd be no way to explain it. Ever. To anyone. What she was involved in was too unbelievable for words.

What a fool I was, how could I not have seen this coming?

Hannah Hunt Everett was scared. She wanted out. The allure of the noble cause was gone. History would have to move along without her. She didn't want to be involved in the lives of so many innocent people. And then, inevitably, being part of changing the course of humanity.

The wild merry-go-round had to stop. Today she would put an end to it. She would meet with him and tell him she was done.

2

Ca' d'Zan

Hannah sat at the light at the end of University, nervously strumming her fingers on the steering wheel. Before her, the digital marquis announced that The Ringling Museum of Art was proud to extend the Salvador Dali Exhibit through the end of December. *Dali,* she thought, *my life is as bizarre as one of his paintings.*

The light changed and she drove forward across Tamiami Trail and into the palm-lined entryway of John and Mable Ringling's museum. She thought it an odd place to meet.

The Ca' d'Zan Mansion was built by John Ringling, the circus magnate, for his wife Mable. The fifty-six room, thirty-six thousand square foot residence sits on the shoreline of Sarasota Bay casting its gaze beyond the thin barrier island called Longboat Key and out into the vastness of the Gulf of Mexico. It was completed by Christmas of 1925. Today the mansion, with its grand ornate rooms and original paintings by the Old Masters is an awe-inspiring tourist attraction.

Hannah didn't know why he wanted to meet there, but she had agreed to it. She wanted to get it over with – to finally be free of the nightmare. She couldn't keep the secret any longer.

She stood in the pre-arranged spot in front of a Salvadore Dali painting, *Red Mangroves*. Dali was born in nearby Clearwater and had been acquainted with John Ringling who had purchased several of his originals for permanent display at the mansion. This particular painting was an early work found after his death, and the death of Ringling for that matter, and had been recently donated to the museum as part of an upcoming tour. Hannah wasn't a fan of Dali's surrealistic style; she could never quite understand what he was trying to say. And in this instance, couldn't for the life of her figure out where the mangroves were. Maybe that was his mystique, she thought. Hannah preferred the plush landscapes and soft, subtle colors of the Impressionists, things she could comprehend.

The security tape would later show a well-dressed man in a straw fedora and tan sportcoat approach her from behind, lean over her shoulder and say something into her ear. Mrs. Hunt turned her head slightly to the man as his hand reached toward the nape of her neck.

The bullet entered the rear of her skull at the tip of the medulla oblongata - the area where the skull sits on top of the neck - and exited her forehead, splattering brain matter, cerebellum fluids and bright crimson blood onto the already colorful canvas of Mr. Dali.

Hannah Hunt Everett dropped instantly onto the marble floor of John and Mabel Ringling's palatial mansion. She never knew what hit her and now the secret she had been carrying all her life, would go with her. She should have warned Carlene Benson.

3
Plane Call

"Ladies and gentlemen, welcome to Sarasota. The captain has okayed the use of small electronics, so you may turn on your cell phones at this time. Please remain seated as we taxi to the gate. Don't forget to check the overhead compartment for …"

Carlene Benson squeezed her husband Ben's arm. "I'm so excited."

Big Ben Benson, chief of police from Bryce Corner, Massachusetts stood and exercised his right leg.

"That bothering you?" Carlene asked.

"Just a little stiff from being cramped up on the flight." He was still favoring his bad knee, an old football injury that was aggravated a year ago when he was chasing a suspect through this very airport. "I think it's the change in air pressure that gets to it." He'd gone through six months of physical therapy, but still had a slight limp when carrying his powerful two-hundred-plus frame around.

Glaring at the big man standing in the aisle, the flight attendant continued, "Please everyone, remain seated until we get to the gate …" Ben sat down. "Temperature today is eighty-four degrees, a lot warmer than the twenty-four we left in Boston, huh folks?" There was some laughter, but most everyone was on their cell phones alerting friends and relatives that they had landed safely and would be inside the terminal in a few minutes.

Carlene Benson turned her phone on and noticed a missed call. "It's a 941 area code. Is that here?"

"Yes."

"I wonder if it's Lorraine MacLaren." She checked her voice mailbox. Empty. "Wonder why she didn't leave a message."

When Ben powered his phone up, it rang in his hand. The screen said MacLaren. He answered it. "Hello, Lieutenant. We're here."

MacLaren was a homicide detective with the Sarasota Police Department. He and Big Ben had worked a case together in Sarasota County a year ago. They had struck up a friendship and the Bensons were coming down on vacation this December in southwest Florida as guests of the lieutenant and his wife Lorraine.

"Carlene with you?"

"Kind of hard to lose her on an airplane."

"Her cell number 508-555-1967?"

MacLaren sounded serious. Ben said, "Yes, it is, why?"

"That's me that called her an hour ago."

Ben Benson didn't like the tone of MacLaren's voice. He turned his head away from his wife. "What's going on?"

"Does your wife know anyone in Sarasota?"

"No. She's never been here before."

"Well someone knew her."

"Knew?"

"I've got a dead body at my feet."

"What's that got to do with my wife?"

"I found a piece of paper with your wife's cell phone number on it."

Big Ben didn't respond.

MacLaren said, "I'll meet you outside baggage claim in fifteen minutes. We're going to the museum."

4
Teddy

Funny thing about money. When you've got it you can get most anything you want. When you haven't got it, you'll do most anything to get it. Teddy Platt didn't have it. What he did have was a failed marriage, a pink slip from the auto parts store he'd sweated at for twenty-two years, zero checking and savings, and a dingy third-floor apartment in an old brick building next to a run-down strip mall.

But things were looking up. Within the last three months Teddy had gotten a job, stopped smoking, began walking every morning and met a woman who thought that pudgy, balding men were a turn on. He'd had more sex in the past month than he'd had in his whole marriage. And that was no lie. Ursula was a godsend. Who would have ever expected to meet such an angel at Frank's Pub?

Ursula was hot. She had a heavenly body and dressed in skin-tight fashions that Teddy and his bar buddies greatly appreciated. And even better, she drank beer and swore at the flat-screen when the Red Sox got stupid, and she was truly amazing at Keno. Teddy had become enamored with her the very first time she had bought him a beer. His buds were damned envious.

But Ursula was unhappy. Not with Teddy, but her life in general. She told him she enjoyed her job as receptionist for

Collier, Collier, Woodbury and Oakes with their prestigious address in Downtown Crossing, but she had aspirations. She wanted to become Administrative Assistant and then take courses at B.U. to become a Paralegal. To get there she knew she had to project and maintain the proper image, and that meant clothing, and hair and nail salons, and that took money. In addition, Ursula wanted the finer things in life. Starting with a car so she and Teddy could go for drives, maybe a weekend on the Cape. More money.

"Wouldn't it be nice if we had a little house on Cape Cod?" she said to him as she sat in bed spooning into a cup of yogurt. Teddy was lying next to her, sexually exhausted and hoping he could get it up one more time before he had to go to his night-shift job.

"Or a nice condo in Back Bay or something near the Common?"

These were all the things swirling inside Teddy's head as he made his midnight security rounds at AbioGenetix LLC in Cambridge. *I could get her all the things she wants, he thought, and we could be really happy. All I've got to do is rob a bank!* He chuckled out loud and his laughter echoed off the stainless steel walls lining the corridors of the fifth floor labs. *Fat chance.*

Teddy meandered down the hallway going through the motions at the checkpoints with his little hand scanner, oblivious to what he was doing, his mind caught up in the elusive dreams of life for the better with his new bride Ursula. Did he say bride? Wow. He *was* infatuated with her. Finally a woman in his life who actually cared about him, liked hanging out at the bar with him, and more amazingly, enjoyed - hell, even initiated - sex. He was on a high. Nothing could stop him now. Except of course the money thing. But that made an appearance too.

"What are you talking about?" Teddy asked her.

"I went into the conference room to drop off their coffees and I couldn't help but hear what they were talking about." His mind played back the earlier conversation with Ursula.

"They who?" Teddy asked, digging one hand into a bag of Cheetos and pausing an old Clint Eastwood movie with the other.

"This new client they have. He's some sorta big shot lawyer from the North Shore who says he wants to file a class act suit, whatever that means, against a bunch of high tech companies in Boston, and AbioGenetix is one of them."

This got Teddy's attention. "What?"

"Haven't you been listening to me?"

Teddy had not been listening to her. He was waiting for that classic Eastwood line to come up ... "Do you feel lucky? ...Well do ya punk?" He loved that line. Every guy did.

"How is AG involved?" he asked.

"I don't know. Alls I know is it's a big deal, something in the millions or even hundreds of millions. All the partners were talking about it hush-hush-like after that other attorney left. They were so excited they sent me out to buy a bottle of scotch."

His ex-wife's attorney had raked Teddy Platt over the coals. "F'n lawyers," he said. "They make all the money no matter who wins." Teddy clicked the movie back on. Clint was walking across the street with his 44 Magnum at his side. "I shoulda been a lawyer," Teddy mumbled.

Ursula finished her yogurt and placed the empty cup on the nightstand. She snuggled into Teddy and ran her fingers through his chest hair. They watched the scene as Clint stood over the bad guy and pointed the Magnum at him.

"That big gun makes me horny, Teddy," Ursula teased. She moved her hand down below his beach ball stomach and began stroking him. "Ohh, I think this one's reloaded."

Teddy moaned and forgot all about Clint Eastwood as Ursula's head disappeared beneath the sheets.

5
Landing

When Big Ben walked through the tinted airport doors he was hit by a sheet of hot air, like opening the oven door on Carlene's famous brownies.

"Ahh," he said to her, "*This* is Florida." He inhaled deeply and spread his arms wide. "Tell me again why we live in New England?" The cold air and dreary skies they had left a mere three hours ago already seemed like a distant memory.

Sarasota is a tropical city on the Gulf side of the Sunshine State. Lots of palm trees, colorful flowers, white sandy beaches - and no snow.

"Do you see him, Bennie?" Carlene was nervous. Ben had told her about MacLaren's conversation. She couldn't imagine why some woman, a dead woman, would have her cell phone number.

Ben scanned the cars idling at curbside. MacLaren wasn't there. Then he saw him. "There he is." A gun-metal gray Dodge Charger with dark tinted windows was roaring towards the terminal on the outside of the line of cars. The car cut into the curb and pulled to a screeching halt directly in front of Big Ben.

The inconspicuous four-door sedan was a conspicuous cop car. The dark windows hid the interior light bar across the back window as well as the computer rig positioned in the passenger seat, but Ben could still see MacLaren's grinning face through the windshield.

The lieutenant got out. Ben noticed that his hair had whitened a touch more since the last time he'd seen him a year ago, but MacLaren still had the ruddy face permanently tanned from his forty-plus years in the sun and the moderate potbelly from his long relationship with all things ale. The two men hugged and slapped each other on the back.

"Good to see you again, my friend."

"You too."

Ben had dressed for the trip in a Hawaiian shirt worn outside khaki cargo pants. MacLaren had felt the metallic weight inside Ben's right cargo pocket as it brushed against his knee during the greeting hug. He wasn't going to ask him how he got that aboard the plane. MacLaren's weapon was holstered on his belt, his badge hanging on a lanyard from his neck outside his white polo shirt. He always wore it visibly like that at a crime scene. The museum was only a mile down the road from the airport.

Carlene was introduced and gently shook hands with the Lieutenant while holding her navy blazer over her left arm. She had dressed conservatively in a poly/cotton skirt suit. She was looking forward to going shopping with Lorraine to acquire some Florida fashions.

"Lorraine was planning on coming with me to the airport, but I got the call while she was still in the shower and had to move quick. We'll meet her at the house." He grabbed the luggage and opened the trunk. "Let's get out of this heat, the car's cool." He hoisted the carry bags into the trunk. "You guys take the back seat, the equipment's in the front," he smiled at Ben. "As you know, Chief."

Exiting the airport, they chatted politely about the flight and the weather and plans for the week. When they stopped for the light everything got quiet.

Ben knew what was on MacLaren's mind. He said, "Do you need Carlene at the scene?"

The Lieutenant fixed his eyes into the rear view mirror and slowly, apologetically, nodded to Ben. Carlene squeezed her husband's hand and spoke into the front seat, "I'm okay with that, Lieutenant. I'm just as curious as you are as to who this lady is, and how she knows me."

"I'm sorry I have to put you through this, but it would be a great help."

"I'll be fine. I'm a cop's wife, remember?"

Ben squeezed her hand and smiled at her. He was proud of his wife.

The light changed. MacLaren turned west onto University. Carlene said, "You haven't told me her name."

"Oh, hang on," he reached over to his sportcoat folded over the passenger seatback and pulled out a small leather notepad. Flipping it open with his right hand, his left on the wheel, he read, "Last name Everett, first name Hannah."

Ben watched his wife for a reaction. Carlene furrowed her brow and thought, "Hannah Everett ..."

MacLaren continued, "Lives here in Sarasota, married, two kids, husband Clayton Everett III, Financial Analyst, don't have her vocation yet, but we'll have a full work-up on her soon."

"The name doesn't ring a bell, I'm sorry."

"Ben says you're a Veterinary Technician. Any chance you know her from those circles? Schooling, seminars, on-line stuff?"

"No."

"Facebook? Twitter?"

"No, nothing like that."

"Well, maybe once you see her ..." MacLaren's eyes found Big Ben's again in the rear view mirror.

Ben took the signal and said to his wife, "She was shot through the head. It won't be pretty. You don't have to do this."

"I know, but she's a mother of two, and has a husband and a life that was taken from her. That's me Bennie - mom, two kids, you - I want you to find the bastard that did this. I know that's what you and the Lieutenant do. And thank God there are people like you who have the courage to do it. I would like to help."

The Ringling Museum of Art is pretty much your average museum; big rooms, high ceilings, humongous spotlighted canvases in ornate gold frames, cold marble floors, and an understood reverence for silence. Today, however, the room Hannah Hunt Everett was murdered in was brightly lit and noisy.

There were uniformed cops and street-clothed detectives huddled inside and outside the Exhibition Room. Bright yellow crime scene tape cut through the expansive square footage like lasers heat-seeking an illusive target. In the center of it all, stooped over a white sheet, was the ME with his gloves on.

MacLaren approached him and said, "You remember this big guy don'tcha?"

"Oh, yes," the ME stood, removed his right glove and shook hands with Ben. "Last year, the supermodel case at the Ritz-Carlton."

"That's right, good to see you again, foregoing the circumstances, of course." Ben introduced his wife.

MacLaren mentioned the note with Carlene's cell number. "We'd like to have Carlene take a look at her," MacLaren said. "If you think it's okay."

The ME knew he was referencing the visual condition of the victim. "Well, I'm done here and the photographer has completed his end of it, so if you'd like, I can get her down to the lab and cleaned up. Say about an hour?"

Big Ben and MacLaren both looked at Carlene.

"I'm okay," she said. "I can do it here."

The ME took Carlene's elbow and walked her away from the body. "Just give me a minute to get her onto a gurney, okay."

He left her and returned to the white sheet, motioning his assistant to join him. He said something to Ben and the Lieutenant and they moved to join Carlene. The ME wanted to get the body off the floor, away from the dark pool of blood surrounding the head.

"You're shaking," Ben said to her. "Maybe it would be best to let him get her downtown first."

"No, I'll be alright. Just hold me a minute."

They got the body onto a stretcher and rolled it to the far end of the room near the exit. The ME tried to fashion the hair, wet and matted with blood, so that it wasn't so gory. Impossible. He gave up and folded a separate sheet over the hair and top of the forehead. It looked like a Nun's habit. He nodded to MacLaren.

The two men walked on either side of Carlene and brought her to the stretcher. She took a deep breath and gazed at the lifeless woman. Ben had his big arm around her.

"I ... I'm sorry, I don't know who she is. I've never ..." Carlene's breath caught in her throat. She leaned in closer. Her trembling hand went to the sheet and raised it higher above the face, above the hairline.

"Oh my God," her voice was barely a whisper. "It's Hannah."

6
Set Up

The man's name was LeBeau. Although Teddy didn't know that. Very few people did. He was an intimidating figure, dressed in black, standing outside the AbioGenetix building. He had appeared at the front doors at exactly the prescribed time and had just stood there. He gave Teddy the willies.

"What did you do?" Ursula asked. Teddy was huddled in the glassed-in security room in the corner of the ground floor lobby speaking nervously into his cell phone. "I let him in and he just walked right by me. Didn't say a damn word."

"Where is he now?"

"I don't know. He got on the elevator. Ursula, he doesn't look like no insurance investigator to me. He gives me the creeps."
"Don't worry about it. They said he only needed ten minutes. Remember? Did you get the money yet?"

The money. That's what this was all about. The other night Ursula had laid out the plan. It sounded simple enough - too good to be true - but never look a gift horse in the mouth, as they say.

"How much?" he asked her.

"A lot. Mr. Collier said we'd have enough money to disappear with and never look back. He said we would be rich beyond our wildest dreams."

Teddy sat up in bed and clicked the movie off. The apartment fell dark. The pink and blue neon lights from the all-night diner across the street blinked incessantly on the white interior walls. "They're in on this? All the partners?"

Ursula reached over and flipped the switch on the lamp on the nightstand. "Yes, I sat with all four of them and they assured me it would work. All you have to do is let their insurance investigator into the building and he'll do the rest."

Teddy got up and began dressing for work. He was quiet. He always got quiet when he was thinking hard. Ursula watched him robotically take the white shirt off the hook on the back of the door and put it on. It had a big AG logo on the crest with *AbioGenetix* embroidered beneath it.

"When?"

"This Friday night."

"Why AG?"

"They said they just need to get some information that AbioGenetix has been withholding from the attorneys. Some kind of proof of evidence or something like that that they need for their case."

"But what if they find out how they got it?"

"They won't. Once Collier, Collier, Woodbury and Oakes have the information, it'll be too late for AG. They can never admit to having it in the first place. It would be an admission of guilt. Mr. Collier says AG will settle for huge money out of court to keep things quiet."

Teddy Platt stood at the foot of the bed in the two-room apartment buttoning his shirt, looking at Ursula's bare breasts with the alternating pink and blue neon flashes highlighting her nipples. He really didn't want to go to work.

"I'm not gonna do this for no measly few hundred bucks, y'know. This is serious stuff. I could get into deep shit."

Ursula sat up on her knees on the bed, her breasts swaying with the movement. "Come here," she said.

Teddy went to the edge of the bed and stood in front of her. She drew his necktie up to his collar and adjusted the knot. "This is our chance, baby. We wouldn't have to work again, ever. We'd be rich. We could do anything we wanted."

"How rich?"

Ursula cupped his face in her hands and whispered into his ear. Teddy's head jolted back and his eyes became as big as saucers.

"Are you fucking kidding me?" he said.

Ursula bit her lower lip and made a huge smile. She started jumping up and down on the mattress. Teddy hugged her and together they jumped up and down, laughing and giggling like two little kids.

That night, after completing his initial rounds at work, Teddy had spent time in the fifth floor library going through the travel literature that the bigwigs were always bringing back from their exclusive trips to exotic places. He wanted to find a place for Ursula and him to start their new life. She'd mentioned the Cape, but that would be impossible. They'd definitely have to get out of the country. So maybe something on the ocean, like the Mediterranean, or Costa Rica. Where was that anyway? He'd have to look that up.

7
LeBeau

When Teddy had let LeBeau in, the man had brushed by him like a cold breeze. Teddy said hello, but LeBeau didn't respond nor acknowledge him at all. He went right to the elevators.

Teddy went cowering back to his post and called Ursula. When she asked him if he had gotten the money, he vaguely remembered the man placing a briefcase on the floor in front of the security office before he went over to the elevator bank. He stood up and peered over the counter and saw it sitting on the floor. "He left a briefcase here."

"Well open it, silly."

Teddy snuck through the doorway, looked both ways and then quickly grabbed the briefcase and returned to the safety of his seat.

"I've got it."

"Open it, Teddy."

"I'm afraid."

"Afraid of what?"

"What if it's a bomb?"

"Teddy, for chrissake, it's not a bomb. Go ahead and open it."

"Okay, okay." He scrunched the cell phone between his shoulder and ear, closed his eyes, snapped the latches open and waited for the explosion. When none came, he opened his eyes and looked at the contents.

"Holy shit, Ursula!" He exclaimed. The briefcase was full of money.

"It's full of money. I mean FULL."

Ursula giggled uncontrollably like a schoolgirl. "Oh my God! Oh my God! Count it!"

LeBeau exited the elevator on the fifth floor and walked down the long hallway. The offices had etched glass doors with polished brass handles and LeBeau could see into the plush rooms with the rich mahogany, dark carpeting, and the floor-to-ceiling windows overlooking the Charles. The lab doors were opaque, thick stainless steel with huge numbers on them, 1, 2, 3, and so on. Ten labs and two offices per floor, twelve floors. All locked and protected by an elaborate million-dollar security system entrusted into the greedy hands of a minimum-wage security guard. LeBeau laughed at the stupidity of American big business.

He moved quickly and deliberately to the door marked Library, directly opposite the one marked Cafeteria. These were the only two doors perennially unlocked. Supposedly there was nothing of value in them. But tonight, something of immense value, cleverly hidden in the open for years, would be stolen and delivered into the wrong hands.

This had been his easiest job to set up and pull off, but the toughest to research. It had taken him more than a year of mind-boggling research to discern the whereabouts of the target. Of course he had been looking in all the wrong places, as the professor had intended. Now, in the small library room, he walked over the Oriental rug, around the leather couch and found what he was looking for on the bottom shelf of books.

LeBeau held the notebooks in his hands admiring the brilliance of the man who had baffled him for more than a year. How clever of Professor Montgomery Fairmont; scientist, entrepreneur, billionaire and current recluse - a man of Einstein-like genius - to realize any attempt at espionage would focus on computer hardware securely locked away in an impregnable, high-tech fortress. To "hide" the biogenetic bounty in dusty old notebooks in clear visibility to all was one more remarkable idea by a man known for remarkable ideas.

But, LeBeau thought, how foolish of him to leave the notebooks behind. Of course the professor didn't need them, he had all these notes and formulas in his head, wherever he was. For the elusive professor was nowhere to be found and was widely believed to be dead. But if these notebooks didn't satisfy his clients, LeBeau vowed he would find the professor, even if he had to dig him up from his grave.

The money was banded in $50,000 increments and stacked in twos, five rows across the top, five rows across the bottom.

"There's a million fucking dollars here! This can't be happening."

"It's happening, Teddy, believe me, it's happening. We're rich! A million dollars to them is nothing. They'll make hundreds of millions on this case. We're rich, Teddy! We can do anything we want now."

"I'm outta here," he shut the briefcase and snapped the latches shut.

"No, no, no! Don't screw it up. You've got to finish your shift, remember? Just two more hours, baby. Everything as usual. Then come home to me. I'm packing right now. In just a few hours we'll be on a plane to Costa Rica and nobody will ever hear from us again. Oh Teddy, I love you, I love you."

"We did it, huh?" Teddy was catching her enthusiasm. "We did it, Ursula! We did it! I can't wait for you to see this, baby."

"Finish your shift and then hurry home. I'll be waiting for you."

"I'll be home in two hours and ten minutes."

"Okay. Bye."

"Bye."

Teddy wrapped his arms around the briefcase and squeezed it like a newborn baby.

The elevator doors opened and the man in black walked out. Teddy sprang to his feet, laid the briefcase flat on the desk and held his breath. LeBeau came toward him. There was something in his hand. Teddy felt a chill. His shoulders began to shiver. It was a black nylon bag. LeBeau hurried at him, then walked right past him and went to the doors. Teddy's eyes were riveted on the man's back as he stood in front of the glass doors as stiff as a statue.

LeBeau waited for several seconds and then turned his head slightly over his shoulder. Teddy jumped and remembered what he was supposed to do. He pushed the button beneath the desk and held it as the buzzing sound echoed throughout the lobby. LeBeau held his glaring profile at Teddy for several long seconds. Then quickly he faced forward, kicked the door open and disappeared.

Teddy sat down and took a deep breath and exhaled it slowly. He could hear his heart pounding. He looked at his lap. There was a urine spot on the front of his trousers.

8

Celebration

Teddy Platt had never been so pumped-up in his whole life. He was carrying a million dollars – a million fucking dollars – clutched in his arms, as he sat anxiously on the T, smothering the briefcase to his chest and nervously fanning his legs like a frightened butterfly.

He was freaking out. He couldn't wait to get to Ursula. It was like a dream. Holy shit! Holy fucking shit! They were out of here. Tomorrow morning, no, this morning, they were on a flight to a new and unbelievable life. Costa Fucking Rica. Paradise with mucho bux. He had looked it up. The value of the dollar was something like ten to one. He had the equivalent of ten million dollars in his hands. A brand new Cadillac - no, fuck it – a brand new Mercedes. Convertible. A wicked-cool house. On the beach. With servants and a monster fucking flat screen as big as a wall. Teddy was giddy. People on the seats opposite him were staring, but he didn't care.

He was going to buy Ursula the biggest diamond ring ever made. And a big-ass gold necklace for himself, like Mister T. Remember him?

The train made its stop and Teddy raced off and clambered up the steps, two at a time, to street level. He ignored the early morning traffic with the blaring horns and ran across the street to his apartment, mastering the third-floor walkup like a high school track star.

Ursula pulled the door open and sprang into Teddy's arms.

"Oh Teddy, Teddy, Teddy," she showered him with kisses.

"Wait, wait," he slammed the door shut. "Come here! Look at this!"

Teddy upended the briefcase on the bed. The money fell out in thick packets and made a beautiful green mound on the naked white sheets.

"Oh my God," Ursula breathed through her hands fanned across her face. "I can't believe it!"

"Believe it, baby. We're rich!"

They started with champagne. Ursula had it chilling in ice in the kitchen sink. They toasted their good fortune, each other, their upcoming flight, the fools they were leaving behind, the weather in Costa Rica. When the bottle was empty, Ursula pulled out another surprise - a bottle of rum.

"It's actually made in Costa Rica, Teddy."

They sat on the bed with the money spread all around them doing shots with beer chasers. They began opening the bundles of cash and throwing the crisp new bills into the air above them like confetti. They were ecstatic.

"This is the happy-sssht day in my life," he slurred, now foregoing the shot glass and drinking directly from the bottle.

"I can make it happier," Ursula teased.

"Oh, yeah?"

She pushed him over on the bed and grabbed his belt buckle. She pulled his pants off and threw them on the floor, leaving him in his boxers.

Ursula frowned and pouted her bottom lip, "You've got too many pants on, Teddy," and she pulled his boxers off and threw them in the air.

She helped him with his shirt and held the rum bottle for him as he pulled his arms free of the sleeves and yanked his T-shirt over his head. Teddy lay naked on the bed with only his sox on. He grabbed the bottle and took another swig.

Ursula was wearing a long terry cloth robe. She stood up, undid the sash and let the robe drop to the floor, exposing her naked body to him.

"Yummy," he said and tilted the bottle back.

Ursula took another chunk of bills and ripped off the band. Carefully she began placing them, one by one, all over Teddy's body, clothing him in crisp hundred-dollar bills.

She smoothed them out like a mosaic over his chest and tried to get them to stop sliding off his pudgy belly. They laughed each time one fell off. Then she took the bottle from him and spread his arms out and covered them with the bills end to end. Teddy was getting turned-on.

"More rum, mommy," he said.

Ursula propped his head with a pillow and tipped the rum into his eager mouth.

When she got to his legs he began to harden. By the time she got to his feet, Teddy was fully erect. She tucked some bills into the tops of his sox and then folded one in half and placed it on the tip of his penis. It looked like a rooftop and they laughed.

Teddy's laugh was loud from the alcohol.

"Shhh," she said. "You'll wake the neighbors. It's still early." She gave him one more swig of the rum and then stuffed a handful of bills into his mouth and placed one over his eyes like a blindfold.

She took the little rooftop off his penis and began fondling him. Teddy squirmed and moaned through the gag of bills in his mouth. When she put her lips over his penis and began flicking her tongue, Teddy's moaning increased and his breathing became quicker and quicker.

When she was ready, Ursula climbed on top of him and gave Teddy Platt the ride of his life.

She rode him long and hard, grinding her pelvis into him and gyrating her hips in circles, first one way, and then the other. She was driving him crazy and she knew it. When he was about to cum she would abruptly stop and then slowly start all over again.

"Oh my God, you're going to give me a fucking heart attack," he moaned through his gag.

Ursula smiled and said, "Not yet, baby, not yet," and rode him harder and harder. Eventually, when she had him where she wanted him, Ursula allowed Teddy to have his mind-blowing orgasm.

Then she pulled the gag from his mouth and kissed him hard, all the while continuing to grind on top of him, riding him until he became flaccid and slipped out of her.

Teddy was comatose. She climbed off him and began gathering the bills and tidying them into their neat packets again and placing them back into the briefcase.

When Teddy's snoring took on a deep, steady rhythm, Ursula slapped him hard across the face. Nothing, not even a flinch.

She pulled the last of the bills from the tops of his sox, placed them in the briefcase and closed it.

Ursula went to the closet and got her bag and extracted a silver cylinder from an inside pocket. It looked like a cigar holder. She twisted the top off and carefully tipped it at a downward angle allowing a slender hypodermic syringe to slip into her palm. She removed Teddy's sox and knelt on the floor at the foot of the bed.

She listened again to his snoring and shook his leg to wake him up. Satisfied that he was out, Ursula pinched Teddy's big toe between her fingers and expertly pushed the long needle under his toenail and depressed the plunger.

After she extracted the needle, she waited a full two minutes to be sure there was no bleeding, no blood trace. She replaced the syringe into its holder and dropped it back into her bag and went to his side. Teddy's snoring became softer and his breathing was taking on a slower pace. She patted him gently on the cheek and said, "Okay Teddy, you can have your heart attack now." Then she bent down and kissed his forehead and whispered into his ear, "Thanks for the ride."

Ursula pulled her cell phone from her purse and checked the time. Perfect, right on schedule. She had exactly an hour to pack her things and make sure the stage was set before LeBeau picked her up. Their flight back to Europe was leaving Logan in two-and-a-half hours.

9
Clean Up

Ursula stood inside the apartment surveying the room, her back against the door, arms folded below her breasts. She wanted a feel for the way the incoming authorities would initially view the scene.

They'd get here shortly after she made the 911 call. The lights would be off but there'd be daylight filtering through the Venetian blinds. The apartment wasn't much more than a motel room, so they'd see Teddy's body right away, naked and dead on the unmade bed. They'd tread cautiously into the room so as not to disturb anything.

The dispatcher would have played the 911 tape for the officers on their way to the scene, so the voice of the hysterical woman saying, "Oh my God, I think he's had a heart attack," would be fresh in their minds, as would the false cause of death, immediately plausible once they saw no physical disturbance in the room, no marks of foul play on the body and the peaceful look on the countenance of the deceased.

The cops would probably chuckle about how happily Mr. Platt "went out" and then casually wait on-scene for the Medical Examiner to arrive. They'd figure the girlfriend had panicked and fled, thinking she had killed him with sex and might somehow be liable for his demise.

The Potassium Nitrate Ursula had injected into Teddy Platt would show up in an autopsy as a normal physiological by-product of a Myocardial Infarction. She had learned about the drug from a physician in Germany who had contracted her to dispose of his wife. Ursula had had a brief fling with Herr Doktor while she picked his brain and then she had done him in in exactly the way he had suggested to her to murder his wife. Unfortunately for the doctor, his wife had outbid him.

But Ursula didn't think an autopsy would be performed on Teddy Platt. She had set the scene perfectly, leaving Teddy exactly the way he was on the bed, naked and sweaty, with an adequate amount of vaginal juices on his genitals to suggest the type of wild and rigorous sexual activity that would raise his heart rate to overload. That, plus his pudgy physical condition and the fact that he had been a life-long smoker, would mask any suspicion of foul play. Also, there was plenty of alcohol in his system. So even if they did just the basic work up on him - the visual body inspection for signs of blunt trauma and the minor blood work for evidence of a drug overdose - they would still assume no foul play. Ursula felt satisfied that the ME would deduce what she wanted him to: death by sex.

As for her, she knew she wouldn't be caught. Her planning and execution was meticulous. Ursula was leaving no reason for anyone to suspect her of any wrongdoing or have any need to find her for questioning, just a spooked girlfriend who panicked and ran. She hadn't hidden anything. Her prints were all over the apartment and her DNA, her vaginal secretion, was all over the deceased. By leaving traces of her existence, she was in effect leaving no traces at all. She was clean. Her prints were not on file anywhere.

Only amateurs would leave traces behind. Amateurs, thinking they were clever, would have wiped everything down, washed the body, vacuumed the bed and carpet, scrubbed the bathroom, removed hair from the sink drain, et cetera, et cetera. All of which would have raised eyebrows and led to a more thorough investigation.

Now, by leaving the scene amiss as it would have been under normal circumstances, Ursula knew the detectives might spend no more than half a day talking to neighbors, who wouldn't know anything, and to Teddy's family and friends, who wouldn't know much more. Hence, they wouldn't chase her. And if they did, they'd probably try to locate her employer and get nowhere fast.

Her work number that Ursula had programmed into Teddy's cell phone when their relationship had gotten hot, was actually the number to her store-bought track phone. She had never been a receptionist for Collier, Collier, Woodbury and Oakes. In fact, the law firm didn't exist. And, if anyone noticed the excessive amount of calls Teddy had made to that number - and bothered to contact her - they'd get no response from the phone that she would toss into Boston Harbor on her way to the airport.

The clandestine activity at AbioGenetix would never be discovered. They'd hire another Teddy Platt to watch over their elaborate security system and corporate life would go on. No one would ever know LeBeau had been there, nor would anyone ever miss the dusty notebooks he had stolen.

Teddy's buddies at the bar would raise a toast to him, call him a lucky bastard and tell each other they hoped to go out the same way Teddy had.

It was an open and shut case.

She only had one more thing to do. Place the call. She would do that en route to Logan. She knew exactly how it would go. After entering a lengthy series of numbers known only to her, she would wait for the click. There would be no dial tone nor ringing as the transmission scrambled simultaneously amongst one hundred different cell towers across the globe. She would have no more than ten seconds before the line went dead and unreachable again, forever. After the click she would say:

Done.
Gut. Unt LeBeau?
Mit mir. He's with me.

Sehr gut. Have a safe flight.

And the phone would sink slowly into the murky depths of Boston Harbor.

Ursula walked confidently out of the apartment with an overnight bag containing all her belongings and a briefcase full of money.

10
Mi casa es su casa

The MacLaren's lived in a nice home in a section of Lakewood Ranch called The Yellow Creek Estates. They had upgraded from their modest house in South Sarasota a few years ago when MacLaren had made Lieutenant. Without being saddled with the expenses of raising children, the MacLaren's had parlayed a decent amount of monetary security and allowed themselves some extra creature comforts. Like the three bedrooms the two of them really didn't need, the over-sized three-car garage with the twenty-one foot Southwind sitting in it (that MacLaren hardly ever put into the water) and the extra-lush, time-consuming acre of tropical landscaping. But the lot at the end of the cul-de-sac backing up to the preserve, and the extra dough they'd spent on the towering screened-in lanai had been well worth it. The four of them were inside of it, comfortably shaded from the sun blazing above them.

The girls were at the patio table getting acquainted over frozen daiquiris. Big Ben and MacLaren were at the grill, holding onto ice-cold bottles of Fleming's Pale Ale. The fresh grouper was grilling nicely next to the veggies.

"Whenever I'm around at night," MacLaren said, "Lorraine and I like to sit out here and watch the sunset. The birds cruise in and roost in the trees of the rockery over there by the water's edge.

There are egrets and cormorants and herons and even a few pelicans."

"You've got a nice place here," Ben said. He flipped the veggies over with the tongs and sipped his beer.

"The other night a gator was sitting prone on the shoreline and a cormorant was drying his wings right next to it. I thought for sure the gator was gonna get it. But they just stood side by side paying no never mind to each other."

"Nature."

"Yeah."

A tropical breeze brushed the nearby palm fronds.

"Got about another five minutes on this grouper. Want another beer?"

"You bet."

MacLaren disappeared into the house. Big Ben went over to the women. They were engrossed in conversation about clothes and Florida. He stood behind his wife and squeezed her shoulders affectionately with his big hands. Carlene leaned back and placed her hands on his. The lady's conversation was pleasant and Ben felt assured that Carlene was okay. He knew the events of the day would be troubling her and he also knew she needed time to spend on girly talk, a respite from the anxiety unexpectedly draped upon her. He squeezed her shoulders tenderly again and left her to her distraction.

Back at the grill MacLaren asked his houseguest, "When are you going to see Chief Ray?"

"I've got an appointment to meet with him and the selectmen tomorrow." Ben, at MacLaren's urging, had thrown his hat into the ring to be considered for Chief of Police of Myakka City, about a half-hour west of Sarasota. Chief Ray Burati, MacLaren's former mentor, was retiring from his position as head dog in Myakka City.

"Right off the bat? You just got here."

"I know, but I wanted to get it out of the way first thing so that we could enjoy the vacation - one way or the other."

MacLaren raised his eyebrows, "You still haven't told your wife?"

"There's a lot to consider and I don't want to get her any more riled-up than I have to. If the interview goes well, I'll lay the cards on the table. If it doesn't go well, then we'll enjoy a ten day vacation away from the kids and go back to reality."

A year ago Ben had been involved in a murder case pointed at his best friend Dodge Maddison, an internationally famous fashion designer who had been involved in the death of a supermodel murdered during a fashion shoot on the sunny beaches of Sarasota. The case had taken some interesting twists and turns and had more than tested the patience of Big Ben (best friend of the accused) and MacLaren (investigating and glory-hungry homicide detective). Yet, during the course of the case, Ben and MacLaren had established a professional rapport, and had become good friends.

Something else also happened at that time. Chief of Police Ben Benson of Bryce Corner, Massachusetts, had been unexpectedly seduced by the wiles of la Floridita.

Ben wasn't exactly hiding the vacation's underlying purpose from his wife. After all, they, like most New Englanders, had often dreamt about moving to Florida. He just wanted to be sure he had a job lined up before he broached the topic of relocating as Chief of Police from a snow state to Chief of Police of a sunshine state.

"What'll we tell the girls?" MacLaren asked.

"Nothing. They're going shopping and we're going fishing, right?"

MacLaren slid the steel spatula under the blackened grouper and carefully turned it over. "Another sixty seconds. Here," he handed a large plate to Ben, "you can load up the grilled veggies and bring 'em to the table."

Dinner was excellent. The food was tasty, the weather perfect and the conversation hearty. When the patio table had been cleared the four of them sat content with their after dinner drinks (coffee and Bailey's for the ladies and single malt scotch for the men). A great white egret soared over the high lanai and descended on the edge of the pond. The big bird preened its wings, nestled them comfortably into its side and then strutted almost motionlessly into the water's edge.

"High school," Carlene said.

They looked at her.

"Hannah Hunt and I went to the same high school."

It was the first she'd mentioned the dead woman since the revelation at the museum that afternoon. MacLaren looked at Ben. His eyes were on his wife.

"It was my junior year. Right before my family moved to Massachusetts from Vermont."

No one spoke. Ben and MacLaren were cops and Lorraine, like Carlene, was a cop's wife. All at the table knew how important it was for Carlene to get this out. They gave her room to remember.

11

Science Fair

St. Johnsbury, Vermont, "Crossroads to New England" they say. Although geographically it is nowhere near the central point of the six states and in fact lies so far north that it practically borders Canada. Surrounded by vast multi-generational farmland (it is still a fact that there are more cows in Vermont than people), it is a quiet rural town with a hilly center of old brick buildings and a not-so-busy-anymore railway yard on the flats. Bustling commerce has long since moved further south along the greater Boston/New York City corridor, as did Carlene's family twenty-some years ago.

St. Jay (the local's moniker) has a grand fieldstone edifice built in the early 1900's functioning to this day as the high school.

"We were friends. Not close. Actually, we were rivals."

"Oh?" Lorraine poured more coffee into Carlene's cup.

"There was this boy that all the girls were goo-goo over."

"Let me guess," Ben interjected, "star quarterback?"

"No, track star, actually. They said he ran so fast because the girls were always chasing after him."

Ben looked to MacLaren and rolled his eyes.

"Roland Briggs," she said raising her coffee cup. "He was quite cute." She smiled at Lorraine and took a sip.

"Anyway," Carlene continued, "Hannah and I dated him at the same time. Not knowingly of course. He was kind of a rogue and played the two of us."

"Would this Roland Briggs character have anything to do with Hannah's murder?" MacLaren was in cop mode.

"I have no idea. I haven't heard from any of my old Vermont classmates in over twenty years. Although …" she hesitated.

"What?"

"I was just thinking, my cousin, who still lives in St. Jay, Facebooked me about our upcoming reunion. I wonder if that's why Hannah had my number. Maybe she's on the reunion committee or something."

"Hang on," Maclaren got up from the table, went into the other room and returned a second later with a small leather notebook and made a note. "I'll check that out. What's the name of the school?"

"St. Johnsbury Academy."

"You said you left in your junior year?"

"The summer after that."

"Then you graduated from?…"

"Bryce Corner High."

"In Massachusetts? Ben's home town?"

"Yes, that's where I met this big lug."

"Best day of her life," Ben grinned.

"Of course, Darling," Carlene patted his knee.

MacLaren continued, "Why would you be on a reunion list to a high school you didn't graduate from?"

"Well, even though I didn't technically graduate from St. Jay, I was still part of that class. Small town. Everybody knows everybody. And I'm not sure I am on the list. I think my cousin Susan thought it would be nice for me to attend and hook up with the old gang."

"Okay," MacLaren sat back, gathering his thoughts. "When was the last time you spoke with Hannah Hunt Everett?"

"In high school. As I said, we weren't close." She laughed.

"What?"

"There was this statewide Science Fair competition between all the high schools in Vermont. Each class would pick a team to represent them. Ironically, Hannah and I got partnered together. We were the science teacher's rising stars and he wanted us to come up with some brilliant idea that would blow away the other classes.

"At first, because of our rivalry over Roland, we didn't even talk to each other. We didn't give a shit about the Science Fair. All either one of us wanted to do was kill the other so that we'd have Roland to ourselves. But ironically we became friends and decided to plot revenge."

"How did you do that?"

"We decided to clone him."

"Clone him?" Hannah laughed. "I'd like to kill him."

"All I'm saying is that if you two are so crazy about this jerk, you should clone him. That way you'd each have him." Montgomery Fairmont was the high school geek; nerdy looking, thick black-framed glasses, disheveled hair - like it was a waste of energy to use a comb. Always wore a suit and tie and carried a briefcase. Sat by himself in the cafeteria. He had been picked to be the third member of Mr. Grogan's Science Fair team because he was ... well, brilliant.

"You're a funny one, Monty," Carlene said.

Monty ignored her comment as he did all the petty comments and snickers that he was constantly barraged with. He sat at the table in the Science lab with the two girls and scribbled frantically in the notebook he was always writing in.

Hannah laughed again. "Y'know, that wouldn't be a bad idea."

Monty was oblivious. Carlene said, "What do you mean?"

"I mean, if we had an exact replica of him and we had total control over it, we could embarrass the shit out of the little prick."

This got Carlene's ire up. "Yeah, we could make him act like a queer when he's with his friends."

"And make him come on to them," Hannah added.

"And dress him up like a girl and walk down the hallways singing like Mary Poppins." They giggled.

"It's doable, you know," Monty said.

The girls looked at him, then at each other, then back to him. "No sir," they said simultaneously.

Montgomery Fairmont looked at them over the top of his thick glasses with an eerie smile.

"Don't even try to tell me you cloned someone in fucking high school," Ben said.

"Obviously we didn't pull it off, or we'd have been world famous. I mean of course it didn't work, but it was fun trying. We felt as if we actually got close. Like if we had more time it might have been attainable."

"Close like actually a body?"

"No, close in theory and formulas. We didn't know how we were going to produce an actual body, so we faked it. We dressed Monty up as Frankenstein's monster and he stood at the booth growling at people as they went by."

"Did you win?"

"Naw, everyone thought we were crazy, especially the judges. We all got D's on the project. They thought we were mocking the whole Science Fair thing. But we didn't give a shit. Or at least Hannah and I didn't. But Monty was pissed that he wasn't taken seriously. He was convinced that if we'd had more time we could have pulled it off."

"Bullshit," Ben said and reached for the bottle of Oban and poured two more fingers.

MacLaren shook off the offer of more scotch, saying, "That must have been pretty advanced stuff for three high school kids back then."

"Hannah and I were smart in Chemistry and Biology and such, but Monty was the real genius. We followed his lead. It was after that whole "Dolly" thing in Scotland had been in the news, where they had actually cloned an animal."

"I remember that," Ben said. "They duplicated a cow."

"Actually it was a sheep. Scottish scientists were the first to clone a mammal," MacLaren said with pride.

"Leave it to the Scots to yearn for more sheep in their lives," Ben jabbed at MacLaren's heritage.

"Before that," MacLaren brushed off Big Ben's comment, "genetic replication had been accomplished only in the plant world. Orchids were the first I think, splitting the genetic codes and cross-pollinating the strains."

"And when Dolly came along," Carlene said, "it naturally led to speculation of 'what could come next?'"

"Sure," MacLaren said. "But there had been earlier experiments of human cloning by Hitler and Stalin and other whack-jobs. You know, all that master-race bullshit. Clone an army of warriors."

"How do you know all this shit?" Ben asked.

"'Cuz I'm smarter than you." MacLaren got up and went into the kitchen to get more coffee for the ladies. They could all hear him laugh, "The Scots have always been smarter than you Swede's," he hollered back.

"Yeah, yeah," Ben grumbled. "I still think it's bullshit."

MacLaren returned, poured coffee and set the pot on a ceramic tile in the center of the patio table. The four of them sat quiet.

Carlene Benson stared into the coffee cup she held with both hands. "How our paths would one day cross in Sarasota, Florida is a mystery to me."

Ben could hear her tears in the filtered darkness of the guest bedroom. He put his arm across her midriff and pulled his wife into him. The bed was high and comfortable and broad enough to accommodate his muscular bulk and Carlene's medium stature. They had slept together for over twenty years and Ben never stopped marveling at how good she felt in his arms. Their closeness gave them a special awareness of each other and, like the instinctual radar evident in the animal world, the couple could easily sense emotional disturbances in each other.

Ben knew Carlene as a strong woman, not only of will, but also of compassion and sensibility. As a mother, those were inherent traits. As a Veterinary Assistant, those traits were a necessity. You had to be strong of heart to help euthanize those helpless animals with the sad eyes pleading to you at the end of their life. So he knew she was okay, or would be. But now he could sense her trepidation and knew it was due to the unexpected events of the day at the onset of their vacation. Softly he said, "Talk to me."

Carlene took her time gathering thoughts. She felt secure in the big arms of her husband and calmed by the rhythmic rustling of the palms in the night breeze outside the open window.

In a whisper she said, "I didn't know her that well, but she was a person that I had known. It's not right for anyone to go out that way. She looked so … so …"

Ben squeezed her tighter and rubbed her shoulder. "It's an awful thing to see. You didn't have to do that."

"To die like that, with her head so … and all that blood. It didn't affect me at the time, but now I can't get the image out of my mind."

"When the image comes, try to think of her laughing. Think of another time when you knew her in school and picture her laughing. It'll help."

There was a loud, disturbing sound outside. Animal sounds, not close, but from the distance. A sharp splashing of a reptilian tail on the water, then a brief horrific squawking that cut through the black air and faded to silence.

"Ben?"

"Yeah, babe?"

"What would we ever do if we lost each other?"

Ben rose over her and kissed her lips. "Don't worry about that Sugarplum, that will never happen."

Carlene wrapped her arms around his neck and kissed him hungrily. Holding the kiss, Ben unbuttoned her sleepwear and climbed on top of his wife, gently pressing his massive chest onto her hardened nipples. Carlene's hand slid the length of his torso and reached between his legs.

Outside, the night was quiet, but a steady stirring arose in the guest room of the MacLaren house.

12
Gramps Ramp

"Good morning."

"Mornin'," Big Ben responded.

"Didn't expect to see you up this early." MacLaren blew into his fresh cup of coffee as he joined Ben standing at the edge of the preserve.

The sun wasn't yet above the horizon but the bright dawn was. The final stragglers of the rookery stretched their wings and lifted off to the east, skirting the pink ribbon of sunrise as they flew into their new day.

"This is what I'm talking about," Ben extended his arms and took in a deep breath.

"What time you meeting the Board?"

"Nine."

"What happens if they offer it to you?"

"Guess I'll tell 'em I need a few days to think about it then lay it all out to Carlene."

"You're a brave man, Benson. If I tried to pull something like that with Lorraine, she'd have a fit."

"Well, the way I look at it is if they don't offer me the position, then it's a moot point. Why stir up the pot if there's nothin' in it?"

The sun poked its head into the sky. MacLaren squinted and turned his back to it. "It's early. The girls will probably sleep in and then I guess Lorraine's going to take Carlene shopping on St. Armands Circle. Then lunch and maybe the beach. I told her we'd be back by sunset for dinner."

"Fine." Ben stood enjoying the warm sun brush across his face.

"So, I thought we could hook up the boat and get an early start. I know a great breakfast place on the way to Myakka."

"You're coming?" Ben said.

"Fuckin' A. I'm on vacation too, remember?"

"Not with this new homicide you're not."

"Yeah, well, I'm on it. But I can be on it from my boat."

They hooked MacLaren's twenty-one footer, *Sea~Nile,* to the hitch on his Ford pickup, grabbed a couple to-go mugs, left a note for their wives and headed out of the enclave, down I-75 and took the exit for SR 70 East. Big Ben was straight-faced. He was going over the upcoming interview in his head. But MacLaren was smiling. He had fishing on his mind.

A half hour later on the long, desolate stretch of state road, well east of the city of Sarasota, *"Gramps Ramp n Grub"* appeared like a mirage out of nowhere. "If you didn't know it was coming up, you'd drive right by it." MacLaren pulled into the gravel lot.

There were several trucks with empty trailers parked out back near the boat ramp. The Peace River flowed casually in the morning sun behind the old shack of a restaurant. A teenager was securing a pontoon boat to the dock. He saw MacLaren's rig coming in and went over to it.

"Hey, Lieutenant."

"How you doing, Josh? Can you drop the boat in and unhook the trailer for me?"

"Sure thing."

MacLaren handed him a couple of bills. "Thanks. And pull the truck up front. I've gotta travel into town for a bit, but I'll be back before noon to take the boat out."

"Need some bait and ice? The snook are hitting out by Pelican Point."

"Yeah. Thanks. The old man here?"

"Everyday."

Inside a scruffy old man with an eye patch and a well-worn leather cap said, "Hey Lieutenant! How da fuck are ya?"

MacLaren went to the counter and grabbed onto Gramps' hand. "I'm fine you old bastard, how are you?"

"Livelier than a dead man!" he yelled. His hearing was as weathered as his looks. "Who's yur body guard?"

"Big Ben Benson," he said. "Might be your new Chief of Police out here."

"Yup, heard 'bout you," Gramps said, grasping Ben's hand. "Grab a seat, grab a seat." He motioned to the cracked red vinyl stools at the low counter. "Got a shit load of runny eggs and greasy home fries to dish out to ya."

A minute later the two men were sipping coffee amid the ever-present aroma of sizzling bacon and grilled fish, a staple on Gramps' one page menu.

"You think Carlene knows more than she's saying?"

"What kind of a question is that?" Ben was offended. "You think she's holding something back, MacLaren?"

"Don't get huffy. I mean do you think she knows something that she doesn't know?"

"What the hell are you saying?"

"Look, she goes to high school with this woman, has a minimal relationship with her in some weird science project, loses all contact for twenty years and then all of a sudden the woman is murdered and just happens to have Carlene's cell number in her pocket on the last day of her life? That doesn't warrant any suspicion? Try to think of it outside your relationship. Be a cop for a minute."

"I am a cop."

"Good. Tell me what you think."

"I think there's something going on that Carlene is unaware of."

"Okay, so do I."

"But what?"

Gramps dropped two heaping plates in front of them. "Bun ape-a-tit," he mocked in a horrible French accent.

Ben gobbled half his plate before he realized how hungry he was. His analytical mind had kept him up most of the night. Carlene had woken up in the middle of the night and they had spoken about Hannah Hunt Everett and gotten nowhere.

MacLaren had slept well, but by first light his mind had been racing too. He said, "Okay, here's what we know." He put his fork down, sipped his coffee and wiped his mouth with a paper napkin from the chrome dispenser in front of them. "One," he started counting on his fingers, "Yesterday afternoon Hannah Hunt Everett is shot to death in the middle of the Ca' d'Zan. In her pocket is a slip of paper with your wife's cell number on it. Two, her husband says he doesn't know your wife nor recall Hannah ever mentioning her." He picked up his fork, stabbed a sausage link and chewed. "Three, the husband says Hannah told him she was going grocery shopping and has no idea why she would be at the Ca' d'Zan. Four ..." MacLaren forked into a piece of the grilled Mahi-Mahi and contemplated. "I don't know what four is."

"Okay," Ben said. "Let's take Carlene out of the equation for a minute. We've got the surveillance tape showing the shooter coming up behind Hannah, whispering into her ear and then, bang. That shows us someone wanted her dead."

"No shit, Sherlock."

"This wasn't random. It was set up; day, time and place. Premeditated. Who would do that?" Without waiting for an answer, Ben continued, "Two perps come immediately to mind. Her husband or a boyfriend."

"The husband has an air-tight alibi," MacLaren said. "A neighbor verifies she saw him washing his car in his driveway *and* he signed for a UPS delivery at almost the exact time Hannah was killed. The neighbor saw the UPS truck and we have verified the husband's signature on the delivery log. So he's out."

"Not necessarily. He could have hired the shooter."

"Long shot," the Lieutenant nodded, "But maybe. We'll look into the relationship."

"A disgruntled boyfriend would tidy things up nicely. She would have met him at the predestined location."

"Maybe not if he was disgruntled."

"She may not have known. Maybe he was jilting her. Had found someone else, didn't like her perfume anymore, whatever. She thinks she's meeting him for a date, he comes up behind her, says, 'Bye-bye, Cup Cake,' and pops her."

"I dunno. Odd spot for something like that don't you think? Public place ... middle of the day ..."

"Unless the perp wanted to leave a clue."

"Like?" MacLaren went behind the counter and took the coffee pot off the burner and refilled their cups.

Ben finished his meal, pushed his plate forward and took a sip of the fresh brew. "Like maybe the Art Museum is significant."

"Or the Dali. *Red Mangroves*. Maybe that's a clue."

"If he is leaving a clue, then that usually means there's going to be other killings." Ben was jumping ahead. Fearful for his wife, Carlene.

MacLaren picked up on this. "Let's not panic. We don't have anything to suggest this is serial."

"We need to factor Carlene back into this. The phone number in her pocket is too coincidental. There's something going on here and I don't like it."

"So then, if in fact the last communication the girls had with each other was back in high school in Vermont, then we may need to start there." MacLaren looked at the clock on the wall. "But for now, we gotta get going. It's almost nine o'clock, big guy."

13
Vultures

The stretch from Gramps Ramp to the center of Myakka was a long straight line with the narrow white road bordered by green prairie foliage fading into a minimal point on the eastern horizon. MacLaren had his foot into it as the pickup sped along. There were no other vehicles in either direction for as far as the eye could see.

A dark lump appeared in the shimmering mirage far ahead of them. Closer and closer it began to take shape.

"What the hell is that?" Ben said.

"Something in the middle of the road. Big looking. Might be a boar. Lots of them around here." He began to slow down.

When they got within fifty yards of it, the image shrank and became clearer. Buzzards flew off the carcass and they could discern what it was. MacLaren slowed almost to a stop as they maneuvered around the huge black vulture lying in the road. "Poor bastard," he said. "Being eaten by his own kind." He sped up.

"Pull over," Ben said.

"Huh?"

"Pull over."

MacLaren did so. "You gotta take a piss?"

Big Ben got out of the truck. The silent heat of the prairie morning surrounded him. The air was hot and quiet and still, the road a barren gray ribbon. He walked back to the bird and stood over it. Shiny, bright-red blood oozed onto the sun-bleached pavement from a wound where the other buzzards had been picking. The bird was still alive. The black feathering, glistening purple in the sun, rose and fell as the bird struggled towards its last breath. Ben looked to the side of the road where four vultures were perched on an old cattle fencing, like the scavengers of death that they were, waiting patiently for him to leave.

He drew his gun from the cargo pocket of his khakis and looked down at the suffering bird, its glossy black eye, like a polished onyx marble, pleading to him for the quick advent of death. Ben fired two bullets into the bird. The other vultures jumped into flight. MacLaren burst out of the truck and came running. Big Ben fired two more rounds at the retreating buzzards.

"What the fuck is the matter with you?!" MacLaren grabbed onto Ben's arm and wrestled the gun away from him.

"Are you nuts?! You can't go discharging a weapon out here. Geesus, Ben."

The big man was breathing heavily. MacLaren walked away shaking his head, the gun in his hand. "Come on."

Ben stood over the dead bird for a moment and then walked back to the truck.

14
Myakka Mafia

They were to meet the five member Board of Selectmen at Ray's place just outside of town. Ray Burati was the current Chief of Police for Myakka, Florida.

"We're not going into town? Town hall or something?" Ben said.

"Naw, no one's that formal out here. In fact, I'd bet those boys will be playing poker and drinking beer before ten o'clock."

Ben had met Chief Ray the year before when he'd helped MacLaren on a case which had stretched into Ray's territory. When they walked into his rusty, tin-roofed shed, Chief Ray Burati was hunched over an old Harley V-twin motor anchored onto a greasy engine stand. He was focusing on the rising needle on his torque wrench, as he pressure-tightened a head bolt.

"Howdy Ray."

"Chief to you, Lieutenant MacLaren," he replied without looking away from the torque gauge.

"Yes Sir."

They waited until Chief Ray finished his surgical procedure. He had a friendly face and a sweeping white mustache ala Richard Farnsworth. He came around the workbench rubbing his hands on a clean rag. He extended his hand to Ben. "Welcome back, Chief. Good to see you again."

"Good to see you too, Chief Burati." Ben looked at the motorcycle Ray was working on. "Panhead?"

"Good eye. It's my baby. Been working on her forever."

"She's looking good."

"Yeah, coming together, slowly but surely. You a bike enthusiast?"

"Soft Tail."

"Good bike. Still ridin'?"

"Nope, sold it years ago after the first born."

"Miss it, don't cha?" Ray smiled and twisted his handlebar moustache. He went to the edge of the lean-to and lifted a blue tarp off of a black and silver Fat Boy.

"Wow. Centennial. You buy it new?"

"Yup. Ordered it two years before the anniversary. Only got five-thousand miles on it."

Big Ben circled the 2003 Harley-Davidson. "She's a beauty."

"Thanks. If you ever get settled in down here, come on by and we'll take these iron horses for a ride."

"Deal," Ben replied and gave Ray a hand wrapping up the Fat Boy. "What are you going to do with them?"

"Well, I'm close to getting the Panhead together, and I can't ride two at the same time, so I'm thinking I might sell the Fat Boy. You interested?"

Ben laughed. "You never know. Mid-life changes change a lot of things. Keep me in mind."

Ray gave MacLaren a welcome slap on the shoulder. "You look healthy Lieutenant MacLaren." Turning to Ben, he said, "The Lieutenant and I go way back. He was my rookie partner on the Sarasota P.D. I taught him everything he knows."

"I'd like to say he's full of shit, but he's absolutely right."

"Haven't seen you two boys since that fiasco we had last year at the State Park. Terrible thing."

"Yes, it was."

"Anyway Ben, the way you handled yourself and brought about a quick resolve to those homicides got the attention of the Board. That, along with the Lieutenant's recommendation, brings us to where we are today. I hope you're ready to make the move from Boston to Southern Florida because I'm sure as hell ready to get on this here motorcycle and ride into the sunset."

Just then a metallic-silver Jaguar XFR with mirror-tinted windows roared into the driveway. It looked like a giant chrome torpedo.

"Here comes the Myakka Mafia," Ray Burati chuckled. "Let's move this party over to the back porch out of the sun. Too damn hot in this lean-to."

As they crossed the yard they were joined by five men exiting the Jag. All were dressed casual in tees or polos over shorts and sneakers.

They gathered on the wide veranda beneath a lazy spinning ceiling fan. Ray Burati said, "I'll do the intros. You all know Lieutenant MacLaren and this here's our guest of honor, Ben Benson, Chief of Police from Bryce Corner, Massachusetts. The mob here are," he pointed one by one around the group, "Dave Nauman, Don Trudeau, Jim Goodrow, Bob Tromblay and Billy Borowik." All shook hands and took seats around a large white resin patio table.

"Before we start conducting business," Ray said, "I've got coffee on and a fridge full of water and sodas."

"I'll take a Bloody Mary," Trudeau said. "In a tall beer mug with extra Tabasco."

"Yeah, and Ray," Goodrow added, "I'd like a little Jack on the rocks. Tiny splash of water."

"This your typical board meeting?" Ben asked.

"Pretty much," Tromblay said. "It'll get better after the first cocktail though," he chuckled.

"Dave?"

"Ah, just give me an O'Doul's."

"Pussy piss."

"Don't give me any shit. You know I gave up drinkin' and I can give up you guys too."

Billy looked at his watch, shaking his head, "It's only nine-thirty. I'll just have coffee, Ray."

MacLaren piped in, "Okay, let's get this shindig underway. I've got to get out on the water."

An hour later Maclaren was racing back to Gramps Ramp anxious to get *Sea~Nile* into the tributary and drop his lines. "Well, that went well, huh? Hell, I thought Ray was gonna hand you his badge and gun right then and there. And then when you said you'd take the job, I thought Ray was gonna either kiss you or cry or both," he laughed. "Can't ever remember seeing him so happy."

"I didn't actually say yes, y'know. I said it sounded good and I'd give them an answer within the week."

"Same thing." MacLaren reached over and slapped Ben's shoulder. "It's gonna be great. We'll bust the bad guys in the mornings and go fishing in the afternoons."

"Boy, I hope my wife is as enthusiastic as you are."

"How do you think that'll go, big guy?"

Ben rode quiet for a long while, running the upcoming conversation in his head. He hoped it wouldn't turn into a confrontation. There was a lot to consider, uprooting not only themselves, but also their two teenagers. But at least it wouldn't be a new conversation; they'd talked about relocating before. Ben only hoped Carlene had genuinely meant it. He knew they would all adjust and be happy. Right?

They came to the spot in the road where the dead vulture lay. The buzzards were back to their feasting. As the truck passed by them they flew off the carcass and circled low above their carrion. Ben turned in his seat and watched them through the rear window. When the truck got far enough away, they alighted upon the road and waddled back to their feeding frenzy.

Big Ben watched the scene as it dwindled into an unrecognizable black mass in the retreating distance. He turned forward in his seat.

15

Hannah's Twin

The two officers of the law stood at the helm of *Sea~Nile* breathing in the tangy air of high noon on the river. They had bait, beer on ice and a smooth sea ahead of them.

"Here, take the helm," the Lieutenant said and reached for two ice-cold bottles of beer. He popped the tops, squeezed them into cozies, handed one to Ben and sat back in the captain's chair.

"Here's to luck and pleasant conversation," he said, clinking his bottle against Ben's. "You think she'll go for it?"

Ben knew what his buddy was talking about. He took a long swig on his beer. A pair of great blue herons flew over them, their wings spread taut on the heat of the thermal above the water. "I think so."

"Think or hope?"

"Both."

"When are you going to tell her?"

"Sooner the better. Maybe I'll go for a walk with her when we get back to your place."

MacLaren downed the rest of his beer and went aft to grab two more. "Few more minutes upriver and then we head into a hidden vein that runs south down to Clay Gully Lagoon. We've got some good fishin' comin' up."

Ben adjusted his cap against the sun. He felt good standing at the helm, cruising the bright river in the sunny Florida December. He was happy and he believed Carlene would be too. He couldn't wait to tell her and to have her join in his excitement. She'd probably want to check out real estate while they were down here. And maybe the veterinary clinics for jobs. She loved her job and had always said it was one she could take anywhere. Vets were always looking for qualified assistants, and people were never at a loss to provide for their animals. Ben smiled to himself. It was all going to work out. He finished the first beer and started on the second.

Big Ben throttled *Sea~Nile* down to idle and held her steady, close to the southern shoreline. MacLaren was straddled on the point of the bow, his toes dragging in the water. "It's been awhile since I've been out here. Lotta new growth. Learned about this spot from old Ray. One time we were … there it is!"

"Where?"

"Ten yards up. Pull out a bit and then cut it hard to starboard and head straight in."

Ben maneuvered into an invisible opening in the foliage. MacLaren stood on the prow raising the mangrove branches and palmetto fronds as *Sea~Nile* slowly disappeared into a long lost tunnel.

The sunlight drifted lazily through the canopy and lingered bright at the end, a hundred yards away. Big Ben laughed.

"What's so funny?"

"I was just thinking of how this reminds me of the airport tunnel in Boston," Ben said. "Only tropical."

"And safer from what I hear."

As they came through the mouth, the water opened and spread into a small pond that had tiny tributary streams scattered around it like a sunburst. "That's where the best fishing is," MacLaren glowed. "Let's get the lines in."

They cut the engine and let the boat drift. The wind was down and the lagoon was small enough that they could fish the edges easily from either side of the boat.

Big Ben hadn't fished since he was a kid, and it showed. MacLaren laughed and helped him with the baiting and showed off with his superior casting. "It's all in the wrist." He sent his line out and reeled it in slow.

"I know, I know," Ben slung his line towards one of the narrow streams snaking off into the foliage. It went much farther than he had anticipated and got snarled in the overgrowth. MacLaren roared and dropped his fishing pole as he held onto his knees laughing.

Ben tugged at the line and shook his pole like a Jedi light saber. His attempt at freeing the line only secured it faster.

"Here," MacLaren grabbed the pole from Ben, "Let me see if I can reel us into the trees and you can undo the line. Step out on the bow and try not to fall in," he laughed.

"Nobody loves a smartass," Ben said, but he was laughing too. "Don't worry, my second cast will be better."

"Yeah, if you take the hook off."

The body had washed in with the rising night tide and gotten tangled in the spider roots of the mangroves. Naked, Caucasian, female, not a blemish on her. With the late morning tide low, she was out of the water, stretched on a thin, tan blanket of sand beneath the shade of the mangroves. She looked like she was snuggled in for a nap. Her hair was long, butterscotch blond, and fell across her dry, crusted back, with the ends thin and spread out and dipping into the murky green water.

Neither man said anything. Big Ben slid over the gunwale and sank into the water to his knees. MacLaren grabbed an oar and pushed the boat into the sandy strip of shoreline and jumped out. Ben was kneeling next to the woman with his fingers on the side of her neck. "She's gone, probably not too long, maybe only a couple of hours. Early morning or pre-dawn."

"Geesus," MacLaren said, looking around the small lagoon for a boat or a canoe or something. "What the hell was she doing in here?"

Ben gently turned her by the shoulders and carefully untangled her hair to get a better look at her face. He squatted there for a full minute and then slowly rose to his feet.

MacLaren stood with his mouth open. Big Ben looked over to him. His look said, *You've got to be shitting me.*

16

Walk & Talk

The ME team concluded their on-scene work in a timely manner. They bagged the body and placed it onto a johnboat and hastened through the tropical tunnel to get the lifeless form out of the blistering sun and into the coolness of the mortuary and the steeliness of post-mortem autopsy. Like Ben and MacLaren, the ME's curiosity was more than piqued and he wanted some immediate answers.

By the time Big Ben and MacLaren got back to the house it was nearing sunset. The wives were on the lanai with cocktails and shopping bags, anxious to show the guys what they had bought. MacLaren went straight to the bottle of Elijah Craig 18-year-old bourbon and poured two fingers each for him and Ben.

Ben took his snifter and sat down next to Carlene and gave her a kiss on the cheek. "Looks like you had a fruitful day," he said.

"A fabulous day actually. Wait 'til you see what I got." Carlene got up and placed a big pink bag on her chair. "This was on sale." She opened a white cotton blouse with a lacy v-neck and held it against her.

"Pretty."

"Annnd," she reached into the bag, "matching shorts." Next came the wide white belt and the coordinated sandals to complete the outfit.

MacLaren's cell chimed and he took the call in the other room.

Lorraine said, "I'm going to go change for dinner. We thought we'd take you to our favorite waterside pub. They have a band and great food. It's a perfect night to dine outside. It'll be fun."

"Oh, that sounds wonderful. I think I'll wear this outfit then. Is it too casual?"

"No, it's perfect." She left her guests at the table.

"Want to see what else I got?"

"Um, yes," Ben hesitated. He didn't wish to interrupt her obvious excitement, but with the discovery of the second body he had some newborn questions for her about Hannah Hunt Everett. And there was the other thing. One topic at a time. "How about we go for a little walk first, while it's just the two of us?"

"Okay."

They walked along the silent streets of the enclave in the comfort of the early evening air. The sky was morphing through the various shades of blue and purple that make Florida twilights the spectacular experiences that they are.

"What did you want to talk about?" Carlene asked

"Who said I wanted to talk about anything? Can't I just enjoy a leisurely stroll with my wife?"

They were holding hands, enjoying the oneness they have shared since high school.

"I need to tell you something," Ben said.

"I know you do. You only take me for a walk when you have something to tell me."

Ben took a deep breath and exhaled it loudly. Carlene snickered. She said, "And you always get so uptight about it. That's the Virgo in you. I'm a Taurus remember? Just blurt it out like I do."

"Okay, I'm having an affair."

They kept walking, hands together. Carlene didn't even flinch.

"You're not falling for it?" he said.

"Nope, not for a minute. I know you're hopelessly in love with me and only me."

"Damn, I hate it when you're right."

She stopped them and turned into him. "Tell me."

He looked straight into her eyes and said, "Y'know how we've talked about someday pulling up stakes and moving to a warmer climate? Getting away from the horrendous New England winters?"

"Yeah, go on ..."

"Well, I think I've found a way to do that."

There was a shine in her eyes that Ben couldn't discern from an eager excitedness or the reflection of the sun behind him. He told her about the meeting with the Myakka selectmen and their offer.

"Since last year I've been thinking heavy about it. Not only us relocating, but the case I broke last December down here made me feel like my old self again. I mean Bryce Corner's a great town and everything, but I need more."

She wasn't saying anything, so Ben kept going. "I know there's a lot to figure out, but I think this would be a good move for all of us. You, me, and the kids. Brenton's been accepted at a few colleges and FSU is one of them - the best choice actually for his curriculum. And Penny's a carefree kid, always looking for new adventures. And you know you can get a job anywhere."

Still no response.

One of the neighbors pulled into their driveway, got out of their car and waved. Ben waved back.

"It's important to me, babe. You know how stifled I've been for the past couple of years."

They walked on until they reached the end of the street abutting the preserve and turned back, now facing the setting sun as they walked slowly with a nervous silence between them. Ben knew Carlene was thinking how to word her response. They got halfway back to the MacLaren's and Ben couldn't take it any longer.

"Say something."

Carlene squeezed his hand and took in a small breath. "I think I'm being followed."

17

Followed

Ben stopped dead in his tracks.
"What do you mean?"
"Remember that lecture you gave at the high school last year? Danger Awareness?"
"Yeah?"
"That part where you said always go with your gut instinct? If you feel you're in danger then you are in danger?"
Her husband squared in front of her and put his hands on her shoulders. "What's going on?"
She looked at him. The cop in him could see a twinge of fear in her eyes. "Well, when Lorraine and I went shopping on St. Armands Circle we parked the car down at the Tommy Bahama end and went in there for lunch. We got seated at a booth across from the bar and I noticed this woman as she came in and went straight to the bar like she'd been there a hundred times before. Like maybe she was meeting someone."
"What made you notice her?"
"Her boots."
"Her boots?"
"Yeah, you know how I am with boots."
"Yeah, me and my credit card."

"Funny. Anyway, they were very nice. Knee-high black calfskin. I had half a mind to ask her where she got them. Then I thought it kind of odd. Every other woman was wearing open-toed pumps, strapless sandals or flip-flops."

"What did she look like?"

"Tall, attractive, stylish. Short-cropped blonde hair. Expensive clothing. Very European."

"A model?"

"Mmmm, maybe, but I don't think so. She didn't walk like one. You know how models are always on stage? This woman didn't seem like that. She was more self-assured. Walked with a purpose, a determination."

"Then?"

"Then I forgot about her. We finished lunch and went boutique shopping."

"Did anyone show up to join her?"

"Actually, I didn't notice. I really did forget about her."

"Why do you think she was following you?"

"Because about a half hour later, she was in the same shoe store that Lorraine and I were in. No big deal, I figured it was just coincidence. I mean, obviously she's a shoe freak, right? But when we were in Chico's, I saw her standing outside looking at the window displays. Lorraine tried on a few things, so we were in there for at least thirty minutes and when we got back outside, there she was sitting on one of the benches just down the way."

"Go on."

"When we passed by her she bent down and rummaged through a shopping bag at her feet, like she was avoiding us. And then it seemed everywhere we went, there she was."

"Well, if she was following you, sounds like she's not very good at it."

"Or, she figured I had no reason to be suspicious. After all, there were hundreds of people walking the Circle shops. So, thinking I'm being too paranoid, you know, still shaken by what happened to Hannah and wondering why she had tried to contact me, I decided I was just being silly. So to get this mystery lady off my mind, I said to Lorraine, 'Hey, let's cut across the way, I want to check out that bookstore over there.' So we cross and when I look back, she's still on the bench going through her bag. Fine."

"And then what?" he said.

"We went into Circle Books - oh, and I bought you that mystery novel you wanted, *Sarasota Sunrise*, which is in my bag if you want it later - and anyway, I walk outside and there she is, walking into the jewelry store right next door."

"Okay, I'll play Devil's advocate, so she's shopping the same place you are. It may very well be coincidence."

"Ben," she turned and looked straight at him, "You know St. Armands Circle. It's a roundabout of boutiques and restaurants and funky gift shops. Everyone meanders around it in a *circle*, like that circus guy designed it."

"John Ringling."

"Yeah, him. But don't you get it? We cut across the street and through the tiny park to get away from her, and she followed us."

"Okay, okay. So when did you feel the danger?"

Carlene thought. She knew Ben was cataloguing what she was saying and needed to input things in his analytical mind. "Maybe an hour or so later. We shopped, stopped for cocktails; we were having a good time. I kept an eye out for her, but I didn't see her again so I brushed it off and went on with the afternoon."

She leaned her head on his shoulder and continued, "And then, we decided to sit at a sidewalk table at The Columbia and have an espresso before we went home. That's where I got the chill."

"How so?"

"She walked past us on the sidewalk and looked directly at me with a little smirk."

Ben drew his wife into him and held her tightly. "Did Lorraine notice her?"

"I asked her afterward if she had seen her, but she said 'Seen who'? The only reason I noticed her is because of what you have taught me."

"Where did she go from there?"

"She disappeared. I didn't see her after that."

He held her close in his big arms, inhaling the fragrance of her shampoo and the whisper of her favorite perfume, the scents of the woman he loved. Ben caressed the nape of her neck and drifted into that momentary trance where nothing else in the world mattered except feeling how lucky he was to have this woman in his life. He would do anything to protect her and keep her safe.

"Don't worry so much. It was probably nothing, Sugarplum. You know how those European women are jealous of attractive, free-spirited American women." He smiled into her eyes and kissed her. "Relax, okay? We're on vacation. Let's have a good time."

She smiled up at him and said, "Okay," and kissed him gently on the lips.

They continued on to the house in silence. Ben hoped he had relieved his wife's anxiety enough for her to be mulling over his job offer. Carlene was awfully quiet. Meanwhile, Ben was thinking of something else. When they got to the driveway he stopped and said to her, "Do you know if Hannah Hunt had a twin sister?"

"What?"

18

Woodstock 1969

In 1969 no one knew what a phenomenon Woodstock was going to be. Not the promoters, not the performers, not the participants and certainly not Winifred Adele Vanderlene.

The outdoor concert in the rolling farmlands of New York State was marketed as three days of peace, love and music. To Winnie, that translated into a long weekend of sex, drugs and rock & roll. Right up her alley.

Winnie was a rebellious girl as much by nature as by heritage. Her grandfather, Wallace T. Vanderlene, had blemished the nobility of the family name - long established in the prominence of southern cotton plantations - by absconding with an early inheritance and joining forces with a man by the name of Flagler who had a crazy notion of building a railroad reaching all the way down to that desolate, God-forsaken peninsula called Florida.

Grandfather Vanderlene had not only made a name (and lots of money) for himself, but had also developed much of the southern Gulf side of the state. By the time Winnie had come along, there was too much money to spend and no need nor desire to work. She was a free spirit, a self-proclaimed hippie, a renegade from all things socially correct and an embarrassing heartbreak to her parents.

Winnie was born to be wild and thrived on the rebellious culture of the sixties. So it came as no surprise to her parents when their spoiled, only child drove off in her colorful VW micro bus (adorned with obligatory peace symbols and flower stickers) to some foolish rock concert up north. Resignedly, they stood on the portico of their stately home with the tall white Corinthian columns, shaking their heads, as they watched their daughter disappear down their long, winding driveway.

Winifred was her own woman now and no matter how hard her parents had tried to groom her with dignity and respectability (attributes for becoming the inevitable matriarch of the Vanderlene dynasty) she had cruised into her thirties with nary a care in the world, and certainly no desire to settle down with a husband and have children to further her parents' control over her.

Sure she'd misbehaved a few times; three DUI's and more than a few stints at different rehab centers, but she didn't care. She was still alive and ready to party. And the money and wealth was hers no matter what. Her beloved grandfather, God rest his soul, had generously provided for her in his will.

Winnie decided to bring some friends along for the adventure. It would be fun, plus they could help with the driving when she got too stoned to drive. Joining her on the expedition was her best friend Joanne Lincoln, a stay-at-home mom of Winnie's age who badly needed a getaway from the kids and her good-for-nothing husband; Joanne's younger brother Ned, fresh out of college and up for a good time his last summer before entering the U.S. Air Force; and Ned's college buddy Conrad Lawrence (the Con Man as Ned called him) who Winnie thought was exceptionally cute and couldn't wait to get between her legs. So, on a hot, sunny morning that August, the anxious and happy group clambered into the microbus with their bedrolls and knapsacks and their stash, and onward they went to Woodstock.

During the course of that muddy weekend, inside a smoky, rain-battered tent - somewhere between Janis Joplin's bourbon-soaked set with Big Brother and The Holding Company and Jimi Hendrix's classic rendition of the star spangled banner - little Montgomery was conceived.

But Winnie would not know this for several weeks. Long after the summer had vanished and separated the entourage like dissipating clouds over different horizons: Joanne returning to her deteriorating marriage; Ned to the USAF to be shot down over Viet Nam a year later; The Con Man to Tallahassee interning with a prestigious group of attorneys that would whet his appetite for a political career; and Winnie, well, Winnie would disappear for a decade and try to spend an inexhaustible trust fund traveling all over Europe and the shores of the Mediterranean. But not before dealing with the unwanted development growing in her belly. She would not abort it, nor would she keep it. But she would make sure that no one would know about the baby. Especially her parents. And certainly not Conrad Lawrence Esq. The father would never know about the son he had sired at Woodstock. Well … almost never.

19
ME Baffled

"Preliminary and off the record ..."

"Goddamn it! That's what you always say."

"... I don't have a clue."

The ME's comment didn't bode well with Lieutenant MacLaren. He was pacing the carpet in his study.

Big Ben walked in. MacLaren said, "Listen to this," and punched his cell onto speakerphone and set it on his desk.

"What do you mean?" MacLaren continued.

"Two things. First of all, the two bodies couldn't be more identical. Not only in looks, but also height, weight, structure, everything. The mangrove lady is a perfect match to Hannah Hunt Everett."

"And secondly?"

"I can't readily find a cause of death. Nothing. No bullet holes, no blunt trauma, no marks on the body, nothing awry in her system ..."

"Then how ..."

"Not a heart attack, not a stroke, not a bolt of lightning, nothing."

Ben sat on the edge of the desk and leaned toward the phone, "Water in her lungs?"

"Nope."

"Poison?"

"No toxins in her system."

"Aw, come on, Quincy," MacLaren was exasperated, "you've got to give me something better than that."

The ME said, "I'm going to run her DNA. That'll take some time. But there's something amiss here. I've already sent in the swab from Hannah Hunt Everett, and because of the startling visual and physiological similarities between these two women, I've put a priority on it and I'm hoping to get both samples pushed through ASAP."

"Okay, okay. Let me know as soon as you get something."

"Will do. And Lieutenant ..."

"What?"

"My name isn't Quincy."

"Yeah, I know." He hung up.

MacLaren flopped into his desk chair and reached for his snifter of bourbon. Big Ben rubbed his chin. "Curiouser and curiouser," he said.

"None of this makes any sense."

"I asked Carlene about a twin sister."

"What did she say?"

"She said Hannah Hunt was an only child."

"That jives with the ME. He did a quick search and found that Mrs. Hunt did in fact give birth to only one child."

"Falsified records?"

"And what?" MacLaren spread his arms. "The mother has twins and gives one away at birth? That's a *real* long shot."

"Don't be so skeptical. Shit like that happens."

"And they both end up dead at the same time in the same place on the planet? I can believe in coincidence, but not when it's preposterous."

"So where does that leave us?"

"Hungry," MacLaren downed the rest of his drink and rose from his chair. "Let's go eat."

20

Woody's Roo

Usually there's not a problem finding a parking spot at Woody's River Roo. Especially since the new owners leveled the decrepit low-lying motel structure next door, doubling the size of the parking lot of the riverfront pub. But tonight it was crowded. They even had valet service.

"What the hells going on?" the Lieutenant said, bypassing the valet and maneuvering through the dirt lot.

"I remember this place," Big Ben said. He pointed to a Grand River Oak with its big bushy branches and silver-gray ponytails of Spanish moss standing on the north side near the bridge. "The white van was parked right beneath that tree in front of the motel room where I kicked in the door."

"Yeah. That's where you almost blew the case with your unorthodox search-and-seizure methods. Have you since learned about things like 'just cause' and 'search warrants'?"

"Aw come on, those guys were as guilty as hell and you know it."

"I knew it and you knew it, but the law unfortunately, is always on their side. Civil liberties and all that bull."

"Well we kicked some ass and got some answers, didn't we?"

"Hmmph," MacLaren squeezed into a spot just vacated by two

Harley dressers. He put the car in park and turned his head to the back seat. "Your over-zealous husband has a problem staying within the perameters of the law."

Carlene smiled, "He gets very excited about his job sometimes."

The outdoor restaurant fronting the Manatee River offers a great view of the western sunset across the water. It is a popular spot for locals and tourists alike. Good food, good music and good times.

"Looks different," Ben said as they approached the entrance of the pub that began its life as a fish shack a century ago.

"New owners."

"Debbie sold The Rusty Anchor?"

"Yeah, not long after you broke up the place and beat up her cook. Actually, Convict Rick still works here."

"No shit? Maybe he's here tonight and I can go beat the crap outta him again."

They looked at each other and both men laughed.

"What?" Carlene and Lorraine said at the same time.

"He's just kidding," MacLaren said.

"I'll bet," Carlene responded.

There was a table at the front next to the big lit-up Kangaroo jumping out of the palm fronds. A cheerful couple adorned in Mr. & Mrs. Uncle Sam outfits were handing out campaign buttons that said "We *Luv* Our New *Guv*". Above them stretched a red, white and blue banner proclaiming congratulations to Governor Conrad Lawrence.

An attractive woman approached from the patio. She wore a strapless black sundress that accentuated her lithe form and gave credence to her native Floridian tan. Her long, dark hair was pulled back in a ponytail away from a stern, yet pleasant face that didn't require makeup save for a thin line of lip gloss spread across her welcoming smile. She looked every bit like the professional woman, tastefully dressed down for a casual evening out, that she was.

She extended her hand to MacLaren. "Good evening, Lieutenant," she said.

"Good evening, Counselor," he responded. "I don't believe you've met my wife Lorraine before. Lorraine, this is Lydia Lawrence, daughter and law partner of our newly elected governor."

"Nice to meet you, Lorraine." They shook hands politely.

"And this is our guest from the cold and snowy city of Boston, Carlene Benson."

"Hello, welcome to Sarasota," she offered Carlene a soft grip.

"Nice to meet you, Lydia."

"And of course you know ..."

"Big Ben Benson," Lydia finished, stepping closer to Ben and grabbing onto his hand with both of hers. "So good to see you again. I hear you're going to be our new Chief of Police in Myakka City."

"Well, that's still up in the air." He gave Carlene a conciliatory glance. "Lydia was Dodge's attorney last year."

"Yes, I remember you mentioning that."

Carlene noticed Lydia still had her hands wrapped around her husband's and there was a slight flush on Ben's face that wasn't there a second ago.

MacLaren picked up the conversation, "This is our favorite restaurant and we thought we'd bring our guests over for dinner. We didn't know about the fanfare. I hope we're not intruding on a private party."

"Not at all, Lieutenant. It's just a little celebration for my father before he heads off to Tallahassee next month. You're all welcome to jump into the festivities."

"Thanks, we will."

To Carlene's relief, Lydia finally released Ben's hand.

"Come along, there's room at our table up front."

They weaved their way through the crowded alfresco patio to a table before the raised stage, where a five-piece jazz ensemble fused their cool jazz into the evening.

Lydia did the intros, starting with her dad, guest of honor, Conrad Lawrence, seated next to Christina and Woody, owners of The Roo, and another couple (a bit overdressed and flashy for the suggested casual dress code), Jake and Ruby Curtis. The band went on break and Woody and Christina excused themselves to go mingle amongst their other guests, surrendering their seats to the MacLarens. Lydia dragged over two seats from an adjacent table for the Bensons, placing Big Ben's next to hers.

Lydia kept the conversation lively, like the litigator that she was, with tales of the campaign, her dad's plans for relocating to Tallahassee and his bountiful ideas for their state and the constituency thereof. Lydia, like her dad, was a Sarasotan and very proud of her city on the Gulf. As a conciliatory gesture, she offered to show Carlene the sights and charms of Sarasota County in anticipation of their potential relocation. Carlene found Lydia to be friendly and articulate and a pleasant enough person, but she was certain she wouldn't take her up on the offer. Besides, even though everyone seemed to be taking it for granted that Ben was going to accept the new job, she had not yet given her blessing.

Drinks came, orders were placed and the ladies continued on in cordial conversation. The Governor was huddled over a page of notes with Jake Curtis, his campaign manager.

21

Jake the Snake

Jake Curtis was, in the parlance of the political world, a Groomer, an Image Maker. He groomed people for success. To him, winning a political campaign was done by visuals. Looks and presentation could stuff more votes into the ballot box than all the past accomplishments and future promises combined. People didn't give a shit about that stuff. Good looks, charm, and a sexy smile for the female vote was paramount in achieving the gold medal. Look what it had done for JFK and Bill Clinton.

Jake didn't care what type of an impression a candidate brought to the table. Real impressions didn't impress him. The fabricated one, the one he could create, the one he could win with, that was his adrenaline, his fix, his drive. Success was Jake's ultimate rush.

His image-making career had, of course, started with himself. He had always been an egomaniac, a Narcissus in the true sense of the word. (He had a framed GQ cover in his office with his own picture on it – self-pasted). As a kid he had driven his parents and siblings crazy with his self-centered ways and the constant fussing over his hair, his clothing, his overall appearance. His childhood friends (with whom he no longer associated) had never believed his constant, self-professing, lies and bullshit, and figured he would grow up to be nothing but a cunning used car salesman with the perfect false smile. Or, more suiting for Jake, *a pre-owned vehicle sales specialist.* They had nicknamed him "Jake the Snake". But he didn't care. He knew he had something going, when, in high school, he took the dowdiest looking couple, did a total makeover; looks, fashion, etiquette and even walking and speech lessons, and had gotten them voted King and Queen of the senior prom. (With a little ballot-stuffing thrown in for good measure, of course). That was when the bell rang in his head. He set his lofty goals and began strutting down the runway to his rich future. After schmoozing his way through an Ivy League college with a degree in Political Science, Jake the Snake headed to the vanity capital of the world. No, not Hollywood, California - Washington, D.C.

Years later, after making an unscrupulous name for himself, he was hired by a nefarious group to get Conrad Lawrence into the Florida Governor's Mansion. "The Group" (very select and vehemently anonymous) had been so impressed with Jake's handiwork and subsequent results, that they retained him for the second aspect of the Conrad Lawrence project – the grooming of a president.

Luckily, Conrad's image, even before Jake's finessing, was quite favorable. Presidential timber actually. The aristocratic Sarasota lawyer was tall and handsome with a healthy, charismatic countenance beneath a neatly coiffed crown of white hair that showcased his native Floridian tan and easy smile. He was an accomplished man, successful and believable, who projected a sound public image. And, as a widower of ten years rarely seen in the accompaniment of any other woman save his daughter and law partner Lydia, Conrad projected a private family image that tugged at the heartstrings of every voting-age female in the state.

Jake played heavy on this, making sure his man was touted as the most desirable bachelor in the state, and soon, the nation. He had successfully wowed the rich and bored society femmes of the Sunshine State - the ones who lived out their futile fantasies by unscrupulously doling out tons of money to their favorite cause du'jour. He planned to stroke their eccentric egos and dig into their Coach purses for the next four years – all the way to the White House.

So here he sat, at a table at *Woody's Roo* with the stage being set behind him, readying his latest accomplishment, the Governor Elect, for his upcoming "impromptu" speech.

Meanwhile, Jake's wife Ruby had captured the attention of Big Ben and MacLaren as they sipped away on their beers taking in the scenery. They couldn't help but notice (as they were sure everyone else couldn't help but notice) the extremely low-cut bright-red dress that Ruby Curtis was wearing. It was the attention getter that she (more accurately, Jake) had wanted. Ben thought if she hiccupped, her bought-and-paid-for boobs would certainly pop out.

Ruby sat there like the neon wallpaper Jake wanted her to be. Bright hair, bright clothes and bright smile, the eye candy trophy wife that he had handpicked to cruise the on-camera political parties and off-camera soirées, specifically designed to bring the limelight to him. Ben realized everything he did was for show, even his wife. The man took vanity to new heights, and Ben was close enough to Jake to occasionally overhear his coaching of Conrad Lawrence. He chuckled to himself at the lines of bullshit coming out of Jake's mouth and wondered how anyone actually got paid for that kind of "consulting". Right off the bat, Ben didn't like him.

Food arrived with another round of cocktails and everyone settled into their plates. The sun had dropped and the night air rolling in from the south end of Tampa Bay was pleasant.

The pub manager Melissa (Woody and Christina's daughter) came over and spoke with the Governor. At the thumbs-up from her husband Kenny, who had set up the lectern on stage, Conrad Lawrence grabbed his notes and excused himself from the table.

Lydia patted her lips with her napkin and placed it on her plate. "Excuse me everyone," she rested her hand on Big Ben's shoulder as she rose from her seat, "I've got to go introduce my father."

After Lydia's introduction, as everyone was standing and applauding Conrad, Ben gave Lieutenant MacLaren a head signal. When the ovation was over and everyone was retaking their seats, Ben said to his wife, "I'll be right back."

Carlene gave him a curious "Where are you going?" look. Ben kissed the top of her head and said again, "Be right back."

22

Convict Rick

"Hello Rick." Convict Rick jumped at the sight of Big Ben and MacLaren standing in the kitchen.

"How the hell are ya?" Ben said.

"Get away from me you big bastard." Rick grabbed a knife and wielded it at Ben.

"Ah, Rick. Is that anyway to greet an old friend?" Ben said.

"With a friend like you I don't need enemies." He looked to the rear door and MacLaren moved to cover it. Ben advanced toward the cook with an outstretched hand.

"No hard feelings from last year, eh? Let's let bygones be bygones."

Rick pointed the knife directly at Big Ben's stomach. "Come any closer and I'll filet you like a piece of fish."

Ben held his hands up in surrender. "Listen Rick, I'm just here celebrating with the new Guv and I thought I'd stop in and say hello, that's all." He spread his hands wider. "Okay?"

Hesitantly, Rick lowered the knife and swapped it to his left hand, extending his right for a handshake. "Okay, okay."

In an almost invisible motion, Big Ben grabbed Rick's right hand and cranked it up behind his back while he expertly disarmed him.

"Ow,ow,ow," Rick groaned from his tiptoes.

"Geez Rick, I think you've gained some weight." Convict Rick, with his kitchen whites hanging off him and an oversized apron tied tight around his skinny waist, appeared to weigh all of perhaps ninety-seven pounds. Big Ben was well over twice that much.

MacLaren laughed.

"What?"

"Standing there, you two look like a big-ass grizzly bear and a scrawny-ass prairie dog on his hind legs."

"Yeah? Hey Rick. How about a picture so I can take it back to Massachusetts with me and show all the guys at the station my new Florida buddy?" Ben released his hold on the cook and placed the knife onto the prep table.

"Wow," Rick answered, turning back to his grill, "I wish I could be a cop so I could be as funny as you guys." They laughed. "Besides," Rick said to Big Ben, "I hear you may not be staying up north anyway. Rumor has you putting on Chief Ray's hat over at Myakka."

Big Ben looked at the Lieutenant with a *How does he know that?* expression. MacLaren shrugged.

Convict Rick had gotten his nickname from being in and out of jail more often than he could remember. He was an easy-going, likeable guy who wouldn't hurt a fly. But he had two uncanny attributes, neither of which he could control. One, he was a sap. Crooks would befriend him and then use him to run the drugs he never did and to fence the merchandise he never stole. And he was the one that always got caught and did the time.

Secondly, and far more attractive to law enforcement, Rick was a clairvoyant, a cosmic magnet to the underworld. Word of anything unlawful or unusual going on in Sarasota County found its way to him like blood flowing into a leach. How? No one knew.

"Some say he's got ESP," MacLaren had told Big Ben a year ago when he'd used Rick's uncanny ability to help crack a case. "I had him evaluated by our shrink. She said he exhibited behaviors similar to that of a psychic or a savant or an Indigo Child."

"What do you think?"

"I don't know. Maybe he got struck by lightning when he was a kid. All I know is he perceives things differently than you and me."

What Convict Rick actually experienced were synesthetic perceptions. He could sense distressed energy passing through his over-active mind via colorful cognitive pathways. Sometimes, if the energy was dynamic enough, it would appear as precise locations in space, kind of like a supernatural Global Positioning System.

MacLaren had busted him so many times that he had finally offered him a deal. He'd stop arresting him in exchange for occasional information from an "unknown source". Rick had taken him up on it, gotten the job at Woody's Roo and was clean. Sort of.

Rick slid some grilled grouper onto a plate, added fries and slaw and placed it into a little window at the end of the grill. "Bar food," he yelled.

Ben said, "What can you tell us about a body that was found out in the mangroves this morning?"

"Nuthin'. I don't know nuthin' about it."

"Don't forget our deal, Rick," MacLaren said. "I've got more on you than you can shake a stick at."

"You can't touch me, Lieutenant. I'm clean. I got a good thing going here. You ask Melissa or Christina, they'll vouch for me." He disappeared into a walk-in cooler.

"Come on, let's go," MacLaren said.

"Wait a minute." Ben was playing a card. If he was going to take over the Chief's job, he wanted to set a precedent. They waited. Ben didn't know if Rick knew anything or not, but he had a hunch.

Convict Rick came out of the walk-in with more fish. "You still here?" He laughed.

Ben took a threatening step toward him.

"Okay, okay," Rick said. He spread the filets on the grill. "All I know is a body was found in the 'groves and that you were the guys that found it."

"Rick, you can do better than that. That's public knowledge. Anyone listening to the news knows that much. Come on."

Rick turned to MacLaren, "Is he takin' the Chief's job? Am I gonna have to deal with this big baboon?"

MacLaren shrugged.

Ben took another step closer to the cook and this time he grabbed the knife.

"What? You gonna fuckin' stab me now?"

"Just holding onto the knife, Rick. I was afraid it might fall off the table and get stuck in your foot."

"Okay, listen. I really don't know. I heard about the twin that isn't a twin that was found without a scratch on her. Not even the gators wanted her."

Big Ben and MacLaren looked at each other. That stuff wasn't public knowledge. Only they and the ME and the wives were privy to that info.

"What the hell are you saying?"

"I'm only repeating what comes in off the river. Some say there's voodoo in there."

"What?!" MacLaren said. "There ain't no voodoo here. This is Sarasota not New Orleans."

Convict Rick threw his hands in the air and turned back to his grill. "You asked. I'm tellin' ya. That's all I got." He flipped the filets over with a spatula. "You don't like the answers? Don't ask the questions."

The two cops knew they weren't going to get any more out of him. Ben put the knife back on the cutting block and went up behind Rick. He pulled a couple of bills out of his pocket and stuffed them into the cook's apron.

"What the hell is this? You settin' me up?"

"Nope," Ben patted him on the shoulder, "If the Lieutenant did that it might be called a bribe and you and he would both be in trouble. But I'm just a citizen on vacation that came back to the kitchen to give the cook a tip." He turned and walked away. "I'll be in touch, Rick."

"Yeah, keep in touch with yourself, big man." Rick laughed.

Back on the deck, the speeches were over, the band was playing and the patrons were dancing.

"What was that all about?" MacLaren asked.

"If I'm going to be working down here, I think I'm going to have to rely on Rick's intuition from time to time. I just wanted to show him I care."

"Yeah, well don't let anybody else see you care like that."

23
Devil's Leap

"Hey Cutie, you come here often?" Ben spoke into his wife's ear from behind.

"Only when I'm looking to get lucky." There was that smile that still melted him. "Where have you been? All these men keep coming up to me and asking me to dance." Carlene giggled.

He noticed a half full martini glass in front of her and an empty one beside it. "Then why aren't you out on the dance floor?"

"Becauuuse," she said in a sexy voice, "I was waiting for just the right man to come into my life, annnd here you are!"

Ben bowed and extended his arm, "May I, dear maiden?"

Carlene gave her husband her hand and rose from her seat. They squeezed onto the crowded dance floor in front of the stage. The music was lively, the night air cool and the mood festive. There was laughter all around. Everyone was having a good time. Especially Carlene. Ben could tell by her loosened mood and wild, sexy gyrations on the dance floor that the martinis were kicking in. She needs to unwind, he thought. She's been through a lot. What a way to start a vacation. Dead bodies, stirred memories from her past, a potential life-style change dropped in her lap (courtesy of her husband's mid-life crisis), and let's not forget the anxiety, true or not, of being followed by some mystery woman that afternoon. Yeah, Ben said to himself, she deserves this night out.

Governor Conrad was dancing with Lorraine MacLaren, Jake had partnered with Lydia Lawrence and Ruby had dragged Lieutenant MacLaren out on the floor. She was twisting and turning and spinning around to the music, somehow managing to keep her breasts contained. MacLaren was smiling.

"Whoa!" Ben grabbed onto Carlene as she lost her balance. "That's a new move." She wrapped her arms around him and held onto him tight.

"I think that second martini just hit me," she said.

"I think it's the third one, Sugarplum. Come on, let's sit down."

"Whew," Carlene plopped into her chair, fanning herself with her hand. Ben poured her a glass of water.

"You okay?"

"Yeah, I'm fine." She chugged half the glass of water. Ben raised his eyebrows.

"All right," she said. "Maybe everything's hitting me at once."

"You want to go?"

Something about the way he said that made her feel good. She squeezed his hand and said, "Okay."

Big Ben pushed his way through the dance crowd to MacLaren. "I need your car keys."

"You gonna go make out in the parking lot?" He reached into his pocket.

"Better than that."

"Oh," he handed his keys to Ben. "Then I'll make sure we get home late."

"Seventy-five south, exit 203, right?"

"Yup. Then you …"

"I think I've got it from there. You got a ride?"

"Yeah, don't worry. Lydia can drop us on her way downtown."

"Thanks." Ben walked away.

"Hey," MacLaren smirked, "don't wake the neighbors."

The highway on the Gulf side of the Florida peninsula never quite gets dark at night, not like in New England where it gets pitch black two seconds after sunset. Big Ben was cruising with the A/C on low and the window cracked to let in the refreshing night air. It was twenty degrees and snowing back in Massachusetts. He had his arm around his favorite girl and her head rested comfortably on his shoulder.

"Remember your old Ford. The one where we first made love?"

"Was that you?"

She slapped his chest. "I remember that shifter that always got in the way."

"Until we got smarter and went into the back seat."

"Yeah. Then that other big shifter would appear."

"And I liked the way you shifted it."

Carlene's fingers loosened a shirt button and slid inside, making smooth circular motions on Ben's chest.

She snickered.

"What?"

"Remember when you got it stuck in your zipper, that night up on Devil's Leap?"

"Hey, that wasn't funny. I think I still have a scar from that."

"No, actually you don't," she smiled up at him. "I would know." Her nails scratched his nipples.

"If that fucking cop hadn't come out of nowhere …"

"And if someone hadn't ripped off your underwear …"

"And I had to sit there grimacing with my dick in my zipper while he fucking interrogated us."

"And now you're the cop harassing the kids up there at night."

"Irony."

They both laughed.

She snickered again. "Then when he finally left we had to unzip it."

"Ow, don't say that. I'm having a flashback and it hurts."

"Let me rub it and make it feel better," she said. "Oh, there's something hard in your pants, officer."

"Hey Carlene. I'm trying to drive, here."

It only took another ten minutes to reach the MacLaren's house. Ben pulled into the driveway at the end of the cul-de-sac. The enclave was dark and quiet. There was a row of bougainvilleas on the side nearest the neighbors.

Carlene's hand was inside Ben's pants. His right hand had found the softness of her breasts, his thumb and forefinger gently squeezing her nipples, first one, and then the other. She moaned softly and squeezed his hardness.

"Wait a minute," he said and took his hand from her blouse to turn the car off and put it into park.

"Kiss me," she said and Ben drew her into him and kissed her. In a moment they were teenagers again up on Devil's Leap. And all the fresh love and passion that had surrounded them there came back with a flourish.

"Let's go inside," he said.

"Why?"

"Because I want to get you in the sack."

"Why do we have to go into the house?"

"Because we're civilized."

Carlene broke from Ben's embrace and crawled into the back seat. "We don't have to be civilized all the time." She pulled her top over her head and unsnapped her bra from the front.

Ben shook his head smiling and got out the driver's side. His old knee injury didn't make it favorable to jump over the seat bench anymore. He opened the rear door. Carlene threw her panties at him. Ben slid in.

24
Naked Man

The naked man wandered helplessly through the brambled foliage with no sense of direction. In the intense heat of the afternoon unknown creatures stirred and scurried away from his staggering footsteps.

Sometimes a clearing would appear and he would stand in it, alone and bewildered beneath the scorching sun, twisting his head side to side, looking for a way out. There was a tall tree in the distance and he went to it and climbed it. His breathing became shallow from the climbing.

At the top he searched the horizon and screamed into the vast green panorama untouched by civilization. But the screaming just faded away without even an echo, succeeding only in ripping through his vocal chords and leaving his throat raw and dry.

No one heard him. By the time he regained the ground he was gasping – his lungs painfully squeezing together in his chest.

Although the day was hot and the air humid, he could not sweat. The eccrine glands were malfunctioning and thermoregulation (the body's cooling system) was shutting down. He could breathe but his body couldn't.

The naked man chose another untrodden path and disappeared into the web-like foliage, earnestly hoping that this one was the path to salvation, freedom and life, and not just another false start choking to a dead end in the ever-thickening overgrowth.

The day wore on. The repetitious wandering to no avail. The quest losing its illumination and a fog of despair gradually overtaking him. His tired legs became limp and he sat down on the ground.

The man's body was spent and exhausted from the fruitless hours of fatigue. His mind, overworked with fear and disorientation, had stalled, and he no longer knew what to do, where to go, nor how to move on.

So he laid down and he died.

25

Conrad's Twin

Six-fifty-three a.m. Big Ben's cell phone buzzed. MacLaren.
"You up?"
"I am now." Ben yawned. "I'm on vacation, y'know. I'm supposed to be enjoying myself and sleeping late."
"No time for that."
Ben swung his heavy legs over the side of the guest room bed. "Where the hell are you?"
"In the kitchen."
"You're calling me from the kitchen?"
"Well, I was gonna knock on the bedroom door, but I didn't want to interrupt anything." MacLaren chuckled. "Come on. I've got coffee on."
Ben leaned over and kissed the top of his wife's head. Gently, he pulled her hair back and whispered into her ear, "I love you, Sugarplum."
Carlene stirred and murmured, "Mmmmm." The house was cool with the central air-conditioning and he pulled the soft cotton sheets over her shoulders.
Outside, the sun was breaking the horizon and spreading colorful sheets of new color across the landscape, awaking it gently, like a new baby, to the new day.

MacLaren stood fully dressed on the lanai. Two to-go mugs sat on the table. Steam rose from the small holes edged on their tops. His shoulder holster hung snugly over his polo top. Ben didn't like the seriousness of that.

"What's up?"

"Got a text from Chief Ray Burati. Take a look."

The text read: *Good morning, Lieutenant. Found another body in the mangroves. Already got it bagged and down at the morgue. ME requests our presence ASAP. Bring your friend.*

When they pulled into the parking lot of the Sarasota County Forensics Facility, they saw Lydia Lawrence and her father Conrad Lawrence getting out of a Lexus SUV.

"Good morning," Ben said.

"What are you two doing here?"

"We aren't sure, Governor. Are you here at the invitation of the ME?"

"Yes. Are you?"

"Seems so."

"Do you know what's going on?" Lydia asked.

"No."

A glistening gold Audi Cabriolet screamed into the lot and screeched to a stop in the handicap parking space. Jake Curtis jumped out. "Governor!" He ran to meet them at the door. "What is going on?"

"I don't know, Jake. I guess we'll find out soon enough."

They entered the building single file. Ben was holding the door. When everyone was through except Jake, Ben closed it halfway. "I'm curious, Mr. Curtis. How did you come to know about this?"

"Oh, I ..." Jake hesitated, "I got a text message forwarded from Conrad."

Ben gave him a curt look of disbelief.

"I *am* his campaign manager, you know. I *do* need to keep abreast of things." Jake went to brush past Big Ben, but Ben held firm on the door. Their eyes met in a moment of mutual defiance. Ben released his hold and Jake Curtis charged through.

Inside, the ME went directly to his work. Preamble was not necessary. Everyone knew each other. He went to the draped corpse on the metal gurney and gestured for all to gather around. Then he acquiesced to Chief Ray Burati, who began, "At 4:30 this morning I was awakened by a text message on my cell phone. It showed a set of latitude/longitude coordinates followed by a line saying, 'You should check this out.' So, I set the coordinates into my phone's GPS, loaded my old pump, grabbed a box of shells and headed out. About forty-five minutes later and a mile into the mangrove forests off of 70, this is what I found." He nodded to the ME

The Medical Examiner pulled the sheet down to the waist of the naked man.

"Oh my God." Lydia's knees gave out. Big Ben grabbed onto her.

They all looked back and forth from the corpse to Conrad Lawrence. The Governor-Elect's gaze was frozen on the man's face. It was like looking in a mirror.

Jake Curtis said, "What the fuck?"

26

Mangrove Crime Scene

They were stunned. No one was able to draw any logical correlation between the dead body and Conrad Lawrence.

The Governor-to-be walked out of the room. His daughter followed close behind.

Jake Curtis said, "We need answers,ced gentlemen. And fast."

The ME responded, "I'll complete the autopsy this morning."

"You do that," Jake said. "And call me as soon as you know what the fuck is going on." He handed his business card to the ME, Chief Ray Burati, Lieutenant MacLaren and Big Ben. Ben didn't move to accept his. He stood with his hands to his sides.

"Listen, big man," Jake Curtis stuffed his card into Ben's shirt pocket. "I don't know who the fuck you think you are and I really don't give a rat's ass. But if you get in my way ... I *will* take you out. You got that?"

Big Ben smiled.

Jake Curtis turned to the others. "We need to keep a lid on this. I'm assuming - due to the fact that this guy was found naked without any ID - that you've got him under a John Doe. Keep him there. If anyone comes forward don't do *anything* until you contact me first." Jake exited.

"Uptight little bastard isn't he?" Chief Ray said.

"I'd like to see the location, Ray," Ben said.

"Great. You're sounding like my replacement already. Follow me." Chief Ray Burati turned quickly and disappeared through the door, Big Ben and MacLaren close behind.

"Ah, Lieutenant? Before you leave, a moment if you will." The ME walked to the far corner of the lab and opened a small tabletop refrigerator. By the time the two men reached him, he had extracted three half-inch vials approximately four inches long. They were filled with varying colors of liquid and were held upright on a little wooden stand that reminded Ben of his grandfather Percy's pipe holder.

The ME raised the first one. "This is blood from the first victim Hannah Hunt Everett. As you can see, it is crimson in color and exudes a rudimentary metallic odor." He twisted the plastic top off the vial and held it so that the Lieutenant could sniff it. He then held it to Ben, who reluctantly took a short whiff.

He replaced the first vial and picked up the next. "This blood, taken from victim number two, the one we are calling Hannah's Twin, although only by conjecture, is clear and is completely odorless." Again they sniffed and nodded their heads in agreement.

"Now the third vial, from our Naked Man over there, is colorful, yet not as dark as the first. The striking thing about it is that *it also* has no odor." The ME allowed them each a smell.

"Now, here's what's perplexing…"

"Wait a minute," Ben said. "You took a clear fluid from the vein of that dead woman?"

"No. It was red when extracted. It morphed from dark red to clear over several hours, in the tube."

"What the hell are you saying?"

"I'm saying that that doesn't happen. And I now suspect that the third vial is beginning to lose its red tint also."

"Impossible."

"Exactly. Blood is red. Arterial being scarlet and venous more crimson. But both are red. Initially, once I got past the fact that I could not rationalize how blood could turn clear, I thought plasma. Plasma in its rawest form is like water and is odorless. Human blood is roughly sixty percent plasma and forty percent erythrocytes, leukocytes, and thrombocytes – red cells, white cells, and platelets."

"Could it be some rare blood type?"

"No, I don't think so."

"Synthetic blood?"

"No such thing."

"Then what is it?"

The ME replaced the samples into the refrigerator and leaned against the closed door. He rubbed his chin and slowly shook his head side to side. "The first one is clearly human blood. The other two? I don't have a clue."

Big Ben and MacLaren looked at each other and then in unison to the ME. He was still rubbing his chin. "In the area where the last two were found there are lots of carnivores; gators, boars, panthers, vultures. To them the scent of blood is a potent lure. Even though there were no signs of external bleeding, blood scent escapes through the skin cells and can attract a scavenger from miles away. Yet nothing advanced upon those two bodies. Not even a mosquito."

"Then how can you explain it?"

"That's it. I can't."

"Oh, what the hell have we got then?" MacLaren was exasperated. "Aliens dropping out of the sky?"

"Don't know, Lieutenant." The ME pushed his back off the fridge and headed towards his desk. "I'm only the medical examiner, you're the detective. Go detect."

Outside, Lydia was waving to her father and Jake Curtis as they drove away. She turned and saw the men exiting the building. She approached MacLaren's pickup truck. Ben was opening the passenger door. "My dad's gone with Jake to keep his round of appearances today. Status quo. Where are you going?"

"We're going to the crime scene."

"I'm coming with you."

"Why?"

"Why? Because this is freaking me out." Before he could rebuke her, Lydia climbed in and sat in the middle of the bench seat. MacLaren shrugged his shoulders and started the vehicle. Chief Ray pulled his cruiser around and motioned them to follow.

The ride out Fruitville, down 75, and east on SR 70 had been silent. Ben thought it must have been tough for her to view that man's dead body. The remarkable resemblance to her father had to be unsettling. "You all right?"

"Yeah." Her leg was against Ben's in the cramped cab of the truck. He patted it.

"Wouldn't the cell phone number of the Chief of Police be protected?" Lydia was in lawyer mode.

"Yes. Law enforcement, FBI, CIA, politicians, none of their information is available to the public."

"Then how would …"

"They nabbed a fourteen-year-old kid in Idaho last week for hacking into the Pentagon's 'highly-encrypted' computer. You hear about this stuff all the time. If it's out there in cyber-space, it can be found."

MacLaren said, "How would you do that? I couldn't do that."

"Well first of all Lieutenant," Ben said, "you'd have to be smart."

"Real funny, big guy."

"Okay," Lydia continued, "So we're looking at someone clever enough to get Chief Ray's private cell number. I'll postulate that he or she or they covered their tracks by what? Getting a throw-a-way at Wal-Mart and then …" she lapsed into thought.

MacLaren leaned forward, past Lydia, to catch Big Ben's eye. "Postulate?"

"She's an attorney."

Chief Ray's blinker signaled them off the asphalt and onto a narrow dirt road that came to a quick end at a metal fence. A sun-bleached sign said, 'Warning: Agricultural Crime Watch'. There was a seven-digit phone number for the County Sheriff's Dept.

They got out and followed Ray into the thick brush hiding beneath the early winter sun. He seemed to be moving along some invisible path. Ben looked at Lydia's shoes with the high heels.

"I can manage," she said.

He laughed.

"What?"

"When you sprain your ankle I'll give you a piggy-back."

"Don't tempt me," she smiled at him.

Occasionally, as they swiped the green foliage away from their faces, they heard a stirring or a sound that reminded them that they were out of their natural element and into another.

"Tell me how the perp got in here with a dead body." Lydia was in cross-examination mode.

"Easiest way would be to walk in together."

"And kill him. Take his clothes off and walk out?"

"Almost there," Ray said from the front.

Ben was taking up the rear. He was anxious. Excited. In a foreign land much different than what he was used to up north. The thrill of the hunt was caressing him, luring him into a new world of adventure and arousing his predatory senses. He wanted very much to assume control of this investigation. He wanted very much to show off his superior skills and bring a resolve to the things that were happening around him, for him.

When they got to the remote crime scene they found the yellow tape stretched around the tight perimeter of the mangrove marsh. They learned nothing. No disturbance. No blood. No sign of a struggle. No evidence whatsoever. If the tape hadn't been there, there would be no evidence of humanity. They took the tape down and retraced their steps back through pristine wilderness.

The hour was approaching noon. No one had eaten breakfast yet. They climbed back into the vehicles and moved east. A few miles later they pulled into Gramps Ramp.

27
Game Plan

"Okay, I'm going to Vermont."

MacLaren almost choked on his food. "What are you talking about? You just got here."

They were seated at a table on the back deck overlooking the river. The three of them: Big Ben, MacLaren and Lydia Lawrence. Chief Ray had driven on to his office in Myakka. Gramps had waved to them from the square hole to the kitchen. He was cooking today. His granddaughter, Alice, was waitressing.

"Look," Big Ben began. "We've got three bodies in three days. I don't care what you and yours from Sarasota County spend days coming up with. In my mind, whatever's happening here started in that high-school Science Fair in Vermont long ago."

"How do you figure that?"

Ben finished the rest of his omelet in one huge forkful. He placed the utensils on his plate and pushed it to the edge of the table. Leaning back, crossing his arms over his ample girth, he said, "One, let's talk common denominator…"

The granddaughter passed by with a fresh pot of coffee and refilled their cups. Respecting their hushed conversation, she moved along. "Here's what we've got…"

"Wait a minute," Maclaren cut in. "You ain't *got* anything yet. And you certainly don't have anything even *close* to an involvement in this case. This is way out of your jurisdiction, my friend. You're a visitor. Let's let the local cops - as in me and Chief Ray - handle this. Okay."

Ben felt the territorial inflection in MacLaren's voice but couldn't help himself.

"I'm not trying to step on your toes, Lieutenant, but my gut is telling me that because of my wife's involvement in this fiasco, there's something going on that I have to investigate - whether you like it or not. Carlene was contacted, or I should say attempted to be contacted, by an old high school friend, who …"

"You don't have to go to Vermont," Lydia was scrolling on her phone. "He's dead."

"Huh?"

"Or … *presumed* dead." She picked up a piece of toast and crunched - reading them the info from Google: "Montgomery Fairmont. Born, St. Johnsbury, Vermont … blah blah blah," Lydia scrolled thru all the essentials looking for something that jumped out at her. She had their uncompromised attention. "Here's where it gets good … At the age of twenty-seven, Montgomery Fairmont left his position of assistant professor at Harvard University to start up his own biotech engineering company in Cambridge, Massachusetts … AbioGenetix. Then, ten years later, he disappears, leaving in his wake a multi-billion dollar business."

Lydia continued scrolling with one hand and sipping her coffee with the other. "Hmmm."

"What?"

"The company still exists. Statute of limitations on 'Missing and Presumed Dead Persons' was reached a year ago and Fairmont was declared legally dead. With no family or heirs, all shares and entitlements in the company transmigrated to his business partner, Elroy Leland. Looks like Fairmont and Leland were roommates at Harvard."

"More coffee?" Alice offered. Lydia and Big Ben shook their heads no. MacLaren said, "Sure," and held his cup to her. "Why aren't you in school today?"

"Lieutenant, I graduated two years ago."

"Oh," he said. "Alice used to live across the street from us when we lived down this way."

"Yeah, and now I'm stuck here with Gramps." She started clearing the table. "Actually started here when I was eleven." She looked out over the watery landscape with the reeds swaying in the light wind out to the horizon and said, "But it *is* a beautiful place to work. Gramps keeps me here by telling me it's all going to be mine someday." She smiled. "With one condition."

"What's that?"

"Says I'd have to rename it 'Alice's Restaurant' – whatever that means. Each time I ask him about that, he just laughs and walks away."

"Hey, get those dirty dishes into the kitchen, girl." Gramps came to the table wiping his hands on his long white apron.

"Yes sir!" She winked at her guests and retreated.

"Gramps," Ben said. "I expect you've heard about these mangrove murders out here."

"'Spect I have."

"What's your take on it?"

"Ain't got one, Chief. Whatever happens out there can stay out there, longs it doesn't hurt my business."

"Who owns the land?" Ben asked.

MacLaren answered quickly. "That's all state protected land out there, and a lot of it."

"Well, that ain't quite right, Lieutenant," Gramps said. "True, it is a vast land. Goes on and on forever. Thousands and thousands of acres stretchin' damn near coast-to-coast, right down to the Glades. Everybody thinks it's a state preserve, but it's actually privately owned."

"What are you talking about?" MacLaren challenged.

"Didn't know that did'ga?"

"So, who owns the land?" Ben asked.

"Some old broad named Winnie Vanderlene."

Lydia's ears perked up.

"What does she do with it?" Ben said.

"Nothin'. Not a damn thing. Let's the skeeters and gators roam it. Probably let it all go to the state once she kicks off. Ain't got no kids or relatives to leave it to."

"She live on it?"

"Nope. She's a recluse. Lives by herself on a little strip of land in the Gulf. Locals call it Two Can Key. Out there at the tip of Longboat or Siesta or Casey Key, one of them barrier islands out there somewhere." Gramps scratched his stubble. "Might be down by Midnight Pass, now that I think of it. Real secluded. Half sand, half trees. Probably the only cay left out there that's not developed." Gramps went back into his kitchen.

"I've heard of her," Lydia said.

"Yeah, well I never have," MacLaren countered.

"Her grandfather was Wallace T. Vanderlene, the guy who funded Flagler's railroad expansion."

"Tell me more about Mizz Vanderlene," Ben said.

"There's not much to tell. She's a very mysterious woman."

"Rich and mysterious," Ben said. "Sounds like my kind of woman."

"And old." Lydia teased.

"Well, like I said, rich and mysterious." Ben signaled to Alice to bring a check. "I got this."

"Good," MacLaren said. "Let's get a move on."

"I'm moving on to Cambridge."

"Oh Christ, Ben. What do you think you're …"

"I want to meet the partner of Carlene's high school Science Fair geek. Like to ask this Elroy Leland/AbioGenetix guy a few questions face to face."

"We could just as well call him."

"No. I want to meet him. I need to read his eyes. Find out how he fell into a billion dollars and what the fuck really happened to his partner."

Lydia said, "There's got to be some connection between Hannah Hunt Everett, Carlene Benson, Montgomery Fairmont, Hannah's twin, the naked man, and, I'm scared to death to say this, my father."

Alice brought the check and said she was glad they had stopped by and looked forward to seeing them again.

Lydia rose from the table and gathered her things. "I'm going to hunt down Winnie Vanderlene."

"Lydia, you've got your law practice and your Governor-to-be dad to think about. You're not a PI. Let us handle this," MacLaren said.

She glared at him with a seriousness in her eyes. "I'm spooked Lieutenant, and I want some answers. You saw that guy - spitting image of Conrad Blake Lawrence. As a trial attorney, I'd say that two bodies found on property owned by the same person is relevant. We don't know if the first body at the art museum ties into this, but it does tie into Ben's wife Carlene through the phone number found on the body, which might - I say might with a capital M - bring us to a connection to their high-school classmate, Montgomery Fairmont. Are you guys following me?"

"Yes, Counselor."

"Good, because we don't have much to go on and we'd better start investigating what we've got. So, if Ben wants to follow the partnership lead, I think it a good idea. Seems like full ownership of a billion dollar company fell into Elroy Leland's lap. That may be legit but I'm suspicious." Lydia donned her sunglasses and said, "I'm going to the ladies room. I'll meet you in the truck."

The two men watched her stride down the deck and turn the corner.

MacLaren said, "What's got her so riled up?"

"I think it's the naked guy's uncanny resemblance to her father."

"Yeah, you're probably right. But I'll tell you one thing, I wouldn't want to be on the other side of her in a courtroom."

"Me either."

28
Google Earth

Just then Chief Ray Burati walked around the corner of the deck. "Gramps said you guys were out here." He sat in the empty seat. "Where's Lydia?"

"Ladies room."

"What's up?"

"We're thinking of splitting responsibilities," MacLaren said. "I'll work with you to paste these murders together, Lydia's thinking of tracking down the elusive owner of the property - do you know Winnie Vanderlene?"

"Heard of her, never met her." He smoothed his bushy handlebar mustache and looked at Ben. "And you, Chief?"

"Gonna make a quick trip to Cambridge and have a chat with an Elroy Leland."

"Who's he?"

"Business partner to the guy who was in high school with my wife and Hannah Hunt."

"How's he figure into this?"

"Not sure that he does, but I'd like to find out."

A broad smile spread across Ray's face. "Sounds like you're getting into this. You thinkin' hard about taking over my job?"

Ben could feel the eyes at the table upon him. He could also feel the unmistakable presence of renewed excitement in his bones. He found himself saying, "Yes sir, I believe I am."

"Good, goddamn it!" Ray leaned forward and slapped Ben's shoulder. "I can't wait to get away from this shit. First thing I'm gonna do is fire up the Harley, cross the Alley and cruise the Keys all the way to Key West. Get drunk for a week." Ray smiled wide and stroked his mustache again, "But now," he pushed his chair back, "I gotta get down to the county office in Sarasota and file some goddamn paperwork."

They were leaning against the tailgate of MacLaren's pickup waiting on Lydia. Big Ben said, "Ray, what's the proximity of the second scene to the first one in the lagoon?"

"I'll show you." They moved over to Chief Ray's cruiser parked in the shade.

Ray slid into the driver's seat, started the car, turned the A/C on and brought Google Earth up on the computer screen. MacLaren sat on the passenger side. Ben looked over his shoulder from the back seat.

Ray zeroed in on the vast marshland all around them. "There's Gramps Ramp, and this little open area here is the lagoon." He zoomed out to expand the screen. "And over here is the latest crime scene."

"So, what's that? A mile or two between them?"

"Little over a mile."

Lydia tapped on the side window glass. Ben opened the door for her and she slid in next to him. "What are we looking at?"

"We're checking out the proximity of the two mangrove murder scenes."

Ben reached over to adjust the monitor. "Do you mind?"

"No, go ahead."

Ben manipulated the program, zooming in and out several times from the two areas to the wider view of the entire county.

"Pretty desolate looking," MacLaren offered.

Ray said, "Two naked bodies in two days out in the middle of nowhere."

"Maybe you've got a nudist colony out there, Ray," MacLaren chuckled.

"If there was one, I'd sure as hell know about it." He winked at Lydia and twisted his handlebar mustache.

"Look at this," Ben said. "From on high the resolution is clear. But when you zoom in closer," he clicked into the foliage. "The lagoon and area where the naked guy was found are clear, but this area over here becomes blurry."

Lydia skirted closer to Ben. "Do that again. Zoom back out and then click back in slowly."

They all focused intently on the computer screen. "There!" She said. "Go back one click." He did. "Now forward one click." She squeezed Ben's knee. "See it?"

"Yeah."

"What?" MacLaren said. "See what?"

Lydia pointed to a spot in the center as Ben clicked back and forth.

"It looks like a smudge," MacLaren said.

"Yes, but watch this." She reached over and held down the arrow key, zooming quickly from one extreme to the other. "When you do it fast like this, the smudge isn't noticeable. But when you get close to ground level, it appears out of nowhere, blending in with the green foliage."

MacLaren actually tried to wipe the smudge with his shirtsleeve. "Hmmm. Could be a glitch. Either with the computer or Google."

"I don't like glitches," Big Ben said. "I'd like to walk that crime scene again. You up for it?" he asked MacLaren.

29

Aqualung

MacLaren decided to leave the boat and trailer at Gramps' and the two cops climbed into the pickup truck and headed back to the mangroves. Lydia was catching a ride back to town with Chief Ray. She needed to touch base with her father and she wanted to prepare a few things for her confrontation with Winnie Vanderlene that she was planning for tomorrow morning.

"I feel like the Three Musketeers and I don't like it." MacLaren was driving. "I've got to start piecing this thing together coherently and I'm not sure you jaunting off to Cambridge and Lydia seeking out the Vanderlene woman is going to help." He looked over at Ben.

"Your point?"

"My point is, we're a little out of bounds and the three of us could get our asses into one big sling."

"I'm going to tell Carlene my game plan and grab a flight to Logan. I'll be gone only a day or two."

"I want you to know up front that I don't think that's a wise idea." He glared at Ben. Ben turned his head and looked out his window. "So you'd better keep everything by the book."

"Listen," Ben said. "I've got to follow this hunch. I need to get ahead of the curve on this thing. And to be honest, I'm worried about Carlene. I need to prevent anything happening to her."

MacLaren found the spot off the roadway where they'd entered the backcountry earlier. He pulled up to the rusted metal fence and shut the truck down.

Ben seemed deep in thought. Finally he said, "We'll give Lydia some latitude on this, but remember, she's not a cop. She shouldn't be involved in this, but we both know why she wants to be. So, let's let her run with the property thing, but I think we should cut her loose after that."

"Agreed."

The afternoon heat was on the prairie beyond the metal gate. There was no clear path out to where the naked man had been found and they spent a long sweaty time snaking arduously through the dense foliage. Finally they reached the spot. They stood there in silence, visually searching the landscape, each man lulled into an investigative karma by the remoteness and uncanny logistics of the crime scene. Finally Big Ben broke the reverie. "How far away from the lagoon do you think we are?"

"Don't know." MacLaren lifted his head to the sky, getting his bearings. "Think it's that way." He pointed to a narrow animal trail leading into the overgrowth.

They wandered around for another thirty minutes feeling lost most of the time and waiting for a break in the green mesh of mangroves that would present them with the lagoon where they had found Hannah Hunt's twin.

"I hate to tell you this Chief, but I think we're lost." MacLaren looked at his cell phone. No reception. Ben was ahead of him, invisible in the brush.

"Hey," Ben said in a guarded whisper. "Check this out."

There was a cypress copse stretching before them and then a flat open space with a circular carving in the tropical meadow, like one of those alien mazes in a Midwestern cornfield. At the far end a ramshackle shack sat beneath an elaborate camouflaged netting that spread like a spider's web across the tundra for several acres like the netted tobacco fields in Connecticut.

Several figures milled about in the foreground of the structure. There were more walking in the clearing. Everyone wore a loose fitting robe of various colors that, in the light afternoon breeze, made them look like fluttering windsocks.

RRR...RUFF!

A low guttural growl emanated from behind them. It scared the shit out of MacLaren. He jumped and spun around. Big Ben already had his gun out in a two-handed grip. A six-foot alligator was sitting up on its hind legs growling at them. Calmly it lowered itself and crawled towards them with its tail wagging. The gator cautiously approached Big Ben and sniffed at his feet.

"Ah … Chief?" A mystified MacLaren said, as he stood frozen in place. "Don't fucking move."

Big Ben had his .38 pointed at the middle of the creature's head, but was unable to shoot. Suddenly it snorted, turned, and skipped off into the meadow.

The two men stared at each other with apprehension.

"That was fucking *weird*," MacLaren said.

"Yeah." Ben returned his gun to his cargo pocket. His hand was shaking.

The gator made a beeline to the front of the house and again sat up on its hind legs. A man in white took something from his pocket and tossed it to the gator. It ran off.

"I've never seen an alligator do that."

The man in white started walking towards them. He wore a white linen Guayabera shirt over white linen trousers. His long hair and equally long beard matched the color of his ensemble that was topped by a wide-brimmed white straw hat. His feet were bare. "Welcome," he said. "May I help you gentlemen?"

"Is this your property?" MacLaren asked in an authoritative voice.

"No."

"Whose is it?"

"It is owned by The Foundation."

"The Foundation?"

"The Woodstock Foundation."

"And you are?" Ben asked.

"Curious as to who *you* are and why you are here."

"Touché." Ben said, extending his hand. "Ben Benson. And this is Lieutenant MacLaren, SPD."

"Anderson," the man said and they shook hands.

"And what does The Foundation do?" Lieutenant MacLaren asked.

"It protects its interests." Anderson smiled. "According to the United States Constitution."

Ben realized the man was guarded against authority. He decided to take a different tact with this guru. "You've got a nice place here." He looked around nodding his head approvingly. "Serene. A little off the beaten path though."

"It is our spiritual refuge. Our tropical Walden Pond, so to speak. The remoteness separates us and allows an untainted peace of mind away from the trappings of our primitive and barbaric civilization."

MacLaren turned his head so that no one would see him roll his eyes. When he turned back his voice got serious. "Mr. Anderson, this is official police business. I would like to ask you a few questions, and if need be I can return with a warrant." He glared, defying him.

"No, no. There is no need for a warrant. Please, come," he gestured toward the house. "Let us enjoy a refreshing drink on the porch. You must be thirsty from the long walk. There is no direct way in from whence you came."

As they walked to the house, Ben asked. "How *do* you gain access?"

"There is a little road, a rural pathway that comes up from the south off of Nocatee Road."

"That's quite a distance away."

"Yes, it is."

The remainder of the walk was silent. Ben took in the surroundings all around them. And all above them. The high netting spread as far as he could see in all directions. Ben realized it was not as much netting, which is fabric-like, and tightly woven gauze, but rather a web-like canopy, as a spider's web that has a large airy displacement throughout. Close up and directly beneath it, it was actually very thin, almost translucent and had a slight metallic sheen to it. He believed he had found the smudge.

30

Gandhi et al

The house, which from the distance had appeared as a ramshackle structure, was actually a well built CBS edifice raised upon strong, thick pilings that looked formidable enough to withstand a category five hurricane. A large outbuilding with eyebrow windows and an adjacent turret stood at the rear. Solar panels slanted on the southern side of the roof. On the veranda, long windows with louvered shutters were open to allow airflow. The wide front door was screened. A woman exited it.

She could have been twenty-seven, thirty-seven, or forty-seven. Hard to tell. Her countenance was as ruff-hewn as her cut-off denim shorts, or her faded denim shirt that she wore open and braless with the tails cinched in a knot above her navel. Her long sandy hair needed shampooing . Her "Hello" was so gravelly that Ben could have sworn he felt the floor vibrate.

"JJ, this is Mr. Benson and Lieutenant MacLaren." Her handshake was rough and powerful.

"Nice to make your acquaintance. Would you like some iced tea or lemonade?"

"Lemonade would be great," Ben said.

"Ditto," MacLaren said.

"Ian?"

"I'll have iced tea, thanks."

"Mind if I use your bathroom, Ma'am?" MacLaren asked.

"Not at all. Follow me." They disappeared through the screen door.

Anderson outstretched his arm to the Adirondack chairs lining the porch and offered Big Ben a seat.

"The lieutenant said you're on police business? Are you an officer too?"

"Incoming Chief of Police for Myakka."

"From?"

"Boston area."

"Be quite a change."

"For the better I think."

"And what brings the two of you scouting through the wilderness?"

"Murder."

"Not mine I hope."

Ben, who touted himself as an excellent reader of human responses, could not tell if he was serious or smirking.

"We are investigating the discovery of two bodies not far from here that we believe have met foul play." Ben was leaning back into the comfort of the Adirondack, but his eyes were focused on his host.

JJ brought out the drinks on an old tin cocktail tray and set it on a round wooden end table. She had thoughtfully brought pitchers of backup. MacLaren was still inside. Ben knew he was doing as much snooping as possible.

"I could fix some snacks and fruit if you'd like."

"No, thank you," Ben said. "This is fine."

She reentered the house. Anderson sipped casually on his iced tea. Ben downed his lemonade in one gulp and refilled his glass.

"How many guests do you have here?"

"One dozen."

"Anyone missing?"

"No. No one is missing."

MacLaren came out to the porch and grabbed his lemonade. He stood at the edge of the steps looking at the property and the individuals walking about. "Mind if I meander a little?"

"No. Feel free," Anderson said, and then added, "Please don't be disappointed if the guests do not converse with you. This is our afternoon meditation hour."

MacLaren descended the steps and walked off with his lemonade.

Big Ben conversed with Mr. Anderson. He explained the situation and the reason that they were here. He treaded lightly, asking open-ended questions, attempting to get Anderson to trip up or to offer some insight as to why two naked bodies were found out in this wilderness. But the man was cool, responding to Ben's questions with short, curt answers that told him nothing.

The wind picked up and brought a light shower with it. The sun was still out and the raindrops fell like fireflies drifting in a blue sky. Some caught on the silver webbing, hung there for an instant, then fell heavy to the ground. Diamonds dropping from heaven.

"I'm kind of curious about your web, here. Doesn't do much to keep the rain out."

"That is not its purpose. It's an experimental apparatus. Designed much like an umbrella without the cloth covering. The strands allow the natural elements to pass through while at the same time capturing valuable ions from the sun that are passed along as energy to our solar panels."

"I noticed that all the strands, as you call them, seem to connect to that turret on the back side of the house."

"Yes. That is our conductive point. Where the solar energy is collected and transformed into electricity."

"Sounds fascinating. Mind if I take a tour of your transformer shed?"

"Actually, I must say that I do. You see the concept is in its formative stage. Not yet proven nor patented." Anderson gave a wry smile. "I'm afraid I'd have to require a warrant for that. But I can assure you; there are no dead bodies in there," he laughed. "Merely a room full of wires and electrodes and such."

MacLaren returned to the porch, wiping the rain from his forearms.

"Would you like a towel, Lieutenant?" Anderson offered.

"No thanks." The rain weighed wet and heavy upon the colorful robes of the meditators. He could tell they were naked beneath them. "The rain doesn't bother them?"

"It is a fast rain. It will be over in a few minutes. Rather than disturb their meditation, they will accept it as a part of it. A cleansing."

The rain was indeed short-lived and a few minutes later the officers of the law thanked their guru-like host for the beverages and descended the porch.

Anderson walked them to the edge of the property and pointed at the clear sky. "You see that line of slow-moving thunderclouds?" They were high white clouds with gray bottoms far off in the blue skyline. "They're due east and traveling straight as arrows to the north. If you keep them in sight and head dead at them you'll reach the road you came in from in about twenty minutes. Save you some time and a few nicks and scrapes battling the brush."

They shook hands and moved off.

A few minutes into the brush, MacLaren said, "WFS."

"What's WFS?"

"Weird Fucking Shit! First of all, I get into the house and I'm living in the sixties. Candles, incense, black lights, psychedelic posters, - I swear there was even a lava lamp in there! Then, I'm in the bathroom taking a piss and the broad starts blasting Janis Joplin on the stereo. Except when I walk back through the living room, the stereo's *not on*. She's fucking singing!"

"Hmph. *JJ*," Ben said. "She even looks like her."

"Yeah and there's more. Out in the field? There's a guy that looks like Gandhi walking around out there. Small man, bald head, distinctive nose, round wire-rimmed spectacles…"

"Yeah, I saw him."

"You did? I'm surprised, because you can almost miss him. He weighs about twelve pounds in a soaking wet sheet. Walks around talking to himself."

The mosquitoes were out basking in the new humidity left by the brief rain. MacLaren swatted one on his neck, leaving a thick red smear on his shirt collar. "Gandhi for chrissake."

"Okay, I'll grant you there are some odd things transpiring here. But we have to remain focused and pragmatic."

"Odd? Focused? Pragmatic? How about bizarre, surreal, and fucking Twilight Zone? Pal, there's something weird going on around here. This place scares the shit outta me. There's an alligator that acts like a fucking dog!"

As if on cue, the alligator jumped out of the foliage, barked at them and ran off.

"Arggh." MacLaren hastened forward.

Ben said, "Did you catch when JJ called him Ian?"

"No."

"My son has a band. Plays guitar, but has recently taken up the flute."

"Great. Glad to hear it." MacLaren grumbled.

"He's been studying flutists. Classic guys like Herbie Mann and Phil Boiteau. He's got all their CD's. And there's another guy he likes. You know Jethro Tull?"

"Sure. The Aqualung guy. Looks like a vagabond. Plays the flute on one leg."

"Know what his name is?"

"Yeah, Jethro Tull."

"Nope. That's the name of the group. From a Dicken's character actually. The lead singer and flute player? The guy on the cover of Aqualung, with the long hair and long beard? Looks like our guru? *He's* Ian Anderson."

MacLaren, who was in the lead, stopped in his tracks and turned to Big Ben. They stared at each other. Finally Ben raised his eyebrows. "What d'ya think of that?"

"I swear to God, if Elvis cruises in here in a pink Cadillac, I'm packing it in, leaving South Florida and never coming back!"

31
The Group

Although they are synched via a sophisticated satellite system that keeps them in contact 24/7, The Group only meets in person once a month. Always in secret and never in the same place. This month's meeting would be held in a Barrow Street brownstone in Greenwich Village, New York City.

At precisely midnight, the final member of The Group arrived. Each one of them had taken different routes, arriving in half-hour intervals, walking alone under the cover of darkness to insure they were not being followed. When satisfied, they descended a narrow staircase and entered a dark doorway beneath the stoop at number 35. If any one of them had been so much as five minutes late, or even five minutes early, the meeting would have been immediately forsaken and held twenty-four hours later in another clandestine location in another country.

The eight member group is code-named Octopus. The lifetime members are wealthy, powerful embracers of despotism. Their credo is tyranny beneath the guise of democracy and their far-reaching tentacles touch and manipulate every country in the world, and subsequently, every human being on the planet.

They are terrorists. Not your run-of-the-mill, bullet-strapped, Uzi-toting, bomb-enwrapped type, but rather the real terrorists.

The Ivory Tower white-collar terrorists who wear Brooks Brother suits and reign supreme from lofty edifices in New York, London, Hong Kong, Shanghai and Dubai. The God they worship is Greed. And the pets they covet are Avarice and Cupidity.

The Octopus Group has the power, the money and the cold-hearted means to control elections, carefully construct social upheaval and promote coups, all with the goal of controlling presidents, premiers, kings, and heads of state of countries all over the globe.

They do not worry about the fluctuations of the markets - the Dow or Nasdaq or Nikea - because they control them. The Octopus Group sets in motion situations and circumstances that influence and control the global monetary bloodstream. This includes, but is not limited to, war, genocide, assassination, installation of puppet regimes disguised as errant dictatorships, et cetera, et cetera. Their power is absolute and ruthless. Their misguided dogma is the embodiment of corruption and false benevolence.

They poured coffees and got settled into the various armchairs and sofas in the large room with the dark paneling and the soft lighting. They would work through the night and hasten back to their corners of the world in the dark twilight of dawn. The meeting began with:

"What is the status of the notebooks?"

"So far, useless. Our clever scientist wrote them in a code we have yet to decipher. We have lost the Hannah Hunt woman. The business partner, Mr. Elroy Leland, has been approached and found incapable of fulfilling our agenda. Professor Montgomery Fairmont is either truly dead or at the very least, a dead end. And now the notebooks are of no help."

"We must crack the code."

They nodded their heads in unison.

"In the meantime, let us proceed with the next alternative. Agreed?"

"Agreed."

"Contact LeBeau and his wife and put the pressure on. We've already wasted a year on this."

"Ursula has already begun some initial work."

"Good, but let's step it up. We must gain the next level soon before anyone else wakes up one morning with our idea."

"I think our idea is too radical for anyone to dream up."

"Perhaps, but don't forget *we* did and there are diabolical radicals elsewhere. Surely we cannot be the only clever ones?"

They all laughed.

"At least the Conrad Lawrence project is progressing nicely. He won by a wide margin and will be a very popular governor and then a very popular two-term president."

"Does he suspect anything?"

"No. Not a thing."

"Good. When the time is right he will be brought into the loop and told where he stands and what to do. That certainly worked well for our Obama."

Again the unison laughter.

"And he never suspected a thing."

"Do they ever?"

"And the W. Bush, don't forget."

"I rest my case." More laughter.

"Yes, but that was close. Luckily the fallback plan worked. A stroke of genius having his brother as Florida governor and manipulating the re-call vote."

"Gore would have been difficult. It would have been necessary to eliminate him if he had succeeded."

"But we made the right decision in not doing so. Much wiser to steal the presidency from the winner and get *our* man into the White House. Assassinating the president of the United States is not as easy as it was for our alumni, fifty years ago."

"Ah, yes, and to cover it so well with the lone gunman and the single bullet theory. How stupid the American people are."

"Lucky for us," the American members laughed.

"Precisely why this Florida thing with Conrad Blake Lawrence will work. Coming from Florida, if need be, with our padding - for lack of a better word - of the electoral college, a recount would never be brought into question. They'd never imagine Florida would do it twice."

"But I have a queasy feeling about Mr. Jake Curtis."

Grunts and head nodding of agreement.

"He is an opportunist. And opportunists have no loyalty."

"I think he's on a high now that will sustain him for the next leg. As long as he's glued under our wing he will cooperate. He's got a lot of work to do and four years is a short time. If we keep him challenged and properly compensated I think he'll get the job done. Then we can eliminate him."

And so it went, for the next several hours, topic to topic around the world until the Octopus was satisfied and the meeting broke. They felt assured they had everything under control.

And they did, with what they knew. But there were two things they did not yet know. They hadn't heard of the bodies found in the South Florida mangroves and they didn't know about Big Ben Benson and his aggressive investigative nature.

32
Salty Dogs

Ursula had spent the last two weeks canvassing the local watering holes around Sarasota looking for a pair of unsavory characters to employ. She kept returning to The Old Salty Dog on the water at New Pass Channel and to the same two discontented old salts that appeared there everyday for five o'clock happy hour.

Jay Gaunt and Dwayne Martin had known each other a long time. They had worked together in corporate America at high-level positions for a retail conglomerate until its demise a few years back. In the end, they had opted for a buy-out package and early retirement, left St. Louis behind and settled into South Florida for the sunshine and laid back life-style. Three years later, the golf and fishing had become monotonous and unsatisfying. Hence the daily sojourns to their favorite gin mill to drown their sorrows. They would arrive at 5:00 pm each day and pre-pay for three beers each to get the happy hour prices, clever ex-businessmen-on-fixed-incomes that they were.

With her killer looks and cunning wiles it had been easy for Ursula to lure the old dogs into her clutches. After a few rendezvous the three of them had gotten quite chummy. Jay had taken to wearing after-shave and a new shirt each day and Dwayne had actually trimmed his scruffy beard. The boys were looking dapper.

Ursula listened attentively to their boring tales of past corporate life and daily complaints of how dull their beach bum life-style had become. She was pleased. She knew they were ripe for adventure. It was time to weave her concocted tale of woe of a disloyal husband.

Carefully and convincingly (complete with an Academy Award worthy performance of misery and tears) she begged them to help get her marriage back on track, not only because she still loved her wayward husband, but more importantly for the stability and future of their three children.

"How can we help do that?" Jay said.

"I need to have a conversation with the bimbo that's ruining my marriage without anyone knowing about it."

"So?" Dwayne asked. "What does that have to do with us?"

Ursula looked around the bar. They were at the end facing the water and she was seated between them. She motioned them to lean closer and whispered, "If you could pick her up and bring her to me, I would be forever indebted. And I will be happy to compensate you for your troubles."

Jay was startled, but managed to keep his voice low when he said, "Kidnap her?"

"No, no, no. It wouldn't be like that. If I ask her to meet me somewhere she'll just blow me off. And the only way to resolve this thing is for me to meet her face to face in private. I just need you to get her to me and then everything will be fine."

"Yeah, so, basically kidnap her," Dwayne said.

"Nothing's going happen to her. I just want to get that floozy away from my husband and out of my life."

Jay said, "And how are you going to do that?"

"I'm going to pay her off. But I can't get near her without someone recognizing me." She had told them she was a successful real estate broker with a high profile in the area. "All I need is to get her alone for five minutes."

Jay said, "And then what are you going to do?"

"I'm going to threaten the shit out of her, give her a bunch of money and tell her to get lost."

Jay got up and went to the men's room.

The bartender came over and asked if they were ready for another round. Dwayne waved him off.

Ursula figured Jay was pondering her offer and she remained quiet next to Dwayne as it all settled in. She didn't know which way this was going to go. But she was prepared. Her husband LeBeau was close by, in disguise at the other end of the bar, seemingly engrossed in the game on TV. She hadn't bothered using a disguise or pseudonym, because she knew the two men wouldn't live to describe her to anyone anyway – whether they took the job or not. They were destined to have a fishing accident far out in the Gulf of Mexico.

She said to Dwayne, "It would be easier with the two of you, but if your buddy doesn't want to get involved, you could do it yourself and all the money would be yours. You've got the truck." Dwayne did have a truck. He wondered how she knew about his old Chevy clunker. He expressed a reluctance to do it alone. Who would hold the woman down while he drove? He needed Jay. He was the bigger, ex-basketball player who would have no problem wrestling her inside and keeping her quiet.

Jay was on his way back to the bar. "Think on it and let me know," she said and patted Dwayne's knee.

The day was calm and the wind was down. Pleasure boats cruised the No Wake waters by Mote Marine and pelicans dove into the sea capturing dinner in their large pouches.

The trio continued into happy hour in hushed, alternating conversation - three baseless strangers as smooth and slick as the sea passing beneath them on the other side of the railing.

After the fourth beer, the whole escapade was sounding like it - as Dwayne put it - "Might be kinda fun."

"Okay, let's do it," Jay surprised them.

Ursula smiled and held her glass up. They toasted and she motioned to the bartender, "One more round."

33

Two Can Key

Two Can Key had been nicknamed such by the local anglers who would drive over to the tiny private key and park their cars at the sandy end next to the No Trespassing sign. With their fishing poles and tackle boxes (and usually a child or two in tow), they would gain entrance by ducking under the heavy chain that was tethered between two fifty-five gallon cans - hence the name.

Wallace T. Vanderlene, Winnie's granddaddy, had procured the coastal strip of land during his real estate expansion in the early twentieth century. He didn't mind the anglers encroaching on his property, but had put up the chain and barrels to discourage the kids who would come to drink, do drugs, have sex and then leave behind their beer cans, used condoms, and torn panties. The fishermen were respective and tidy.

When his one and only granddaughter arrived, he further secluded his little key by planting a wide mix of palms, Australian pines and red mangroves. Then he built her a grand dollhouse where she could play while he was getting away from his wife, enjoying a few beers, and fishing in the shoreline waters of the Gulf.

Many years later, when the Vanderlene estate passed to Winnie as sole heir, she sold off the family mansion and forfeited residency in any and all of the lavish condominiums available to her. Then she built a quaint, expanded dollhouse of her own on her favorite little place in the sun ... Two Can Key.

Winnie had removed the rusty weathered chain, but had kept the two big cans in their usual place. Lydia drove through them in an early morning wind.

She knew she was arriving unannounced, and had no idea if Ms. Vanderlene would even be home and half-hoped that she wouldn't be. But the events of the previous day, especially what had transpired at the morgue, had gotten her adrenaline spiked and she was running on gut intuition. Lydia Lawrence drove along a narrow, crushed-shell road beneath the shade of towering pines whispering in the wind and pulled up to a quaint, sun-bleached cottage surrounded with colorful tropical plants and flowers. A yellow Jeep Wrangler with a big peace sign on the spare wheel cover sat on the side. A pink bicycle with a crooked wicker basket leaned against a coconut palm. Lydia parked her car and ascended the low steps to the porch.

"Hello," she spoke into the screen door with the open room behind it. After a minute, she spoke into it again and rapped on the wood frame. After a third time without response she didn't know what to do. One part of her wanted to leave a note and another part of her wanted to turn and run like hell.

She opted to walk around back. Maybe Ms. Vanderlene was out back and didn't hear her. Off to the side there was a narrow overgrown pathway leading to a smaller cottage a short distance away. It looked abandoned, with the shutters closed and windswept debris cluttering the frail looking porch.

Then she saw her. Winifred Adele Vanderlene, reclusive heiress to the vast and rich Vanderlene estate. There had been very few pictures of her since her school days and that would have been over fifty years ago. Yet, as she approached from the beach on the Gulf side of little Two Can Key, clad in a long pink towel, Lydia could see beyond the aging. There was something timeless about her: the way she carried her petite, yet powerful frame with a strong and purposeful stride. Her hair was white and wet and hung long and straight from the weight of the water, the wetness giving it a younger, platinum blonde look.

Lydia realized she was frozen, transfixed by the lady, her stature growing taller as her bare feet padded over the powder white sand toward her.

"Hello," Winnie said in a soft voice as soft and smooth as the sand beneath her feet.

For a moment Lydia couldn't respond. She was mesmerized by Winnie's sparkling pale-gray eyes that seemed so young and alive with wonderment, like a little girl who had just gotten a pony from Santa on Christmas morning.

"I've just come in from my morning swim," Winnie continued. "Would you like to join me in a cup of tea?"

"I'm Lydia Lawrence."

"Yes, I know who you are dear. Come along."

Lydia followed the older woman back to her cottage and took a seat at the bistro counter poised between the kitchen and the open living room. Winnie filled a teapot with water from the tap and placed it on a gas burner.

"How do you know who I am?"

"Oh, just an old lady's whim. I like to keep abreast of the goings-on in my hometown. I know you are a successful attorney and I also know, of course, of your involvement in your father's campaign."

Winnie reached into a tall cupboard for a box of teabags. Her towel slipped from her shoulder and she took a moment to re-wrap it. Lydia caught a quick glance at her naked body, quick enough to see that her body was lithe and toned, another anomaly to her age, or testimonial thereto.

"Um," Lydia couldn't help but snicker, "do you always swim like that?"

"Naked? Oh yes. It's the only way to swim," she smiled.

"Aren't you afraid people will see you?"

"Who cares. Let 'em look at an old naked lady if they want. Besides, the fish don't mind, and really it is very private here on my little key."

Lydia got a sense of her "free-spiritedness". She thought it was cute, but she returned quickly to her serious mission.

"Do you know my father?"

"Why, yes. I voted for him. I know he'll make a fine Governor."

"No, I mean do you *know* my father?"

Winnie could feel a chill crawling up her back. She took two teacups from the mug shelf above the stove and placed them side-by-side on a silver serving tray. She added fresh cut lemons from the fridge and a jar of honey from the windowsill.

Lydia was waiting for an answer.

"I've got to freshen up, dear." Winnie walked through the living room and disappeared into her bathroom. As the door was closing, Lydia could hear her say, "When the water's ready, help yourself. I'll only be a minute."

Lydia noticed that Winnie's soft, powdery voice of a few minutes ago had turned a little sandy, a little grainier. She wondered why. She had a feeling she was about to find out.

34

The Retreat

Winnie stepped into the shower and stood perfectly still as the fresh water rushed over her body, washing away time and bringing her back to that rainy day at Woodstock, that wild and rainy day inside the tent with a young Conrad Lawrence.

The memory stirred her and made her wonder if she had made the right decisions in dealing with the consequences.

After Woodstock, after she stopped cussing herself for getting pregnant, Winnie knew things had to change. She was thirty something now. Time to stop fucking off, clean up her act. Get responsible and settle into a long and rewarding life, like her mother had done, sponging off the money that the family name had brought her. She wouldn't have any problem finding a man to marry her, even in enough time to convince everyone that the baby was his. Money had its privileges. She was a lucrative target: wealthy, attractive, and sexually lascivious. What man wouldn't want to crawl into bed with that?

But Winnie was also free-spirited and stubbornly independent. Her conundrum was thus - Do I conform to society's clutches or do I say fuck it, and just be me? The latter won out.

Yet, as liberal as she was, Winnie couldn't bring it upon herself to have an abortion. And she also knew that, even though she could amply provide for a child, she couldn't possibly handle motherhood. So, she devised a plan. Have the baby in secret. Keep the birth from her parents (who she feared would take over and control the baby for the rest of its life) and find a home and hearth that her child could live happily in and not suffer the ridicule, disdain and emotional scars that her parents had laden upon her.

Her friends, and the unknowing father, had all gone off to their respective worlds and nobody would ever know she was pregnant. She wasn't showing yet, so it was easy, and not out of the ordinary, for her to pack up the microbus and disappear. And, after some shrewd trust fund shuffling, that's exactly what she did. First stop – rehab.

The Brattleboro Retreat, nestled in the woodlands and meadows of southern Vermont, was well renowned for its therapies and successes dealing with alcohol and drug abuse. The cluster of grand brick edifices (originated in 1834 as The Vermont Asylum for the Insane) sits on over one thousand acres of pristine Vermont topography and exudes the appearance of an Ivy League campus. Admission was expensive (not a problem for Winnie) and patient confidentiality strictly guarded (perfect).

Winnie drove from Florida to Vermont, stopping only two nights at roadside motels. She wanted to visit party friends in Savannah, Virginia Beach, New York City and Northampton, but didn't trust herself to stay on the straight and narrow. She was determined to give the baby a fighting chance - free of the drugs and alcohol that had captured her. So, she had driven hurriedly past all of them and arrived three days later in Brattleboro, Vermont. She hoped to seclude herself at the serious looking retreat for a few months to dry out. *The College of Hard Knocks*, she mused. But as she drove through the tall fieldstone pillars with the imposing wrought iron archway, Winnie was really craving a joint and a pint of Captain Morgan.

At The Retreat she befriended and confided in her counselor BettyAnn who worked part time at an adoption and placement center. BettyAnn had been working with a couple from St. Johnsbury for some time, and, on a late night when she and Winnie were alone in the solarium, Winnie bared her soul to her. A sympathetic BettyAnn took it upon herself to breach protocol and talk to Winnie about the Fairmonts.

"They're a lovely couple. Mr. Fairmont, Norman, works at St. Jay Manufacturing as a wood pattern maker and Doris is an R.N. at Brightlook Hospital there. They aren't able to have a baby on their own and very much want one. They've already cleared all the pre-screening and have been waiting for a baby for over a year now. Your baby would be perfect for them, and I know they'd be perfect for her, or him. Whatever it is I'm sure they'd love it to death and provide a wonderful home for your baby." BettyAnn smiled a sincere smile and took Winnie's hand. "I don't think you could find a better home."

The Fairmont's were a kind, compassionate and caring couple, genuinely in love with each other – everything Winnie's parents were not. She moved into their warm and cozy Colonial on Cross Street in St. Johnsbury and settled in to bring the baby to term. For the next few months Winnie experienced the only real feelings of a happy family she'd ever had.

For the sake of all concerned, they had worked out a mutual deal. Winnie had initially offered to pay for all expenses and set up a trust fund for the baby, but the Fairmont's wouldn't hear of it. True Vermonters, they wanted to shoulder all responsibilities and would have it no other way. They thought it best that when the umbilical cord was cut, so would be the ties to Winnie and the Vanderlenes. The father would be listed as "unknown".

So it was. And after the baby was born, Winnie stuck to her promise and her plan. She kissed little Montgomery Fairmont good-bye, sold her VW Microbus and grabbed a flight to Europe, where she would shake off her heritage, assuage her guilt and reconnect with her wild side. The free-spirited haunts of Amsterdam, Italy and the French Riviera beckoned to her.

A decade later, her resolve to sever all ties with her parents, only brought more guilt upon her when she was made aware of their mutual demise via the morning newspaper delivered to her suite at the Chateau Simoneau in St. Moritz. It had come, really, as quite a shock. For Winnie had thought her parents, even with all their faults and misgivings, were indestructible.

So, over her morning breakfast tray, Winnie read the feature front page story in the French papers of how the world was wondering if the estranged daughter and only heir would show up for the funeral of *Mr. and Mrs. Wallace T. Vanderlene II, flamboyant executors of the vast Vanderlene estate in southern Florida, who met a tragic demise when their yacht,* The Sea Jewel, *capsized in a freak storm off the Bimini Islands*. Winnifred Adele Vanderlene didn't want to return home, but she did.

Back in the States, she resumed her life-style as a happy and steadfast mystery woman, roaming and mingling freely around the beaches and bars of Sarasota, no one the wiser. No one would ever guess that this old hippie woman from the sixties was the one who wielded hard-handed control over the Vanderlene estate, was an anonymous philanthropist, and the woman who kept a close eye on her biological son, Montgomery Fairmont, following his life and career from a respectful distance.

None of this would she tell Lydia Lawrence. Winnie figured she'd kept the secret for forty plus years; she could keep it awhile longer, hopefully indefinitely. It had been her mistake, and her promise to the Fairmonts. No need to disrupt the lives of the innocents. No need to reveal a son to the new Governor. No need to reveal a long lost brother to Lydia.

35
Lydia/Winnie

Winnie came out of the bathroom wearing a loose cotton tee shirt and beige shorts. She was scrubbing her wet hair with a towel and shaking her head like a young colt in a sudden rain. "So, what brings you to me? Are you representing someone?"

"I came to ask you about some property you own." Lydia waited while Ms. Vanderlene fixed her tea and took the stool across from her. "But first, I would very much like a response to my last question."

The women sat eye to eye. "You're persistent. I imagine you are a good attorney."

"So, I've been told."

Without further pause Winnie said, "I know of your father. But your tone seems to imply more to it. Am I right?"

Lydia took a deep breath, "My mother died eleven years ago. My father loved her very much, as did I. I helped him box her belongings and store them in the attic. Just recently, while preparing for the move to the Governor's Mansion in Tallahassee, I went through them looking for a remembrance of her to take with him. The pictures were the hardest. They had shared a wonderful life together and the three of us were very happy."

Winnie sipped her tea, keeping the rim of her teacup level so her eyes didn't leave Lydia's.

"I found some pictures of my father when he was young. Taken at Woodstock. He has spoken of it from time to time, always glad that he and his friends got to experience it. There's a picture of him with a woman. An attractive, older woman. On the back is an inscription in a female hand – *Remember our day, Winnie.*

Winnie sat back and held her teacup on the edge of the tabletop.

"My father and I are very close, but his personal business is his personal business. And his past is certainly *none* of my business." Lydia sipped her tea cautiously. "I have not asked him about the picture and I'm not sure why it was in my mother's belongings. Only surmising the pictures had gotten mingled together as those things sometimes do over the course of a long marriage."

Winnie started to speak but Lydia raised a hand to her. "Please, let me finish." She placed her cup forcibly onto its saucer. "I really don't care what transpired between you and my father back then, nor since then, only if it had intruded upon my parent's marital years." At this, Lydia raised her eyebrows as if to say, *did it?*

Winnie shook her head. "Other than bumping into Conrad from time to time at a charitable function or such, I haven't had any contact with him since Woodstock. That was a long time ago." She had a glaze on her eyes that seemed to look right through Lydia. "I did have occasion to meet your mother once. I believe it was at the dedication of the Selby Library. She seemed like a nice lady. They looked happy together. Your mother was very attractive, I can see her in you." Winnie smiled. The unexpected compliment broke Lydia's affront.

She felt embarrassed. "I'm sorry," Lydia said, leaning forward and rubbing her temples. "I didn't mean to seem harsh or ambivalent. It's just that ..." Tears began to well in her eyes and her lower lip began to quiver.

Winnie rose from her stool and reached a box of tissues from the counter. She went around and placed the box in front of Lydia and pulled a tissue for her. Lydia took it and dabbed her eyes. "I'm sorry. I don't know what's gotten into me. I shouldn't be ..." and then her shoulders began to shake and Winnie put her arm across them and held onto her like her mother used to do. Lydia felt the warmth and compassion of an old woman's arms comforting her and she began to sob.

Winnie's cottage had sliders on the Gulf side that opened onto an infinity deck that reached across the white beach and grasped the emerald waters hovering like a mirage beneath the noon sun. An umbrella hovered over a low table surrounded by sun-scorched wicker chairs. She had set out a plate of fresh veggies and cheese with a homemade veggie dip. Winnie poured two glasses from a chilled pitcher of Margaritas. "To the day," she said, and they clinked glasses and sipped like two close friends on a reunion. Although they weren't. This was the first time they had met and Lydia had an agenda that suddenly swept back to her.

"There's an investigation going on. A man was found in a mangrove marsh. Dead. No identification on him, in fact he was naked. No apparent cause of death." Lydia looked helplessly at Winnie Vanderlene. "He looks like he could be my father's twin."

"Oh my."

"He was found on your property."

"What?"

"In the mainland out by state road 70."

"When?"

"Yesterday morning."

Winnie seemed to take a moment to register this. "I haven't been out to that land since ... Lord, I don't think I've ever been out there. Due to the vastness of the land holdings of the Vanderlene Estate, I've never gotten around to actually viewing all the land - nor ever wanted to. I plan to leave it all to the state anyway as a preserve. My last "fuck you" to the cancerous urban sprawl eroding our beautiful state."

"So, you have no idea what someone would be doing on your land?"

"None. And I must say that, over the years, there have been squatters that have come and gone. I never took any action against them because, well, first of all I didn't care and secondly I was always a bit afraid of reprisals if I had them forcibly removed. I certainly didn't want some disgruntled squatter setting fire to those prairies."

"If I may ask, how many acres do you own?"

"The Vanderlene estate covers a little more than 200,000 acres."

Lydia raised her eyebrows.

"And it's just me. So you can imagine how impossible it is for me to police it."

"I had no idea it was so vast."

Winnie laughed. "No one does, really. The land has been there for eternity. It's just part of the scenery. I'm very reclusive and I don't like to brag. The only acreage I give a damn about is the four acres right here."

"But haven't you ever been approached by developers?"

"Oh, lots of times. But I never return their phone calls and eventually they leave me alone."

The day lulled and the conversation was comfortable. Eventually the pitcher of Margaritas was exhausted and Lydia felt it was time to go.

"Thanks for seeing me and for your generous hospitality."

"Oh, you're quite welcome, my dear. Come anytime."

They walked off the decking and strode through the shade along the side of the house. Lydia looked over to the small cottage hidden in the tropical greenery.

"What's that little house over there?"

"Oh, that's my little doll house. My grandfather built that for me to play in. We used to come over here together. He'd fish," she entwined her arm into Lydia's as they walked, "and drink his beers away from my grandmother." She smiled. "He said this was our secret place that only he and I knew about. He was quite the dreamer, old Wallace T. I loved him very much. More than my own father."

"It's cute. Looks a lot bigger than a doll house, even big enough to live in."

"Oh, it is. I actually resided there for several months after I returned from my European sabbatical and was having my new cottage built here. It was fun."

"Do you use it now?"

"Oh, I'm afraid it's just a place for old dolls and cobwebs."

They reached the car. Lydia took her hand and said, "You are an amazing woman Winnie Vanderlene."

"I'm just a happy old lady living her life the way she wants to," she smiled. "But I have been blessed. The wealth has allowed me to be a carefree spirit all my life. And I have encountered many wonderful things and wonderful people. Your father was one of them."

Lydia knew she had just received the answer she had come for.

36
Tasers

Five o'clock Happy Hour was in full swing at The Old Salty Dog. Amy Blair, the manager, was setting up a twenty-top on the rear patio for a group of writers attending a Mystery Florida Conference. Their reservation was for 5:30. She was angling the umbrellas against the sun lingering hot above the New Pass drawbridge. The crew from Marine Max next door was stationed on their favorite stools at the bar.

Jay Gaunt walked in along the outside deck and sat at the far end closest to the water. Without asking, the bartender pulled a Yuengling draft and set it on a coaster in front of him. "New hat?" Shannon asked.

"Yeah, it's a Panama."

"Classy. You solo today?"

"Nah, Dwayne'll be right along, in fact I see his pickup pulling into the parking lot now. You may as well set him up."

A minute later Dwayne was at the bar with a mischievous eye.

Jay said, "What's with the shit-eating grin?"

Dwayne took a long draw on his beer, wiped the froth with his forearm and said, "Wait'll you see what I got us."

He placed a men's travel kit on the bar, unzipped it and pulled out something that looked like a brass screwdriver with a long pointed end.

"What the hell is that?"

"It's a window-punch."

"A what?"

"A window-punch. It's a special spring-loaded tool designed to instantly pulverize a car window. You just jab this pointed end against the center of the window and presto! The window's in a million pieces. And here," he pulled another one from the bag, "I got one for you too."

Jay grabbed the tools and the bag and hustled them into Dwayne's lap beneath the bar top. "What the fuck is the matter with you?" He looked around hoping that no one had seen what had just transpired. "Keep that shit out of sight."

"Don't be so jumpy." Dwayne took another long draw and then opened the bag wide in the space between their stools. "Check this out."

Jay reluctantly leaned back and looked down into the bag. "I'm afraid to ask."

"Tasers."

"Tasers! Geesus, Dwayne."

"And I've got ski masks in the truck."

Jay shook his head and donned his sunglasses from the lanyard around his neck; a not so subconscious move to hide from everyone and everything around him.

Dwayne surreptitiously palmed one of the Tasers. "These stun guns are really cool. They shoot out an electric current that incapacitates the neuromuscular .."

"I know, Dwayne, I watch TV."

"Yeah, well I bet you don't know where their name comes from, smartass."

"And I'll bet you're gonna tell me."

"The guy who invented them was a fan of the Tom Swift adventure stories and Taser is an acronym for Thomas A. Swift's

Electric Rifle. I used to read that stuff when I was a kid. The story is about …"

"Please don't enlighten me further."

"Man," Dwayne put it back in the bag and zipped it up, "you are such a party-pooper."

"Hmmph."

They finished their beers and motioned for a second round.

A twenty-eight-foot Grady-White with twin Yamaha 250s pulled up to the dock. Two couples were onboard. One man jumped onto the dock and secured fore and aft as the other man held fast at the helm. A slight swell rocked the boat against the pilings. The attractive ladies were primping in a mirror dangling from the Bimini top. Jay recognized one of the men as a local writer from Longboat Key.

"I think that's Terry Griffin."

"Who?"

"And the guy with him is Matt Royal. He's a lawyer or a private investigator or something."

Dwayne looked over at them.

"Don't let them see us." Jay turned his back to the water.

"How do you know them?"

"I read his books and I just saw Griffin's picture on the poster out front for the writer's conference. Here they come. Turn around."

"You are way too paranoid, my friend."

The foursome passed by them with no incident.

Dwayne shook his head. "Jay, you need to chill out. They don't know you from Adam."

"I just don't want to attract any unwarranted attention, that's all."

"Like I said," Dwayne raised his glass, "way too paranoid."

The popular waterside restaurant was quickly filling up with sunset patrons. To the east, hundreds and hundreds of black sea crows were flying high above the tall masts of Sarasota Sailing Squadron and skimming the fading sky towards an early roost in the tall pines of Quick Point Preserve. This pre-nocturnal dance would continue until the twilight captured the few remaining strands of daylight and the birds could rest comfortably into the evening.

Jay was oblivious to the wonders of nature. His concentration was fixed on the parking lot.

"She's not coming today," Dwayne said.

Ursula had told them she needed a couple of days to work out the particulars. That she would set everything up for them. Not to worry. She'd be in touch. But Jay wasn't exactly worried - although Dwayne's crazy Butch and Sundance enthusiasm was making him wonder if the two of them weren't going over the edge.

Jay was hoping Ursula would show. She hadn't been there the last two days and he was missing their cocktail hours together.

"Are you having second thoughts?" Dwayne asked.

"No. I want to help her. And her kids." Jay had told himself he was doing it for humanitarian reasons. But Dwayne thought Jay was harboring a simmering infatuation.

Nevertheless, Dwayne was excited. For him it was all about the thrill – Gardner McKay, *Adventures In Paradise*.

A black Lincoln Zepher, sparkling like a polished onyx on a bed of crushed, sun-bleached shells, rolled into the parking lot. Jay straightened his posture, lifted his hat and smoothed his thinning hair. He adjusted the straw fedora just so. "She's here," he said.

The driver's door opened and long, bare legs with bright red toenails slithered out. Ursula sauntered towards the bar, her tanned legs disappearing into a short skirt that fluttered when the breeze caught it. The accompanying white top clung to her well, pleasantly accentuating her cleavage.

"Just once," Jay said.

"You're fucked up. You're old enough to be her father. Grandfather actually."

Jay was undeterred. "Just once."

Ursula saw them and waved. Jay lowered his sunglasses and stood to give her a welcome hug. Dwayne remained seated and rolled his eyes to the ceiling.

"I thought I'd find you boys here," she said, amidst the plume of perfume wafting around her.

Jay slid his stool out and held it for her, taking up the next one to his side so that she was sitting between them. He motioned to the bartender and turned to face Ursula.

"I didn't think we'd see you today."

"Things are speeding up," she said. "I think tomorrow will be the day. I really want to get this over with and get my life back to normal again."

Two more beers and a Grey Goose martini, one olive, arrived. Ursula took a quick sip and replaced her glass onto the bar top. "I can't tell you how much I appreciate your help and concern." She squeezed both men's forearms as she said this.

"Did you get the toys?" She addressed Dwayne.

"Yup, right here," he tapped the bag in his lap. "Got the window-breakers at an auto parts store and the Tasers from ..."

"I really don't want to know," she broke in. "I know they're illegal." She sipped her martini and thought, *Men are such saps.*

Jay was a little perturbed that he had been kept out of the loop about this. Apparently Ursula and Dwayne had instituted some things on their own. Truth be told, Ursula was having second thoughts about Jay. But she liked his size and needed his muscle. And she knew she had him wrapped around her finger. She looked at him and gave him a sweet smile and patted his thigh.

"Okay," she lowered her voice, "here's how it should go tomorrow."

37
Cambridge

Big Ben had left his car in long-term parking at Logan just three days earlier. Luckily in covered parking so he didn't have to brush off the light snow Boston had received last night. His plan was to have a dialogue with Elroy Leland this afternoon and then drive home to Bryce Corner and spend the evening with the kids and Uncle Bob who was staying at the house during his and Carlene's absence. He was anxious to broach the Florida relocation topic with them. His return flight was the next morning.

Ben exited the airport in the cold afternoon sun and drove through the sparsely lit Callahan Tunnel. What a difference from the tropical mangrove canopy he and MacLaren had putted through two days ago. Yesterday, under the ruse of an old college buddy passing through town, Ben had called AbioGenetix to ascertain if Leland would be in today. He would. And it had been easier than he thought to enlist Leland's personal secretary as a silent partner in his "surprise" visit.

Boston is a cool town, but it's a navigational nightmare. Streets have been thrown together over the centuries like pieces of a faulty puzzle ever since our forefathers landed at Plymouth Rock – and *they* hit a rock! Their aptitude for laying out a suitable blueprint of thoroughfares didn't get any better.

Ask any cabbie or Bostonian on the street for directions and the first thing they'll ask is, "What time is it?" Another thing about Boston – if a route sign or a street sign falls down, gets stolen, or axed by a snowplow, it's never replaced. So, even a GPS system is rendered fruitless and just as confusing as the traffic patterns themselves. Fortunately, Ben knew a bit about Beantown traffic.

The digital readout on the dashboard said 12:30 pm. Ben calculated: weekday, noontime, major congestion. The normal twenty-minute route through the city and over the Longfellow Bridge into Cambridge would now take an hour. If he circumvented north over the Mystic River through Charlestown and cut west through Somerville, he could reach the western edge of Cambridge in less than thirty. Better idea.

However, per usual, no matter how traffic-savvy you thought you were, Murphy's Law took precedence. Ben was stuck in bumper to bumper on the Tobin Bridge.

They were roommates at Harvard. *Hahvahd*, he thought. Montgomery Fairmont and Elroy Leland. Where did they get these names, he wondered. Did they come to Harvard and meet with the Dean of Names to decide on a moniker that would better further their career? Montgomery Fairmont. Elroy Leland. Like they had some book with only last names in it that you had to choose from to become your first name. Whatever. People might say the same about his name, Benjamin Benson, or MacLaren. He suddenly realized he didn't know what MacLaren's first name was. Or how about William Williams, or Adam Adams, or Gregory McGregory, or a guy he knew that was actually named Jameson Jameson … the third, mind you. These were the inane things you thought about when you were bogged down in Boston traffic.

He was also wondering what was wrong with him. Why had he interrupted his vacation so hastily to go chasing a lead that would take him not only back to where he'd just come from, but also away from the woman he was trying to protect?

"Why do you have to go, Ben? We're supposed to be on vacation, remember?"

"It'll be just for two days. One overnight. I can stop in and check on the kids."

"Ben, this isn't your case."

The Chimera fireplace in the corner of the MacLaren's lanai was facing them. They sat in matching chairs extending their feet to the warmth. The dark night wind was coming down from the north and dropping the temperature to fifty degrees; December winter was hitting south Florida. Already Ben was regretting going back to Boston tomorrow.

"I can solve this thing, baby. Down here I get excited about my job again. I feel alive and charged up. Bryce Corner is a great little town, but I'm just not challenged there anymore. I mean, nothing happens there. I haven't even handed out a parking violation in over a year."

Carlene knew how stifled Ben had become of late. And his lethargy and unease had begun to affect their relationship. She'd love to have him happy with his career again. He was a damn good cop, like his father and uncle Bob before him. But she loved Bryce Corner, Massachusetts and wasn't sure what a sudden move towards the place of their retirement years would do to the family.

MacLaren and Lorraine had gone off to their bedroom, giving Big Ben and Carlene the house to themselves. They knew they were going through a sensitive time.

Ben set his beer on the floor and reached over to massage his wife's left breast.

"What's gotten into you lately?"

"You."

Carlene, her wineglass wavering in her left hand, moved it to her right hand and leaned back, allowing him to massage her other breast. He squeezed her thick nipple. "Mmmmm," she responded.

Ben took her glass, set it on the floor and raised Carlene's top over her head.

"I think it's a Florida thanng," he drawled.

He took her down on the floor and....

"Ohmygod ..."

The air was cool, but the tiles in front of the Chimera were warm against her naked back.

"Ohmygod ..." she said again beneath the purple twilight.

A taxi blared at him from the stalled traffic behind and brought him out of his sexual reverie. Ben realized he had his hand in his lap and embarrassingly grabbed the steering wheel with both hands. *God, I love that woman.*

38
AG / Elroy Leland

Leland's office was perched on the top floor of the twelve-floor granite and glass building on the Cambridge side of the Charles. The building exuded a distinctive air of nouveau-riche prosperity.

The receptionist inspected Ben's ID and placed a check mark next to his name in her logbook. Leland's executive assistant had already cleared Ben.

Edna Gochie was an attractive granddame whose congenial personality and warm smile were as pleasant as her looks. Ben noticed her keen, professional sense of fashion that she wore in a classic Ann Taylor reflection. Edna had been with AG since its inception and Ben would learn later that she was Leland's most valued employee. Edna loved everyone and everyone loved Edna. Her pleasant personality and exceptional work ethic awarded her a level of respect she wholly enjoyed. Leland admired her so much that he told Ben he would gladly fire his entire staff before he let her go. For Edna had one endearing quality that he particularly enjoyed; she knew everything about everyone in the building.

She extended her hand to Ben and whispered, "You're exactly as I pictured you, Mr. Benson. Well," she snickered, as Ben loomed before her, "perhaps a bit larger. Leland will be thrilled to see you again. He's alone in his office. Allow me to present you."

"Oh, that won't be necessary, Edna. I'd like to catch him off guard if you don't mind." Ben's smile was loaded with charm.

It worked. "Be my guest," she said, pointing to the office door. "Just buzz me if you'd like refreshments."

Ben nodded and walked in on Elroy Leland.

Elroy Leland was a clean-shaven man. Lean and athletic looking, in his early forties, crisp in his presentation, immaculate in his Louis of Boston attire, with not a hair out of place or a speck of dust within ten yards of him. He sat stoically behind his well-organized desk intent on his computer monitor.

After a long moment (and *one second* before Ben was going to throw something at him) Leland sat back in his ergonomic chair and glared at his unannounced guest over the top of his half-glasses. He said nothing. He waited, as if people popped-in on him unannounced all the time.

"I'm Chief Ben Benson from Bryce Corner."

"Bryce Corner? You're a little beyond your jurisdiction aren't you Chief?"

"Just a little." Ben helped himself to a seat. "First of all, let me apologize for my intrusion and assure you that your assistant is free of any wrongdoing. I'm afraid I duped her into being an unknowing accomplice."

Leland seemed to take that pretty well, but when he placed his glasses on the desk and moved his hands towards his lap, Ben wasn't sure if he was going to reach for a hidden security button or a gun. Instead he leaned back and folded his hands, as if to say, "Go on."

"I am here to talk to you about your partner, Montgomery Fairmont." This seemed to get a rise out of him.

"Monty?" he said. "I'm afraid he's been dead for several years."

"But first," Ben continued unabated, "I need to ask you if these two names mean anything to you." Ben divulged his wife's maiden name and that of Hannah Hunt. Leland had no recognition of them and stated he couldn't recollect Fairmont ever mentioning them.

"The three of them went to the same high school in Vermont. Are you sure your partner never mentioned them?"

"Monty was very closed about his past. I'm afraid it was a topic he chose to bypass."

Ben hesitated a moment and then continued, "Time is of the essence, and you're right, I am outside jurisdiction. If I had gone through proper channels I'm not sure I would have been able to talk to you. I'll be up front with you Mr. Leland, I'm caught up in an investigation where my wife is peripherally involved and may be in danger."

Leland scratched his chin. "I admire your candor in speaking with a complete stranger. Please call me Lee, everyone else around here does."

"Call me Ben, then." Ben had rehearsed his conversation on the flight. Being an extremely cautious investigator who held the belief that everyone has something to hide, he had decided to craft it in such a way as to trip up Mr. Elroy Leland and hopefully elicit a crack in the case before any further discomfort or harm came to his wife. He held a strong gut feeling that Fairmont/Leland/AbioGenetix was a key to the goings on in Florida and the trauma Carlene was experiencing. However, now being face to face with the man, Ben reevaluated his prepared stance and hit him with his true feelings and trepidation. "I'd like to keep this as close to the vest as I can, Lee. Let me bring you up to speed on why this is so important to me personally."

Ben told him as much as he could without jeopardizing the case. He didn't want MacLaren and Chief Ray Burati chastising him when he returned to Sarasota. After all, this was merely a fact-finding mission he had taken upon himself.

Leland listened attentively. Although he did not know this man, he felt for his circumstance - having himself recently been acquainted with a taste of fear. "I'm not sure how I can be of assistance, Ben."

"Maybe we could start with some background on Fairmont."

Leland rose and went over to the credenza. "Would you like a drink?"

"No thanks."

"Scotch? I've got a smooth twenty-five year Glenfiddich."

"Black coffee if you've got it."

Leland poured two fingers of scotch into a snifter and added an ice cube from a chrome ice bucket. He opened his office door a crack and spoke to Edna, then he took his glass over to the floor-to-ceiling windows of the penthouse suite. The day was bright with a mild temperature that had already melted most of the previous night's light snowfall. Crews were rowing on the Charles. Stalwart joggers padded over the Longfellow Bridge.

Leland took a healthy sip. Ben thought he noticed a slight quiver to his hand. "I was fortunate. I had Monty for a roommate at Harvard." In the skyline beyond the river, he could see the slate roof and lofty gables of his Ivy League alma mater. He paused and took another sip. Edna brought Ben his coffee and retreated from the room.

"Describe fortunate."

With his back still to Ben, Leland swirled his snifter and took his time. "He was the focused one. I was the fuck-up. I came from money. Went to Harvard because dad and grand-dad were alumni. Had no interest in grades. Hardly went to class. My only real interest was getting laid. I knew that being a Harvard under-classman would spread a lot of legs for me."

"And?"

Leland turned around and smiled. "It did. I was young, spoiled and sowing my oats. Nights were for partying and days were for sleeping off the hangover. But Monty …" he began to pace in front of the windows, "Monty was incredible. He didn't have a silver spoon in his mouth. He'd come from grass roots. So, initially I thought his incessant studying was an attempt to prove himself worthy of being accepted to Harvard. But I was wrong. His mind was constantly on overload. He couldn't help himself. He studied twenty-four seven, like a man possessed. And to a degree, I think he was. When he wasn't in our dorm room, he was in the lab. I couldn't budge him from his work. Couldn't get him to go out and have some fun. I couldn't fix him up on a date. The only extracurricular activity I knew him to have was trout fishing. But other than that, he was so focused on his theories and formulas that it stirred my curiosity and I got caught up in it. We forged a partnership. It began in our dorm room and several years later it brought us here." Leland held his arms out. "Monty was the scientist and I was the socialite. He brought the brains to the table and I brought the bankers."

Big Ben spread his arms, "And what exactly is all this?"

Leland kind of smirked. "What do you know about bio-technology?"

39
AbioGenetix

"It started in plant life. Orchids actually." Leland sipped his scotch. Ben noticed a slight change in his attitude. A little arrogance coming on with the scotch? "Apparently people are quite enamored with their flowers. Monty and I always thought that was quite humorous. Anyway, being as crazy as we were in the scientific realm of things, we followed the development of regeneration. He of course was way ahead of me in theory and practice, but I had the business acumen, or as Monty liked to call it, the gift of bullshit." He laughed out loud. "Anyway, it was new. Cutting edge. And we were on the forefront. We started small. He was still teaching at Harvard when we set up our first lab. Do you know what abiogenesis is?"

"I have no possible idea, educate me." Ben blew across the top of his coffee cup, steeling himself for what he thought would be an upcoming 'tit-for-tat' conversation.

"Well ..." Leland returned to his chair and rolled it forward, leaning into his desk, "Let me start with *bio*-genesis."

"Please do." Ben was getting the impression that this Hahvahhd-breed brainchild with the fancy name was toying with him, or maybe just showing off.

"Biogenesis, in laymen's terminology," he winked (Ben hated guys who winked), "is the development of life from pre-existing life. Much the same as pro-creation. You know, man impregnates woman; living things fuck; life-goes-on, type of thing."

Ben winked back, "Gotcha."

Leland was in his glory. He loved talking big to little people. "Well then, *A-biogenesis* is the hypothetical development of living organisms from non-living matter." He smirked at Ben. "The operative word here is hypothetical."

"Or perhaps 'non-living'."

"Precisely."

Ben wanted to feed into Leland's ego here, so at the risk of sounding too country bumpkin, he said, "Does this have anything to do with the sheep thing?"

"Ah, very astute, Chief Benson." He leaned back in his chair and clasped his hands behind his head. "But Dolly was merely a sheep in sheep's clothing. Today, the advancements in biotechnology are happening at an acceleration never before imagined. In the field of livestock farming alone, cloning produces animals with leaner meat, bigger milking potential and enhanced disease resistance. And when you can select animals that produce so much more meat per kilo of grain feed, the logic of cloning is inevitable."

"And this is happening now?"

"Has been for years. In 2008 the FDA declared food from cloned cattle, pigs, goats and their progeny safe to eat."

Ben didn't want to ask, but he did, "Progeny?"

"Their offspring."

"A clone can reproduce?"

"Cloning and breeding techniques are becoming mainstays in the industry. Sperm and embryo banks exist, and are growing – literally. In Spain they have cloned a super-bull, a Pedraja, the crème de la crème for bullfighting. The price tag for stud service is two million dollars."

Ben whistled. "Was your company involved in that?"

"Not that one. But there are things we are involved in outside the strict parameters of the United States."

Ben raised his eyebrows, "For example?"

"We're working with a company in South Korea on pet cloning. Perhaps you saw the story in the news about the woman who paid $50,000. to have her dead dog cloned?"

"Nope, must have missed that one."

"True story." Leland rose from his chair and refreshed his drink. Ben wondered why he was banging down scotch in early afternoon.

"I'm smart. I wouldn't be in this position if I weren't. But Monty?" Leland hesitated here, slowly shaking his head side to side. "Montgomery Fairmont was brilliant. Genius actually. Godlike, depending on your view."

"What do you mean?'

"His capabilities were astounding." Leland again returned to his desk. "Let me give you an example. Several years ago we were contracted by a conglomerate of Texas cattlemen. They were having problems with red ants. Nasty critters. Toxic. Stinging and eating their way right into the flesh of the steer, killing thousands a year. They'd tried everything to get rid of them; pesticides, burning, bulldozing, flooding. Nothing worked." He swirled the snifter and seemed to get lost for a moment. Finally he took a sip and placed the glass on his desk and looked directly at Ben. "Monty mutated the genetic material of a fly and engineered it to lay its larvae into the body of a red ant. The larva would then eat the entrails of the ant for nourishment and when it was mature, the head of the ant would fall off and the new fly would emerge. Then the process would start all over again. No small feat of genetic engineering."

Elroy Leland rose to refill his glass. That's number three in less than twenty minutes, Ben thought. Something is up with this guy.

"And then there's the Modified Mosquitoes. Initially only an experiment, but Monty was pushing its fruition. Ever the do-gooder, he felt certain that eradicating disease-carrying mosquitoes would help mankind. We could eliminate West Nile for instance. We disagreed on that one though." Another sip. "There's pros and cons in upsetting the balance of species on the planet. Mosquitoes serve their own purpose in the overall scheme of creation, whether we like them or not."

Ben was intrigued with not only the stories, but also by the scotch-induced outpouring coming from Mr. Leland. He decided to keep him going and see where it led. "Modified Mosquitoes?"

"Yes. Foregoing the ethical boundaries, it was actually another brilliant idea. In this case, Montgomery Fairmont altered the sperm of the male mosquito so that once the female was impregnated; the sperm would kill off the progeny."

"Then why would they continue fornicating?"

Leland laughed, "Because they wouldn't know. The male is happy fucking and the female is happy getting pregnant. It satisfies the wants and needs of the species and kills it off at the same time. And they don't have a fucking clue. They just keep fucking away." He laughed heartily and gulped his scotch. *"And into the valley of death rode the six-hundred!"*

"Was this ever introduced?"

"Unfortunately the entire body of work was stolen during the patenting process."

Ben raised his eyebrows.

"There is a fair amount of espionage in this business, Chief Benson. One can imagine what certain extremist groups could do with such knowledge by altering the genetic codes to affect other species."

"Including our own?"

Leland sat quiet.

So did Ben.

Leland said, "There are many things we cannot understand. We are a neophyte species, Ben, which does not have the developed mental capacity to understand even a fraction of the miracles of life nor the perplexities of the universe. AG made its mark, and wealth, through bio-engineering. That is still true today.

But Monty wanted to take it further, to make abiogenesis a reality. It was his idea to name the business AbioGenetix."

"Are you saying he had his head in the clouds?"

"No. Further than that. Off the planet. Beyond the realms of the galaxy. There's a fine line between brilliance and lunacy, and Monty walked that line like a Walenda tightrope."

Leland went back to his mini-bar. Ben thought he was going to pour scotch number four of the afternoon. He picked up the bottle and held it for a full minute. Slowly, without pouring, he put the bottle back onto the counter. He turned to face Ben and hung his head. His arms were at his sides, his gaze on the floor.

"I haven't told anyone about this, and I'm not sure why I'm going to tell you. It may or may not have some bearing on your investigation." He raised a hand to his chest and rubbed in a circular motion, like maybe he was having heartburn from the scotch. Leland looked at Ben and said, "Last week I was accosted at my home."

40
Monty vs Science

"I live alone in the burbs north of the city, and have since my divorce last year. It was late, nine-thirtyish, so it was dark. I clicked the garage door open and pulled in. The door closed automatically behind me. So I thought it odd when I entered the house and flipped the switch and the lights didn't go on. I remember thinking just that when, in the span of a half-second, a hood went over my head, my arms were trussed behind my back and something very cold and steel-like was jammed into my temple. There were two of them. I was pushed into a kitchen chair. The one holding the gun to my head said, 'Do not resist'. It was a female voice. The other was a man. He had an accent, European or Middle Eastern, I don't know. I'm not good at accents."

"What did they want?"

"A code."

"A code?"

"The man said, 'We have the notebooks, Mr. Leland. Now we need the code.'"

"What notebooks? What code?"

"I had no idea what he was talking about. I told him that, but he drilled me for a long time. It felt like two hours, but it could have been only minutes. I was petrified. I knew they were going to kill me."

"Then what happened?"

"It got quiet. I pleaded with them. I offered them money. Lots of it. I told them I hadn't seen their faces so I couldn't identify them. I begged them to take my money. But they didn't answer. After a while I realized they had gone."

"How did you get free?"

"I got up and grabbed a kitchen knife and cut through the plastic ties. Then I ripped off the hood. I just stood there, my heart banging in my chest. Finally, once I was convinced they were not there, I went into the bathroom and took a shower. I had soiled myself, and I thought I was going to vomit."

"Did you notify the police?"

"No. That's what Edna said I should have done."

"I thought you said you hadn't told this story to anyone."

"Well, no one except Edna."

Ben raised his eyebrows.

"I was scared. I needed to tell someone. I trust Edna like a mother. She wanted me to call the police."

"Why didn't you? Do you have something to hide?"

"No, I have absolutely nothing to hide. It's just that I've had a bad experience with the police. I'm not very fond of them, ever since I was under scrutiny regarding Montgomery's disappearance."

"You would have been a suspect if any foul play was involved."

"Even without foul play, even without a body, I was still their guy. Monty had no heirs to scavenge his wealth; no wife, no kids, no siblings, no parents, not even a dog. So, yeah, I was scrutinized. Harassed even. It literally took years for them to leave me alone and I'd bet they still have their eye on me."

"What happened to Fairmont's corporate assets?"

"All went to me. That's how we had set it up. The predeceased partner's shares go to the survivor."

"A pretty penny I'll bet."

"Lots of pretty pennies."

There was a tap at the door. Edna walked in. She carried a cup of coffee to Leland's desk and set it down in front of him. Ben didn't recall him ordering it. "Mr. Benson, a refill?"

"No thanks, I'm fine."

"Okay then. I'm going down to the mail room. Be back in a few minutes." She took Leland's empty scotch glass from the credenza and left the room.

"I can see she is the motherly type," Ben said.

"Yes. She treated Monty and I like her own two sons. Now I get all the mothering." It would have been a good time for him to snicker, but he remained contemplative.

"How long has he been gone?"

"Six years. Statute of limitations was up a year ago and he was declared legally dead."

"So they never found his body?"

"No."

The cup of coffee remained untouched on the desk blotter.

Ben said, "Do you think he's dead?"

"I really don't know if Monty is alive or dead. But I do know he's definitely gone and he's not coming back."

"You must have a feeling."

No response.

Ben said, "Okay, if he's dead, he's dead. If he's alive, I've got two questions. One, you say he's brilliant. Do you think he's brilliant enough to engineer his own demise? And if so, for what purpose?"

Leland looked over to the scotch bottle but remained seated. "Yes to the first one. The second question, I can only speculate on. I have not heard from him since the day before he disappeared. He was different back then. For months prior to his disappearance, he seemed more and more introverted. I thought it was a mild depression. He'd been having some go-arounds with the inner circles of the scientific community, particularly the ethics committees. He was frustrated and complained constantly and vehemently about their ignorance. He tried to enlighten them.

There was a major conference in Geneva, 'Unethical Advancements in Biotechnology'. Monty was one of the guest speakers. His presentation was simple, I was there. I heard him say, *'Can you imagine creating a heart or a lung or a kidney or any organ of the human body via non-living matter? Without dealing with the stem-cell debacle? Medical Science could leap a century ahead of itself in just a few years.'* Do you know how they received that? They booed him. Can you imagine?"

"What happened next?"

"He stormed out of the meeting calling them insipid, short-sighted cowards who would have criticized Galileo and Einstein. He returned from that conference greatly disheartened. He moped about for weeks. He felt gravely misunderstood and ranted on about a conspiracy against him. I thought he was just burnt out and overworked and needed some time to himself. I said as much to him."

"Then what?"

"Then he went fishing and never came back."

Leland got up from his desk and went to the wet bar. He retrieved another snifter from a cupboard and made another drink. He took a sip and summarized his thoughts. "So to answer your second question - if he is still alive and out there somewhere, *A*, he doesn't want to be found. And *B*, I'd bet he's still working like a madman."

"On what?"

"Abiogenesis, of course."

41
Quabbin

The Nipmuc Indians of Massachusetts would turn over in their graves (if any of their graves could be found) if they knew what became of their precious "valley of many waters" - what their people called Quabbin. Regrettably, by the 17th century, decimated by war and disease (both brought on by the British and European colonists) their tribe had disappeared and their fertile valley, rich in soil and water for farming, passed into the hands of the settlers.

However, with the explosion of industrialization in the 20th century, people began leaving the farmlands and flocking to Boston. As the population in the city grew, so did the need for fresh drinking water. So, in 1927, the Massachusetts legislature passed a bill appropriating money to build a reservoir.

Quabbin Reservoir is the largest man-made body of water in the world. It exists in the center of Massachusetts 66 miles due west of Boston. Its pipelines provide fresh water to that metropolis and forty-six towns and cities along the way. The massive project began in 1927 and ended in 1946. Houses and factories were moved or razed. Vegetation was clear-cut. Cemeteries were dug up and over 7000 bodies were reburied elsewhere. Then, after the residents said farewell to their hometowns, the four quaint picturesque New England hamlets of Dana, Enfield, Greenwich and Prescott were submerged beneath 412 billion gallons of water. The Quabbin Reservoir was born.

Today it is a grand preserve of eighty-one thousand acres with one hundred-eighteen miles of shoreline and a maximum water depth of one hundred and fifty-one feet. Dave Sanders lives on the northern fringe in the small town of Petersham - one hamlet that survived the flooding merely by its hilly topography. He drives a Kenworth eighteen-wheeler on a three-hundred-mile round-trip route through Massachusetts and Connecticut in a twelve-hour day, five days a week. That's how he noticed the car.

The white Mercedes-Benz SUV was still parked off the road by Gate #35 of the reservoir as Dave Sanders wheeled by in his rig. It was dark at six p.m. as it had been at six a.m. that morning when he had begun his daily delivery route for Sysco Food Services.

Hardwick Road is narrow and desolate and twists for miles without any lighting. Dave's headlights had picked up the white car, both times, when coming around the hardy curve at the turn-off where fishermen, hunters, bird-watchers and hikers would leave their vehicles and trudge into the vast woodlands leading to the water. This particular area was the farthest access north and seldom used. So Dave thought it odd to see a Mercedes sitting there for what he guessed was at least twelve hours. But, it didn't necessarily alarm him. Until the next morning.

This time he stopped. Walking to the car, he harbored a bad feeling that he was going to find someone hunched over the steering wheel, the victim of a heart attack or, please God, not murder or suicide. But the car was empty. The ground around it undisturbed since last night's rain.

He should report it, but knew he was out of cell-phone range for the next fifteen miles. His house was only five minutes away, where he could use his land line, but cruising back into his driveway at this early hour would only alarm his sleeping wife. He decided to continue on and stop at the state police barracks in

Belchertown. They had jurisdiction over Quabbin. He wrote down the plate number and drove away.

A few clicks on the Mass State Police's computer revealed the car to be registered to the corporation of AbioGenetix of Cambridge. They established that one of the corporate principles, a Montgomery Fairmont, had driven the car to Quabbin for some trout fishing.

By the time they amassed a search team, Monty was several states away, comfortably snoozing in the seat-back position of a southern-bound Greyhound bus.

42

Mrs. Fairmont

When he had gotten word of his mother's death, Monty had no idea what a godsend it would be. Not that he didn't love her, for he truly did, but her death bed revelation, entrusted to her lawyer for the reading of her will, would change everything.

Mrs. Fairmont's husband had predeceased her and her son, Montgomery, had grown into a man, a Harvard grad and then professor thereof, who had gone on to establish an enormously successful bio-tech business and a reputation as a man-of-science unparalleled in the world community.

Doris and Norman Fairmont had done a remarkable job with their son and had never broken the promise they had made to his true mother. But at the end of her life, alone and weakening as her time drew near, Mrs. Fairmont crafted a letter to her only child. In it was revealed the hard truth that the parents, who had brought him up, the ones he loved and cherished so dearly, were not his biological parents.

Montgomery felt remorse for having put Mom Fairmont through the agony of carrying such a heavy secret to the end of her life. He should have told her that his biological background never bothered him. Not since he was fifteen and found the adoption paperwork secreted in a cubbyhole of her Governor Winthrop desk. He never told the Fairmont's that he had discovered the truth. Nor that it hadn't bothered him in the least.

He never had a desire to look up his real mother. He didn't hold anything against her, people did what they had to do, and she probably had her own reasons. Monty had been content with Mom and Dad Fairmont. Plus, he was far too busy with his experiments.

But now, with them gone and no one close in his life, he felt alone. The paradox was that his business was flourishing, he liked his partner and admired the determination and professionalism of his employees, and he had more money than he could ever want - but he was unhappy. Chastised by the scientific community, bogged down by a host of archaic laws and ethical restraints, Monty yearned to do more. He didn't have the time or forbearance to wait for science to catch up to him.

The only one who truly believed in him, who constantly encouraged him and made him happy, was his mistress. And his mistress was his research. So he devised a plan to spend more time with her.

In the letter of disclosure, Mom Fairmont said she had sent a similar note to Winifred Adele Vanderlene of Sarasota, Florida telling her, "I know I agreed to never reveal you to him, but he has turned out to be such a fine person and we should all be proud. I have done as much as I could for him. Now, if you desire, would be a good time to get acquainted." Montgomery agreed.

The reunion with his mother started with a phone call.

"Hello?"

"Is this Winifred Vanderlene?"

"Yes, it is."

"This is Montgomery Fairmont."

There was a heavy pause that concurrently spanned fifteen-hundred miles of geography and a gap of four decades.

"I want to meet you."

"Okay."

"Tomorrow."

"Okay."

"Two p.m."

"Okay."

"Is that all you have to say to me?"

Winnie realized she wasn't breathing. She took in a short breath. "I'm not sure what I have to say to you."

Monty nodded into the silence on the airwaves. "Okay, then. Two p.m. I'll find your place."

"Okay."

He hung up.

Winnie kept the cell phone to her ear, holding onto his voice.

Montgomery Fairmont wanted to meet his mother, but not for an emotional mother and son reunion. He had another agenda. He had done extensive research on Winifred and the enormous Vanderlene estate and had crafted an idea that would give him the time and anonymity he desperately desired. But he had to be careful. Something in the back of his mind told Monty not to use conventional means of transportation. Conventional in the sense that his footsteps could be traced.

Thirty miles northwest of Boston's high-profile airport, Aerodrome Aviation offered chartered jet service that could get him from Bedford Airfield (BED) to Sarasota International (SRQ) in under two hours. The *"economical way to fly privately"* would cost him twenty-thousand dollars, round trip. For an additional twenty percent tip to the pilot, the flight plan could be blocked. No security checks, no I.D., no hassle. As the literature proclaimed, *"simply drive up and board your awaiting jet."*

Upon landing at SRQ Monty spoke into the cockpit, "I'll be back in three hours for the return flight."

"Fine," the pilot replied. "I'll be standing by."

Monty de-planed the Cessna Citation SII and walked directly to the hanger on the edge of the concourse. Inside he found a mechanic standing at his workbench.

"Do you have a car?" He asked.

The mechanic gave him a wary look. "Yeah. Why?"

"I'll give you five-hundred dollars to borrow your car for three hours."

The mechanic laughed and went about his business.

"Seriously. Five hundred bux for three hours. Nothing will happen to your car, except it will be light a couple gallons of gasoline."

"Who the fuck are you?"

"Just a man with an interesting proposition."

"You come in on that Citation?"

"Yes."

"I know the pilot. He vouch for you?"

"He's standing by for my return flight. You can ask him." Monty took five one-hundred-dollar bills from his pocket.

Five minutes later he was on his way to meet his mother for the first time.

43
Hide

Winnie was sitting on her porch in a wicker rocking chair. At precisely two p.m., she heard a car coming along the approach road to Two Can Key. A dark blue Crown Victoria, with tinted windows and a throaty dual-exhaust system, pulled to a stop. She thought it was a detective's car. She didn't know it belonged to an airplane mechanic. But she did know the man who exited it. Seeing him for the first time caught her breath. He was the spitting image of Conrad Blake Lawrence.

Montgomery Fairmont walked to the porch and stood at the base of the stairs. Winifred Adele Vanderlene rose from her chair. They took a moment surveying each other: mother to son; son to mother. An unmistakable resemblance was there, most notably in their identical pale-gray eyes.

"Hello, Montgomery." The sweet sound of her voice instantly soothed him, as it had done when he was in her womb. That secret and pleasant sound between mother and child, once experienced, never forgotten.

"Hello. What should I call you?"

"Call me Winnie, I guess."

"Hello, Winnie." He climbed the three short steps and shook her hand. She held onto it.

She looked remarkable. He hadn't known what to expect. He had no pictures or reference points. But now, seeing her face-to-face, in her tee-shirt, shorts and sandals, he could tell she had held onto an athletic body and smooth skin only lightly tinged by the Florida sun. He could not help but feel a sense of pride that his mother was so beautiful.

"Mom said you and she were the same age. That would make you …"

"Seventy-seven."

"You don't look it."

"Thank you. Hard living has done me well," she laughed.

"So, you were …"

"Thirty-five when you were born."

She grabbed his elbow and said, "Come inside."

"I'd rather not. I won't be staying long."

"Oh," she was disappointed. "Well, then have a seat. Would you like a drink? Iced tea or coffee?"

"No thanks. I'm fine." He sat in the adjacent rocker and continued, "I don't want this to be awkward for us. I'm sure you have some trepidation and I want to say up-front that I am not here to blame you for what you did. No one is to blame. I had a wonderful upbringing by wonderful parents. I wouldn't trade that for anything."

"I appreciate those words. Your mother said you had grown into a fine man. I can see that."

Winnie began rocking. The chair squeaked on the worn flooring. "I'm curious, how did you find me?"

"It wasn't easy. You're very reclusive. You have hidden yourself and your past exceptionally well. I guess I'm a living testimonial to that." He didn't mean this as a jab, but it could have been interpreted as such.

She drew her legs into a lotus position and the rocking chair stilled. "I know of your career and accomplishments. I know I wasn't part of it, but I followed your life. It was difficult in the beginning, the Internet wasn't available yet and the word Google wasn't even in the vocabulary. You were little and living in

Vermont and I was ..." her eyes scanned the tops of the nearby palm trees and settled into the blue sky, "I was adjusting, I suppose you could say."

"From a distance from what I understand."

"Yes, after I left you with the Fairmonts, I spent several years out of the country."

Monty got up and began pacing the porch. "I saw you once. I didn't realize it until just a few minutes ago." He stopped and placed his hands on the gingerbread railing and looked out at the small key. The sound of the ocean came to him through the tropical foliage wrapped around the house.

"It was at my graduation from Harvard. I was descending the stage with my diploma in hand. Mom and Dad were there seated midway in the audience. I could see them smiling as I pumped the diploma high above my head. The three of us were so proud. But I remember this woman standing off to the side on the lawn near where all the grads were seated. She stood out because she was dressed all in white. She wore a big floppy hat and sunglasses and had a blazing smile. She looked right at me. When I got back to my seat I looked for her but she was gone." He turned and looked directly at Winnie. "I can still picture her now. It was you."

Her eyes began to water. "I was proud too."

"Do you know who my father is?"

She didn't answer.

"Is he still alive?"

"Yes."

"Does he know about me?"

Winnie cast her gaze to the floor. Embarrassingly, she shook her head.

"I don't need to know. Maybe someday we'll talk about it, but right now I don't want to know anymore." He turned away from her.

"I thought you said we weren't going to do this."

"I didn't think we were."

"What do you want from me? An apology?" Winnie had thought about having a drink before her abandoned son showed up.

Or maybe a toke or two to calm her nerves. But she hadn't. She wanted to be clear-minded in order to weather whatever affront her son was going to bring her. Now she wished she'd taken a hit.

"You *are* harboring anger towards me."

"I guess I am discovering a little suppressed animosity."

Winnie stood. She leaned against the railing and crossed her arms. "I'm sorry. I don't know what you want from me. Is it money?"

Monty laughed. "Let's not be so mundane. I know you're rich and you know I'm rich. If it's one thing we have in common, it's that neither one of us gives a damn about money."

"Then what is it?"

A flock of green parrots flew by and punctuated the air with their screeching. Somehow the high-pitched intrusion was welcomed.

"What?" Winnie said angrily and immediately wished she hadn't been so disdainful.

That's where I get that from, Monty thought. Then he faced her and said, "You weren't there to help my past, but you can be there to help my future."

"And how can I do that?"

"You can hide me."

44

The Getaway

Monty chose Quabbin Reservoir to launch his disappearance plan for two reasons. One, it was vast and remote. People had gotten disoriented and lost in there for days. Some had suffered mishaps with black bears, bobcats or coyotes. Some even drowned.

The second reason was because he was familiar with the territory. He had fished catch-and-release there for years. He knew the streams and the dense contours of the land and the rural roads that spun away from it in every direction. He figured a parked car at one of the access gates wouldn't raise any suspicion for at least a day if he left it in a distant, less-traveled area. This would give him plenty of time for a clean getaway.

In preparation he had set up off-shore accounts with monies that he'd grown from personal investments over the years. He had ample money to build his laboratory. If he fell short, well, his new mother was loaded.

So he packed his car for a day of fishing and headed west. But before leaving Boston he made one quick stop at a costume house in the theater district - to purchase a beard.

Montgomery took the Mass Pike west and exited at Worcester. He cruised casually along route 9 through Cherry Valley, Leicester and Spencer and ultimately stopped at The Copper Lantern Motor Lodge in West Brookfield. It was a mom and pop operation at the edge of town, set back from the road on open acreage. A waft of home cooking came from the back room as Montgomery paid cash and told the woman with the apron that he'd be leaving early in the morning.

Inside the motel room he engaged the double lock on the door, closed the curtains, stripped, and went into the bathroom and shaved his head. He flushed his hair down the toilet and took a shower and toweled down. When he held the beard up to his face, even he didn't recognize the guy in the mirror. So far so good. He'd apply the adhesive in the morning. For now, it was time to rest. The bald-headed guy had a long day ahead of him.

At four a.m. Monty was up and out the door. He drove west along Ware Point Road past The Salem Cross Inn, The Rock House Reservation, took a right onto Five Town Road into Gilbertville, then north past the Barre Cutoff into New Braintree and circumvented the reservoir to remote Gate #35 in Petersham. He hadn't encountered a single vehicle in the one-hour drive.

In the rising morning light he hoisted his back-pack onto his shoulders, grabbed his rod and tackle box, locked the car and entered the preserve. Two miles in, at a favorite stream, he sat his pack on a boulder and extracted a pair of Sperry Top-Siders and a plastic IV bag filled with a pint of his own blood.

Monty scuffed up a wide area around the water's edge and into the stream. He pulled off one of his hiking boots and dripped blood in and outside of it and wedged it tight into the base of the boulder. The fishing pole was smeared with blood and thrown to the side. The remaining blood was scattered around where the "scuffle" would have occurred. He stuffed the remaining boot into his pack and donned the boat shoes. Not the best for hiking, but the flat soles would not mark the bed of leaves he planned to walk out on.

It would take him all morning to walk through the forest and then a few hours more along the abandoned Norwottuck Rail Trail down to Amherst where he would board his first bus. Monty took out an energy bar and a bottle of water and began his journey to a new and anonymous life.

The second leg of the journey went from Port Authority Bus Terminal in New York City to Washington, D.C. Then onward to Richmond, VA, Atlanta, GA, Orlando, and finally Sarasota, Florida. At each stop Monty had changed buses and purchased new tickets with cash.

Winnie was sitting in her yellow Jeep at the downtown bus terminal when a bald-headed man with a black beard climbed into the passenger seat. She said, "Ohmygod. You look like Shel Silverstein."

"Who?"

Winnie laughed, shifted into first gear and drove away.

45

Elevator Call

Ben was wrapping up his Cambridge visit. "Thanks for your time, Lee." They stood and shook hands.

"I hope I was of some help to you. I wish you luck in resolving the case and keeping your wife out of danger."

"Well, I'm not sure if you have been a help or not. But I appreciate your time. It's a weird case. Asking questions is the only way I know to get to the answers."

Leland had the distinctive look of one who had more to say but was afraid to say it. Ben held his stare to him in this recognition, almost as a dare, but Elroy Leland backed down and turned away.

Ben passed Edna's desk and went to the elevator bank and punched the down arrow. A minute later the door opened and Edna stepped out.

"Oh, are you leaving?"

"Yes. Thank you for your help, Edna, I appreciate it." Ben shook her hand politely.

"Glad to have been a part of your reunion. I'm sure Leland enjoyed it."

Ben got into the elevator, pushed L and waved good-bye to her.

On the way down, his cell-phone rang. MacLaren.

"Hey, what's up?"

MacLaren responded in a markedly different voice. "How are you doing?"

"Okay. I'm just leaving AbioGenetix now. Had a long chat with Leland."

Ben began filling him in on the conversation. Abruptly, MacLaren cut in, "Tell me about it later. How fast can you get to the airport?"

"What's going on?"

"I don't know how to tell you this and I hate like hell that you're two thousand miles away."

The elevator stopped. The doors opened. The lobby was busy.

"Carlene's been kidnapped."

46

Kidnapped

"She's awake."

"I can tell."

"I thought you said she'd be out for at least an hour."

"I thought she would be."

"Pull over, I'll stun her again."

"No, we're almost there."

Carlene was kicking and banging and screaming bloody murder from the trunk.

"I told you you should've taped her mouth," Jay said.

"Woulda, coulda, shoulda, but I didn't okay?" Dwayne snarled. "Now hurry up."

"Speed limit, remember. We don't want to get pulled over."

"There's no one out here."

"Ain't taking any chances."

Jay was driving. They were east of the interstate out in cow country, the only car traveling Red Toad Road.

The abduction had gone smoothly. Ursula had gotten them a Mercury Grand Marquis because she liked the size of the trunk and she said, "It's gold. Do you know how many gold Grand Marquises there are in Southwest Florida?"

Dwayne had wanted to use his truck but Ursula had nixed the idea. "Too recognizable. No offense, Dwayne, but an old beat up Chevy Silverado stands out."

He thought it would be cool to throw the woman in the pickup bed and cover her with a tarp.

Ursula's husband, LeBeau, had stolen the car the night before off the dealership lot on Tamiami Trail, leaving it behind the new Publix being built on Bee Ridge Road. Construction was ongoing and the external security cameras had yet to be installed.

The next morning Ursula was parked on a side road where she could monitor the rear of the new building unseen. When she saw Dwayne's truck enter the back lot, she placed a call.

"Yeah?" Dwayne answered on the cell phone she had given them to use.

"You there yet?"

"Just pulled in."

"The car is at the end near a big bucket loader."

"Okay, I see it."

"Good. Park next to it. It's locked but the keypad code is 12345. Keys are over the visor. When you get in let Jay drive. You've got the stun guns and the window breakers?"

"Yup, right here." He patted the bag sitting between him and Jay.

"Okay, let me talk to Jay."

Dwayne handed the phone to Jay and maneuvered his truck between the loader and the Grand Marquis.

"Hi Jay. You doing okay?" Her voice was soft to his ear, even a little sultry.

"Yes, I'm fine."

"Okay, I want you to drive and I'm going to give you directions now. Are you ready?"

"Sure."

Ursula told him to take 75 North to exit 213, then east to Lakewood Ranch.

"I know where it is."

"Good. About two miles past the main entrance you'll come up to Yellow Creek Estates on your left. Go towards it but don't go through the gate. The first road to the left, Bluewater Lane, will have a Do Not Enter barrier. Go around that. It's an unfinished road. Drive to the end and turn the car around to face the way you just came in. Then wait. I'll call you when she's approaching. Do you think you've got that?"

"Lakewood Ranch to Yellow Creek Estates, go around the road barrier to the end, turn around and wait."

Ursula smiled. "Good boy."

Jay smiled too. He was nervous, but he wanted to please her. "We're all set, Ursula. Don't worry, everything will go fine." He hoped he sounded brave.

LeBeau, in a bright neon vest and matching hard hat, detoured cars away from Bluewater Lane. When he saw Lorraine MacLaren's car exiting the front gates, he removed the barrier and directed her into the dead end road. He could see the ladies laughing and carrying on as they passed him. He replaced the barrier and called his wife. "Go."

She immediately punched off and hit redial. Jay answered.

"Okay, here they come," she said. "Be calm. Stay focused."

"We're good." He hung up and looked at Dwayne. "Show time."

Lorraine drove on unaware anything was amiss. She was chatting up her houseguest. Until she got to the dead end. "What the hell? Wasn't that guy holding a detour sign?" They didn't see the men approaching from behind, one to each side.

The sound of the windows exploding was earsplitting. Both women grabbed their heads and screamed. A second later their neurological systems were short-circuited and their brains shut down when Jay and Dwayne zapped them with the stun guns. They left the unconscious Lorraine MacLaren slumped in the driver's seat and pulled Carlene Benson from the car and dropped her into the trunk of the Grand Marquis. Jay drove cautiously down the road, around the Do Not Enter barrier and steered toward the rendezvous point a half-hour away.

"Wow! What a rush!" Dwayne drummed his knees and whooped. The whole thing had taken less than a minute. "That was awesome!"

47

Leland Confrontation

MacLaren gave it to him all at once, cop to cop. "Lorraine and Carlene were going shopping. They exited the enclave and were diverted to a dead end road. Two assailants in ski masks smashed the windows and Tasered the girls. Left Lorraine unconscious in the driver's seat and kidnapped Carlene."

Intense and immediate shock overpowered Ben like a tidal wave crashing over you as you stood with your back to the ocean unaware of danger approaching. Unable to grasp what MacLaren had just said to him, Ben fell into an abyss where there was no rationality. No comprehension. A blank desperation and a wish that he was in a dream. A bad dream. Then his ingrained cop reflexes fired up and took control.

"They took Carlene?"

"Yes."

"And your wife? Is she hurt?"

"Shaken up, but she's fine. Home."

"Does she know anything?"

"It happened fast. She only remembers a split second after the windows exploded. Saw the two figures and then passed out cold. Came to about an hour later and reached for her cell phone. It was still in her purse. I think they wanted her to alert us."

"Any communication?"

"Not yet, but I'm sure there will be."

"How long has it been?"

"Little over an hour."

"And you're *just* getting to me?"

"Hey, take it easy."

"Take it easy? Fuck you take it easy! My wife has been kidnapped. Get me the next flight out of Logan and text me the info."

"I'm on it."

"You stay on it!" Ben said, and killed the connection.

Ben lit the floor number for Leland's office. As the elevator rose he stood still - adrenaline, nerves, and sparking emotions, all combining in an explosive mixture like a time bomb on its last second. He smashed his fist into the wall. The elevator jarred to a stop. Big Ben moved like a linebacker down the hallway, stormed past Edna and charged into Elroy Leland's office.

Leland was at the wet bar. Ben came at him like a loaded barge out of control, grabbed the snifter of scotch from him, threw it on the floor and spun him around.

"I'm going to give you about three seconds to give me some *real* answers."

"Whoa. Wait a minute, you can't ..."

Ben pushed him hard against the credenza. His big hand covered Leland's mouth. "The next words out of your mouth better be something better than that. I want to know about the notebooks. And don't even *think* of saying you don't know what I'm talking about." He pressed his hand so forcibly onto Leland's face he could feel his teeth on his palm. He gave him a few seconds to let the seriousness sink in, then he let go.

Leland rubbed his lips and looked at his hand. There was blood on his palm.

"I've just got word that my wife has been kidnapped and I am in no mood for any bullshit. There's something you're not telling me and I need to know what it is. *Now.*"

"I'm sorry to hear about your ..."

"Save it! Why did they let you go?"

Leland loosened the knot on his tie and drew it off his neck. He unbuttoned his shirt, pulled it from his pants and lifted his tee-shirt, revealing a nasty series of raised welts on his chest and stomach. They were red burn marks that would certainly scar.

"They tortured you."

"There's more in places I'd rather not reveal. If I had known the answers to their questions I would have told them. I would have told them anything."

Leland buttoned his shirt.

A trickle of blood seeped from the corner of Leland's mouth. There was a roll of paper towels suspended above the mini bar. Ben tore one off and handed it to him. Then he poured himself a half shot of whiskey and one for Leland and went to the window.

Leland wiped the blood from his mouth and picked up his drink. "Thanks." He took a sip. "I'm sorry for your misfortune."

In the sky beyond the Pru an airliner was banking over the harbor and settling into its approach pattern to Logan. Ben was thinking he'd have to tell the kids, but he wasn't going to. He wasn't about to put them through this type of torment. Carlene wouldn't want him to either. He knew the first twenty-four hours were crucial in a kidnapping. He needed all his wits about him and dealing with the kids' hysteria would only get in the way of what he needed to do – whatever that was going to be.

He dumped the whiskey in the sink and called Uncle Bob at the house in Bryce Corner. After filling him in he said, "Keep this quiet. Don't mention it to anyone. Not even the kids. Status quo. And for God's sake don't let them out of your sight." Bob understood. He told his nephew not to worry – he'd keep it under control. "And Ben," Uncle Bob said, "keep a cool head about you."

Uncle Bob hung up, went into Ben's office, snatched the hidden key to the gun cabinet and grabbed a .357 Magnum and loaded it.

48
Cracker Trail

The Cracker Trail (a name derived from the cracking of bullwhips from generations of Florida's hard working cattle ranchers) stretches eastward into Hardee County, cutting through the flat landscape of citrus groves and herd ranches spread out to the horizon. The only traffic Jay and Dwayne encountered was large trucks loaded with oranges heading west to the Tropicana plant in Palmetto. The Grand Marquis moved smoothly along with its precious cargo.

When she regained consciousness, Carlene knew immediately the dark, confining space surrounding her was the trunk of a car. She screamed and yelled and banged and kicked, to no avail. Mercifully she was not bound and could move with a certain degree of freedom. She pushed on the trunk lid, felt for an escape latch, fumbled for a tool to pry with. Nothing. Helpless. She was locked into an inescapable struggle, enwrapped in heart-racing fear. She was freaking out and needed to calm down. Carlene heard Ben say, *try to relax, breath evenly, control the adrenaline. Tell me what your senses are saying.*

She heard the rush of the wind above her and could feel the humming of the road beneath. The ride was smooth and level. She imagined a highway and strained to hear other vehicles nearby. But there was no swooshing of passing cars or the stop and go of streetlights and intersections. The steady smoothness of the ride was hypnotizing. In her mind she tried to piece things together. Her first quandary was why. Why? Then, What? What did she have that was so important to someone that they had kidnapped her. And killed Hannah. And, Ohmygod, where was Lorraine?

From the darkness flashed the image of the woman who had followed her on St. Armands Circle. Who was she?

The road droned along and Carlene could hold her fear at bay no longer. She was terrified. Fear puts your mind off kilter and then you think not about the reason you've been kidnapped (and soon might be dead by some psycho) but oddly enough you wonder if the trunk of the car you're imprisoned in will be crushed by a school bus or rammed by a tractor trailer. Carlene thought of her children and wondered if she'd ever see her son and daughter again. Tears flooded her eyes and she screamed at the top of her lungs, "BENNNN!"

At the county line, at the end of an arrow-straight one mile gravel road, sits an abandoned aggregates quarry. Mined and extracted to extinction, the landscape looks like an excavated moon. Nothing around for miles except white dust and deep craters. The tall silos that used to be filled with cement fly-ash to make concrete, stand empty and huddled together like deserted rocket ships ready to launch to Mars. Huge hoppers, gray and thick with soot, loom above frameworks of metal stilts. Silent conveyor belts crisscross at forty-five degree angles to awaiting cement mixers, dormant now with their bright swirling colors faded by the intense sunshine of Central Florida. The whole scene looks like something out of a science fiction movie.

From one of the observation towers, Ursula watched the car approaching along the road, with the white dust swirling behind like a jet stream. She stood on an exterior catwalk and waved them over. Jay got out and clambered up the steel staircase.

"We've got her."

"Great job," she hugged him. "You have no idea how much this means to me."

Jay took the liberty to hold her close and tight. She kissed his cheek and said, "Bring Dwayne up. I've got a celebration surprise for you," and went into the building. Jay leaned over the railing and called to Dwayne. A minute later the two men stood in the cramped office with her.

"I've got some beer on ice in the back room. Help yourselves. I'm going to go let her out of the trunk."

"That sounds great," Dwayne said and he and Jay went through the adjacent door, slapping each other on the back, happy and high from their successful adventure.

LeBeau was waiting for them.

49
Edna's Story

Ben knew it would be futile, but he called Carlene's cell anyway. It went directly into voicemail. In a deliberate voice he said, "I WILL FIND YOU." It was not meant as much as a message for his wife as it was a message to the kidnappers whom Ben knew had possession of her phone.

Leland heard his tone and felt his pain. He pressed the intercom. "Edna, would you come in here please?"

She must have been standing at the door because she entered immediately. "Is everything alright?"

"No." He motioned her to a seat. Leland explained Ben's real identity and purpose of his visit.

"Tell him about the notebooks, and the security guard."

"I've known the boys since day one of AbioGenetix. So I got to know quite a bit about them and their habits. I never had children of my own, so they became my surrogate sons."

Edna was seated on the leather sofa in the center of the office. Two matching chairs and a walnut coffee table were arrayed before it on an Oriental rug. Big Ben was nervously pacing around the setting, inputting her information while simultaneously working up a game plan for Sarasota.

"When it became apparent that Mr. Fairmont was not going to return, we decided to convert his office into a conference room."

Ben said anxiously, "What about the notebooks?"

"Yes, well, I was just getting to that. When Leland told me what happened to him last Friday night, and mentioned the notebooks, I remembered how Montgomery had this habit of carrying a notebook with him and constantly writing in it. His mind was so full of ideas that he didn't want to miss one when they came to him. I joked with him once and asked if he carried one into the shower with him." Edna snickered. Ben glowered.

"Anyway, I took it upon myself to clean out his office. Most of the furniture was placed throughout the building in appropriate settings and the personal items - there weren't many, mostly fishing memorabilia and pictures and such - I boxed and stored in the basement."

"The notebooks, Edna," Leland said.

"Yes, well, I discovered some of his notebooks in a drawer, two or three I think, and I thought it odd that he'd left them intact. He always shredded them when they got full. He was meticulous about that. But these were underneath a stack of new ones still in cellophane, you know, those spiral notebooks that you can buy at Staples by the bundle? He must have forgotten they were in there."

"Did you inspect them," Ben asked.

She looked at Leland. He nodded his head.

"Yes I did, but I couldn't figure them out. They were written in gibberish. I couldn't make any sense out of them."

"What did you do with them?"

"I put them in binders and placed them in the library and made a mental note to tell Leland about them, but then I completely forgot about them until just the other day." Ben was getting impatient. He rolled his hand.

"And then," Edna continued, "when Leland mentioned his terrible misfortune, I went to get them but they were gone. And I thought, now that's odd, they've been here for years undisturbed and all of a sudden they're missing. And I know they were there just the day before because I had gone looking for something and would have noticed the vacant spacing on the shelf."

"Did someone borrow them to read perhaps?"

"Well, I thought of that, so I asked around and no one had."

Ben was still pacing. His mind a whir.

"And, of course, the Teddy thing," she added, "just blew me away."

Ben stopped pacing. His head twisted from Edna to Leland and back to Edna. "The Teddy thing?"

"Yes. Teddy Platt was our night security guard and he ... well, he died."

Ben raised his shoulders. What does that have to do with anything?

"I just thought the timing was odd, that's all," she said. "He was in charge of security and had his evening rounds to do and the only rooms in the whole building that were not locked up tight each night were the cafeteria and the library. So I thought he might know about the missing notebooks. But when I went to ask him about it, I found out he had died unexpectedly."

"How so?"

Leland replied, "He had a heart attack. He'd only been with us for a few months so I don't think he had any real idea of what AG was about. I think his death was coincidental."

"When was this?"

"About two weeks ago."

Ben thought out loud, "So, in the course of two weeks, Fairmont's notebooks that have been untouched for years disappear, your recently hired security guard dies, you're tortured for information that you don't have, bodies start piling up in Florida and my wife is kidnapped."

Ben's cell phone chimed a new message from MacLaren. *Southwest Flight #1101, non-stop. Lv BOS 3:15pm Arv SRQ 5:53pm*

"I've got to go." Ben extended his hand and helped Edna up from the couch. "Thank you. You've been very helpful." He ushered her towards the door.

"Well then, goodbye again Mr. Benson."

Ben closed the door behind her and growled to Leland, "Okay, so nobody has the code, but you must have some idea of what the notebooks are about and who would want them. Why are they so fucking important?"

"I can only surmise."

"So surmise."

"I don't know who these people are but I do know they're not nice. I don't believe they have the best interest of humanity or medical science on their agenda."

"Give me your best guess."

"Replication. Monty was obsessed with human cloning. I think their intent is evil, horrific evil." Leland looked grave. "Think one hundred suicide bombers, or one thousand, or ten thousand, strategically placed throughout the western world wrapped in C-4 or biological canisters, maybe even nuclear. All going off at the same time."

"*Manchurian Candidate.*"

"*The Boys From Brazil.*"

"Fiction becomes reality?"

"If they break the code and get the formula, couldn't it?"

50
Plan Hatching

Big Ben punched a key on his cell phone as he rushed through the AG lobby.

Two seconds later a gruff voice responded, "Hey, Benson, how the hell are ya?"

"I've been better," he said but didn't elaborate.

Tom Ford was captain of the Boston PD's Tactical Terrorist Team (TTT or Triple T) and a longtime acquaintance of Ben's.

Ford immediately realized the tone of the conversation wasn't going to be light. "What have you got?"

"Need to know. Couple weeks ago. Teddy Platt - probably Theodore – a security guard at a company called AbioGenetix of Cambridge found dead in his apartment. Can you pull up the sheet?"

"What's it got to do with Triple T?" Ben could hear Ford already clicking his computer.

"Maybe nothing, maybe something."

"Hang on."

Ben came up short behind an old lady with a cane. He reached over her shoulder with his free hand and pushed the door open for her.

"Thank you, young man."

Before he could say you're welcome and brush by her, something caught the corner of his eye. In the atrium of the lobby, two framed portraits of the company's founders hung on either side of a grand AG logo. On the left, above a brass plaque etched with his name, was a younger Elroy Leland. Montgomery Fairmont was on the right. There was a peculiar familiarity. Ben crooked the cell phone between his ear and shoulder and used his left hand to cover the picture above the eyebrows and his other hand to cover below the nose.

"I'll be damned," he said.

"What?"

"Nothing, Tom." He exited the building and started to jog through the parking lot. His bad knee governed his pace.

In the phone, Ford laughed. "I remember this one. Had nothing to do with Triple T, but it got around. Guy had a heart attack while having sex with his girlfriend. Went out with a bang!"

"Official cause of death?"

"Acute Myocardial Infarction."

"What did the girlfriend have to say?"

"Nada. They couldn't find her. Must have spooked and split."

"Is there an inventory?"

"Wasn't treated as a homicide, so I don't know how thorough they were."

"Could you check, Tom?"

"This important?"

"To me it is." Ben purposefully refrained from mentioning his wife's kidnapping.

"Okay. Looking for anything specific?"

"Notebooks. Hand written in scientific jargon."

"Give me a few. I'll call you back."

Big Ben's personal car was a Ford Expedition, equipped with a siren, blue grill lights and a red clip-on roof-light. He had them all activated as he sped through Boston towards Logan International.

The Beatles chimed into his Blue Tooth system. *Here Comes The Sun.* His wife's ring tone. Ben answered, "Carlene?"

A cold and unfamiliar female voice said in a foreign dialect, "She gives us what we want, we give her back to you. Tell her to cooperate."

"Listen you bitch, if you even ..."

"Ben?" It was his wife's voice.

"Carlene? Are you alright?"

"I'm okay. I'm tied up. They have us on speaker." (She was telling him three things: *I'm Okay* - her voice was level, she was saying, I'm coherent and not panicking. *I'm tied up* – I am unable to fight back. *They* – there are multiple kidnappers.)

Ben and Carlene, like most Americans, had seen many movies where kidnapping was part of the plot. Unlike most Americans, however, Ben analyzed the scenes as an investigator. She remembered him once saying, "Most abductors do not allow the victim to communicate in any way. But if they do, the victim needs to remain cool and try to give out information without being suspect." A good lesson learned.

"What do they want?"

"They have a couple of notebooks." (*A couple*: one man, one woman.) "They're hand-written in some language I don't understand, Arabic or Russian or something," Ursula raised an eyebrow, "with equations like from a science project." Carlene would have to be careful. Ben knew she was telling him the nationalities of her captors. *Science project*: Carlene believed her abduction was linked to Hannah Hunt and Montgomery Fairmont.

"Enough!" Ursula shouted. Speaking into the phone she said, "We will get the information we want one way or the other. If she breaks the code for us perhaps we will not have to break anything on her. You have ten seconds left to encourage your wife Mr. Benson. And please do not waste your time foolishly pinging this cell phone signal. You will not find it. Ten seconds."

"Carlene, give them what they want."

"I do not have what they want, Ben."

"Give them something. Stay strong, Sugarplum, I'm coming for you." He heard the other woman laugh and then the line went dead.

A darkening rage was forming over Ben Benson like an errant black cloud on a cloudless day.

Tom Ford called back. "Nothing. No books, no notebooks, no magazines, no newspapers. The only thing even close was a takeout menu from a Chinese restaurant."

"That's what I figured."

"What's this all about?"

"Can't get into it right now, but you need to check out a guy by the name of Elroy Leland at AbioGenetix. You'll find his story interesting. It could involve your task force. Also, run a check on a male/female kidnapping/assassin team. One Arabic, one Russian." Ben knew he was spreading things around more than he should, but he didn't want to further involve MacLaren for reasons of his own.

"This better be good, Ben. You're being awfully cagey."

51

Covert Partners

The pilot's voice crackled through the overhead speakers. The usual welcoming spiel followed by the flight information: route, altitude, flight time and speed. Four hundred and twelve miles per hour. It wasn't fast enough for Big Ben.

Halfway down the coast, he texted MacLaren telling him the flight had been delayed forty-five minutes. Ben wanted to be in and out of the airport before MacLaren arrived to pick him up. He hoped the Lieutenant wouldn't check flight status. MacLaren was a good cop, but he played too much by the rules. For what Ben was planning, he needed to circumvent his involvement, both for the freedom he needed to traverse the borders of law and order, and also to protect the Lieutenant's career. Ben was going to do what he had to do to get his wife back safely into his arms. He needed to move fast. He made some calls then willed himself to get some sleep. He would need his strength.

The descent woke him. From the airplane window Ben located Woody's Roo by its blue tin roof and colorful table umbrellas perched on the edge of the Manatee River. From the air the distance southeast to the mangrove prairie didn't look to be that great. The airport stood roughly in the middle of them. Gauging by the fading sun over the Gulf, it would soon be dark. The timing was good.

Ben's car rental was waiting for him outside the terminal. A black Hummer HX. He wanted the big machine for its strength, durability, and four-wheel drive. He'd requested the color and had taken out maximum coverage.

Sixty minutes later he pounded on a motel door.

"You ready?"

"Fuck no, I'm not ready. You need to tell me what the fuck's going on."

Ben pushed his way into Convict Rick's sparse abode adjacent to Woody's Roo. He threw some bags on the bed and started to remove his clothes. Ben had made a stop at the outlet mall down the road at exit 224.

"Rick, I told you as much as I can." He pulled a black sweatshirt out of one of the bags. "Here, put this on." Rick was already wearing a black tee-shirt, black jeans and black sneakers. "The more I tell you, the more you'll know and the more apt you'll be to suffer legal consequences if they arise."

"*IF* they arise?"

Ben had ripped off the clothing tags and was putting on black jeans. He slid on black socks and boots and a black long-sleeved top. He placed his hands on Rick's shoulders. "I do appreciate this Rick and I promise you won't get hurt and if we're lucky MacLaren will never know of your involvement. But the less you know the better. I need you for your size."

"And my covertness, right? We're doing black-ops, right?" Rick was like a little kid, he was so excited he actually made Ben laugh. He needed that.

Soon, under the cover of darkness, the unlikely partnership of Big Ben and Convict Rick set out to rescue Carlene Benson.

Ben was sure he knew where she was. It was just a matter of remembering how to get there. He figured Rick could help.

"From here it's easier to go down 675 and cross over SR70 at Myakka Road and head south past Gramps Ramp. It'll be a couple miles after that." Rick knew the area. "But I gotta tell ya, I'm not looking forward to crawling through that thick prairie growth in the dark. There's some nasty-ass animals in there man."

"Don't worry. We won't be crawling much. That's why I got the Hummer."

The night had darkened well. No moon, partial clouds, dry. Traffic was sparse. At Rick's signal Ben turned off the tarmac onto a narrow dirt path leading south into the vast land. He pushed the Hummer as far inland as he could. The ground was flat and sturdy and the undergrowth was no match for the big all-terrain tires and the wheel height. But the brush got thicker and thicker, screeching the sides of the vehicle like sharp venomous fangs sucking them further into the black nocturnal jungle until even the 4x4 Hummer could no longer advance. They sat at a wall so thick with vegetation the headlights were rendered useless.

Ben looked at the digital compass, SW, and killed the engine.

"I think we're dead on course. It's at least another mile. Here, put this on." He handed Rick a tube of black face paint.

"Cool."

Ben retrieved his S&W .38 from his cargo pocket and checked it.

"Where's mine?"

"You don't get one."

"Come on. Give me something. This is gonna be dangerous."

Ben smeared his face.

"You gotta be shitting me. Is that all you brought? One little gun?"

"All I need."

Rick laughed and shook his head. "You are one fucked-up cop, you know that?"

"Just stay behind me and try not to make any noise."

The compound was quiet. The main house was dark save for faint, flickering lights downstairs. Candles. Maybe Anderson and JJ were getting it on or stoned out of their minds or both. The back building with the turret was all dark.

Big Ben checked his silenced cell phone. Four missed calls with messages. All MacLaren. *Not a happy MacLaren I'll bet.* He'd deal with that later.

Time was just before midnight. He whispered to Rick, "We'll wait ten minutes. See if anything happens. Then we go in."

Rick nodded. He looked scared.

Ten minutes later they sneaked to the back building and huddled against the tower. The eyebrow windows were just below the roof line and were propped open a few inches for air flow.

Ben kept his voice low. "Okay, hot shot. Here's where you earn your keep."

They had gone over the plan several times on the drive. Ben crouched down and Rick climbed onto his shoulders and was hoisted up to the tiny window. He looked inside and perused the space from end to end.

"I don't see her," he whispered. "It's too dark, can't see anything."

"Okay, go in. Be careful and be quiet."

Rick stepped off Ben's head and slithered through the window. His mission was to get inside and open the door for Big Ben. The heavy metal door faced the rear of the house and looked too challenging to break into. Plus it would take too much time and raise suspicion from inside the house. If Rick could unlock it, Ben could slip inside in a second. He waited at the corner of the tower. He knew his wife was in there somewhere. He hoped they had the element of surprise with them. He also hoped Rick wouldn't blow it. It was taking forever.

Suddenly he heard movement. Lights came on all around him and the big door swung open.

Montgomery Fairmont said, "Welcome, Chief Benson. Won't you join us?"

52
Coordinates

Carlene was not there. Never had been. Fairmont had nothing to do with her kidnapping. Ben had been wrong. Way wrong. He had been convinced Carlene was in the secluded mysterious building, captive of a fanatical fringe group presided over by a whacked-out scientific guru. Not the case.

But he had been right about the identity of Ian Anderson/Montgomery Fairmont, something he'd like to get into, but not now. Now he was disillusioned and desperate. And it showed. He never took failure well and certainly couldn't now with his wife's life still at stake.

"I'm afraid I saw you coming quite a while ago. We enjoy a rather elaborate security system here," Montgomery sat in his usual white-on-white garb at a chrome and glass table in the middle of the grand room. Ben sat opposite him. Convict Rick slouched in a nearby Barco Lounger apparently asleep.

"I took the liberty of rendering your little friend unconscious before I turned on the lights. Didn't want him to be shocked by the surroundings."

The room was right out of NASA, with a bit of Twilight Zone sci-fi thrown in. Computers, flat-screen monitors, walls of whirring electronics. And vats. Tall clear tubes complete with bodies standing upright immersed in a phosphorescent green liquid: John Lennon, Jimi Hendrix, Jim Morrison, JFK, MLK, RFK, Mahatma Gandhi, even Marilyn and Elvis.

"My array of dead poets, philosophers and peaceniks."

Ben realized these must have been the shrouded figures he and MacLaren had seen walking the property before.

"I'd really like to add Socrates but DNA from 300 B.C. is impossible to acquire. I am working on Nelson Mandella though."

"I'm surprised Janis isn't here."

"She's in the house, already gone to bed."

Convict Rick stirred. Montgomery went to him and lifted an eyelid. "Should be out a while longer."

He regained his seat. "I'm assuming by your commando garb, you came to bust me."

"Look Fairmont, I know who you are and I have an idea of what you're doing. I met with your partner Elroy Leland at AbioGenetix. It looks like you have advanced beyond all probability." He motioned around the room. "You should be commended. But let me tell you this, as intriguing, and perhaps disturbing, as all of this is, I don't give a shit."

"So then, what is the meaning of your presence here?"

"What you are involved in has led to the kidnapping of my wife."

"Your wife? I don't understand."

"Carlene Heath, high school, Vermont. Ring a bell?"

It did.

"Hannah Hunt is dead," Ben said.

"Yes, I ... I know."

"And I believe that whoever killed her has taken my wife and I also believe you know why."

They sparred back and forth, Fairmont claiming his innocence and Big Ben angrily emphasizing his disbelief.

Finally they came to an understanding when Montgomery said, "I haven't had any contact with the real world for years now, not since I sequestered myself in this isolated land. My work requires the strictest solitude. I am a peaceful, non-violent man, but

I realize there are those who would stop at nothing, including violence, to garner my knowledge and to twist it to advance their own evil purposes."

He lapsed into deep thought. "And then there is society with all of its fears and castration for anything new and astounding …" he shook his head and made a dismissive hand gesture, "… but that is another topic entirely. Unfortunately, the bettering of humanity must be done in cautious steps. Personal sacrifice is only one of many prerequisites. Security is another. The lavish metallic netting you noticed the other day, keeps me off the radar."

"But I got through."

"I had a feeling you might return, and I allowed you to do so."

"Why?"

"Lately there have been certain occurrences, bewildering and unexplainable. I am a believer in Chaos Theory and when you unexpectedly appeared, I took that as an omen. I had no idea it would revitalize my past. But I needed to see where it would take me."

"Fairmont, you are talking in circles to me. I would love to stay and chat with you, but I need to go."

"Yes, yes, sorry. Haven't had many real people to talk to lately. Do you know where you are going?"

"No, but it's not here. I need to get back to Sarasota and regroup. May need to bring in some reinforcements." He was thinking he'd have to bring MacLaren and Ford into the loop. He had wanted to handle things solo, his way, and thought he'd had it figured out. But now, Carlene was still in danger and the clock was ticking.

Unexpectedly, Fairmont said, "Perhaps I can be of help. Have you had any contact with the abductors?"

"Yes."

"How did they contact you?"

Ben thought it odd that Fairmont asked *how* and not *what did they say*. "They called my cell from my wife's."

"Then there'll be a trace."

"No. They said it wouldn't be traceable."

"Ah, for mere mortals maybe." Fairmont grinned and went to a computer and began tapping a long series of numbers.

"The beauty of the Global Positioning System is its simplicity. Air is merely an invisible gaseous substance of oxygen and nitrogen. It is pretty basic. Nothing much disturbs it. But it is nonetheless a medium and when radio waves pass through it they leave an indelible trail, much as a knife through flesh. It leaves its mark." Fairmont continued inputting.

"Don't you need my phone?"

"No. Give me the time, the area you were in and the duration of the communication."

Seconds later Montgomery had not only a location, but a visual on the screen. "This is where the call emanated from. I do not recognize it, but it is within an hour from here."

Ben stared at the screen and said, "Print this out with the coordinates and I'll find it." He went and stood over Convict Rick. "I've got to wake him and take him out of here with me."

"Leave him. I will return him to safety. Unharmed, but unconscious. I cannot risk him divulging my work."

"Don't worry. I think he'll be happy to forget the whole experience. I'll make sure of it."

"Take this. I've entered the coordinates." He handed Ben a small, ultra-thin GPS.

"The Hummer's got one."

"Not like this one. Watch." He powered it up. "This little techno-gadget has not only GPS, but also infra-red which can detect body heat by sex, and ENV - Enhanced Nocturnal Vision that gives a near flawless rendering of the topography, buildings, vehicles, et cetera, no matter how dark or cloudy it is. This will take you precisely to her location. No variance factor."

The screen showed a small building with three bodies. One female in an awkward seated position, "This is probably your wife," and a reclined male, "I would think that's one of the kidnappers," Fairmont said. "This one here," he pointed, "is a moving female who appears to be circumventing the building. I would say she's walking around a catwalk." He handed it to Ben. "Push this icon here to zoom."

Ben did and saw that the building was a raised, stilted structure. A readout at the bottom said, 12 x 16, 192 sq. ft., wood/metal. "Now click the 360 button." A 360 degree view of the building swept slowly across the screen. "I put a chip in there that integrates multiple points from multiple satellites on all four horizons." Fairmont chuckled. "Garmin will be developing these in about 20 years."

Big Ben couldn't help but smile. "This is perfect. Thanks."

Fairmont extended his hand. "Good luck my new friend. May we meet again someday."

Ben stopped at the door and looked at the prototype GPS in his hand and then scanned the room with all its bizarre components. "Have you always been ahead of your time?"

Montgomery Fairmont had a sad look in his eye. "It does get lonely."

Lonely enough to live with a clone of a dead rock icon. Ben felt sorry for him.

He left to go find his very own, very real woman.

53
Brutal Release

"What the fuck are you doing?" MacLaren was screaming on speaker phone. "And what kind of bullshit was that at the airport?"

Big Ben was traveling fast on a dark road in the dark night. It was two a.m. Fairmont's GPS was guiding him as steady as a drone. Twenty-four minutes to destination. "I didn't want you to be involved."

"What are you talking about?"

"I've got to do this my way. Your involvement will hinder me and also jeopardize your career."

"I'm a cop. A kidnapping has happened on my turf. *I AM* involved. We need to do this right. We need to follow protocol. Now, where the fuck are you going?"

Ben's voice was hard. A darkening rage was festering. "This is my wife, MacLaren. I am going to rescue her and I am going to do it my way. There is no time to fuck around. These guys don't go by protocol."

"I know how you feel Ben, but …"

"NO! You don't know how I feel. They've kidnapped my wife! Holding her hostage. Tied up and terrified, maybe emotionally damaged for the rest of her life. I need to get to her. I need to save her. And I need to do that right now."

"Don't do this on your own. I don't know where you're headed, but I do know where you are."

"Are you locked onto me?"

"You're damn right I am. Do this right. Wait for back-up. I'm only twelve minutes behind you."

"Stay out of this, Lieutenant."

"Listen you son-of-a- …" MacLaren's voice disappeared as Big Ben threw the cell phone out the window. He stomped the accelerator to the floor. The Hummer jumped to over one hundred-miles-per-hour.

The increased speed got him there six minutes ahead of ETA. He sat idling at the edge of the long quarry road. It was dark but he could still make out the ghost structures half a mile away. Dead ahead stood a shed on tall stilts with a railing around it. On the GPS screen he noticed the female figure was on the back side, away from the entrance road. He killed the lights.

Ben needed to prep himself, to quell his anxiety. He closed his eyes and tried to envision Carlene in a summer dress swinging in their backyard, her hair lightly blowing and the sun on her face as she smiled into his eyes. But he only saw her gagged and tied to a chair, her eyes fraught with terror searching for him. Ben took several deep breaths, attempting to calm his racing heart. They didn't work. He checked his gun and tucked it into his waistband.

Slowly and stealthily the Hummer rolled forward. The woman moved unhurriedly around the building. As he got closer, he could make her out coming around the corner. She stopped. She saw him. Ben hit the gas. She came to the front and rested her forearms on the railing.

The first shot pocked the windshield and Ben ducked. He could see the orange flashes from her semi-automatic weapon. Several of them. All the bullets were hitting the accelerating machine. Ben scrunched down in his seat, his head below the steering wheel, his focus on the roof of the building thirty feet in the air.

He sped non-stop, full-throttle into the structure with maximum force. Half of the pilings snapped. The metal staircase twisted and the building lurched to one side. The Hummer moaned angrily into the night.

Ben reached for the door handle and was startled when Ursula's body crashed onto the hood. The side of her face rested on the bullet-holed windshield. Blood oozed from her mouth and streaked the shattered glass.

Big Ben bounded up the twisted staircase and a split-second later kicked the door in and entered the room. The floor was slanted from the crash and what little furniture there was had slid to the far wall. LeBeau stood propped against it, clutching Carlene to him with his hand over her mouth and a Glock 9mm held to her temple. Ben was crouched in a two-handed pose, his Smith & Wesson .38 pointed at the center of his adversary's face. They were in a classic stand-off.   "Drop your gun or she dies."

Ben rose gradually from his stance and lowered his left arm from the double grip. He hadn't looked at his wife yet. His unblinking eyes were focused on LeBeau.

"Okay. Okay. Don't hurt her." He stood erect, his feet planted firmly to the floor, the weight, luckily, on his good leg to compensate for the tilt. Slowly he brought his gun arm downward in surrender.

The blast resounded loudly in the small room. LeBeau's instinctual reaction to the .38 blowing off his kneecap was to simultaneously drop his gun, release his hold on Carlene, and to drop to the floor clutching his leg.

Big Ben dove at him, ramming his shoulder into his upper torso. They struggled, but Ben got the best of him. He pulled him up, held him against the wall and smashed his fist straight into his nose. The nasal bone broke and blood started gushing.

"BEN!" Carlene had fallen away and scrambled on hands and knees to the open door.

Ben was filled with uncontrollable rage. Not only did this man abduct and terrorize his wife, but he had also accosted Ben's world, threatened his manhood, endangered his ability to provide and care for those he was responsible for. He became unhinged. He sent a flurry of blows into the mid-section. His hard, powerful fists cracked ribs that splintered and punctured both lungs. LeBeau became unconscious and slipped to the floor. Ben picked him up like a rag doll and pummeled his face.

"BENNN!"

The second nose punch jammed the middle concha bone into the front cranial vault.

"BENNN!"

Overwhelmed with primal vengeance, Ben continued to pound away. Somewhere in the beating, as the ME would later conclude, LeBeau's fractured zygomaticofacial bone was driven like an ice pick through the infraorbital foramen and deep into the frontal lobe of his brain.

"BENNNNN!" Finally Carlene's voice got through to her adrenaline-crazed husband.

Ben looked at her for the first time since the ordeal started. He released his grip and LeBeau fell in a bloody heap to the floor.

"Oh, Ben," Carlene went to him and he embraced her with his bloodied hands.

"It's okay. It's okay, it's over."

She held him tightly. "Oh, Ben." She could feel his heart thumping wildly against his chest. *Oh, Ben* she said to herself and began to cry.

With his blood pressure and his senses back to normal, Ben could hear the sirens and see the red lights flashing off the walls of the distorted building. He moved to the doorway and stood with his arm over his wife's shoulders. MacLaren clambered up the twisted stairs, his weapon at the ready. He looked from Carlene to Ben then back to Carlene again.

"Are you okay?"

"Yes," she answered.

He touched her arm, "I've got an ambulance on the way."
"Okay."
"How about you?"
Ben replied, "I'm good. There's one inside, unconscious. The other one's on the hood of the car."
"What car?"
Big Ben looked over the railing. The Hummer was gone.

PART II

... I've been trying to get down to the heart of the matter
But everything changes and I think it's about ...

Forgiveness

Lyrics ... Don Henley

six months later

54

Six Months Later

The Hummer had been found at Orlando International Airport. Ursula was unaccounted for. Her partner LeBeau was dead and buried at county expense.

The mangrove murders remain unsolved. Hannah Hunt Everett was laid to rest in Peaceful Palm Cemetery. Her husband and children were coping as best they could. An anonymous college fund had been set up in the children's names. MacLaren still had hopes of finding her killer.

Nobody claimed the bodies of the naked man or Hannah's twin. Because of the bewildering unknown causes of death, the bodies were kept on ice, becoming popular research specimens for medical examiners, doctors and universities worldwide.

Conrad Blake Lawrence was officially ensconced in the governor's mansion in Tallahassee. Jake Curtis, Jake the Snake, never far behind.

Conrad's daughter and law partner, Lydia Lawrence, was busy with their law practice and currently preparing a tricky defense for a new client.

Montgomery Fairmont and his "experiments" are still under the radar – at least for the time being. His identity is being held in confidence by Big Ben Benson for reasons of his own.

Convict Rick is happily cooking at Woody's, his brief covert adventure a thing of the past. He is now focused on a hot new waitress.

Jay and Dwayne have been mysteriously absent from happy hour.

Elroy Leland remains in sole control of AbioGenetix. The wounds from the torturing are healed as best as they ever will be. He's glad one tormenter is dead, but leery of the other one. He has installed a new security system at his house and has obtained a license to carry.

The Group continues to hold their clandestine meetings.

Ray Burati has stayed on as chief of police in Myakka City. His dreams of riding his Harley into the sunset are on hold.

Big Ben slayed the dragon but lost the damsel. He and Carlene have split up.

She's living back home in Massachusetts with the kids, the dog and, at Ben's insistence, Uncle Bob to watch over the family. Carlene still works at the animal clinic and has sought therapy to help cope with the lingering trauma of the kidnapping/rescue and the more damaging aspect of watching her husband beat a man to death.

Ben is living alone in Florida, stripped of his badge and gun, suspended and under investigation.

Winnie Vanderlene is still swimming naked, smoking pot and enjoying afternoon cocktails on her infinity deck. Her little dollhouse cottage on Two Can Key has been refurbished and rented out.

Lydia Lawrence was headed there to meet with her new client.

55

Beach Shack

A strong blow was coming down from the north, swirling over Two Can Key. The Australian pines were bent in the wind like giant jai-alai scoops. Long, heavy palm fronds twisted and snapped on the front side of the blow. In the lee stood the little beach shack, undisturbed and seemingly unaware of the bristling winds.

Big Ben was on the porch with a beer when Lydia's pearl white BMW Z4 cruised in, coming to rest on the sandy drive next to Ben's Fat Boy.

"Little windy to have the top down isn't it?"

She leaned against the railing next to him pulling off her red cap and twisting her long dark hair into a ponytail. She spoke through her sunglasses in her teeth, "Why have a convertible if you don't like the wind? Besides, the front's on its way out."

Ben smiled at her. She was a pretty lady all right. The hair off her neck revealed tan breastbones and a crisp cleavage that dove into a lacy white top.

"Got a beer for a lady lawyer?"

"I got a beer. Alcohol gonna mix well with sound legal advice?"

She smiled at him with that easy smile of hers. "Probably make it sounder."

"Come on in," he said, "I'll give you the tour."

After Ben and Carlene split up, Ben had imposed on the MacLaren's hospitality anticipating Carlene would soon change her mind about the separation. When he realized it wasn't forthcoming, he began looking for an apartment. He had retained Lydia to represent him for the inquisition and it had been at her suggestion that he met with her new friend Winnie Vanderlene and made her a deal on the beach shack. Winnie agreed to two months' free rent in lieu of Ben's handyman skills – the place needed a little fixing up.

"I never got the chance to thank you properly for hooking me up with Winnie and her cottage here. So, thanks."

"You're welcome."

Lydia looked around the little cottage. The ceiling was open to the rafters and held twin skylights that you could crank open to bring in the breeze from the Gulf. A palm-bladed fan, suspended from a rough-hewn support beam swirled lazily above the open front room where a rattan couch in tropical fabrication accompanied its matching chair. A low coffee table sat atop Pago-Pago flooring. The walls were tastefully adorned with colorful prints by local artists and a makeshift bookshelf hosted a smattering of mystery novels. The kitchen was small and galley-like and separated from the living room by a raised counter with two stools tucked beneath it.

"The bathroom," Ben explained, "is right behind the kitchen but it's not much more than your basic lavatory, as the shower is located outside at the rear of the cottage. But it does have a latticed enclosure," he laughed, "so as not to scare the birds."

"Heaven forbid," she said.

At his suggestion, Lydia took a peek into the bedroom at the back of the cottage and found it cool with a slight breeze seeping through dark, wide Plantation blinds. The wall treatment of light-colored wainscoting had been carried in from the front room and gave the limited space a nice illusion of openness. An open-air closet stood in the corner consisting of a short chest of drawers with several shirts hanging from a bamboo rod above. She smiled at the fresh-made bed and the tidiness throughout. Lydia liked a man who was neat and organized. She sensed he cared about the things around him. She hoped she was one of them.

Ben directed Lydia outside to the porch chairs. He sat down next her and handed her a cold bottle. "Need a glass?"

"Comes in a glass."

"Yeah, I hear that a lot at the bar."

"How are you doing at Gramps'?" Gramps Ramp had converted the back deck into a Tiki bar and Ben had taken Gramps up on a bartending offer.

"Okay. Pretty basic stuff. Drafts and simple mixes. Haven't had to make any fancy margaritas yet, but I'm sure I could figure it out."

Lydia took a sip and looked out into the yard. "I like your new mode of transportation. When do I get to go for a ride?"

"As soon as you get me out of this mess."

Big Ben had lost his bid for replacing Chief Ray, but had gained his Harley - for a fair price of course. That had solved the transportation issue. Bartending would help the income so all he'd needed was a place to live - temporarily he hoped.

Lydia had been right. The wind was dying down, the front fading away. To the west the sun was clearing the clouds and the little key would soon be back in the sunshine.

"Are you ready?" she asked him. The inquest, to be held jointly with the DA and the coroner's office, was scheduled for the next morning.

"As I'll ever be."

"She'd love to fry your ass, y'know. She's had a grudge against you since last year."

Ben remembered her well. Tanya Chisholm, DA, Miss Bitch on Wheels, or "the Chisel" as she was called by her co-workers behind her steely back. The 'murdered model' case had brought international intrigue and notoriety to her domain and she absolutely hated to lose face. But she had, due to Ben's unorthodox bungling.

"You really riled her. She'd love some revenge."

Ben grumbled.

Lydia was thinking of the circumstances surrounding her new client. "She doesn't like people getting killed in her territory. Even bad people."

"I'd do it again if I had to."

"And she really doesn't like renegade cops."

"Listen, he had my ..."

"I know, I know. We've been through this a hundred times. But she's going for 'excessive and deadly force' and if the board finds it that way, you'll at the very least never be a cop again."

Ben got up and went to the corner railing. The waves were not far away and the sound of them on the back side of the front was soothing. The trees had stilled and stood tall in their original splendor. Sandpipers scurried on the beach reveling in the bounty washed in from the Gulf.

"Y'know Lydia, I'm not sure I want to be a cop anymore."

A gush rolled onto the shore and spread quietly over the sand as if awaiting her response.

Lydia pulled off her cap, pulled down the Scrunchy and shook her mane wildly. "And if you're not, what do you want to be?"

"A husband and a good provider for my kids."

Lydia felt a twinge in her stomach. She flung her cap onto the vacant chair. "Come on." she jumped up. "Let's go for a walk."

They walked along the narrow pathway passing by the other cottage. Lydia noticed the yellow Jeep was gone. "Where's Winnie?"

"Don't know. She comes and goes. Sometimes she's gone for a couple of days at a time."

"Maybe she's getting lucky," she smiled.

"Never know with her. She's a secretive lady."

They got to the edge of the path where it meets the white beach. Lydia took her sandals off and left them on the sand and ran ahead of Ben toward the water. Her legs were long and tan beneath khaki shorts. Ben watched the curls of her dark hair dancing on the back of her loose, sleeveless top.

He took his time catching up with her at the shoreline. Her toes curled in the foamy surf. He wanted to embrace her from behind and bury his head in the nape of her neck. But he realized he was only thinking of Carlene. Ben stood beside his attorney.

They were each standing on the edge of something, lost in their own respective thoughts. Lydia knew she should be consumed by the upcoming coroner's inquest but was instead struggling with her emotions. She wondered if she had the courage to just let it out. Tell him how she felt. And if now was the time.

Big Ben standing next to her was two thousand miles away. He didn't give a damn about the inquest, nor its results. He was wondering for the millionth time in six months how Carlene was doing back home in Massachusetts.

56
Therapy

It didn't happen right away. Carlene wanted to finish out their vacation, rationalizing that the Florida sunshine would help her de-stress from the ordeal. So they tried to be happy and make the best of it. The foursome went to Disneyworld; camping in the Everglades; deep sea fishing and even a long weekend in Key West. They had a blast.

But there was an underlying vibe accompanying their journeys that was slowly metastasizing in the deep psyche of Carlene Benson.

The nightmares awaited her in her own bed back home in Bryce Corner, Massachusetts.

At first she thought it was just a delayed reaction to the kidnapping and that it would go away as she readjusted to her normal life routine. She needed to put it behind her.

But it didn't go away. Night after night the nightmares continued. Always the same yet always different. Like different trailers to the same movie. And it wasn't about the trunk or the captivity or the fear of dying, it was always about Ben beating that man to death. Each night she could see him as an enraged animal, his face contorted, his huge arms and fists distorted in the dream. She could hear the pounding of flesh like tribal drums getting louder and louder and louder until she heard the cracking and snapping of bones and saw the blood spurting towards her. And then she'd scream and wake up clutching the sheets to her sweat-soaked body.

On the cushiony couch at her therapist's office she was told, "The damage done is compound. There are two issues here. First, the emotional paralyzing fear of the abduction and the inherent trauma associated with that. Secondly, the over-the-top trauma of witnessing the violent beating death of your captor by your husband - a man you love and trust - but have now seen in an unfamiliar and troublesome way. The violent assault was an extreme traumatic sensor and what you are experiencing now is Posttraumatic Stress Disorder, PTSD.

"Most people who experience a traumatizing event - police, firemen, first responders, soldiers, victims of violent crime or natural disasters, et cetera - will not develop PTSD. However women, because of our deep emotional makeup, are more likely to develop PTSD than men. And sometimes there are patterns. Most PTSD patients have a trauma history or prior anxiety disorders or deep-rooted religious views that greatly hinder understanding of, and hence treatment for, PTSD."

Carlene asked for a glass of water. Her therapist obliged, regained her seat and waited while Carlene took a drink and settled back onto the couch.

"Better?"

"Yes, thank you."

"Okay, let's get into this." She lifted a leg onto her knee and scribbled on a notepad resting in her lap as she continued, "Your reaction of intense fear and helplessness are dual, harmful anxieties born of an extremely traumatic event. Characteristic symptoms of PTSD include a persistent re-experiencing of the traumatic event – i.e. the recurring nightmares."

Carlene flinched.

"Is there a history of violence in your past, your childhood?"

"No."

"Has another family member or friend been a victim of abuse?"

"No. I do not know of anyone."

The therapist was searching for patterns.

"Tell me about your religion."

"Well, I was baptized Protestant and attended Sunday school as a kid, but not much after that."

"No extreme religious activity?"

"My parents weren't church-goers. At best we'd go to Easter services or a wedding here and there."

"Any physical or verbal conflicts between you and Ben?"

"No. Never anything physical. Just the usual marital skirmishes."

The therapist paused and entered some notes.

Carlene lay still with her hands folded on her stomach. They were shaking. Tears seeped down her cheeks. "I still love him but I don't know who he is anymore. How do I deal with that?"

Her therapist reached a box of tissues and handed it to her. "That's what we are going to determine together. There is hope. We can get you through this, but I'll be honest with you, Carlene, there is a degree of personal sacrifice on your and Ben's part. The Posttraumatic Stress Disorder will dissolve over time, but you've got to not let it absorb you, not let it destroy your relationship. It will take time and it will not be easy. The therapy will only succeed if we initiate some strict procedures."

"I don't want to do drugs."

"I'm not talking drugs."

"What then?"

"Avoidance of reminders of the precipitating stressor."

"The kidnapper is dead, doctor."

"You're not dreaming about the kidnapper."

Carlene snapped up and placed her feet on the floor. She looked into the eyes of her therapist. "You mean, Ben?"

"You have gone through a myriad of phases and powerful emotions in an extremely concise time frame: fear, anger, feelings of desperation and emptiness, all followed by an uplifting elation, only to then be diminished by a violent, traumatic event. Your core has been shaken. You need time and distance to cope."

57

Something

"I have something for you."

"A reprieve, I hope."

They were sitting in the sand now. The retreating storm had left the air fresh and clear.

She'd started it, so she figured she'd go for it. "No," Lydia said. "I mean I have *something* for you. But I don't know how to present it to you, or that I even should."

Ben wasn't dumb. He'd known since the year before that she was interested in him, ever since that first day they had bumped into each other at the bookstore/café downtown. And then there had been the time they were out in the boat together, but he thought he'd handled that well. Thought he'd cooled her jets. But he knew now that she was probably going to tell him what he didn't want to know. He knew what she meant by *something*. So he remained quiet and let her run with it.

Lydia took a breath and let it out quietly. "Ever since last year when we were involved in that case and we were almost killed, I can't get you out of my mind. I know that sounds like an old song, but it's true. I've thought about you every day since then, and I know that's wrong. Wrong for you, wrong for your wife, and especially wrong for me. But it's there. In the morning when I wake, throughout my day, and in my restless nights. I don't really know why nor what the reason is for it. I'm a mature woman, a professional, a lawyer for chrissakes. But I feel like a teenager when it comes to thoughts of you," Lydia paused, "and I don't know what to do."

"I thought we were going to talk about the inquiry."

"Dammit Ben!" She turned toward him with a flush on her face. "Help me here. I'm pouring my heart out to you."

An outer band of wind came off the Gulf blowing through Lydia's hair and pressing her loose top against her breasts. Ben couldn't help but notice her nipples standing firm in the breeze. She drew her knees up and stared back at the sea.

"Lydia, I don't know what to say. I like you, I really do."

"Oh, you *like* me."

"Wait. Hear me out." Ben drew his knees up too and quickly got reminded of his bad knee. He stretched his right leg out. "I came down here a few months ago for a nice quiet vacation and yeah, I was interested in the chief's job out in Myakka, but Sarasota always seems to have a different agenda for me. Now, I'm suspended, separated from my wife and family, living in a shack on the beach - which may sound glamorous under other circumstances - bartending and riding a motorcycle - which also sounds wonderful - but I'm facing losing my career, questioning my self-worth, and all I want to do is find the motherfuckers who are responsible for all this shit laid on me and get my life back in order." He didn't even pause when he added, "And yeah, I'd like to jump your bones, but I'm still very much in love with my wife. So, at the risk of fucking you up too, I think we should keep our relationship professional and platonic. I can't even think about tomorrow I'm having such a hard time keeping up with today."

Not necessarily what she wanted to hear, but not necessarily unexpected either.

"I ... I'm sorry," she said and took the liberty of leaning her head against his shoulder.

Big Ben wrapped his arm around her and said, "I'm sorry too. Just help me get out of this fiasco and I'll get out of your hair. Okay?"

She hid the tear in her eye and straightened up. Her defense mechanism kicked in and the attorney in her said, "We don't have to worry. Bottom line is it'll never go to trial. Your wife is the only witness to what happened that day and she cannot testify against you; spousal privileges. The DA knows that. So my gut feeling is that they'll find you 'not responsible'. But you'll never be a cop in the state of Florida and I expect Massachusetts would follow suit. I'm sorry."

"Don't be. I dug my own hole."

They got up and brushed the sand from their shorts and headed back toward the cottages hidden in the shade of the trees.

"What will you do?" she asked.

"I don't know. Maybe private work. Maybe I'll just be a bartender for a while and see how things work out."

Lydia knew he meant between his wife and him. She needed to conquer her infatuation and stop harboring the fantasy that Ben and Carlene would divorce.

When they got to the drive Lydia stopped next to the Harley. "We haven't discussed my fee yet."

"Whatever your normal rates are."

"I'll charge you one afternoon ride on this big boy."

"Fat Boy, actually," Ben chuckled.

She ran her hand along the tank, "Okay, one afternoon ride on the Fat Boy with the Big Boy."

"Deal." They laughed and shook hands.

58

Soul Searching

A band of rogue showers passed through the sunshine and doused Two Can Key one final time for the day. It didn't last long, quick and easy like a sinful summer breeze. In fact Ben hadn't even moved out of its way. He sat with his back against the palm tree on the side of his beach shack, elbow on an ice chest and a beer in the sand, watching the rain cut across the water and brush the key. It was refreshing and dropped the temperature enough so that he was comfortable in his spot in the shade. Or at least his body was comfortable; his mind was in a whir.

Lydia had returned to her office to finalize preparations for his case tomorrow. He didn't feel sorry for what he had done, no remorse. Maybe that was his problem. He loved Carlene more than anything and would do anything for her, and had. After the rescue they had been extremely happy, glad to be alive together. It wasn't until the nightmares began back home that their exuberance waned.

Ben had done what the therapist suggested – given his wife some solo time. And because of his makeup, he'd returned to Florida to appease his obsession, his inflexible need, to solve the case, find the other kidnapper and those behind the scene and bring them to justice - one way or the other. He wouldn't rest until then and he didn't need to be a cop to do it. He had to set his world right and then Carlene would be his again.

Ben knew Lydia was probably right when she told him he'd get more than a hand-slap. So, if he didn't get reinstated, so be it. He didn't care anymore. He'd get through the inquest and figure things out from there. Lydia was a good attorney and Ben knew she'd do her best for him. Lydia ...

He drew his bottle of beer out of the sand, took a sip and replaced it in the same hollow spot. She had flattered him. It's nice to know you're still attractive to a woman. And if things were different between he and Carlene? Well ...

Ah shit, he said, things *are* different between us. He finished off the beer and reached into the ice chest for another cold one. I don't know Sugarplum, he was talking to himself, why do I always seem to fuck things up? Ben wondered if Carlene had someone flattering her. She certainly deserved it. A great lady, damn good looking, a wonderful mother and a loving wife. Ben choked up. *Dammit!* He yelled to the vacant sky.

Reflection
Sorrow
Guilt
Shame
Repentance
Redemption
Surrender

Ben felt them all. From the pit of his stomach to the weight on his broad shoulders. A heavier weight than the biggest heap of linebackers ever to pile onto him. Hard. Emotionally destructive. Not easy to shake off. And not helped much by his increased drinking and lonely, self-pitying nights.

He'd been secluded, emotionally marooned on this little key for five months now trying to sort everything out. He was lonely, adrift on this sea of misery – wasn't that a song? Sea of heartache, heartbreak? Something.

Que sera sera ... he sang into the breeze and realized he was getting a bit tipsy. Big Ben knew his fate would be decided tomorrow. And if he was lucky enough to get his badge back?.. Or maybe he'd be luckier not to. He couldn't worry about it. He didn't give a crap. Lydia had asked him to go over his prepared statement for the inquiry board, but, fuck it. He didn't have to work tonight, so he decided to tie one on and wallow in self-pity.

Que sera sera ...

The afternoon got long and lazy and Ben ran out of beer. He left the empty ice chest and padded heavily through the sand to his shack.

The unknown was calling to him. Deserved or not. Calling to him. Alone. Big as he was in all aspects of his life, he felt miniscule and helpless. He slugged a fresh bottle of beer and leaned his back against the porch railing, anxious for night to fall so he could hide his loneliness in the dark. Although, he had to admit, the sunsets were soothing; beautiful colors swirling above the washing waters beyond the short beach to the Gulf. Changing. Like his life. Changing into a swirl of unknowns above his own horizon.

Winnie's cottage off to the right was quiet. No idea where the old girl was. She was absent recently from their late night talks. He missed her. During the past few months they had struck up a rapport. They'd spent many a night talking and philosophizing, aided and abetted by alcohol and ganja, and now he missed her verbal confrontations, her concurrent support and condemnation for his plight, her crazy ideas. She called them *The Aging Hippie Chick and The Big Man with The Lost Soul* and thought that would make a great movie title.

Ben chuckled. Maybe she was getting lucky. Seventy-seven and still attractive and sexy in her own way. Hell, he thought, if I was thirty years older or she was thirty years younger, like she'd once said to him. He laughed out loud and headed inside to grab another beer.

59

Forgiveness

"Hey," Winnie knocked on the screen door. "You got a bottle opener in here?" Without waiting for an answer she pulled open the old weathered door with the familiar creaking she'd heard a million times since childhood.

Ben came out of the tiny bedroom with only his shorts on. His hair was on end and he looked like he'd been napping. Winnie held two cold beer bottles in one hand and rummaged through the kitchen drawer with the other. Ben leaned against the counter and yawned. She found the opener and popped the tops. "These damn Yuengling twist-tops are getting harder and harder with my gnarly fingers." She handed a bottle to him. "Don't get any easier at my age, y'know."

Big Ben looked reluctantly at the beer, but then took a swig. "Winnie, if I'm half as spry as you are at your age I'll be pleased as punch."

Winnie smiled and lifted the bottle back. "Put a shirt on and meet me on the porch. Sunset's gonna be a beauty."

"Why do I need a shirt? There's no mosquitoes tonight." The night wind was up and blowing the insects over the inlet to feast on the bay side.

"It ain't the skeeters I'm worried about, it's that hairy chest of yours that troubles me." She gave him a wink and pushed the squeaky door open.

A minute later, with his shirt on, Big Ben appeared on the porch with two more beers in cozies. "Back-up," he said and placed the beers between them on the driftwood steps.

"A man after my own heart."

They sat in the breeze listening to the wind trying to howl above the sound of the waves. The breeze felt nice. They didn't talk through the first beer. Ben sat in deep thought, his elbows on his knees, his head bowed, and his fingers absently twirling the beer bottle before him. A dove cooed from the trees out past the sandy drive and another cooed back, nearby, out of view on the peak of the roof above them.

"Miss her, don't ya?"

Ben lifted his eyes to meet Winnie's, but she was staring straight ahead into the twilight shadow of the pines. He matched her gaze and leaned back, resting his elbows on the upper step and crossing his ankles.

"More than I even understand."

"I've had love," Winnie smiled to herself. She didn't elaborate, but she harbored a whimsical look in her eyes.

The cooing from the distance had continued, but the response from above them had ceased. "More than once," she said. "Hell, more than many a once."

They heard a flutter of wings and the sound of flight.

Winnie said, "I think you can love, and maybe love many times. But I think you can only *be* in love once in your lifetime - if you're damn lucky. Being in love transcends everything. Once. That's all you get."

She thought this might have elicited a response from him, but it did not.

"Let me ask you something," she said. "When you look yourself in the eye, which eye do you look into?"

"What? What difference does that make?"

Winnie chuckled and lifted the beer bottle to her lips. It was empty.

"Are you still in love with her?"

The gloss on Ben's eyes told her yes.

"Go get her."

"I don't know how."

"Well, you could fly or drive or crawl." Winnie grabbed one of the back-ups and attempted to twist the top off. Ben took it from her and opened it. She said, "The last option might be the most appropriate."

"That's not what I mean."

"I know."

She handed Ben the beer he had just opened for her and grabbed another for herself, twisting the top off with ease.

"I wouldn't know what to say. I've been over it a thousand times and I don't know how to fix it."

"Try."

"Ah, I blew it," Ben chugged half the bottle. "My temper gets in the way of my feet sometimes."

"You didn't have to kill that man."

"But I did."

"Well, seems like you had good reason."

Winnie got up and walked over to her cottage. She came back with a six-pack in one hand and an amber pint bottle with a red top in the other. Two Dixie cups rode upside down on the end bottles of the six-pack.

"What's this?"

"Makers Mark."

"Ohh boy..." he said with reluctance, then took the cups and held them as Winnie twisted off the waxed top and poured a shot into each.

"To life's perplexities," she held her cup up. "What fun would it be without them?" She downed her shot. "Go ahead."

Ben toasted her and did so.

An hour later they were comfortably inebriated and still sitting on the driftwood steps of the beach shack. The sun had set and a full moon was rising at their backs. They were counting stars opposite it as they dotted into the blue night sky above the Gulf waters.

"Eight, nine, ten."

"Where?"

"Right there," Winnie pointed into the dusking western sky. "The three in Orion's belt."

Ben had a fresh beer dangling from his hand and Winnie was rolling a joint. "I told you it was gonna be a great star night," she said.

"I think you cheat," he said. "You're not even looking up."

Winnie laughed as she licked the edge of the rolling paper. "Same stars, same place, every night."

Big Ben laughed. "How'd I ever end up with a crazy old woman like you sitting on my porch?"

"A ... you were lucky. B ... it's my porch." She lit the joint with a silver, well-worn Ronson lighter. She took a hit and raised her eyebrows at Ben. He shook his head.

"Besides, you should feel honored," she lifted her beer from the decking and raised it to her lips, "crazy old women are hard to come by these days."

She put the beer down and drew the joint to her lips.

"How long you been smoking that shit?" Ben asked her.

"Longer than Willie Nelson," she smirked. Another hit. "Never smoked cigarettes though. No point to it. If you're gonna smoke you may as well get something out of it. Besides, never wanted to support the F'n tobacco industry – giving people cancer just to fatten their wallets. Rather support my sisters and brothers who farm the weed to provide for their families."

"You believe that?"

"Sure I believe it. Besides, it's gonna be legalized soon. You can bet your ass those tobacco boardrooms are already planning their marketing schemes. And the government's already got tax laws lined up to make sure they get their piece of the pie. Bastards."

They sat silent awhile looking into the west and listening to the rush of the night waves onto the shore. Anterius broke through the dark blue veil and they both saw it at the same time. In unison they said, "Eleven," and slapped each other a high five.

After a while Ben said, "Do you think there's life after death? Y'know, God and Heaven, some type of afterlife? Or just a black hole?"

"Some say it's Heaven, some say it's Hell, then some say it's nothin' at all. You want to know what I think comes after life?"

"Yeah."

She held the joint out to him, but Ben again waved it off. Winnie took a toke, held it in for several seconds and then slowly exhaled a faint stream of smoke through her pursed lips.

"Forgiveness. Pure forgiveness."

The wind had moved on and left in its wake a clear stretch of ocean for the moon to illuminate. The beer was gone, along with the whiskey, and the conversation had run its course.

"Wanna swim?" She punched him in the arm. Hard.

She went to do it again and Ben caught her wrist and looked at her hand. "Gnarly fingers, my ass."

Winnie smirked, grabbed his hand and pulled him off the porch. "Come on!" She ran toward the water, stripping her clothes off as she went.

"Crazy old broad," he said, then yelled, "what about my hairy chest?"

"Bring it with you," she hollered back and ran naked into the waves.

Ben laughed, took his shirt off and lumbered his big frame to the shoreline and plowed into the ocean.

60

Inquest

Usually a coroner's inquest was held at the ME's office above the county morgue east of the interstate on Clark Road. This one however had no need to delve into forensics or science and was only concerned with the behavior of an officer of the law. So, at 9:00 am Chief Ben Benson accompanied by his lawyer, Lydia Lawrence, made their way into the DA's office in the recently restored Spanish-Mediterranean building downtown which housed the Sarasota County courthouse, municipal offices and police complex.

The ME was already there seated at the conference table on the right of DA Tanya Chisholm. He held a mug of coffee and she a cup of herbal tea. Her ADA, Tyler Tate, cowered on her left fastidiously organizing tomes of law journals in anticipation of her any need for references involving the meeting. He was new and young and well aware that "The Chisel" blew through ADA's by the dozens.

Ben and Lydia entered. "Well, Mr. Benson. We meet again." Tanya Chisholm gestured to three empty seats opposite her. "Take a seat and let's begin." She was setting a quick pace for the inquest. "Counselor," she said to Lydia, "may we get you tea or coffee?"

"Thank you, just a glass of water would be fine."

"Tyler …" she addressed the ADA as a butler. He noticed she made no beverage offer to Ben Benson.

Tyler knew the circumstances surrounding the morning's inquest and actually admired Chief Benson for the way he had resolved the kidnapping. He thought Ben was courageous and should be given a medal and not an inquiry. But he knew the DA had it in for him, some past history.

"May I get you something, Chief," he asked Big Ben, purposefully using his formal title and irking his boss.

"Black coffee would be good, Tyler."

Tanya Chisholm would have scowled at both of them if she wanted to admit their little interplay had affected her. Luckily MacLaren entered the office and she could scowl at him. "You're late, Lieutenant."

"Good morning to you too, Tanya." He had walked over from his office on the other side of the building with his prized *Tampa Bay Devil Rays* coffee mug – with the old logo before they had to drop the word "Devil". He nodded to all the participants and took a seat next to Lydia.

"Okay, let's get to it," DA Tanya Chisholm began in her typical no-nonsense manner. She opened her file on the iPad propped before her.

Once Tyler had delivered the drinks, she held a hand, palm up, over her shoulder and said, "Tyler…" Obediently he placed a small recording device into it, which she snapped on and positioned in the center of the table. Methodically she dictated the date, time and place, the names and titles of all persons present and then outlined the purpose for the joint District Attorney/Coroner's Inquest.

"Chief Benjamin J. Benson, you are being charged with…"

"Ahem." Attorney Lydia Lawrence cleared her throat.

"Excuse me," Tanya said and rephrased, "You are being *interviewed* concerning the cause of death of an unidentified person in Sarasota County, a probable suspect of the kidnapping of your wife, Carlene Heath Benson."

Ben didn't like the word probable.

DA Tanya Chisholm quickly outlined the specifics of the case and then said, "This conduct is unbecoming an officer of the law, a chief of police nonetheless, who was way out of line, way out of his jurisdiction and had no *official* involvement in this case, *who in fact*, acted on his own in the manner of a crazed vigilante, exhibiting a defiant and blatant disregard for the proper procedures of law enforcement."

"Grandstanding so soon, Ms. Chisholm?" Lydia Lawrence mocked.

"And furthermore," the DA glared at the attorney, "behavior of this sort is beyond reprimand and bordering on criminal. Perhaps charges of misconduct and police brutality should be considered."

Big Ben's face reddened and Lieutenant MacLaren thought he saw steam coming from his ears. Tanya Chisholm held her ground.

"Please everyone," the ME beseeched, "let's remember this is only an inquest not a trial."

Lydia Lawrence said, "We have a statement which Chief Benson is prepared to read." She looked at Ben who sat absolutely motionless.

"Fine," Tanya Chisholm barked. "But before he does, allow me to present my recommendations…"

"No," Big Ben said, a demonic grin spreading on his face, his eyes locked onto the DA. "This is my statement …" He slapped his hand onto the tape recorder and turned it off. "… Fuck you, Madame DA."

Everyone was stunned. The ADA turned his head and covered a guffaw with his hand.

Tanya was shocked as if she had been physically slapped in the face. "Mr. Benson," she raised her voice and ranted, "this type of behavior is absolutely unacceptable and exactly the type of …"

Ben raised the palm of his big right hand, stretched it across the table and held it directly in front of the DA's face. Tanya Chisholm flinched and lost her voice. Her eyes widened and the color drained from her face. She thought he was going to hit her.

Still holding his palm in place, Ben gently rose from his seat, then slowly turned and walked out of the room.

Everyone was dumbstruck.

"Well," MacLaren pushed his chair back, "I guess the inquest is concluded."

61

MacLaren's Office

Two minutes later MacLaren entered his office. "Smooth. Very smooth," he said. "You put on a good show, maybe you should take up acting as your new career, 'cuz it sure as hell ain't gonna be law enforcement."

Big Ben was sitting in a side chair with his feet up on the edge of MacLaren's desk. "You got anything stronger than coffee in here?"

The lieutenant sat in his swivel chair and opened a bottom drawer. He pulled out two shot glasses, wiped them with his tie and then unscrewed a pint bottle of Knob Creek. He filled them and passed one to Ben. "Try to sip it."

Ben downed it in one gulp and held the glass out for a refill. "I'll sip the next one."

The lieutenant refilled Ben's glass and took a small sip of his own. "What the fuck is the matter with you?"

"Awww shit, I dunno." Ben got up and paced.

A uniform came to the doorway. She was holding paperwork in her hand. MacLaren shook his head and motioned for her to shut the door.

Outside the building, palm trees swayed in the tropical breeze. Colorful birds rode thermals over the Gulf. Cars rode the causeway to sunny beaches on the nearby keys. Sailboats skimmed the bay and the sun made diamonds sparkle atop the rocking green waters. Paradise was in motion.

Inside, Big Ben was rubbing his temples and silently cussing himself. "I have a big mouth."

"No argument there."

"Carlene needed to get back to her security; the kids, house, job, friends, Bryce Corner and all I did was fall into a black hole. I can't seem to let this thing go. It keeps haunting me. It's like those vultures on the road that day. No matter how hard I tried to scare them off, they kept coming back."

MacLaren watched Ben circle the room for the hundredth time and then plop his big frame back into his seat.

"I gotta figure this out," Ben grumbled.

"Look, Ben, take some advice. Go see your wife. Patch things up. Get your life back in order."

"There's still someone out there. Still a threat."

"Or it could be over. We haven't had a single lead since you killed our only one six months ago."

"The woman's still out there."

"No, she's gone. Poof. I doubt she'll ever surface. She may even be dead. Whoever she worked for probably wasn't impressed with the performance. Whatever they wanted from your wife, they never got."

"But there's something still unfinished out there. I can't let it go."

"Let me deal with it."

"You're not any closer than you were six months ago and I know you've got more on your plate now."

"And the resources and manpower to handle it. Go away, Ben. Get it off your mind. R and R, my friend."

Ben got up and stared out the window. A squall line drifted off the western edge of Longboat, stretching south to Casey Key. Gray sheets of rain fell off the end of it and he figured Venice was under the downpour a half-hour away.

Lieutenant McLaren thought he had talked some sense into him until Ben said, "I want to see the video again."

"What video?"

"Where it all started. The museum. Hannah Hunt's murder."

"That would be unorthodox and you know it."

"Roll the tape, Lieutenant."

The security video from the Ca' d'Zan was in MacLaren's computer. He brought it up. Ben stood beside him. He'd relinquished his second bourbon untouched and had found a cup of hot coffee. Hannah Hunt Everett came into view from the left side and turned, facing the Dali. They were watching her back. The cameras were set to focus on the artwork and record in five second intervals. The perpetrator entered the same way as Hannah had and stood beside her to the right, placing his hand on the nape of her neck.

"Freeze it," Ben said.

They stared at the still shot that they'd viewed hours on end in the initial days after the murder. Nothing had changed.

"Dammit." They were still unable to see the weapon.

"Totally concealed in his hand," Ben said.

"Yup, Colt Derringer .22 Short. Brass stays in the chamber. Expertly placed shot too. She was dead before she hit the floor."

"Rewind it again."

MacLaren went to do so but hit fast-forward by mistake. "Whoops, wait a minute," he said and went to adjust it.

"No, hold it there." Big Ben leaned in closer and pointed at the monitor. "Can you enlarge it here?" It was the perp exiting the room. "Right there. The hat."

"What?"

Ben touched the screen. "Right here, below the wide brim."

"It's a shadow."

"Nope, look closer."

The lieutenant squinted. "It's a shadow."

"Nope, it's hair."

"Huh?"

"Long hair tucked into the hat."

He looked again. "Maybe. If it is I can't tell the color. The picture is too grainy at this resolution. Still looks like a shadow to me."

"Who do we know that has long hair?"

"Lots of people have long hair. Shit, half the derelicts in town do."

"This is no derelict, Lieutenant."

"A woman?"

"Perhaps, but think. In the initial phase of the investigation, who did we encounter that had long hair?"

MacLaren scratched his chin. "The guru?"

"Montgomery Fairmont."

"But he had a long white beard. And we met him *after* the killing."

"I know."

MacLaren looked at the beardless person in the video. "Nobody grows a beard like that in only a few days. It can't be him."

"Probably not," Ben said in frustration.

62

Group Octopus

Au Petit Hotel is in the heart of Vieux Quebec on Ruelle Ursulines, a narrow, quaint cobblestoned lane of lantern streetlights and pastel shops with worn store-fronts and colorful flower boxes. The charming little hotel began life a century-and-a-half ago as a boarding house for adventuresome French ladies plying their wares in the new Canada. Not too unlike its early residents, it is slender and alluring. Four thin stories of a dozen revamped rooms are positioned above a lovely old-world bistro. Off-the-beaten-path and very discreet, it is a perfect place for The Octopus Group to take a holiday.

Octopus occasionally breaks tradition and spends more than their usual monthly twenty-four hour meeting in one place - if it is an exciting place to be. This was one of those occasions. Ever conscious of security, they had reserved the entire hotel and were treating themselves to a three-day weekend. One day for their formal meeting and the next two for frivolities. They wished to partake of the many amenities of Old Quebec City: cultural, with the Theatre de Quebec and the Orchestre Symphonique; lively at the Jazz L'Empress or the Cigar Lounge at Chateau Maurice; intimate and quiet at the 'Boutes a Chansons; or alternative and discreet at the darkest clubs such as Grand Allee Est, hidden in the deepest shadows of Vieux Quebec where you could get whatever your libido desired, male or female or trans, for a lavishly exuberant price.

The Group was feeling good about their overall accomplishments. The direction they were engineering was well on course - except for one particularly annoying bump. Comforted in the dark-paneled bar, post entrees, with snifters of cognac and illegal Cuban cigars in hand, they confronted it.

"What do you mean we have no choice? We make the choices!"

"Listen. There is an American saying, 'Shit happens.' And that is exactly what is going on."

"And going on for far too long. We may have to cut our losses and re-think this plan. One way or the other Conrad Lawrence needs to be positioned in the American White House for the upcoming term. I say we devise a new approach."

"No, that would take too long. The cloning itself would take two to three years. We must gain the formulae and set things in motion now."

"Yet we are drifting further from our goal and all due to one setback. Let us 'stop beating around the bush' - another foolish saying - and take increased action."

"I agree. There is something astir with this bungling Big Ben fellow. He must be addressed or eliminated or both."

"Let's evaluate where we are. We know that Hannah Hunt was collaborating with Professor Fairmont. For unbeknownst reason she is now out of the picture. Carlene Benson and the ex-partner Elroy Leland are clearly unknowledgeable and we have not even ascertained if Professor Fairmont is alive or dead. We have only his notebooks which are rendered useless due to a seemingly unbreakable encryption. The key to success is to break that code. I believe Mr. Benson may be an asset for us."

"How so?"

"He has shown himself to be very tenacious and I think we can use that to our advantage. Whether he knows it or not, due to his relationship with Carlene Benson, familiarity with Elroy Leland and now these mangrove murder victims, he is closest to the code. In a coincidental way, he may be our best hope."

"Hmmm."

"Further, he is currently estranged from both his wife and his career, living alone and disheartened. This is a vulnerable time for him."

"Too bad Lydia Lawrence is not in our employ. She is close to him and from the looks of it she'd like to get closer."

"We cannot disrupt the Conrad Lawrence project. We need her to remain as an unknowing pawn for that plan. Besides, as you say, she is not in our employ."

"But we have someone who is."

"Ursula."

"Yes."

"She is our best asset."

"Would it not be too risky? Two reasons: first, Benson is the one who beat her husband to death. Do you not think revenge will hinder her mission?"

"The woman has no heart. She is the coldest person I have ever met. She exists without emotions. Her relationship with LeBeau was purely a business transaction. Money is her one and only aphrodisiac. She will perform ruthlessly as always."

"Then, secondly, there is a recognition factor. Ursula was recognized at the melee in Florida by Carlene Benson and perhaps by Ben Benson also."

"Not to worry. She is a master of disguise and a consummate actress. There is every confidence she will pull it off."

"Perhaps, but she must be watched very closely. If she cannot deliver soon, we must move on without her."

"Then I propose we let her loose on this Big Ben fellow and see what she can net us. Time is marching on. The presidential election is now only three-and-a-half years away and we need to set things in motion quickly."

"Agreed?"

They all acknowledged in the affirmative.

"Any further discussion?"

There was not.

They adjourned.

Night life awaited.

63

Georgia

Big Ben unlatched the long wooden shutter suspended above the bar, eased it down and attached twin padlocks, one to each end, securing the Tiki bar at Gramps Ramp for the night. The restaurant occupied the front of the ramshackle building on the roadside. That always closed at ten. The deck bar on the riverside stayed open 'til midnight. It had been a slow night and Ben had been by himself for the last hour accompanied only by the breeze roaming in from the prairie beyond the thin, blue river.

He fired up the Harley and eased into the night, the distinctive thundering of the pipes the only sound on the desolate county road. Blinking red hazard lights appeared in about a mile. As his headlight washed over the car pulled off to the gravel shoulder he saw a tall, thin man standing in the middle of the road waving his arms. Ben throttled down and glided to a stop before the car. He left the headlight on, aimed at the man. His cop eyes scanned the embankments and checked his mirrors. He had been forced to surrender his service weapon months ago when he'd been suspended, but was glad he had held onto his personal weapon. He felt the weight of his .38 S&W in his cargo pocket.

"Thank you. Thank you so much for stopping." The figure approached.

Ben was idling in first gear with the clutch in and his hand on the throttle. His feet were firmly planted on the pavement. He was prepared for a quick getaway if someone jumped at him.

"Stop there," he shouted above the idling bike. The figure obeyed and Ben held the high beams on it. "What seems to be the trouble?"

With the high beams he could see that the figure was a woman. Tall, slender and bald. White shorts, white Crocks and a rose polo top that held the evidence of her womanhood. She had a hand in front of her in an apologetic gesture. "I'm sorry, I didn't mean to startle you, but I'm stuck. I've been here for twenty minutes and you're the first one to come by."

Ben noticed more things about her. She spoke with a southern accent. Carolinas or Georgia, but her voice was shaky. Her head wasn't bald as first assumed, but rather short, fuzzy-like, only a quarter of an inch long. Blonde or white, difficult to tell in the thin light. Her unexposed hand was curled at her side and he recognized the object in it. She was scared and the pepper spray was more frightening than consoling to her. A woman alone, broke down on a dark night on an unfamiliar road.

She continued, "I haven't been able to get cellphone reception."

Ben shut the bike off. A dead silence permeated the air. He lowered the kickstand and got off the bike, leaving the light aimed at the car. He approached cautiously. The woman backed away.

"You won't get any reception out here," he said. The car was a Mercedes. Georgia plates. Driver's door open, hood up, flashers going.

"It just stopped," she said. "I was going along listening to my music and it just stopped."

"What did you notice?"

"Notice?"

"Did the check engine light come on? Did the car shake? Anything?"

"No, it was like someone turned the key off. Then the steering got hard and I pulled off the road."

Ben said, "Why don't you get in and give it a try." She looked leery. "Go ahead, I'll stand back."

He moved away from the car, alert to the roadside. She got in and closed the door. When she turned the key, nothing happened. Ben pulled on the door handle and the woman arched back in a defensive manner and raised the pepper spray.

"Listen, I know you're afraid, but remember, you're the one who flagged me down. If you'd rather, I can leave you here and when I get to reception in about ten minutes I can call for help."

His voice must have seemed honest enough to calm her. She relaxed. The pepper spray went into her pocket.

"I'm a cop." He realized he should have said retired or ex or something else, but it came out as it did naturally. "I bartend part-time down the road. I could give you a lift back there and we could use the bar phone to call a tow truck. Do you have triple-A?"

"Yes, but ... you don't think it's flooded or something? Maybe if I give it a few more minutes?"

"It's not turning over. I think it's electrical. It'll probably have to be towed." Ben looked both ways on the road. Darkness was at both ends. "Where were you headed?" He knew she had out-of-state plates. "Do you have friends out this way?"

The woman answered shyly, "No, I'm ..." she stopped, as if thinking of what to say to this big stranger on a motorcycle out in the middle of nowhere. "... I'm on my way to Miami and I got off the interstate awhile back for a rest room and a coffee and then I think I got disoriented and went the wrong way. I thought this road was Alligator Alley, but by the time I realized I was getting lost, my GPS wouldn't work and then the car slowed down and then ... well, here I am, I guess."

"Well, you're about fifty miles north of the Alley, and there isn't much out this way for about a hundred miles."

Big Ben swung the door open. "Let me give it try. She vacated the seat and stood leaning against the open door. Ben got into the car and turned the key. Nothing. He beeped the horn. It worked and the lights were still bright. He was thinking it might be the car's computer. "She's not going to start."

"Ugh." She ran her hands over her fuzzy head in reminiscence of longer hair. "I knew this was a lame idea. I always hated driving at night."

Ben tried the key one more time. Nothing. He moved to get out.

"Would you hand me my purse please?"

He lifted it from the passenger seat and got out.

"Thank you."

She dug into it. Ben thought she was looking for a cigarette but instead retrieved a pack of gum.

"Would you like one?"

"No thanks."

She popped a stick of gum into her mouth and set her purse on the rooftop. She chewed and looked around at the surroundings. "Well, I guess my choices are limited."

"Look, if you're unsure, you could lock yourself in the car and wait for the next person to come by, but it's not too safe for a lady alone on this road, or anyone for that matter."

"No, no. I don't want to wait here and I do really appreciate you stopping." She was trying to be brave with the gum-chewing, but it wasn't working. She took it out of her mouth and flung it into the night.

"Then of course there are the gators …" Ben smiled.

"Ohmygod, I didn't even think about that."

"Not to mention the wild boars and the bobcats."

"Okay, I get your point." The woman's lips moved into something between a smile and a pout. "I'm a little afraid …"

"I'm not going to rape and murder you." The comment was blunt enough that it broke the ice and they both laughed in relief.

Ben spoke first, "Have you ridden on a motorcycle before?"

"Yes, my husband has … had a Harley."

64

Stranded

"Remember that plane crash at O'Hare last year?" Ben didn't need to answer her. She was into her second Chardonnay and beginning to chill out from her roadside mishap. "My husband was one of the two hundred and twenty two." She twirled the glass by its stem in a slow circle on the bar top. Her eyes dry and focused on the night moisture clinging like a faded memory to the polished teak bar.

"I buried my husband and started chemo the same week," she raised her glass to her lips and finished off the wine.

Without asking he replenished her glass.

"At first I noticed there was more hair in my brush. I would sit at my vanity every night and do my usual one hundred strokes. Then the next morning there was more. More than usual. They told me to expect the hair loss. But you hope they're wrong, hope you're the exception. Then as the days wear along, and the hair keeps falling out, you reluctantly give in. The female vanity takes over and rather than hiding beneath a cheap wig I decided to woman-up and shave it off. Wear my chemo-coiffure as a statement. Hey, I'm bald and I'm proud."

They had left the Mercedes' flashers on and ridden the Harley back to Gramps. Ben had opened up the deck bar. She sat on a stool. He was on the bar side. "Wine? Martini? Beer?"

"I'd love a glass of Chardonnay." She brushed her fingers through her non-existent hair again. Her back was against the bar top, her gaze on the silent river, illuminated by underwater flood lights beneath the dock. "It's pretty here." She shook her head; her imaginary hair flowed in the breeze behind her. "I've had an interesting day."

Ben uncorked a bottle of Kendall Jackson Vintage Reserve. He poured it just above halfway and handed it to her. Then he grabbed a Diet Coke for himself.

"Aren't you going to have one?"

"Don't drink when I ride." He raised his glass and said, "To midnight rescues." They clinked glasses and sipped.

The tow truck was on its way.

"Georgia," she said.

"Yeah, I saw your plate."

She snickered. "My name. My name is Georgia."

"Georgia from Georgia?"

"Cute, eh? My parents had a warped sense of humor."

"Ben. Some call me Big Ben."

"Like the clock beside Parliament, or because of your stature?"

"Both I guess. Old football name."

"Pro?"

"Almost. Had a contract with the Patriots 'til my knee blew out." Ben squirted more Diet Coke into his glass from the soda gun.

Georgia sipped her wine and put the glass on the bar and bowed her head, massaging the back of her neck. "I can't believe how foolish I am."

He waited.

The air was warm, as summer would be on a quiet night in Southern Florida. The nocturnal sounds wafting along the dark and invisible breeze suggested an impervious distrust of human intermingling. The mangrove night thought it had been left alone. A flat-bed carrying the Mercedes pulled in and circled the back parking lot beneath the halogen lights. The lettering on the side said CHUCK'S TRUCK. Below that in fancy red cursive against the white door read, *You Holler and I'll Haul'er*. Ben knew Chuck as a local afternoon customer at the bar.

Chuck shut his truck down and approached them. He was way over three-hundred pounds, most of it hanging over his belt. He'd been in bed when Ben had called him. It was now an hour after closing time. Big Ben had a cold beer ready for him when he stepped onto the deck.

"Thanks Chuck." Ben handed him his beer. Chuck took a long swig, wiped the froth from his beard, burped and said, "Much obliged."

"This is Georgia, the lady in distress."

"Pleasure to meet you ma'am," he nodded and grasped the bill of his cap even though he'd forgotten to put it on.

"Likewise," she responded.

"What do you think?" Ben asked.

"Welp, I put the scan tool to it and got a real interesting code. Best as I can tell, there's a substantial problem in the fuel injectors. Not uncommon for a Benz. How old is that car ma'am?"

"Um, I just bought it brand new a month ago." Georgia gave Ben a worried look.

"Hmmm," Chuck surmised.

"Is it something you can do at your garage, Chuck?" Ben asked.

"Nope." He took another long draw and burped again. "Got to go to the dealer."

"And the nearest Mercedes dealer ?..."

"... is in Naples." He finished the beer and handed Ben the empty glass.

Ben pulled him another draft.

Georgia said, "So, what are you saying?"

"Welp, if it's what I think it is, dealer ain't gonna have parts for it yet. Too new. 'Spect it's a factory thing. May be a recall on it, but you're probably one of the first ones to have a problem. Usually when new cars have ..." Ben knew Chuck as a long-winded talker from his daily visits to the bar. He broke in, "How long will it take to fix it?"

Chuck went to lift his cap up, realized again he wasn't wearing one and scratched his head. Ben had never seen him without a cap before.

"Welp, first off, it's gotta get down to Naples Mercedes, and I ain't gonna do that in the dead of night. Tomorrow mornin'd be as soon as I could. Then if you're lucky they'd have parts for it but I doubt it. That's a new eco-green motor for them and I'd bet they'll have to send to Germany to get parts. And it's the weekend coming up and their service department's closed all of that."

"So are you saying I'm stranded?"

"Yes ma'am. For a few days at least. Now I don't know their policy but they should give you a loaner car and I'm sure you'll be covered under warranty for the work and the towing."

Georgia gave Big Ben a forlorn look. "What do I do now?"

65

Gunshots

The gunshots woke him. Two. Shotgun. Ben grabbed his .38 and ran outside barefooted in his boxers. It was a very dark night, but he saw a figure running in from the beach and another one close behind. They scrambled through the dark foliage towards the narrow entrance to Two Can Key on the northern side.

"Halt!" Ben yelled. "This is the police. I will shoot." To emphasize this he fired a round into the dirt beside him. The figures bolted further into the darkness.

"Don't bother," she said. "I've scared them away. The bastards." Winnie stood at his side holding onto a double barrel shotgun. She was stark naked. "Poachers. They come out here to get the eggs." She was talking about sea turtles.

Big Ben glanced at her then looked away, shaking his head. "Are you always naked?"

"I swim naked and I sleep naked." She poked him with her elbow, "and I do other things naked too." She laughed.

They heard a vehicle start up and the crunching sound of tires spinning away on the crushed shell road. "Well, those two won't be back," Winnie said proudly. "Get dressed and come on over. I'll put some coffee on."

"What time is it?" Ben asked.

"Close to sunrise, it's the perfect time to ..." Winnie saw the woman standing on Ben's porch with a blanket wrapped around her. "Oh, never mind. I didn't realize you had company."

"It's not what you think. Start the coffee, I'll be right over."

Ben returned to his cottage.

"Were those gunshots?" Georgia asked.

"Yeah. Poachers. They're gone now."

"Who is that woman?"

"My crazy landlady."

"Was she ...?"

"Yeah, naked and holding a shotgun. She's a bit eccentric."

"Is everything all right?"

"Everything's fine. Listen, why don't you go back to sleep. I'm going to throw some clothes on and go over and have a cup of coffee with her."

"Okay," she yawned. "I think I will."

Dawn was scratching on the eastern windows of Winnie's cottage as they sat at the kitchen counter with their coffees. Winnie had a joint smoldering in an ashtray.

"Know anything about turtles?"

"Um, I had a couple when I was a kid," Ben replied. "Little green ones. They lived in a plastic bowl with a palm tree in the middle. They died though."

"Store bought." She took a hit. "I'm talking about sea turtles, Loggerheads. When I was a little girl I'd come out here with my grandfather during nesting season. We'd sit quietly late at night and wait for the females to come out of the ocean. They crawl onto the beach and dig holes to lay their eggs then cover them with sand. A couple months later the hatchlings crawl back to their ocean following the light of the moon and stars."

"I've seen their tracks in the sand. Pretty neat."

Another hit. "Only one in a thousand makes it into the safety of the seaweed. Sharks think they're pretty tasty and even before they can get to the perils of the sea, there's birds and raccoons and such, but that's nature. The ones I hate the most are the fucking poachers. Those are the ones that have put them on the endangered list."

"Isn't it against the law to hunt turtles?"

"Hell yes. But you can still buy tortoise shell sunglasses can't you? And turtle oil is still used in skin moisturizers. Then there are those sons-a-bitches like those guys tonight who hunt the eggs to eat."

Winnie tried for another toke of marijuana but it was out. She decided not to relight it and placed it back onto the ashtray. "Luckily there are turtle watch groups who discourage people from disturbing the nests."

"Do they all carry shotguns?"

Winnie just smiled at him. "I heard them scraping the sand and I jumped up and fired a couple rounds from the deck."

"At them?"

"Maybe."

Sunlight stretched into the room and spread across Ben's back. Winnie squinted against it and relighted the joint. By now she knew it was fruitless to offer it to Big Ben. But she was feeling good.

"So?"

"So, what?" she said.

"So, are you going to ask me about her or what?"

"None of my business."

Ben let out a hearty laugh. "There's nothing going on." Ben told Winnie the story and then added, "I called a couple hotels for her but the town is booked up for the regatta this weekend. And with me flying up to New England for a few days, I was hoping you wouldn't mind if she house sat. Her car will probably be fixed by the time I'm back and she'll be on her way."

"Fine with me."

"Don't give me that look."

"What look?"

"I offered her the bedroom but she insisted on the couch. That's all there is to it. Nothing happened."

"Like I said, none of my business."

Winnie got up to replenish their cups. She reverted to her prior conversation. "I'm working with some people who, in lieu of shooting the poachers and beach developers, are trying new ways to expand the turtle population."

Ben thought, some people? Then said, "And how would you do that?"

Winnie smirked. "We're going to clone them."

There was that cloning word again. "Tell me about it."

"Not now. It's time for my morning swim." She went into her bedroom. "You up for it?"

"No thanks, but I'd better get out of here before you take your clothes off again."

"Chicken."

As Ben got to the door he heard her yell,"Hey, how you getting to the airport?"

"I was going to take a cab."

"You want a ride?"

"I was hoping you'd say that."

"What time's your flight?"

"Noon."

"Okay, come on over at ten-thirty."

"Thanks, Winnie. You're the best."

"I know."

66

Departure

Ben smelled the bacon halfway to the cottage. "Wow, you're up?"

"Something about shotgun blasts at dawn that disrupts my sleep pattern."

"Welcome to South Florida."

"You all coffee'd out?"

"Never enough coffee."

"Nor beer apparently." Georgia poured Ben a fresh cup. "Your fridge has a limited inventory. Beer, four eggs, more beer, six pieces of bacon and a very moldy half-sandwich of, I think, tuna fish."

"So that's where that was."

"Next time you should wrap it in Saran Wrap."

"What's that?"

Georgia was already showered and dressed. She set two plates on the short coffee table in front of the couch. "I would have prepared home fries and toast and jelly, but, you know …"

"Yeah, that damn maid just can't seem to find a supermarket lately," he smiled. "Thanks, this is nice."

"Your landlady okay?"

"Oh yeah. Maybe a little disgruntled that she didn't kill anybody this morning, but she'll get over it."

"This is a cute place. How'd you come by it?"

Ben told her the story, including the reason he was there.

"That's why you're heading to Boston today? To patch up your marriage?"

"Well, that's the intent. I don't know how well I'll do."

He finished off his plate and poured more coffee for them both. "I'm sorry for your misfortune and your loss," he said to her.

Georgia dabbed her lips with a napkin and sat back into the cushions of the couch. "Doctors say the cancer is in remission. Hair's growing in and I'm putting my life back together. As for my husband, it was a shock. He was a good man and we had a good life together. It would have been nice to have children, but we couldn't. Do you have any?"

"Yes. Two teenagers. A boy and a girl."

"Must be hard for them."

"Oh, I don't know. They're too involved with their friends and teenage stuff to wonder about their crony old parents. Besides, they think I'm on a case."

"I guess we all go through our own trials. I hope you are successful back home. You seem like a nice guy."

Ben didn't know what to say to that so he just said, "Thanks."

At ten-thirty Ben slung his luggage into the back of Winnie's jeep and introduced the two ladies. Georgia was riding with them to the airport to pick up her rental car, courtesy of Mercedes Benz. When they pulled up to the terminal at SRQ, Georgia thanked Winnie for the ride, said good-bye to Big Ben and headed to the rental counter. Winnie leaned over and gave Ben a kiss on the cheek.

"What's that for?" he asked.

"Luck."

He smiled at her then grabbed his bag and walked towards the sliding doors.

"Hey," she said. "Don't be a jerk."

"Too late," he laughed.

67

Ebenezer's

The Publick House Historic Inn is a landmark destination located in Sturbridge, Massachusetts. It was built by Colonel Ebenezer Crafts in 1771 along the old Boston Post Road - originally a system of mail routes between Boston and New York City established by postmaster general Ben Franklin. On the common, just across the heavily rutted road, the colonel had trained local Minutemen to fight against the encroaching British troops. History states that George Washington did indeed sleep there.

The Bed & Breakfast-style main house has a dining room with a majestic open-hearth fireplace joined by a host of smaller function rooms and a huge converted barn perfect for weddings and other grand festivities. Adjacent to the barn, located in the old rustic stables, is Ebenezer's Tavern, offering a lighter pub fare and a relaxed, casual feel. This was one of Carlene and Ben's favorite restaurants. Carlene had chosen it for their rendezvous.

Ben's flight had gotten him into Logan at four-thirty p.m. Another hour and a half in bottle-neck traffic got him to Sturbridge at six. He was meeting Carlene at seven.

"Hey, Big Ben! How the hell are ya?" Don Juan extended his hand across the bar.

"Good. How have you been?"

"Great. Haven't seen you in a dog's age. IPA?"

"Yeah, thanks." Ben settled onto a bar stool.

Don Juan, with his period garb and seasoned ponytail exemplified the look of the founding colonists and had been bartending there – as he liked to say – "Since Sam Adams, Johnny Hancock and I were drafting the Declaration of Independence right here at the bar." He and Ben had struck up a kindred friendship several years back.

Don Juan slid a coaster in front of him and put a frothy pint of beer on it. "Heard you moved down to Florida."

"Well not exactly."

"What's up?"

Ben took a healthy swig of the local pale ale. "I'm meeting Carlene here for dinner."

Don Juan leaned toward Ben and lowered his voice, "Yeah, I heard you guys were kinda split up. Sorry."

"Well, I'm hoping to resolve that."

"Good man. I hope you do. I hate when my favorite couples split up. You still a gumshoe?"

"On the sly, but you're not going to believe what I'm doing now."

"Okay, lay it on me."

"I'm following in your footsteps, I'm a bartender."

"Get the fuck out." And they high-fived each other.

Ben glossed over the story as carefully as he could to bring his bartending compadre up to date.

"Wow, that's an interesting story. If you need me to play Watson, I'll shit-can this gig and move down in a heartbeat. Be back." He moved off to tend to the servers' drink orders.

Ben sat quietly by himself. He was only going to have one beer to calm down from the flight and to steel himself for the upcoming conversation with his wife. He thought of Winnie's parting comment and laughed. *Don't be a jerk*. He hoped he could adhere to that advice.

She walked in.

"Hi." She was stunning. Ben hadn't seen his wife in five months. If his knees weren't already weakened from his football days, they would be now. Summer was a beautiful time in New England and Carlene fit exceptionally well in it. Ben noticed a fresh exuberance about her, his wife, the lady he had given his heart to, the girl he was still very much in love with. *God*, he inhaled her perfume, *she smells fucking delicious.*

He pulled the chair out for her and gave her a peck on the cheek. "It's great to see you, Sugarplum."

Carlene settled in and squeezed his arm. "You too. You look well."

"Been working out lately."

"And not eating right, I'll bet. You've lost weight."

He wanted to say you too, but held off.

"Hi, Carlene," Don Juan said. "What can I get'cha?"

"Oh, I guess a glass of Malbec, please."

"Sure thing."

"You're early," Ben said to his wife.

"I saw that your flight got in on time and I knew you'd drive right here. Didn't want you to have too many beers before I got here."

"I wasn't planning to."

"You never do."

The bartender placed her wine and left them to their private conversation.

"How are the kids?" he asked.

"Fine, they said to say hi."

"I was thinking I'd take them fishing tomorrow."

"Brenton's band has a two day gig in the Berkshires and Penny is camping with Meghan and her family on the Cape."

"Oh." Ben was disappointed. But then he wondered if Carlene had set it up that way so they'd have the time together. "How's Uncle Bob doing?"

"You know Ben, I love Uncle Bob, but he's gotten to be a cranky old man. I don't think I need him guarding the house anymore." She said *guarding* like it was a bad word.

"I like knowing he's there. He may be a cranky old man, but he's a cranky old man with a gun. The retired chief of police don't forget."

"How could I? He reminds me daily that he was your predecessor."

"He needs to be there, Lene. There's still a threat out there."

"Ohmygod, Ben. It's been six months. If something was going to happen, it would have happened by now."

"Carlene ..."

This was a bone of contention between them.

"Let's get a table," she said.

68

Check Out

They got seated at their favorite table in the back and slipped comfortably into twin wing-back chairs and idle conversation. A server came over.

"Hi, my name is Paula and I'll be your server tonight. May I get you another cocktail?"

Carlene ordered another wine and Ben asked for a diet coke.

Paula recited the dinner specials then asked if they'd like to start with an appetizer.

"Do you still offer the basket of fresh-cut potato chips?" Carlene asked.

"Yes, can I bring you one?"

Carlene raised her eyebrows to Ben. "Please," he said.

The room was dimly lit. Light jazz spread over the tables and swayed the candlelight. Carlene looked at her husband in the amber glow of the evening. She missed him.

"How are you doing?"

"Oh, okay."

"I'm sorry about the inquest."

"Yeah, well."

The server came with their drinks. Ben handed her his empty pint glass and reached for his Diet Coke.

"Paula," Carlene said, "could you bring this big guy another IPA?"

"Sure."

Carlene took a sip of her red wine. "You don't have to impress me by abstaining from a couple of beers, Ben. Relax, just be yourself."

The beer came and he said, "Thanks." They clinked glasses and smiled at each other. Ben felt hopeful.

"Like your new career?"

"Bartending?" He laughed. "Can you believe it?"

"Living on the beach and cruising on a Harley? You should be happy. Life is not always about crime."

Shit, he thought. Now she's starting to sound like Winnie.

"How's therapy going?"

"Fine. I'm doing better."

The chips arrived and they sat awkwardly swirling them in the accompanying ranch dressing.

"You know I ..."

"I can't seem ..."

They spoke at the same moment. It made them laugh. Carlene reached her hand across the table. "I have really missed you, you know."

"I miss you every day and every night," he squeezed her hand. "You think I'm doing okay down there, but I'm not. I miss everything here and at the same time I'm glad to be away from it. Can you understand that?"

Carlene took a slow sip of her red wine.

The server returned and Carlene ordered a cup of New England clam chowder and the Yankee pot roast. Ben got a chowder and the hallmark Thanksgiving turkey dinner that was offered every night of the year.

The soothing ambiance of the old tavern spread over them.

"Lene, come back with me. Come back and let's spend some time together on the beach. It's beautiful there, you'd really like it. We could just hang out and do nothing. Get back to being us again. I miss you, baby. I miss us."

Carlene saw the server and made a motion indicating another round.

"Is it over?" she asked.

"Is what over?"

"The case."

Ben sat back and twisted his beer glass on its coaster. "You're still on it aren't you?"

He took a swig. "I've got some suspicions."

"And what are you going to do with them, Ben?"

Their new round arrived.

Carlene took a healthy taste of her red wine. "This isn't going to end."

"Yes. It will end. I will end it."

Paula arrived with the chowders and a bread basket. They unrolled their set-ups and laid the napkins across their laps. Ben and his wife leaned into the steaming pewter bowls and partook of the thick creamy chowder. It was good, but there was more than the taste and pleasant aroma wafting over them.

He knew the whole experience she had gone through was something she was overcoming with the therapy. And he knew that she knew he couldn't overcome it without a final and absolute resolve. And that was the split, the wedge between them. She could overcome it mentally. Ben had to overcome it physically, head on. So, she knew he really wasn't doing any better than before. His fists were still pounding.

As if he was reading her mind, Ben said, "Y'know, Lene, I don't care about any of that shit. All I care about is you and me and the kids. I want to get back together and be a family again."

"That'd be nice if it were true. But I know you. You are still focused on that case. And you can't let it go, even if you wanted to."

"I want to. I will let it go, for us."

"Say that again, with meaning."

Ben hesitated and that was all Carlene needed. "I'm sorry, Ben. I can't do this yet. I can't regress. You have to do what you have to do and so do I." She got up from the table and placed her hand on his shoulder. "I love you. Please take that with you."

And she left him there, in the corner of the restaurant in the wing-back chair gazing at the flickering candlelight.

After a few minutes the server came and cleared the soup crocks and placed the entrees on the table. "Shall I leave the cover on the lady's dinner?" she asked, assuming the lady had gone to the rest room.

"No thanks, Paula. I'll take a check at the bar."

Ben ordered Elijah Craig 18-year-old bourbon on the rocks and nursed it while Don Juan called the front desk to arrange a room for him. He was cool, didn't ask any questions and shook Ben's hand when he finished the bourbon and said good-night.

The night had clouded and a light summer rain was falling. Ben was walking the meadow with the crickets on the pathway and the bull frogs out along the water's edge. He was struggling with his feelings. He swung back and forth between driving over to their house in Bryce Corner, taking Carlene in his arms and bringing them back together again, or, going back into the tavern and getting shit-faced.

But he was afraid. Afraid she wouldn't accept his embrace. Because he knew she was right. He couldn't let it go. That was his fucked-up make-up. Ego or flaw. Or both. One way or the other he knew he had to deal with it in his own way. Ben still believed he could keep the marriage together. He really loved his wife and knew she still believed in him, in them. Right?

69
Invite

"How'd it go?"
"Don't ask."
"That bad, huh?"
"I should have heeded your advice."

They were driving back to Two Can Key from the airport. Winnie at the wheel and a glum Ben riding shotgun.

"Well, things happen or don't for a reason."

When they pulled up to the cottages, Ben said, "Our stranded guest still with us?"

"Haven't seen her since we dropped her at the airport car rental the other day." Winnie parked in her spot.

Ben thanked her for the ride, unloaded his gear and went over to his beach shack. There was a note on the counter:

> Thanks for the rescue and hospitality. The dealer in Naples says my car will be ready in a few days so I decided to visit there. I took the liberty of augmenting your beer collection in the fridge. Hope the food doesn't take up too much space.

> *Thank you again. I'm extending a dinner invitation. Give me a call if you'd like to accept. Or, now that you actually have provisions, I could cook for you.*
>
> *Georgia (941-555-1953)*
> *P.S. Hope everything went well up north.*

Well, he was glad she was gone. He needed to be alone. He always put a better plan together in solitude. Ben needed to put an end to the torment affecting him and Carlene, one way or the other. Maybe, when it was done, he could convince her to relocate to Florida. Or, if she was reluctant, maybe he could return to New England and hang a shingle: *Ben Benson Private Investigations*.

He was hungry. There was bread on the counter and deli meat in the fridge. Ben made a sandwich and stood eating it at the counter. He was trying to formulate a plan but was thinking instead how nice a home cooked meal would be.

After the sandwich Ben took a nap and then got ready for work at Gramps Ramp. He fired up the Harley and rode down the shell road.

70

Bump

"Asshole." Ben swore.

The high beams stabbed at him from the handlebar mirrors. Ben twisted the throttle and sped into the night. Or actually, the early morning. He'd just closed the bar and the road back to Sarasota was dark and barren past midnight. The car behind him matched his new speed.

"What the fuck?!" He brought the Fat Boy up to eighty, pulling away from the moron who couldn't find the high beam switch.

It didn't work. He brought it to ninety. Again the vehicle raced up behind him and settled into the new speed with just enough distance to focus the blaring lights in the center of Ben's mirrors.

Ben thought of *Duel*, that movie with Dennis Weaver terrorized by the eighteen-wheeler. Wasn't that Spielberg's first? He brought it up to a hundred and held the throttle open. His pursuer faded behind him. One-ten, the Harley gained some distance. Luckily the road was dead straight, the night was clear and dry and all Ben had to worry about was a gator crawling across his path.

The lights grew larger. "You've got to be kidding me."

It happened fast. He was hit from behind with such force that he was immediately airborne. He'd been hard-tackled before and sent flipping and tumbling through the air, but this time he knew he was flailing out of control. And that was all he'd remember for a while.

Something was beeping next to Ben's left ear. His head throbbed. A television was blaring. Someone was squeezing his right arm. A figure stood at the foot of his bed. MacLaren came slowly into focus.
"How you doing, pal?"
"How do I look?"
"Seen you look better."
Ben surveyed his surroundings. "Where am I?"
"Lakewood Ranch Medical Center. You've been out cold all night. They ran some tests, x-rays and stuff. Think you're good."
The nurse relieved the blood pressure cuff. "One twenty-two over eighty. Not bad, considering." She held his wrist and timed his pulse with her watch. She seemed pleased with the results. "I think you're going to make it, handsome." The nurse adjusted the IV drip and silenced the beeping monitor.
"When can I get out of here?"
"Soon as the doctor gives the okay. No broken bones, only a mild concussion, internals and vitals are okay, so, I imagine he'll let you go this afternoon." She winked at MacLaren, "He'll be fine," and left the room.
"Do me a favor, shut that TV off."
The lieutenant complied. The room got quiet.
"Good thing you had a helmet on. But you're gonna need a new one. Yours has a nice big split in it."
"Probably why my head hurts."
"Do you remember what happened?"
"Someone rammed me from behind."
"On purpose?"
"On purpose. Who found me?"
"Anonymous call. You sailed about twenty yards into the prairie."
"How's the bike?"

"Pretty banged up. Chief Ray picked it up and brought it back to his place."

Ben elevated the bed into a higher sitting position.

"How do you feel?"

"Actually, not bad. I think I've survived worse tackles." He stretched his arms, rolled his shoulders and moved his legs. "Except for the knee, as always."

MacLaren moved to the side of the bed. "Crazy people out that way. Especially at night. Lot of rednecks."

"Nope. Wasn't rednecks. Wasn't random. Intentional."

"Who, then?"

"Unfortunately, your guess is as good as mine. But I do have a theory."

"Yeah?"

"It wasn't a hard hit. Not directly from behind. I remember the headlights leaving the mirrors, he moved to the left as if he was going to pass me and then swung in and bumped me from the rear quarter. At that angle I was catapulted away from the asphalt and into the softer ground of the shoulder."

"The bump was a love tap?"

"Didn't want to kill me, just a warning. I think this episode is connected to Hannah Hunt and the mangrove murders."

"Oh, come on. How could you possibly know that?"

"Instinct."

MacLaren rubbed his chin and thought about that. He had a hard time connecting the dots. Then he said, "What's up with this chick I hear you rescued?"

"Nothing's up. Stranded motorist that I gave a hand to."

"And your abode." MacLaren smirked.

Ben grumbled and adjusted his weight in the bed. "I'm going to solve this case."

"Great. Any idea how?"

"Nope, but I ain't gonna do it from here."

71
Knock Knock

She stood in the doorway with a stuffed animal hiding her face. "Knock, knock."

Ben and MacLaren looked at her and responded in unison, "Who's there?"

The fuzzy animal entered the room with the person behind it.

"Boo."

"What's this?"

"It's a teddy bear."

"I can tell that."

"Thought it might cheer you up."

Ben took it in his big hand and wiggled it at her, "I'm cheered."

Lydia took his hand and rubbed his forearm. "If you didn't want to take me for a ride you could have just said so. You didn't have to crash your bike." She smiled and kissed him lightly on the forehead.

MacLaren went and stood looking out the window.

The doctor came in. "You're a lucky man, Ben Benson. No major injuries. Although that bad knee of yours took another hit."

"What else is new," Ben grumbled.

"You'd do well to give it a little PT." He scribbled on his prescription pad. "Here's a script for a mild pain killer. You may have a headache for a day or two. If it persists beyond forty-eight hours stop back in and see us. Keep the knee on ice for a while." The doctor handed Ben a clipboard. "Just sign on the dotted line and you can get out of here."

Ben did so.

The doctor took the clipboard and said, "I'll send the nurse right in to unhook you." He patted the teddy bear and left.

A half hour later Ben squeezed into Lydia's BMW Z4 convertible. He groaned as he lifted his right leg into the car. MacLaren laughed and pushed the door shut for him. "Let's get together and talk, big guy."

"Let's."

"Soon." The lieutenant got into his unmarked and drove off.

Lydia had parked in the shade beneath a row of Queen Palms. The afternoon was sunny and hot. She started the car. "You want the top up?"

"Your car, you decide."

"I like driving with the top down and the A/C cranked."

"I like your style." Ben leaned back in his seat and rested his head against the seat back. He held the teddy bear in his lap.

"You okay?"

"Yeah, glad to be out of there."

"I'm glad you're alive." She placed her hand on his leg and gave it a squeeze. "Where to?"

"The beach shack. I'd like to shower and put on some fresh clothes."

"Okay."

While Ben was in the shower, Lydia took the liberty of searching for refreshment. She found a partial bottle of Kendall Jackson Chardonnay in the fridge, poured a glass and took a seat at the counter.

A few minutes later Ben came out of the bedroom in a short-sleeved tropical print shirt and khaki cargo shorts. He looked like

Jimmy Buffet – only bigger. His right knee was wrapped in an Ace bandage. He took a beer out of the fridge and sat next her.

"When I helped myself to the wine I noticed a change in your refrigerator."

"What's that?"

"There's food in there," she laughed. "Did you actually go shopping?"

"It's a long story," which he didn't want to get into.

"Well, I'm impressed." She sipped her wine and added, "I didn't know you liked wine."

"Always good to try something new." Ben felt a little embarrassed and uncomfortable and he wasn't sure why. He changed the subject. "I need to lease a car. How about you give me a ride to the dealership?"

"Only if afterwards we return here and I cook you a decent meal then tuck you in. You've had a harrowing experience and need a full tummy and a good night's rest. Deal?"

He gave her a blank stare.

Lydia raised her hand in a Girl Scout pledge, "I promise I'll leave right after dinner."

72
Another Hummer

"So, what are you going to do next?" Lydia was driving. Ben was thinking beneath his Tommy Bahama "Relax" hat, subconsciously petting the teddy bear in his lap.

"I've got a hunch."

"Care to tell me about it?"

"No."

"I'm your attorney. You know, as in attorney/client confidentiality? You can tell me anything."

"Not if you are aware that I'm going to commit an unlawful act."

She took her eyes off the road long enough to pull down her sunglasses and glare at him. "Ben, what the hell are you saying?"

"Listen, Lydia," he placed the bear on the console and turned towards her. "I'm going to do what I do best - play out my hunches. I've been mulling this case over for months and now it's getting very very personal. So, as a newly anointed free agent, ala the inquest, I feel more at liberty about the direction I have to take and the reasons for it."

"Ben, I have to say ..."

"Wait. Hear me out. I appreciate everything you've done for me. But I've gotta move fast, and free of encumbrances." She opened her mouth to rebuke him but Ben cut her off. "No, you're not an encumbrance. I just do better when I move alone. Listen, I think you need to focus on your new governor and your law practice and I need to delve deeper into this investigation."

"Okay, I won't pry and I won't get in your way, but there's something you need to do for me."

Ben lifted his eyebrows.

"Figure out why that dead man found in the mangroves looks so much like my father. Dad seems to be able to move on from it – and I'm sure being a busy new governor helps him to do that – but I am still spooked. So, don't forget, I'm on your side and I want answers too."

The Hummer dealership was on Jacaranda Boulevard in Venice. Ben had called ahead and alerted a salesperson to his desire.

Lydia pulled up to the showroom. "Another Hummer?"

Ben restrained a brash comeback.

"After totaling two I'm surprised they'd want to deal with you."

"Two?"

"The one you crashed at the quarry and the one you blew up last year at Marina Jack."

"Oh yeah, but if you remember correctly, *I* didn't blow it up."

"We're lucky we came out of that alive."

Lydia put the shifter in neutral and said, "We still on for dinner?"

"You bet." The idea of a home-cooked meal was still swirling in Ben's head, or more precisely his stomach.

"How long do you think you'll be?"

"Shouldn't take too long."

"Be nice to get back for sunset."

"See you in about an hour."

"Okay," her smile brightened. "You go get your car and I'll head back to Two Can Key and start cooking."

Ben struggled out of her sports car.

"Now I know why you want a bigger vehicle," she laughed. "I'm going to stop on the way to pick up a bottle of wine. Do you have a preference?"

"No, get what you like. I'll stick to beer."

"K. See you," and she raced off.

"Ah, Mr. Benson," the salesman held the door for him, "good to see you again. I've got the paperwork started. Come into my office."

Ben leased a black Hummer HX. He liked the vehicle for its ruggedness and the color for covertness. He was planning on doing some off road four-wheeling, not for pleasure, for surveillance.

"Maximum insurance coverage?" The salesman looked above his cheater glasses.

"Of course."

73

Paring

Lydia cruised into the paver parking lot of the upscale Promenade Publix on Tamiami Trail. She wasn't exactly sure what was in Ben's refrigerator so, to be on the safe side, she gathered some fresh organic vegetables, brown rice, a multi-grain baguette and a nice piece of seasoned Wild Alaskan Salmon. A chilled bottle of Kris Pinot Grigio completed her list.

Her ride over to Two Can Key was contemplative. She had an interest in this man - okay an infatuation - and knew that on more than one occasion he had straightforwardly expressed his desire to keep their relationship professional and platonic. He was still in love with his wife. She told herself to honor that tonight. *Dinner and conversation then go home Lydia.* She shouldn't even be doing this. Should have dropped him at the dealership and split. Who was that poet that lamented about affairs of the heart? *Ohmygod girl*, she said aloud, *get a grip!* Lydia smacked the steering wheel and shouted a nasty four-letter word into the wind.

Pulling up next to the Mercedes in Ben's driveway made her chuckle. So much for the Hummer, she thought, he must have changed his mind, or maybe they didn't have any he liked. Lydia grabbed the groceries and the wine and entered the cottage.

The first thing she noticed was the vegetables and paring knife on the cutting board atop the counter. Then the simmering pot on the stove. She heard movement in the bathroom and, putting down her parcels, said to Ben, "You started without me?"

She heard the toilet flush and a moment later Georgia walked into the kitchen. The two women shared an awkward moment. Lydia knew it wasn't Ben's wife, for she had met her before. This woman, dressed rather casually in denim short-shorts and a provocatively cinched cotton top, this Daisy Mae, appeared too comfortable and familiar with these surroundings.

"Hello," Georgia said. "Are you a friend of Ben's?" she asked as she went back to her work on the cutting board.

Lydia was perplexed and it showed. She didn't like the flippancy in this woman's voice. Gritting her teeth she responded, "I'm his attorney. Are you?"

"An Attorney?"

"No, a friend of Ben's."

"Why, yes."

Lydia couldn't help but notice the air of confidence and the manner in which she sauntered about the kitchen. This *Georgia* was certainly making herself at home, "May I ask what you are doing here?" Lydia said.

"Returning a favor. Ben was kind enough to take me in for a few days and I told him I'd cook dinner for us sometime." She grinned, "I'm surprising him."

Take her in for a few days?!

"Did you have an appointment?" Georgia lifted a stemmed glass of white wine to her lips. Ah, Lydia thought, that would account for the Chardonnay in the fridge.

"Appointment?"

"With Ben, you said you're his attorney, I thought ..."

Lydia could sense an arcane jealousy building within her like a quick fever. And when she saw the pre-set coffee table complete with tapers and fresh flowers - that did it.

"Here," she motioned to her groceries, "add these to your menu. Hope you like Pinot Grigio."

Georgia, speaking to her back, said in a deliberate singsong voice, "I'll tell Ben you stopped by."

Lydia wanted so much to say Fuck You, but she bit it back and instead turned, snatched her bottle of wine and slammed the screen door on her way out.

She jammed the Z4 in reverse then shoved it into first gear and tore out of there, her wake peppering the Mercedes with sand and crushed shells. She stopped at the entranceway where the two large cans were and tapped a hasty text message to Ben.

Seems your dinner guest beat me to the stove. Enjoy your evening.

The teddy bear stared at her from his perch on the console. Lydia grabbed it and tossed it into the road.

74

Fatal Attraction

Big Ben was sitting at the light at Stickney Point Road when his cell phone chimed. He read the message. What? He was confused. What dinner guest? Winnie? He started to send a return text but the light changed. He drove on, he was almost there anyway.

When he came through the two cans he stopped and got out. What are you doing here? He said to the little stuffed black bear lying in the gravel. Ben picked it up and put it on the hump next to him. Here, ride shotgun. And tell me what's going on.

Black Bear just stared back at him as if to say, you'll find out soon enough.

"Hi," she said.

"Um, hi." He stood just inside the doorway. He saw the layout in the kitchen and the table set for two. Ben was getting the gist of Lydia's message now.

"I thought I'd surprise you with dinner, as promised," she smiled. "There's cold beer in the fridge. Would you like one?" Without waiting for an answer, she grabbed a Yuengling and poured it into a chilled mug she had in the freezer. "Have a seat and tell me about your day." June Cleaver was in his kitchen?

Ben, dumbfounded, took the frosty glass and sat at the counter. He didn't remember any "promise", and certainly did not recollect setting a date nor ever discussing it. *And* how the hell would Georgia know he wasn't working tonight. He was beginning to feel a *Fatal Attraction* and he wasn't sure which woman was playing the Glenn Close part. He took a healthy swig of beer.

"Was Lydia here?"

"Ohmygod, I almost forgot. There was a woman who said she was your attorney, although she didn't introduce herself. She dropped off some groceries and then left rather hastily. I told her I'd let you know she stopped by."

Ben could sense a long night closing in. He texted Lydia.

Hey, come on back. There's been a silly misunderstanding. I'd love to have dinner with you. I can explain it all over a glass of wine. I'll have it awaiting you. PS... Black Bear is happily guarding my new Hummer.

Now he turned his attention to Georgia. "I didn't know we had set up a dinner date. I got your note and I thought it said to call if I was interested."

"Well, yes it did. But I got my car back sooner than expected and I'm leaving tomorrow and I thought it'd be nice to show you how much I appreciated your help and hospitality. I hope I didn't intrude on your evening."

He looked at his phone. No return text.

Ben was starting to feel the grueling effects of his last twenty-four hours. He was sore and thought about taking some medication but remembered he hadn't filled the scrip yet. He walked to the other side of the small room where a short selection of booze sat on a table by the window. He'd been saving a bottle of Woodford Reserve Bourbon for a visit from his bud MacLaren, but he hadn't visited his little beach shack yet. He wondered why. Ben pulled the top off and poured himself a shot. He was going to offer some to Georgia but when he looked to her she was taking a sip of her wine and fussing with dinner prep.

He took his bourbon and beer out to the porch and checked his phone. Nada.

There was a sixty-per-cent chance of rain tonight which meant it was going to rain. He could feel the initial winds coming in off the Gulf. Light and warm. A couple hours away yet.

He called her and got her voice mail. Ben again reiterated his text message and pleaded with Lydia to return and enjoy dinner together. He figured he would tell her how innocent this whole thing was and the three of them would end up laughing about it.

A rogue gust of wind passed by and then dissipated into an instant, serene calm. He stood on the porch and it hit him that he felt stranded. Incapable of pulling his life together. He didn't care about losing his cop career but he wanted desperately to be himself again. Strong and focused. Able to reach tall buildings in a single bound. God, he missed Carlene.

Winnie's Jeep screamed into the compound. She clambered out of the driver's seat. Seeing Big Ben standing on the porch she said, "Heeey! Wassup?" She was hammered.

"Hey to you too!" He yelled back, happy to see her no matter what shape she was in. He desperately needed a friendly face.

She wandered over to him. He could see the red ember of her joint glowing in the coming night.

"Whatcha up to?" she said.

"Winnie, I have no idea, but I am sure as hell glad to see you."

They hugged.

"Whose Mercedes? Your lady friend back?" She jabbed Ben playfully in the ribs.

"Did you eat yet?" he asked.

"No, I'm gonna go inside and mic up some slop now."

Ben grinned. "No you're not." He put his big arm around her and guided them to his door, "Get your ass in here."

First thing he did was pour two shots of bourbon and hand one to Winnie

75

Seduction

Ben never did hear back from Lydia and after more bourbon with Winnie he forgot about everything and got happy with his company. The three of them sat on cushions around the low coffee table enjoying Georgia's sumptuous meal.

The conversation drifted from Georgia's interrupted trip to Miami (which she said happily brought her to Two Can Key and dinner with two fascinating new friends), to reminiscences of Winnie's many and varied exploits - laughter-enhanced by the after dinner joint Winnie and Georgia had shared. Even Big Ben was unusually loose and full of mirth which the ladies attributed to the second-hand smoke swirling about the little cottage.

Then the conversation turned to Ben's recent accident and his preoccupation with the mangrove murders.

"Ohmygod," Georgia was intrigued, "tell me."

"Well," Ben began, "let me start at the beginning. Carlene and I were flying down for vacation ..."

Georgia listened attentively to Ben's lengthy recap: Hannah Hunt Everett's murder, the discovery of Carlene's phone number on the body, the twin in the lagoon, the naked man with the uncanny resemblance to the new governor, the unknown causes of death, the torturing of Elroy Leland of AbioGenetix, the missing notebooks and the curious heart attack of the security guard, the kidnapping of Ben's wife, the beating death of one of the two kidnappers and the disappearance of the accomplice, the inquest and loss of his badge, and finally the attempt on his life.

"And that happened on the same road I broke down on?"

"Almost the same spot."

"That is some story."

Ben didn't mention the guru or the goings-on in the compound. He wasn't sure how to deal with that and his gut told him to keep that element to himself.

The weighty conversation lulled. Everyone pacified by their own thoughts. Outside the darkening evening was shadowing their conversation and sneaking in with a promise of an overnight storm.

Winnie seemed reticent.

Georgia put her hand on her shoulder. "Are you okay?"

"Yeah, it's just that I feel I'm involved somehow. I mean those mangroves are on my property. What's happening out there is ... I don't know," she trailed off.

"Okay," Georgia said, "I think we're all crashing. A minute ago we were all laughing. Maybe we need to light up another joint."

"Not for me," Winnie yawned, "I'm starting to nod out. Time for an old lady to go count sheep."

"Oh, don't go," Georgia said, "we're having such a good time."

"Gotta go. Need my beauty sleep. But I do thank you for such a lovely meal." The two women embraced and Georgia walked Winnie to the porch then watched her as she made her way across the shell lane and entered her own cottage.

When Georgia came back into the house, Ben was still seated on the floor leaning against the couch. His eyes were shut. She started to clean up and the sound jarred him. He said, "Let me help," and struggled to his feet and brought a few things into the kitchen.

"Why don't you sit down and relax," she said. "I'll clean up here. Would you like another beer?"

"No. I'm done in. Think I'll take a couple Ibuprofen and hit the sack."

"Do you mind if I stay? I think I shouldn't be driving."

"No, that's fine. You're right. Please stay. Take the bedroom."

"Actually I'd rather the couch. I'm comfortable there. You take your own bed. I'll finish up here, then I'm going to have another glass of wine before I retire."

"Okay, good night."

"Good night."

Ben shuffled towards the bathroom.

"Hey," she said. "Thanks for the conversation. It was a nice evening."

The rain came in the middle of the night. Not loud. Soft patters on the tin roof. Steady and rhythmic and soothing. That's what woke him, the ease of it, a subtle disturbance, like someone approaching. And there was. Her naked form entered the bedroom and moved furtively in the soft glow of the nocturne. Carefully she lifted the sheet and slid in next to him.

76

Embarrassed

He could smell the coffee. It was early. The sun was up. Ben filled his mug and pushed through the screen door. Georgia was seated on the porch steps holding her cup with both hands. The steam rose from it and she blew across it. He leaned against the railing and took a sip.

"Good coffee," he said.

"Thanks."

The wind wasn't up yet and the ocean was quiet. Sunlight peered through the motionless palms, making them look like a snapshot.

"You okay?" He asked.

She didn't answer right away.

"I'm sorry." She wasn't looking at him. "I feel embarrassed."

"Don't be," he said gently. "If either one of us is embarrassed it should be me."

Ben sat next to her on the short steps. His right knee was swollen and he stretched the leg out until his bare heel rested on the sand.

She said, "I admire you. Your wife is a lucky lady." She turned her head to him and chuckled, "I didn't think men like you existed."

He had felt her presence only a moment before she'd entered his bed. And he had seen her body, toned and darkened by the shadow of the night. When the sheet lifted he wanted to say something. But she was quick and slid eagerly against his side.

She didn't know him. Not really. He was a man, yes. But a man with hard beliefs and strict morals.

And he didn't know her. Not really. She said her husband died a year ago. It must be lonely. Especially going through the chemo alone. She's probably been true to his memory, he thought, and now, with the cancer in remission and a new lease on life, she felt good about herself again. And brave. And uninhibited by the wine and marijuana. And here he was, alone and available. Two people adrift.

Except he wasn't. Even though the separation from his wife was lengthy, his heart still held out for her. His love was deep.

He wanted to hold this woman and tell her everything would be alright in her life again. But he knew that would send a certain signal. One he could not express.

He was not afraid of sex and knew it was there for the taking, yet for Ben, sex was an integral part of love and he could not have one without the other.

His best friend, Dodge Maddison, was a famous fashion designer in New York City who, if he desired, could have sex with a different model every night. He had chided Ben many times about his old-fashioned ways and beliefs and thought he was crazy. And he was – crazy in love with Carlene.

So, Ben got out of bed and looked down at her. "I'm sorry Georgia," he said softly, "I am very much in love with my wife." Neither one spoke for a moment and then he said, "I'll take the couch."

"No, I'll go," she whispered and left the bed and the man and walked out of the room.

Wow, she was amazed. Ursula had never failed to seduce a man before.

77
Value

"More coffee?" she asked.
"Sure, thanks."
She retreated into the cottage and was back in a minute with their cups refreshed.
Ben said, "I'm sorry too."
"For what?"
"I feel I disrespected you and I had no intent to do that. You are a beautiful woman and I am sure things will work out for you."
"No, it was my wrongdoing. I should never have done that. That was far too presumptuous of me."
"Blame it on the wine," he laughed.
"And the pot. Ohmygod where does she get that stuff?"
"Hey, I don't ask. I think I got high just being in the room."
"No harm no foul?" she asked.
"No harm no foul." They clinked their coffee cups.
"I hope I didn't bore you with my venting about the case last night."
"Not at all. It seems very exciting, yet perplexing at the same time."
"What do you make of it all?"

No one had ever asked Ursula for an opinion before. She had always been directed, told what to do. No one, starting with her strict Scandinavian parents had ever seemed to care about her feelings or opinions. She had been happy when they were killed – assassins terminated by other assassins. At the age of seventeen she was finally free from their abuse and on her own, honing the only skills she knew.

Her wet work for The Group kept her active and well compensated, but they were a cold lot. She didn't trust them one iota. Of course, she never trusted anyone. Ursula was void of feelings and that fluke was why she did her job so well. She never experienced sadness, nor did she ever remember shedding a tear in her life – unless it was part of an act. Even the loss of her husband did not affect her. That had just been an unfortunate business incident. Yet now, sitting on these steps next to the man who had caused her husband's death, she did feel something. Value.

Last night's camaraderie had been fun, she had actually laughed – another taboo from her childhood. Laughter weakens you, her parents engrained in her, it drops your guard and makes you vulnerable.

But she had had a good time with Winnie and Ben. For a little while she felt part of something. And perhaps, if she could allow herself a flicker of honesty, for the first time in her life she wanted to have sex - not with an assassin's seduction, but a woman's desire.

God, she thought, *is this what emotion feels like?*

"No really," Ben continued, coaxing her, "I'd like to know. Sometimes it does me good to get an opinion from an outsider – someone completely removed from the case."

Ursula withheld a smirk. She had to be careful here. She knew Ben was smart, The Group had warned her of that. And she had to guard her involvement and not jeopardize her mission.

"Well, it seems like a pretty big puzzle. Are you sure all those things are related?"

"Yeah, I am. The murder of Hannah Hunt, the bodies in the mangroves, the abduction of my wife and now this assault on me has got to tie together somehow."

Ursula assembled the pieces in her mind but she only knew her half of the puzzle. Initially she was contracted to procure the dead scientist's notebooks. She didn't care what was in them, she never clouded her mind with why or what – only how. How to succeed and how much money she would get.

She and LeBeau had initially succeeded, but then it got complicated. The Group couldn't decipher the formulas and needed a code. So they had tortured the partner to no avail and kidnapped Carlene, but that operation went south and now she was in it alone to garner the info from Ben Benson. But she didn't think he had it. And Ursula felt The Group knew more than they were telling her and she didn't like that.

As for the murders, well, she certainly knew who had killed poor, pudgy Teddy Platt, but was clueless regarding the two bodies found in the mangroves and had absolutely no idea about Hannah Hunt.

"You said the medical examiner couldn't find cause of death for the bodies in the mangroves, right?"

"Right," he replied.

"I don't get it. What would that mean?" She was pushing him. She still needed to get information for The Group. What did he know?

He'd been keeping his thoughts regarding the mysterious Montgomery Fairmont and his exploits on the back burner. Nothing of any significance had transpired for several months now. Carlene seemed to be safe and off the radar. But there were clearly nefarious elements at work here.

She had just raised a very good question and he thought he may know the answer. It was time to pull the cat out of the bag. He needed a break in the case. Just one break.

And that's exactly what he got.

78

The Break

The break came in the form of a pigeon. It dropped out of the sky and came directly at them, fluttering to roost on the porch railing.

It was gray. The wings were tipped in white as was the neck where its head reared back and opened unnaturally to allow a small black object to emit. Ursula covered her mouth as if to suppress vomiting. The bird was dead-still with one eye blinking red in one second intervals.

Big Ben cautiously reached forward and extracted the object from the bird's neck and it flew away leaving a mechanical whir in its wake.

He held the object in his hand and nonchalantly twisted it between his thumb and forefinger, as if everyday a motorized pigeon dropped off a device for him. Ursula still held her hand to her face in disbelief. Ben didn't seem to be alarmed.

"What is this?" he said.

"Umm,"

"And why do I think I know where it came from?"

"Did you just see that?" she queried in disbelief.

"It looks like a mini flash drive." He held it to her and reluctantly she reached for it. She surveyed the object and said, "That's exactly what it is. How did?… where? …"

"Let's plug it into my computer."

Ursula's quick brain discarded the bizarreness of the occurrence and immediately transfigured the options. "It's too small for a standard USB port." She'd had extensive training with electronics. It came in handy with her profession. "Where's your smart phone?"

Ben led her into the cottage and retrieved his phone. Ursula plugged it into the side opening. Instantly an automated voice said, "You like my pigeon? Crafty, eh? It's a drone. I'm thinking of patenting it and selling it to Amazon." A short chuckle followed. "Anyway, heard you had a bad leg so I thought I'd do some legwork for you."

The screen blinked and a Florida license plate appeared. The voice said, "Avis rental." As the voice continued, the shot panned out to show the back of a Ford SUV moving at great speed toward a motorcycle. Big Ben, the other night.

"I've got a flock of these pigeon drones patrolling my little habitat 24/7. Interesting what they come up with." Another sinister chuckle.

"Anyway ... more legwork. The car was rented by a Mr. Jacob Curtis of Washington, D.C."

They were watching a video of the SUV racing behind Ben's Harley and ramming it from behind. A clear picture, somehow illuminated, showed Ben's "flight" into the shoulder brush.

"Luckily, you survived the mishap."

The screen faded to a daylight shot of a downtown Sarasota skyscraper. The voice-over said, "As of this morning, Mr. Curtis is residing in his condo at Five Points Tower, suite 924. Happy hunting. You owe me one. I will collect."

"Isn't Jake Curtis the Florida Governor's aide?" Georgia asked, already knowing the answer of course. But not knowing why he would be involved with Ben Benson and not liking the indisputable fact that he was. What was going on?

"Yes. Jake the Snake."

"Why would he do that?"

"I don't know but I intend to find out. I think I'll pay him a little visit this morning."

She followed him into the cottage as he went into the bedroom and came out with a gun. He checked the revolver for ammo, snapped the cylinder back into place and put the .38 in his right cargo pocket.

"Shouldn't you call the police?"

"No, I shouldn't."

"I'm nervous for you."

"Don't be. I'll be fine. This is my line of work, remember?"

"Let me come with you."

"Absolutely not. Best thing you can do is move on with your life." He stood in front of her and placed his hands on her shoulders. "Really, Georgia, I believe that's what you need to do."

She stood still and took a deep breath and looked into his eyes. "Yes, I do too."

Ben nodded in agreement and kissed her on the forehead.

"When will you be back?" she said.

"I don't know. I'm on this full time now. Not going to stop until I put all the pieces together. I've asked Gramps' granddaughter Alice (remember Alice?) to cover my shifts for a while."

"Well then, I'll be on my way. Thank you for your hospitality and," she smiled demurely, "your understanding." She stood on tiptoe and kissed his cheek. "Be careful and take care of yourself."

"You too. Let's keep in touch."

79

Snake Eyes

Ben stood with his back to the door so that Jake wouldn't be able to recognize him through the peephole. He knocked. When he heard footsteps approaching he said loudly, "FedEx for Jacob Curtis. Need a signature."

As soon as the door cracked, Big Ben drove his shoulder into it and charged into the room.

"What the fuck are you …?" Jake was in a white terry robe. A young lady sat at the breakfast table in a matching robe. It wasn't Jake's trophy wife, Ruby, it was another trophy.

Ben said to her, "Get your things and get out."

She looked at Jake. He said, "It's okay, honey. He's a friend of mine. Go ahead, I'll call you later."

The men stood eye to eye, neither one spoke. They waited. She came out of the bedroom dressed, carrying an overnight bag over her shoulder. Without acknowledging either of them she walked out, not bothering to shut the door.

"Sit down," Ben growled.

"Listen …"

"No. You listen. I didn't like you from day one. I could smell the stink on you a mile away." Ben was breathing heavy. "I'm trying to contain myself right now because all I want to do is rip your fucking head off."

"It was supposed to motivate you. I did not mean you any harm."

"Motivate me? You hit my motorcycle from behind at a hundred miles an hour! You rotten son-of-a-bitch ..." Ben went at him.

"Whoa! Whoa!" Jake had his hands up in defense. He pushed the chair back and got to his feet.

Ben stopped. Flames were coming out his nostrils. "What's your angle, Curtis?"

"Look. I know things I'm not supposed to know. I didn't get to where I am today without being cunning."

"Nor snakelike."

"Be as condescending as you want Benson, but don't forget, knowledge is power no matter how you acquire it."

"And what knowledge do you have that would require you to bump me off the road?"

"It's more like what knowledge do *you* have?"

Ben took another step at him and Jake backed against the wall still holding his hands in front of him.

Ben said, "Speak English to me."

"All right, all right. Let's sit down and talk this out, shall we?"

"No, we shall not." Ben loomed over him. "Talk while you still have teeth in your mouth."

"I work for some people."

"I know you work for the governor."

"Not him, the people who put him where he is."

"Who?"

"It doesn't matter. They're a very powerful group with an inflexible agenda. They need to know something and they believe you know what that is, or if you don't, that you can acquire it for them. I figured if I riled you up you'd bungle your way onto it and I'd follow you to the answer."

"Is this how you follow me? Shacking up with some blonde in your condo?"

He got quiet. Ben pulled out his gun. Jake Curtis said, "You won't get anything out of shooting me."

"I'll get the satisfaction of not having to deal with you anymore." He cocked the hammer.

"I have a source."

"And ..."

"I'd be alerted when the time came."

"Who?"

"I really can't say."

Ben jammed the barrel under his chin. Beads of perspiration appeared on Jake's upper lip.

"She's someone very close to the governor .. and to you."

She? Ben thought. *Lydia?*

Suddenly Jake's eyes bulged like two black snake-eyes. He was looking past Ben's shoulder. Ben was wise to this ploy and wasn't about to be tricked. Then something hot stung the back of his neck and he went down and out.

80

Pffftt!

"It's you." Jake rubbed his chin where Ben's gun had pressed against it. "The one they send." His bulging black eyes had a red gloss of fear over them.

Without hesitation, Ursula raised a silenced Walther PPK and shot Jake through the fleshy part of his left shoulder.

He screamed and grabbed the wound with his right hand.

"Sit," she motioned to the chair with her pistol.

He complied, stepping over the unconscious body at his feet. There was a splotch of blood on the wall.

"I will speak. You will answer." The Georgia twang was gone and her curt Scandinavian inflection was back. "What part do you play?"

"Part?"

"That is a question, not an answer. *I* question, *you* answer!" She pointed the gun at his other shoulder.

"Okay! Okay!" Although this woman was half the size of Big Ben, Jake was twice as terrified of her. He thought it would be unwise to tell her anything but the truth. "I was initially contracted to ensure Conrad Lawrence won the governorship of Florida." He took a cloth napkin off the table and held it to his shoulder.

Ursula buffered herself a dozen feet in front of him. The gun was at her thigh. She looked at the bloodstain on the wall and saw the bullet embedded in the center of it. "Continue."

"My contract has been extended. They want him in The White House."

"And you can promise that?"

"If need be, yes. I am a warranty of last resort. If he is far enough ahead in the polls, not much will be necessary. But if the election appears chancy, then I need to be prepared."

"How?"

"To coin an old phrase, 'stuff the ballot boxes'."

"And how would you do that?"

"With additional voters. Many additional." He grinned.

He had her interest, but there was something else. "What are you not telling me?"

He leaned back in his chair. The blood was congealing. He availed himself a sip of water. She was a cool customer alright. Ice cold. And she had the gun. Jake was trying frantically to think of a way to get to her but she was holding all the cards. He was trapped. He decided to show his hand. Maybe his raucous charm could win her over.

"I assume, though our professions are different, that we share the same goal."

Ursula raised her eyebrows.

"Money." He saw what may have been a slight smile cross her face.

He motioned a seat to her, but she shook her head. He had nothing to lose, except his life, so he leveled with her. "I'm really not interested in running the world, or care who does for that matter. The governor thing was good money, but the next phase will take over three years and that is a long wait for a big payoff. I'd like to be retired by then. I need faster money."

She stood dead still, unblinking, coercing him on.

He continued, "There's big money to be made. Way more than The Group will offer. There are others who will pay more handsomely and more immediately."

"So, you turn on them?"

"Who cares? They're all evil. Money is the only true thing."

"Don't you have any morals?"

Jake laughed at that. "About as many as you do." He could see her thinking. "We're two of a kind, y'know."

Ursula realized he was baiting her, the con on the make with the sweet talk.

He said, "We could do a deal. Fifty-fifty."

"I could never partner with you."

"Why not?"

"You are not trustworthy."

Jake the Snake conjured up his best shit-eatin' grin and drawled, "I'd never lie to you, darlin'."

"I know."

Pffftt!

81

One More

In the night, the rain came fast across Two Can Key like a runaway train. It was a raucous storm, wild and furious and short-lived – fairly common on the Gulf Coast. As loud as it was, exhaustion from his recent mishaps permitted Ben to sleep right through it.

By mid-morning, Big Ben had cleared the debris from the yard and the cottage porches and was seated at his counter on his second cup of coffee. Before him lay a yellow legal pad where he was jotting down a new game plan.

His cell chimed. He looked at the screen. MacLaren.

"Hey, what's up, Lieutenant?"

"We've got another body. Guess where it was found?"

"In the mangroves."

"Yup, down by Gramps Ramp. Actually quite near where you went off the road. Think that could mean anything?"

"Why would it?"

"It was a friend of yours, Jake Curtis."

Ben was speechless.

"But at least we have a cause of death for this one. He has a perfectly placed bullet hole between his eyes."

Ben's mind was racing, but he stopped it long enough to say, "Have you had breakfast yet?"

"No."
"Meet me at Village Café."
"Siesta Key?"
"Yeah. Twenty minutes. I've got something to tell you."

MacLaren found Ben seated at a rattan table on the sidewalk beneath a broad thatched awning. The usual accoutrements of salt and pepper, sugar caddies, ketchup, etc. were huddled in a square bamboo basket in the center. Tropical print roll-ups were placed diagonally across wickerwork placemats. A coffee carafe and two mugs completed the setup.

MacLaren pulled a chair opposite Ben and sat. He poured coffee and took a sip.

Ben said, "I ordered for both of us."

"What am I eating?"

"I dunno. Whatever the special is."

MacLaren looked around. "Nice place. You come here often?" His attempt at humor wasn't wasted. Ben chuckled.

The lieutenant added another sugar to his coffee. "Get any damage from that storm last night?"

"Just branches and fronds."

"Lot of lightning inland. Half the county lost power."

"Can't believe I slept right through it. Usually I sleep light."

"Probably residual effects from the accident. How's the head?"

"Okay. Headache's gone."

The waitress appeared with a heavy tray. "All-righty," she said. "Two Extra-Everything Omelets, turkey sausage, double home fries, double order of sun-dried tomato toast, fresh OJ, and a stack of papaya pancakes. Good for now?"

Ben nodded, "Perfect."

MacLaren said, "I think I need a to-go box already."

She laughed. "I'll check on your progress in a couple. Enjoy."

They dug in.

When she returned a few minutes later to do her check-back, Ben was already done. "Didn't like it, eh?" she smiled and took his plate away.

MacLaren had only dented his. "Not good to eat like that, y'know. Too fast."

"I was hungry."

"Good, now you can talk while I eat in the proper manner."

Ben leaned forward with his forearms on the table. "What's the time of death?"

"ME says 24 hours. Yesterday morning."

"In the mangroves?"

"No. We think he was popped and dropped. No peripheral blood evidence at the mangrove scene, but his condo was a different story. The place looked clean but when they Luminol'd it the UV picked up blood spatter on a wall behind a picture frame, a chair, and the floor beneath it. Also, there was a hole in the middle of the wall stain where we believe a slug was removed. So, we think he was killed there and then the perp or perps cleaned up, moved a frame over the wall spot and somehow got him out of the building and out to the county road."

"I was there."

"Where?"

"In his condo. Yesterday morning."

MacLaren almost choked on his food. He put his fork down. "Why were you there?"

"Confronting him. He was the one who bumped me off the Harley."

"How'd you come up with that?"

"A little birdie told me."

MacLaren didn't like that answer. "Okay, jerk-off, be evasive."

"He was alive when I was there."

The lieutenant wiped his mouth, threw his napkin onto his unfinished plate and sat back. "I'm all ears."

"I got there around nine-thirty. I knocked, he let me in. He was having breakfast with someone."

"Someone?"

"A chick. They were in their bathrobes."

"So, let me guess. He wasn't expecting you."

Ben raised his coffee mug and answered over the rim, "No."

Lieutenant MacLaren factored in the robe. Jake Curtis had been found wrapped in a bloody robe. "Go on."

"The girlfriend left and Curtis and I had a conversation about the other night."

"Why did he say he bumped you off the road?"

"We were just getting to that when someone got me from behind and I went out cold."

"Hit you?"

Ben twisted in his seat so the lieutenant could see the back of his neck. MacLaren recognized the mark. "Taser."

"Yeah, hurt like hell. Anyway, when I came to, no one was there, so I left."

"Did you get a look at the assailant before you went blank?"

"No, happened too fast. I figured the girl had returned and zapped me and then they both split."

"You didn't notice any blood?"

"No, everything looked normal. Are you sure he was shot there?"

"Yeah. Did you hear anything? Even unconscious you may have heard gunshots. There were two. One in the shoulder, one to the head."

"Naw, I was out. Or they used a silencer."

"You think it could have been the girl? Zapped you, shot him, then dragged him away to the freight elevator?"

"Motive?"

"Jealousy's always a good one. She knew he was married. Maybe he was making promises he wouldn't keep and she got tired of it."

"She was petite. Can't see her lifting him."

"Maybe she had help. Or maybe it was someone else."

"Like who?"

"Oh, I don't know. Maybe a big strong ex-football player who held a grudge?"

"Fuck you lieutenant."

"What have you been doing for the past 24 hours?"

"Are you serious? Why would I want to kill him? Besides the fact that he's an asshole, I mean?"

"Calm down. I know you didn't do it."

The server dropped their check and wished them a good day.

"Here's what puzzles me," MacLaren said, "why drag his body out to the mangroves?"

"Dunno. Maybe to keep to the theme."

"You still think all these things are related?"

"Even moreso."

MacLaren shook his head and stood up. "Who's getting the check? You or you?"

"You."

They walked along the village sidewalk. Big Ben was chewing on a toothpick. "Where'd you park?

"Down at the end of the lane. You?"

"Just past that, near the beach."

"So, what *have* you been doing for the past twenty-four hours?"

"Outlining. I worked up a history of this whole mess starting when Carlene and I got off the plane last December."

"Well, now you can add the body of Jake Curtis."

"Yeah."

"I'd like to read it."

"I'll give you a copy when I've solved the case."

"When do you think that'll be?"

Ben didn't answer right away. They got to MacLaren's car. He chirped the remote. Ben said, "I'll let you know. Thanks for breakfast." He kept walking down the lane.

"Hey," MacLaren called to him. "What's up with you and Lydia?"

Ben turned, "What do you mean?"

"Rumor has it she's in Tallahassee looking for an apartment."

So, that's why he hadn't heard from her.

"It's not good to piss off your own attorney, y'know." MacLaren slid into his car.

82

Friction

Ursula's satellite phone rang. Only one person in the world had that number. She answered angrily, "What!"

"What the *hell* did you do?"

"Did I get your attention?"

"You had no right to terminate him. That's our decision to make, not yours."

"You double-crossed me."

"We did no such thing."

"Lying does not become you."

"Where are you?"

"Far away."

"You need to come in. We need to talk."

"No. Talking is done."

"He went rogue. He was acting on his own. Come in. We can settle this."

Ursula knew what would happen to her if she went in. "Not a chance. I am no fool."

"We have a change in plans. A better offer for you. More money."

"You compromised my operation. I do not like tricks played on me. I no longer want your money. Only to settle this score."

"What the hell does that mean?"

"You sent him to meddle in my mission without even courtesy to consult me."

"Again, we did not."

"I do not believe you. You controlled him. He would not move without your direction."

"Look, none of that matters now. We must move forward."

"It matters to me."

The voice on the other end got harsh. "You *must* come in. Do you understand, Ursula?"

"You were never to use my name in any communication."

"Damn it! This line is secure. Where are you? I can have you picked up anywhere you are within an hour. Then we will sit down and draft a new mission for you."

"Your American contemporaries have a word that seems befitting now… Bullshit!"

"You come in or risk the consequences! That is final."

"There is only one thing that is final and if I were you I would sleep with one eye open."

"Are you *threatening* me?!" he said in an incredulous tone.

"I do not threaten." She ended the call and disposed of the phone.

83

Back to the Lab

Big Ben remembered Montgomery Fairmont saying there was an abandoned prairie road down in Nocatee that ran north for several miles into the hidden compound. The Hummer was rumbling through that jungle now. It sprang through the final thicket and into the clearing before the house. He parked the machine. Ben hadn't been here since the night he and Convict Rick were on their thwarted mission. JJ waved from the porch and pointed out back.

The door was open. Monty's pet alligator lay on the threshold.

"About time you got here."

"You saw me coming?"

"Of course, come in."

Ben cautiously stepped over the gator, relieved that it didn't snap his leg off.

"Have a seat. Lemonade?"

The laboratory hadn't changed; still had that eerie, mad chemist's feel to it. As before, the myriad of tall vats surrounded the room, like giant test tubes, except now they were void of the green phosphorescent liquid and the bodies were once again wandering the field in their long, colorful sarongs.

They sat on stools surrounding a stainless steel table that reminded Ben of a coroner's gurney. The scientist filled two glasses with ice and poured the lemonade. JJ appeared and placed a fruit platter in the center of the table and bent to kiss Fairmont on the cheek before she departed. Ben got a weird feeling from that.

"How did you do that? How did you clone Janis Joplin?"

Montgomery Fairmont sipped the cold drink and leaned back in his seat. "Without getting too technical, the easiest way to clone a human being is to utilize DNA. With Janis, I procured a whiskey bottle from The Hard Rock Café in New York. Janis Joplin was known to covet a bottle of Southern Comfort on stage at her concerts. A fan had stolen one years ago and preserved it. The Hard Rock acquired it, and then subsequently I purchased it from them."

"That simple, huh?" Ben chuckled.

"Easier than raiding body parts from the graveyard and stitching them together as Igor and the good Doctor Frankenstein did."

"You're being facetious."

"Somewhat. There is absolutely nothing simple about it. JJ is a successful one, but the others I am still perfecting. Each one seems to have its own flaw. Like a faulty wire."

As if on cue, the alligator came over to Fairmont and rested its snout on his lap.

"Like a gator that acts like a dog?"

Monty scratched its head and it retreated to its blanket in the corner of the room, circled it several times and then plopped down with a huff.

"Trial and error?"

"You have no idea. Edison went through a thousand prototypes before he perfected the light bulb. This is my life's work. Not only the cloning, but to get beyond the DNA factor with abiogenetics. Notwithstanding modesty, I have pioneered the most advancement in abiogenetics on the planet."

"Seems I've heard that word before."

"The development of living organisms from non-living matter. Before I came along it was only hypothetical."

"And how do you do that?"

"Do you speak Swahili?"

"Um, no."

"You'd have a better chance of understanding that language than my interpretation of your question."

"How did you get this far?" Ben looked around.

"Lot of work, lot of failure, and to be honest, it would not have been possible without my wonderful assistant and guinea pig, Hannah. She literally gave her life to science. She was a brilliant student. When I left the professorship at Harvard to set up my business, I contacted her and she came to work for me. She was a great researcher with a PhD in Biochemistry.

"We worked together in Boston for years, always on the QT. Then when I disappeared to Florida, she was gracious enough to move here. She procured a teaching position at New College of Florida in Sarasota and we continued our clandestine work. All of my initial cloning was done with her DNA. Although it took us years to perfect, her clone was the most successful, because we had unlimited access to Hannah's strands."

"Why would she make that kind of move? She had kids and a husband."

"She was totally committed to the research. We were on our way to change the course of medical science. The benefits to mankind would be enormous."

"Who killed her Fairmont?"

A sheen came to his eyes but he stared right through it to meet Ben's forceful gaze.

"I don't know."

Ben wasn't sure if he believed him.

"And my wife? How does she figure in all this?"

"She doesn't. Not really. It was a long time ago. Carlene was a classmate of ours who once participated in a bizarre high-school science project. It was actually her impetus to clone the boyfriend that got all this started. Hannah believed Carlene had an uncanny knack for contributing biological suppositions that were later proved to be right on. She thought she could be a great asset to our work and suggested I contact her and enlist her help, but I didn't want to endanger anyone else and I doubt Carlene has had any thoughts nor interest in cloning since that time."

"So, the things that are happening, the mystery and the murders, it's all about you isn't it? What you're doing."

Fairmont picked up a twig of grapes and began popping them into his mouth, chewing slowly. He was pondering. Finally, in exasperation, he said. "I believe so."

He took another sip of lemonade. Ben could see he wanted to let something out, to unburden himself. Ben waited him out.

"Things have gotten to a crucial point. There are evil elements at work that I feel are out of our control. Certainly mine. I truly do not know why Hannah was murdered. She didn't have enough knowledge to get her killed. The twin was a clone. Something happened to it once Hannah was gone. A short circuit like. Almost as if it died a sympathy death. Then the trauma your wife and my ex-partner have gone through, and you with the motorcycle accident, and now the murder of Jake Curtis." He looked at Ben questioningly.

"It wasn't me."

"You know, I believe that. But it was somebody." He was slowly shaking his head when he muttered, "Chaos theory."

"You forgot one. The naked man resembling the governor."

"That was also a clone."

"Why would you clone the governor?"

"A topic for another time, my friend."

Fairmont got up and went to a wall of monitors. He was checking the security cameras. Ben could tell he was nervous.

"I'd like to look at your surveillance of state road 70 for last night, same area that your pigeon showed me. That's where Jake Curtis' body was found. I'd like to know who dumped him there."

"Sorry, pal. No can do."

"What do you mean?"

"That storm last night knocked out my surveillance system. Didn't get it back up until just a few hours ago."

"Shit."

"That why you came by?"

"Yeah."

"Well I'm glad you did, because I'd like to collect on that little favor you owe me."

"How so?"

"I need your help."

"With what?"

"With my mother."

"Your mother? I'm afraid I don't know your mother."

"I'm afraid you do."

84
Poets, Prophets and Peaceniks

"Winnie Vanderlene is your mother?"

Monty laughed. "Yup, your eccentric landlady is my dear ole mom. Let's go for a ride. I'll tell you a few things about her you probably don't know."

They walked out of the lab followed by the gator. Monty held his palm up and the gator stopped at the door and took up his position on the threshold. When they got to the Hummer, Monty said, "Can I drive? I always wanted to drive one of these things."

"Go for it."

He pulled the driver's seat to its most forward position, adjusted the mirrors and turned the ignition. "I hope you don't mind a few superficial scratches, I have a shortcut."

"Be my guest. I've got maximum coverage."

Monty smirked and roared along the side of the building out into the field, crossing it at a harrowing speed. "Hang on," he said, but before Ben had a chance to, the Hummer plowed into a wall of greenery. A second later a gravel road stretched ahead of them and the scientist-turned-race-car-driver stomped the accelerator. "This is fun!"

"For you maybe." Big Ben, who usually never wore a seatbelt, suddenly felt it prudent to fasten his.

Monty brought Big Ben up to speed regarding his biological mother, starting with Mom Fairmont's death-bed revelation. He went through his first visit with Winnie and their subsequent collaboration. "She agreed to hide me and said she knew of the perfect place. The building back there was originally a cattle shed and the house was a barn. It was abandoned for decades and fell into disrepair. I totally revamped it internally, leaving the dilapidated outside of the structure as a ruse. It is a great lair for concealment and seclusion …"

"And unchecked experimentation."

"Yes, precisely," he continued, "but the motherly love and support came with a stipulation. Once she found out what I was up to, she decided my 'rent' would be helping her turtle cause by cloning loggerhead eggs. Then it progressed to her cannabis-influenced notion of saving the world by bringing back the poets, prophets and peaceniks of the sixties."

"Hence, the Woodstock Foundation?"

"Ah, you remembered."

"Yeah, but why the infatuation with Woodstock?"

"A couple of reasons, but I don't want to get too far ahead of myself. Hang tight and most of your questions will be answered shortly."

"Where are we going?"

Monty grinned, "Patience my big friend."

A commodity Ben was short on. But he figured he'd go along for the ride. "So, how can I help you with your mother?"

"I need to vanish again. My operation here has been compromised and I fear my whereabouts will be discovered in due time. My work is too vital to fall into the hands of greed and fanaticism. In order to survive and continue, I need to relocate."

"To where?"

"Not sure yet. But definitely another country."

The Hummer escaped the prairie foliage and rumbled along a thin strip of tarmac heading for civilization. Ben chuckled to himself, "Crazy Winnie, the mother of the eccentric scientist. What a coincidence."

"Coincidence and chaos are often willing bedfellows."

"Mm."

"I am worried about Winnie, though. She's become quite fond of our little commune and I'm not sure how she will deal with its demise. The turtle cloning was one thing. It made her very happy and will undoubtedly help her cause. But the peaceniks is another. Winnie's gotten quite fond of our roster and has spent a lot of time with them. She's been schooling them, trying to instill in their memory banks who they are and what their individual philosophies are. Unfortunately I've had problems with their memory enhancements; trouble with postsynaptic density and the transference of neuron signals. So, some of the clones seem like zombies. Hannah was focusing on that, but now …" He trailed off.

They passed beneath Interstate 75 and got into the western edge of Sarasota County that would shortly dip into the Gulf of Mexico.

"Know where we're going yet?"

"Yup. I figured."

"She knows we're coming, but doesn't know my intentions on relocating. Let's keep that to ourselves until the opportune time. For now, she and I need to lay some cards on the table. I've asked Lydia Lawrence and her father, the Governor, to meet with us. Also, Lieutenant MacLaren."

Ben didn't respond. He was tying the pieces together.

85
Theories

Two Can Key reclined in the afternoon sun - its stunning white sand lay in stark contrast to the gradient greens of the lazy palm fronds and the red, sticklike roots of the mangroves. The shell drive was void of vehicles and Monty was instantly disheartened – had Winnie copped out on him? He parked the black Hummer next to her cottage and hoped the yellow Jeep would soon appear.

He felt relieved when he walked through the kitchen sliders and saw the retractable awning extended over the deck and the table beneath it adorned with place settings. Oscillating fans swept a refreshing breeze from side to side. Two silver buckets of ice sat chilling white wine against the blue afternoon. A sticky note said: *Making a quick run to Publix. Don't touch the wine – that's for our guests. Beer in the fridge for you two.* She had scrawled a happy face next to a cursive W.

Big Ben stood on the edge of the infinity deck looking at the ocean. He hadn't spoken since the ride. His beach shack peeked at him from around the corner.

Monty came up behind him with two cold bottles of Fleming's Pale Ale. "She must have known you would show. Your favorite brew."

Ben took a healthy swig. "Before we get into this pow-wow, there's one thing I'd like to know. Where did the idea for the 'roster' come from?"

"The Sixties. Revolution. Woodstock. It was a time of peace and love, man. The message was in the music and Ganga was in the air. All of which you and I missed. But Winnie was there. She lived it, believed in it, was inspired by it, then ultimately disillusioned by it."

They took up chairs at the table facing the ocean. Puffy white clouds drifted above the horizon like cotton balls lined up one after the other.

"Disillusioned? How?"

"By what was happening. She held - holds - a sincere distrust for our government and others of the world."

"A misanthrope?"

"Ah, clever word. I'm impressed. But no. Winnie has a strong belief in humanity and prefers to focus on art and music and those creative spirits who advance our culture in a positive, karmic way. The quest for world peace, man," he pinched his fingers and drew them to his lips like he was taking a hit. "You may have noticed she smokes a lot of pot."

They both chuckled.

Monty picked up his beer bottle, finished it off, and set it back on the table in precisely the same moisture circle he had lifted it from. "So, maybe not so much a misanthrope as a conspiracy theorist. JFK's assassination is one of her favorite rants. She believes there were larger factions involved beyond the 'lone assassin' - and there is some support for that."

"Do you really believe in the 'single-bullet' theory?" They were interrupted by a voice from behind. "Any logically minded person viewing the Zapruder film - excluding politicians of course - would conclude JFK was shot multiple times."

They hadn't heard her approach nor knew how long she had been listening to their conversation.

"Hello mother," Monty said.

Ben stood and pulled out a chair for her. "I had no idea."

"You weren't supposed to." She claimed her seat and produced a joint from her blouse pocket.

Montgomery glared at her, "Please, not now."

Winnie placed it back in her pocket and reached for the wine. She started to get up, "Need a corkscrew."

Ben halted her, saying, "I'll get it. Sit here with your *son*." He patted her shoulder and said, "You're full of secrets, Winnie Vanderlene."

Big Ben pulled on the kitchen drawers and shuffled around for a wine opener. The gun was tucked in the back behind the silverware. A Colt Derringer. Twenty-two caliber. It was small in his palm, easily concealed.

"Did you tell him?" Winnie asked her son.

"Not all of it. I want to wait until the others get here."

"So where were we?" Ben returned, did the production of the wine opening and poured a glass for his landlady. "Professor?" he asked.

"Sure."

He poured him a glass then opened one of the two bottles of beer he'd brought from the kitchen. The other he stuck into the ice bucket. "So? You were saying?"

"I call them 'The Sixty's Conspiracies'. They started with Marilyn."

"Here we go again," Monty chagrinned.

"Marilyn?" Ben said in a surprised voice. "But she committed suicide."

"She committed suicide about as much as Jack Kennedy did."

"Okay, Winnie, indulge me." Ben sat back with his beer in his lap.

"They had to eliminate her first because she was full of pillow talk. Kennedy knew who his enemies were. It wouldn't have worked the other way around. If they killed JFK first, Marilyn would have been emotionally devastated. She was in love with him. She believed Jack and Jackie were on the rocks and she had visions of being in the White House with him for his second term. She would have blown the whistle, maybe not loud enough to prove anything, but she'd have known who to point fingers at."

"Winnie …"

"Hey, disprove it. They got Marilyn in '62 and JFK the very next year. You don't have to be a conspiracy theorist to challenge coincidence.

"Then, less than five years later they get Bobby and Martin. Coincidence? Come on. Martin Luther King is *assassinated* and two months later Robert Francis Kennedy is *assassinated*? Really?"

Winnie reached into her pocket but caught the evil eye from Monty and picked up her wine glass instead. She was on a roll.

"Want more coincidence? Two years after that, in 1970, Jimi Hendrix *ODs*. And just two weeks later, *two weeks*, Janis Joplin *ODs*. Are you seeing the picture yet?"

Big Ben looked at Monty, but the scientist just shrugged his shoulders.

"Wanna talk about Jim Morrison? Seven months after Janis, Jim Morrison dies in Paris? Another *OD* they say, yet there was no autopsy done and some Parisians still believe the grave is empty. So, where is he?"

"I think I just saw him pulling in with Elvis." Lieutenant MacLaren arrived on the deck. "Hello everyone," he said and took a seat.

Winnie acknowledged her new guest with a quick smile and tried to lower her blood pressure. "Glass of wine, Lieutenant?"

"Absolutely not. This beer belong to anyone?" he asked as he lifted it out of the ice bucket and popped the top. "What am I walking in on?"

"I was pulling the wool off the boys' eyebrows."

"Well, don't stop on my account."

"I was almost done with my soliloquy," she smirked. "Anyways, it ended with Lennon in 1980. They would have gotten him sooner had he not gone into seclusion at The Dakota for five years. They had to wait him out. The bastards."

"My mother is very cynical." Monty said to MacLaren as Winnie continued, "The establishment was afraid of them all. Their words, their beliefs, their influence on the youth. I mean, *war is over, all you need is love, give peace a chance* ... are you kidding me? Why would they want to do that? Where's the money in that?"

MacLaren turned to Big Ben. *"Mother?"*

"Long story."

"They feared their free spirit. So their only recourse was to kill the idols." Winnie really wanted to light her joint, but in deference to her son, she held off. It wasn't easy. "Kill their idols and the idealists will conform."

86

Roundtable

"Do you have any idea what this is about?" Governor Lawrence asked his daughter as they passed over the rickety bridge on the approach to Two Can Key.

"Just that Winnie Vanderlene asked me to visit and to bring you along."

"I know of her, of course. She was actually a major contributor to my campaign, anonymously, but we found out where the check came from. I can't imagine why she wants to meet with me." Conrad Lawrence was in Sarasota due to the death of his campaign manager and aide, Jake Curtis.

Lydia looked at the Governor seated in the passenger seat of her BMW convertible. His white hair, still full and wavy, rustled in the wind. "Dad, I know about the two of you at Woodstock."

Conrad gave his daughter a sideways glance. "That was a long time ago, before I knew your mother."

"Dad, it's okay. Everybody has a youth," she grinned. This made him laugh.

Once they arrived and had exchanged greetings, Conrad Lawrence, Lydia Lawrence, Lieutenant MacLaren, Montgomery Fairmont, and Big Ben Benson joined Winnie Vanderlene at her table. She had brought out a platter of hors d'oeuvres and made sure her guests had fresh libations. The ensemble relaxed into a polite banter.

After a few minutes, Governor Lawrence punctuated the conversation. "Pardon me everyone." He gained their attention and said, "Although I am pleased to partake in this lovely cocktail hour," he smiled pleasantly at Winnie and then turned an angry glare to MacLaren, "I am perplexed as to its purpose and miffed that the murderer of my aide is running free. What is the status of the Jake Curtis investigation, Lieutenant? I would very much like some answers."

"Governor, I assure you ..."

Winnie broke in by raising her hands, "Please everyone, allow me to bring some bearing on that and other issues." Respectfully, they gave her their undivided attention.

"Ageing is an interesting thing. It seems the older one gets the more remorseful one becomes. I'm afraid I have made some errors in judgment in my lifetime and all I can do now is make amends and hope you will all forgive my imprudence. Especially you Conrad and your lovely daughter, Lydia." She took a fortifying sip of her wine and forged on.

"First, let me tell you about my guest Montgomery Fairmont, whom some of you have met and some have not. Long before his long hair and long beard turned white - an attractive coloring I must say -" she said as an aside, flipping her own lengthy mane, "he was a professor at Harvard with a doctorate in bio-chemistry. Later he spawned his own company specializing in bio-genetic research and development. More recently, Professor Fairmont has sequestered himself in the mangrove forests hereabouts and has been secretly experimenting with ..." she looked at Monty and asked, "may I?"

"It's your show Ms. Vanderlene," he smiled back at her.

"Human cloning." This got a rise from the Governor and Lydia Lawrence. Big Ben and MacLaren nodded.

"He is a brilliant man, an exceptional scientist and a wonderful person." She looked at him with admiration. "And he is my son." She reached for his hand. "And yours, Conrad."

Conrad Lawrence adopted an understandable look of astonishment, seconded only by his daughter.

Winnie went through the obligatory recapping of the Woodstock event, her decision to surrender her baby to the Fairmonts, her European sabbatical, and led them up to the reunion of mother and son and the subsequent establishment of his secret laboratory.

Monty took it from there. "As you know, human cloning is a very controversial subject. My research necessitated some clandestine preparation and precaution. She didn't tell me about you when we first met, in fact I asked her not to. Mom Fairmont's revelation was enough. And I was focused entirely on my research. It wasn't until last year that I found out. I had vowed never to do it, but I gave in to scientific curiosity. I cloned myself. And the clone, minus the long hair and beard, looked amazingly like you, Governor. Or I should say, dad."

Conrad addressed Winnie. "Why didn't you tell me?"

"I didn't want to burden you with that type of responsibility at such a young age. You were on your way to college and an important career. I am sorry, Conrad. But I did what I thought was best at the time." She looked at Montgomery. "My son has forgiven me and I hope someday you will too." Then she patted Lydia's hand and said, "And I need to apologize to you too dear. I could have revealed this to you years ago, but I did not. I am truly sorry."

Lydia placed both her hands over Winnie's and smiled broadly. "Hey, I should be thanking you. I always wanted a big brother." Winnie and Lydia laughed and the table became contagious with the laughter.

Conrad Lawrence went over to Monty and they stood together in an embrace. Lydia joined them. Big Ben gave Winnie a smile and a wink and she felt relieved and happy.

MacLaren ventured to the edge of the deck, then stepped onto the sand and made his way into the shade. Big Ben joined him with two fresh bottles of beer. They stood as still as the trees next to them.

"So," the lieutenant said, "the dead naked guy in the mangroves was the clone of Montgomery Fairmont."

"And the woman we found in the mangrove lagoon was Hannah Hunt Everett's clone."

"That's why the ME was so baffled as to cause of death."

"Right. The blood thing. Apparently clones don't have real human blood."

"But the woman in the museum did. So then, she was the real Hannah."

"Appears so."

"Now we have two dead clones and two dead people."

"Yup. Two down and two to go."

"Why Jake Curtis?"

"Dunno."

"And who would want to kill Hannah and why?"

"I think we're back to square one on that one, Lieutenant."

"I don't think we ever got off it."

The afternoon came to a close. MacLaren was going to return to his office to close the two cases. Or not. Although he knew what he knew, he wasn't sure how to word his report. He thought about consulting with the ME, but figured he'd think he was crazy. Clones?

Besides, Monty had refused to give him a statement, claiming that he was legally dead and wanted to stay that way. And who was really dead anyway? He was confused. As he headed up Tamiami Trail back into town he came up to the Fillippi Creek turnoff and decided to stop into the bar there and forget about it all.

The reunited family was going to head to St. Armands.

"You're a brave woman, Winnie." Conrad hugged her. "We're going to the Columbia for dinner. Will you join us?"

"You three go along. You've got a lot of catching up to do. I'm gonna stay here and smoke a joint."

"As the governor of this state and a sworn representative of the law, I'll pretend I didn't hear that," he laughed.

When all were gone, Big Ben helped Winnie clear the deck and clean up in the kitchen. "Y'know Winnie, I think that went pretty well."

"Yeah, me too. Let's celebrate with one more." She poured herself another glass of wine and got a beer for Ben. "Outside. It's a beautiful afternoon."

When they were again seated at the table and Winnie had fired up her long awaited joint, Ben said, "Yup, went pretty well. Although I am curious about one thing," He pulled the little Derringer from his pocket and laid it on the table between them."

"What's that?"

"I believe it is called a gun. A Derringer to be precise."

She picked it up and turned it in her hands. "This is my grandfather Wallace T's little gun. Where on earth did you find it?"

"In your kitchen drawer."

"Huh. I'll bet it's been there for years. I can't imagine it still works."

Big Ben took it from her and pointed it at the sand just beyond the deck. He pulled the trigger. Winnie jumped at the sound.

"Well, I'll be damned," she said.

87
Interlude

During the course of the next several weeks, several things happened …

88

Bayfront

Big Ben and Lydia met downtown at her office in the "blue building" at One Sarasota Tower.

"Let's go for a walk," she said.

"No time for coffee?"

Lydia closed and locked the glass door with *Lawrence and Lawrence, Attorneys At Law* stenciled on it.

They waited for the walk signal and crossed Gulf Stream Avenue where the statue of the WW II sailor and nurse stands. Conversation was thin and superficial and Ben could feel a mild tension emanating from his lawyer as they strolled the sidewalk amidst the art sculptures spread along the bayfront.

The slips at Marina Jack were filled with expensive yachts and grand powerboats from ports of call all along the Sun Coast. In the bay, sailboats rocked to the soft swells, the tunes of their lanyards playing like wind chimes in the intermittent breezes.

"I'm moving to Tallahassee," she said.

Ben had heard this rumor from MacLaren. "I heard a rumor," he responded.

"I'll probably stay at the Governor's Mansion with dad until I can find an apartment. There's plenty of room there." She laughed, trying to lighten this conversation she had been dreading.

"What about your practice?"

"Most of the rudimentary stuff I can handle via the phone and Internet from the capital. If I have to appear in court here I'll take a flight down. I plan on keeping my condo downtown."

"Any particular reason you're making the move?"

"Yes. Dad's just getting settled in and even though he'd never admit it, he needs me. We've always been close, moreso since mom died, and the legal partnership was always strong. Now that he has the responsibilities as Governor, I hate to think of him there alone. I worry about him. Besides, I miss him."

"Okay, I'll buy that. But why do I sense there's another, underlying reason?"

Lydia smiled. She knew she couldn't fool him. "Your cop instincts checking in?"

"No. My own. Tell me what's going on."

The sunlight swirled through her hair and dripped off the ends like rich creamy chocolate. Ben could see the amber eyes sparkling behind her sunglasses. Lydia curled her hair behind her ears and took a breath. This was hard for her.

"Look," she stopped him in front of her, her fingertips resting lightly on his forearms, "I wish nothing but the best for you. I really do. But, selfishly, if things don't work out for you and Carlene," she hesitated, "well, you'll know where to find me."

Lydia stretched on her tiptoes and kissed his cheek. "I gotta go." Quickly she turned and walked away.

He didn't go after her. Didn't call to her. Just stood there watching her walking out of his life, and wondering. Wondering.

Ben ambled along the bayfront and into Dog Park. It was only mid-morning but O'Leary's Tiki bar was already open. He grabbed a beer and sat on the retainer wall and let the rolling bay waters splash over his flip-flops.

89

Apology

Her bedroom was dark, save for the moon glow seeping through the lace curtains of the second floor window. Carlene usually drew the shade when she was alone, but recently she'd acquiesced to Ben's style. "Gotta let the moon in, Sugarplum," he'd say as he crawled in next to her.

She was missing her husband and still slept on her side of the bed, but usually awakened with her leg over his invisible body. The several months of therapy had gained her a livable control over the PTSD and she felt ready to be with him again, although the therapist warned of regression at this stage, suggesting a few more months would be more beneficial. But she missed him, missed their relationship and knew the kids were having a hard time of it too. Carlene was tired of her life being governed by the disruptive traumatic event of the near past. It was unfair and she resented the people who had brought it upon them.

Outside the window the trees swayed in the evening wind and the shadows moved in the background of the bedroom. But there was no wind tonight. The shadows weren't cast from the outside. Carlene sprang upright and reached for the bedside lamp. It didn't work. The S&W *Lady Smith* that Ben had given her was absent from beneath his pillow.

The shadow said, "Do not call out. I know of the man in the downstairs bedroom and the two children on this floor. They are unharmed and peacefully asleep. Your dog has been anesthetized and will awaken shortly. I will do you no harm. I only ask that you listen to me and then I will be gone from your life."

Carlene wanted to shout for Uncle Bob, knowing he would be there in a second with his gun drawn. But there was something about this woman's voice. Something familiar. The kidnapper that got away. Why was she here? Suddenly she realized she was holding her breath and she inhaled deeply, attempting to quell her racing heart.

"What do you want?"

"To apologize."

That was probably the last response she would have expected. Somehow it relieved her.

"I have gotten to know your husband of late."

Carlene was disturbed by the words *gotten to know*.

Ursula continued in a soft, subdued voice absent of her Scandinavian accent. "He is a good man with a good heart. I assume you know this. You are lucky. I was sent to extract information from him and to kill him. You would have been next."

Carlene began breathing heavily, her chest heaving with adrenaline and the thirst for oxygen.

Ursula was stone cold calm. "It is strange how fate turns."

"How did it turn for you?" Carlene sensed her therapist speaking through her.

"That does not matter to you. Only to me."

Carlene knew she should engage her in conversation while she planned what to do next. What would Ben do? Keep her occupied as long as possible. Buy yourself time. She feared for her children and Uncle Bob and had to focus.

Carlene sensed the only recourse she had was to draw her into her and then leap at her and tear her throat out. Carlene was bigger than this woman. She had the bulk and maybe the upper body power, but her nemesis had a gun. Hers, in fact.

Ursula said, "I know you want to move against me, but do not. Stay where you are and listen. What happened, happened. You and I live in different worlds."

Ursula approached the darkened bed. Carlene drew her knees up to her chest in a protective manner. She wasn't sure which way this confrontation was going to turn.

"Perhaps if tables were reversed I would have the life you lead and you would be the one always on the run with nowhere to run to. No one to care."

Ursula took another step closer. She was at the edge of the bed, standing eerily silent. Carlene felt a new wave of fear come over her. "Please," she pleaded. A tear hovered in the corner of her eye.

"I envy your emotion. And your husband's. He killed for love. I kill for money. A difference."

Ursula took a step back into the darkness. "No one will bother you now. It is over."

Carlene could no longer make out her form. She spoke into the dimness. "Why did you come here?"

"To tell you my husband is dead. And yours is not."

Then the threat was gone and the *Lady Smith* was back under the pillow.

90
At Sea

She stood at the edge of the sea listening to the cascading tide roll along the shoreline, the soothing sound of it washing over her as it had done her entire life. She closed her eyes and lifted her head, inhaling the sweet salty scent. She was calm. The sea that is. And so was Winnie.

The sky was clear and dark and spotted with diamonds. It was nearing midnight. A fitting time. The end of one day and the beginning of another. Eternity.

So, this is it. *This is the end*, Jim Morrison's deep voice echoed in her inner ear, *this is the end, my friend*.

Winnie was proud of her life. Overall, anyway. Except for the one regret.

And now it was time to go. One last swim. Winnie dropped her clothes and entered the water. She figured she'd come into this world naked and she'd go out the same way.

Winnie stepped into the frothy surf, wading up to her waist before diving beneath the sea. Underwater, in the refreshing silence, she swam as far as she could until her lungs screamed and she burst to the surface.

A lifetime of swimming had kept her toned and healthy. Her strokes were strong and pulled her quickly away from shore, away from her little Two Can Key, away from everyone and everything she loved.

Once Winnie got beyond the breakers the water smoothed and she settled into a more comfortable rhythm. A hundred yards out she paused and turned, looking back to her city of Sarasota with its nightlights aglow. She raised a hand and gave it a wave then turned back to the Gulf.

Usually, she stayed fairly close to shore, traversing the coastline two miles one way and then two miles back. But tonight's plan, as if it was any plan at all, was to swim straight out into the darkness as far as possible with no turning back. *Maybe I'll make it to Mexico.* She snickered. *And celebrate with a salty margarita.*

Half an hour later her arms weakened and she rolled onto her back. The moon was not visible, which made the constellations above all the more brilliant. *Wish I was counting stars with you, Big Ben. Sitting on the porch, cocktails and a little weed. Ah well, gonna miss that.*

She took up the swimming again and didn't allow herself to rest for another long while. When she did, the lights of Sarasota were a dim glow on the black horizon and the lights on the barrier islands stretched like a string of pearls from Anna Maria to Venice.

Something bumped her. A slithering along her thigh. *Oh shit, please be a dolphin. Not a shark. Not yet.* Her adrenaline spiked and she powered on with an awakened fury.

When the fatigue set in, Winnie rested on her back and watched the stars whirl and spin above like a kaleidoscope. The current had taken her. She went silently with it and wondered where it would go. Certainly to the Keys. Around the point in Key West where the Gulf meets the Atlantic at Fort Zack, where she used to walk for hours in the shade of the park on her many visits there. And then it was only ninety miles to Cuba. She had always wanted to go to Cuba.

Had plans to go one New Year's Eve, but something came up. She chastised herself for not going. She would have been there at that historic time when Castro's rebels took Havana. *What a great city and what a waste. So romantic.* Winnie thought of the movie of the same name with Robert Redford and Lena Olin. *Whatever happened to her? I love that scene in the beginning where they're on the ferry from Key West to Havana and she comes out from behind Redford. Great direction. Very romantic.*

Winnie didn't realize it but she was backstroking with the current. Smiling. *And at the end when they meet for their last scene and she says, "Have you been waiting long?" and Bob Redford delivers that classic line, "All my life." Fucking beautiful! They don't write movies like that anymore.*

The sting on the bottom of her foot felt like an electrical shock. It jolted her into a fetal position and she went under. *Ow! Goddamnit!* She yelled and salt water rushed into her mouth and down her throat. She sprang to the surface, spitting and hacking and gasping for breath, flailing one arm to tread water and holding onto her burning foot with the other. The next sting hit her arm and she bolted forward, swimming frantically with the current.

A long time later, or only moments, Winnie stopped, breathing hard, with pain and exhaustion spreading throughout her body. Fearing that whatever it was would soon come up behind her, she left the current and side-stroked further west. Or what she thought was west. For now, the lights were gone, the shoreline invisible and she was totally surrounded by darkness, having no idea which direction was which.

Swimming and drifting, swimming and drifting. Tired and disoriented and unable to feel her left arm and leg, Winnie's mind thought she was swimming but her body was shutting down. She tried to stay awake.

How long has it been? I must be in the Gulf Stream by now. Maybe near Cuba. Hmmm, Cubans. How nice it would be to be in Havana again. With that man I met. Who took his time with me. So sensual. Slow. Titillating. God, how many orgasms? A true romantic. Not like American men. Wham-bam-thank-you-ma'am.

Her memory was fading in and out, taking intermittent precedent over her consciousness.

No, that couldn't have been Cuba. I've never been to Cuba. It was Italy. He was Italian. And so beautiful.

Now she was simply floating, in the ocean and in her mind.

How far does the Gulf Stream go? I know it comes around Florida and sweeps north across the Atlantic. Think it goes above Africa. Into the Mediterranean. I could get there. To Italy again. To the pleasures of Italy again.

So it went. In and out of memory and delusion. In the dark on her back looking up at the black sky unable to tell if she was above the water or sinking beneath it. Dreaming or awake.

And eventually, with the power of eternity behind it, the incessant, unforgiving sea won out and Winifred Adele Vanderlene went down.

91

Departure

Big Ben saw the clean-shaven bald guy coming along the Tiki deck at Gramps Ramp. He pulled up a stool at the bar and said, "Hey."

"Hey."

"Wanted to stop in and bid you adieu." Ben pulled him a beer. The man took a long draw.

Ben said, "If you'd shaved off your eyebrows too, you'd look like David Bowie, *Spiders from Mars*."

"Naw, I'd look too much like an alien. And no matter where you go on the planet that attracts attention. Bald-headed guys are everywhere. Universal male hairdo." Monty chuckled.

Ben placed his big hands on the other side of the wooden bar and leaned into him.

"Monty, don't give in. Your mind is too unique to waste. Fucking vital to mankind."

"I'm burnt out, Ben. I need a break. A different environment."

Ben felt sorry for him. He'd sacrificed a normal life; a wife, kids, friendships, and gotten what in return? Ridicule and ostracism from his peers just by following his unsolicited destiny. In a way, Ben felt a kinship, a parallel – on a much different plane. But wasn't he also going through a redefining of his own life? Two men who'd been lucky in their own ways, only to turn out confused and bewildered at mid-life. Was this what it was all about?

"Where will you go?"

"Far away."

"They'll hunt you down. The kind of guys thirsting for your knowledge don't give up."

Monty sipped his beer and gazed at the water beyond the railing. Ben pulled himself a short glass.

"Did you get a letter from her?" Monty asked.

"Yeah."

Big Ben still carried the folded letter in his pocket. He read it from time to time:

> My Dearest Big Friend ~
>
> Remember that night when we were sitting on the porch philosophizing about what came after life? Well, I'm gonna go find out.
>
> It's been a pleasure knowing you and I will miss our chats.
>
> You did such a good job restoring my doll house I figured I'd give it to you, along with the rest of my little key.
>
> Don't you worry about me - I'll be fine.
>
> Take care of yourself and that lady of yours. Get her down to Two Can Key and let her absorb the feeling. She'll fall in love with it and you too, all over again.
>
> And don't fuck it up this time 'cuz I'll be watching you!
>
> Love you Ben.
> Winnie

> PS ... I'll let you know which one of us was right.

"I'm glad she left you the key."

"You got a note too?" Ben asked.

"Yes. Said she loved me, enjoyed our time together, wished me happiness ... stuff like that. I got the Jeep and the money. The land will become *The Vanderlene Preserve*. Conrad Lawrence is going to see that that happens. Lydia's going to handle the legal end."

Monty raised the pint to his lips, "Well ..." he finished off the beer, put the glass on the bar top and stood.

They shook hands and wished each other luck. Ben followed Monty's back along the length of the bar and watched him stop at the corner. JJ appeared and wrapped her arm in his. Together they, this brilliant ahead-of-his-time man of science, and cloned rock-star-from-the-sixties, disappeared into an unfamiliar future.

The night was closing in. The hot air remained uncooled. Reptilian sounds drifted through the nocturnal humidity. The restaurant was empty. It was closing time. Gramps was long gone and Ben was left solo to wrap it up. A half hour later he was climbing onto the Harley that Ray had repaired. When the blast went off, he flinched. His heartbeat jumped. Instinctively his shoulders hunched and his eyes riveted onto the bright orange fireball on the black prairie.

92

Introspection

It was that kind of morning. The rain was heavy and deafeningly loud on the tin roof and when the thunder came the cottage shook.

Big Ben stood at the corner of the porch where the salty spray churning in off the waves could reach him. He closed his eyes and let the wind bring the water to him. He could feel the hot, salty sting on his face and he wondered what had brought him to this point where nothing seemed to matter anymore.

Winnie was gone. She had bequeathed him Two Can Key, an unexpected gesture that was nice, but it would be lonely without her. She'd been a good friend and he had enjoyed her company. Montgomery was also gone, probably forever on some spit of land or jungle somewhere. The reclusive mad scientist. Lydia was off to Tallahassee. That wouldn't have worked anyway. Ben was consummately in love with his wife Carlene. And if that didn't eventually work out, he'd have to learn how to live with a big hole in his heart. If he could.

He didn't even have bad guys to chase anymore. Monty had accounted for some of the mayhem, but Ben doubted they'd ever know who killed Jake Curtis and Hannah Hunt Everett. His best guess was that they'd been professional hits that would remain cold cases on MacLaren's desk.

So, what did he have left? He had Gramps and the bartending gig. And he had his Harley back. Chief Ray had repaired the damage and given it a new paint job. Still had a friend in MacLaren. Maybe they could go fishing again and find another dead body that would spark his investigative soul and keep his tortured mind occupied.

Big Ben walked the beach in melancholy. He was lonely and cursed the gods for allowing his world to fall apart. But he knew. Ben knew he was responsible for his own loneliness.

The storm was over and the sand, cool and damp beneath his bare feet, would warm quickly with the morning sun and be dry and powdery again.

It was that kind of morning.

93
Retribution

The window on the sea side was open. He had closed it earlier against the rain. Someone was in the beach shack. There were no vehicles in the drive. Ben had left his gun in the bedroom. He approached the porch with stealth and climbed the worn steps by the edges, mindful of their creakiness.

At the screen door, he listened. He heard movement in the kitchen but saw no one. A blitz would take him three quick strides to reach the invisible intruder. Power down like in his football days, break through the line and make the tackle in less than two seconds. He could do it. Unless they had a weapon in their hand. But he had surprise on his side, Right?

He crouched and took a deep breath. Without hesitation, Big Ben yanked the door open and burst into the cottage. A second and a half later he halted as surely as if he'd hit a brick wall.

"Ohmygod!" she shrieked, holding her hand over her heart. "You scared the whup outta me."

She turned and poured the carafe of water into the coffee maker. Ben stood silent and dumbfounded.

When she turned back to him, she said, "Aren't you going to say anything? Aren't you glad to see me, you big oaf?"

They sat at the counter sipping coffee. Winnie was telling her story. She had a blue Crown Royal bag with her marijuana paraphernalia in it. She was rolling a joint. "And then I must have blacked out because the next thing I remember, I was in an elaborate beach house on the reclusive end of Casey Key being pampered by an interesting man with a dog named *Gargoyle* and a fluffy Maine Coon cat named *Sinister*.

"Who was he?"

"We never did exchange names, but I knew who he was and he knew of me. Said he found me on his beach one morning while walking the dog. He was very nice. Let me stay a few weeks 'til I was fully recuperated. The Man-O-War stings were pretty nasty. Then he drove me home. And here I am, back from the dead." She spread her arms and smirked.

Yet she was hyper. Something was off. Ben saw the shakiness in her hands as she rolled the joint.

"Why did you do it, Winnie?"

She didn't answer him, just kept fumbling with the joint.

"Winnie?"

She dropped everything and spread her hands over her face.

"Just wanted to go for one final swim."

"It was you, Winnie. Wasn't it."

She dropped her hands. "Me what?"

"Hannah."

Her eyes welled instantly. Her shoulders began to shake uncontrollably. And in only a moment she was in full breakdown. Tears flowed. Her breathing became short gasps straining to inhale oxygen through a mouthful of sawdust. Ben let her go. His heart sank. He wanted to reach out to her but he couldn't. He didn't understand. He hated being right.

Winnie couldn't get herself under control and sought the safety of the bathroom. Ben heard her hard, wrenching sobs and wished she hadn't come back.

It was way too early for drinking, but he poured a shot of bourbon for himself and one for her, if she ever came out of the bathroom. He waited.

When she returned her face was puffy and red. She held a handful of tissues. Winnie took her seat and took the bourbon in one swift gulp. She took a deep breath and a sip of coffee.

"I didn't know it was her," she began in a whisper. "He was so successful. The clone was perfect. He had perfected her in every way. She could walk, talk, drive, go grocery shopping, hell she even had a cell-phone. She was Hannah's identical living, breathing twin. But it was getting too serious, too crazy. I wanted to support Montgomery, knew he was on the brink of an incredible breakthrough for mankind, but there was an element."

"An element?"

"A dark downside. The science was wonderful, the achievement glorious, but there would be ethical ramifications and the potential for evil consequences was too horrific. I decided to end it. Even Hannah had been openly wondering if they should go on.

"So I set up a rendezvous for the twin to meet me at Ca' d'Zan. Only it wasn't her. I had used Monty's cell phone on the sly to text her, only it wasn't her." She said this again, almost inaudibly. She took up the bourbon bottle and poured a finger into her glass.

"His address book had a listing for *Hannah* and another for *Hannah C*. I thought the *C* was for clone. I found out later it was for cell." Her eyes began to moisten again and she dabbed them with the tissues.

"So it was Hannah who met me at the museum. Hannah who I killed." She began to become unglued again. This time Ben went to her and kneaded her shoulders.

"It was a mistake, Winnie. A terrible mistake."

"Tell that to her kids and husband."

"So you were the one who set up the anonymous trust fund for them."

"Yes. I couldn't bring her back to them, but I could provide for her family. A lousy compromise, but they will never have to worry about money for education or anything. I even set up a substantial land grant." She finished off the shot, then whispered, "But it's not enough."

Ben stood behind her kneading her shoulders thinking about what she had done. And thinking of Monty and himself and even Jake the Snake, whom he hadn't even liked. "We have all fallen from grace, Winnie. Each in our own way."

"You've got to turn me in."

Ben had been thinking about this moment since he had discovered the Derringer. His analytical cop brain had suspected Winnie, but the pit of his stomach churned with an acidic denial. He had kept the suspicion to himself, not only because he was at a loss for a motive, but also, if it was true, he didn't know what he would do. Now the time was upon him.

"Why? What would it accomplish? Years of litigation; a sensational trial; a Hollywood movie? Hannah's family would be drawn and quartered and never the same again. And your son? Monty and his work would be exposed and set back. He might be charged with complicity. More trials. You'd be in prison and probably die there. It would be worse for all of them. Doing the right thing isn't always the best thing. Maybe it would be best to let sleeping dogs lie. Let them go on with their fond memories."

"I should be punished, pay a penance."

"You are, Winnie."

"I'm so fucking sorry." She was standing now, weeping in Ben's arms.

"Let's think on it." He said.

Epilogue

Winnie stayed awhile longer. Declined Ben's breakfast offer of scrambled eggs and bacon. Had another slow cup of coffee then said she was tired and was going to go to her cottage and sleep. She gave him a hug and left.

Ben took eggs out of the refrigerator and cracked them into a bowl.

The screen door squeaked open and Winnie returned.

Ben said, "Change your mind on breakfast?"

"Nope, forgot my stash." She grabbed the little blue bag from the counter and left again.

Ben started the eggs on the stove then placed several strips of bacon on a paper towel and put them in the microwave.

He was wondering if he was doing the right thing. Wondering what that would actually be. He filled his cup with more black coffee then started whisking his eggs. The door squeaked again. He laughed. "What did you forget now?"

When no response came, he turned around. She was standing just inside the door. He had never seen anyone look so beautiful.

"Nice place. Cute. A little hard to find, though."

If his heart had ever beat, it was beating now.

Ben's feet froze to the floor and his eyes dried for fear of blinking the image away.

Carlene placed her purse on a chair and walked to him. Her smile lit up the whole room and when she put her arms around him, Ben thought he was going to faint. Instead, he hung onto her for dear life. He could feel the tears welling behind his eyes.

He said, "I love you so much," and let them flow.

*The imagination is a wonderful thing,
but sometimes it needs a little help from family and friends.
I love you guys for being there. Also ...*

Many Thanx

To Chief Tom O'Donnell WBPD; Attorney Anthony Fernandes; Detective Lieutenant Tom Ford II MA State Police; Chief Tom Ford III SPD; G.L. (the Godfather of Finance); Louis B. Grace, MD; Norman Tonelli LMHC; Donna "Mac" Nauman, RN; Bradford Sherburne, Director Clinical Pathology Hartford Hospital; Dr. Robert Lanza, Advanced Cell Technology; Lou Hawthorne, BioArts International; Hwang Woo-Suk, Sooam Biotech Research Foundation of South Korea; The Guardiola Family of Spain; Viking Genetics; Andrew Pollack, *New York Times*; Rick Trahan and the great staff at The Quechee Inn, Quechee, Vermont; Ebenezer and all the ghosts past and present at The Publick House; Jay Gaunt and Dwayne Martin for use of their names and mischaracterizations; Arlo Guthrie and Alice; and a nod to Mary Shelley for creating *Frankenstein* in 1818.

To pea, for keeping the ship afloat through the Waves of Eccentricity.

Toucann, for invaluable guidance and insight on the research road.

And my daughters, Jennifer and Jill, who keep the rhythm in my heart.

And lastly, to Professor Montgomery Fairmont, wherever you are ... be safe my friend.

P.S. If you ever find yourself at Gramps Ramp, 1st drink is on me. Just tell Gramps to put it on Big Ben's tab.

Also by Donn Fleming:

Made in the USA
Middletown, DE
03 June 2018